EVERYMAN, I will go with thee,

and be thy guide,

In thy most need to go by thy side

BEDE—STEVENSON

An Anthology of
English Prose

ARRANGED BY
S. L. EDWARDS

DENT: LONDON
EVERYMAN'S LIBRARY
DUTTON: NEW YORK

NO. *1675*

SBN: 460 01675 x

INTRODUCTION

THE wide field of English Prose, despite cheap reprints, is as yet an untilled domain to many readers. In the hurry of modern life there is time but to snatch at the productions of contemporaries, or to know from a hasty review of the existence of such and such a "volume of forgotten lore." It is the object of this anthology to help to give the modern reader some conception of the way in which the prose that he devours so eagerly has grown up, and some desire to turn up the soil of this vast domain and discover treasures for himself.

The trend of English prose, always more elusive than that of poetry, and its gradual development from infancy to gigantic growth, afford a voyage of adventure for him who seeks. The temper of the English mind, the growth of its national sensibility, have found an idealized expression in the pages of poetry, but in the realms of prose have been reflected in all their many moods and changes with kaleidoscopic vigour and detail.

It was characteristic of English prose during its earliest period that it should have little universal interest; until the eighteenth century it was the instrument for the individual expression of enthusiasm for a particular religious belief, or a favourite line of thought. What there was of general interest to mankind came into England in the form of translations—most influential of all, the Authorized Version of the Bible in 1611. The writers of English prose ploughed small and isolated plots, while poetry early swept over its head and rained benefits upon rich and poor, learned and *lewd*. Yet the national energy from earliest times has found its expression, fleeting though that was at first, in prose, as well as in poetry; and as the Saxon element absorbed the Norman and all other influxes of alien growth, so English prose has enriched itself from many foreign sources and yet remains thoroughly English.

Perfection of form in prose was attained much later than perfection of form in poetry. Prose rhythm found no natural response in English ears, and it is a far cry from the rough but vigorous diction of the Anglo-Saxon chronicle to the organ notes of Sir Thomas Browne, and the simple dignity of John Bunyan; even such a master of words as Milton lost himself in the mazes of written speech.

Owing to the centering of learning in the monasteries, it was natural that the earliest prose should come from ecclesiastical sources. Nevertheless the element of romance is ever present. Young and impulsive, it leaps forward to embrace all fields of human activity. When all is said, it is the romantic element in prose that holds its own in the minds of Englishmen, more than of any other nation. To certain individuals the philosophical disquisition, the book of scientific speculation, the religious tract, make a greater appeal; but to young and old romance is ever young, romance in its truest and widest sense—the actions of human beings in relation to all circumstances adorned by the art of the imaginative writer whose achievement it is to excite and satisfy the unexpressed aspirations of the human mind. Romance does not find the same outward expression in all ages. We now-adays do not care for Arcadian valleys, or the elegant euphuisms of piping shepherds to their loves; but this was but the veneer of the pseudo-chivalric age; and beneath it lay the real and palpi-tating humanity of Rosalynde and Rosader, made vivid by Shakespeare, the greatest of all lovers of romance. To other branches of literature we go for ideas, for beauty of style, for elegance of thought; but for life, its heights and depths of feeling, let us away with Crusoe to his island; let us join Christian in the fight with Apollyon; let us hie to the golden land by the riverside with Richard and Lucy where there is no "Pilgrim's Scrip" to shadow our natural desires; let us sit with Harry Esmond at the feet of Lady Castlewood; let us ride with Rob Roy in the wild glens of Scotland, or voyage over the high seas with Drake and John Oxenham; "let us drink life to the lees." All that there is in the world of beauty and loveliness, of death and grim calamity; of the clash of war, or of waiting on love in this "piping time of peace"; of adventure, of achievement; of passion, of despair, of hope; all this is the inheritance of Romance, and this dowry is ours through the pages of English prose.

The reader of this volume can trace the growth of the novel from the Elizabethan romance, through the character sketches of the seventeenth century, through Bunyan and Defoe, Richardson and Fielding, to the great artists of the nineteenth century; of philosophical prose from Bacon, through Sir Thomas Browne to

Carlyle and Ruskin; of natural description from Izaak Walton to Richard Jefferies; of historical writings, of criticism, of biography; while the student of style may evolve for himself if he can, the literary ancestry of the periods of *Sartor Resartus*, or the cadences of *Marius the Epicurean*. Where in his search he fails to find satisfaction, as he must inevitably fail, let him turn to the writers themselves in their entirety, and plough his furrow further afield.

The passages in this Anthology have been chosen not only with a view towards enabling the student to trace the growth of English prose, but for their intrinsic interest, that the general reader may pass a happy hour browsing amongst its pages. Limits of space and difficulties of copyright must partly account for the absence of a favourite passage, and no book can please all tastes.

It remains to acknowledge the kindness of those who have given their permission for the inclusion of copyright passages in this Anthology; of Lady Ritchie (and Messrs. Smith, Elder & Co. for confirming her permission), of Mr. Thomas Hardy (and Messrs. Macmillan & Co.), of Mr. Austin Dobson, and of the following Publishers for the works of the authors whose names follow their own: Messrs. Constable & Co., George Meredith; Messrs. Longmans, Green & Co., Andrew Lang; Mr. Wm. Heinemann (and Mrs. Wm. Sharp), "Fiona Macleod" (selected from the Collected Works, Vol. II). If I have unwittingly infringed the rights of any, I must crave their kind indulgence.

It has been thought best in most cases to modernize the spelling of the earlier extracts, but one or two have been left as they originally were written, when the dress of antiquity lends an added charm.

S. L. EDWARDS.

The following is a list of the chief works drawn upon for the selection:

Bede: *Ecclesiastical History of the English People* (translated by J. Stevens, revised by L. C. Jane), 731; *The Anglo-Saxon Chronicle*, translated by G. N. Garmonsway; Alfred: translation of Orosius' *History of the World*, 890; Geoffrey of Monmouth: *Historia Regum Britanniae*, 1132–5, 1147; *The Ancrene Riwle, c.* 1220; Mandeville: *Travels*, 1356? (oldest MS. in French, 1371); Caxton: *Recueil des Histoires de Troye*, begun 1471, printed 1474, *The Game and Play of Chess*, 1474; Berners: translation of Froissart's *Chronicles*, 1521?; Malory: *Morte d'Arthur, c.* 1470; More: *Utopia*, 1516; Latimer: *Remains and Sermons* (ed. 1844–5); Tyndale, Foxe: *Acts and Monuments*, vol. v., 1838; Elyot: *The Boke of the Gouernour*, 1531; Ascham: *The Scholemaster*, 1570; Holinshed: *Chronicles of England and Scotland*, 1577; North: translation of *Plutarch's Lives*, 1579; Hakluyt: *Voyages*, 1589; Raleigh: *History of the World*, 1614; Hooker: *Ecclesiastical Polity*, 1594; Sidney: *Defence of Poesie*, 1581; Lyly: *Euphues His England*, 1580; Lodge: *Rosalynde*, 1590; Greene: *A Groat's Worth of Wit Bought by a Million of Repentance*, 1592 (pub. 1740); Bacon: *Essays*, 1597, *New Atlantis*, pub. 1627; Dekker: *Gull's Horn Book*, 1608; The Authorized Bible, 1611; Overbury: *Characters*, 1614; Hobbes: *Leviathan*, 1651; Walton, *The Compleat Angler*, 1653, *Lives*, 1670; Earle: *Micro-Cosmographie*, 1628; Browne: *Religio Medici*, 1635 (pub. 1642), *Urn Burial*, 1658; Fuller: *Holy and Profane State*, 1642, *Church History of Britain*, 1656; Milton: *Reason of Church Government*, 1642, *Apology for Smectymnus*, 1642, *Areopagitica*, 1644; Clarendon: *History of the Rebellion, c.* 1684 (pub. 1707); Taylor: *Sermons, Holy Dying*, 1651; Cowley: *Prose Works*, 1667; Evelyn: *Diary*, 1641–97 (pub. 1818); Bunyan: *Pilgrim's Progress*, i. 1678, ii. 1684; Temple: *Miscellanea*, 1680–92; Dryden: *Essay on Dramatic Poesy*, 1665, Preface to the *Fables*, 1699; Pepys: *Diary*, 1659–69 (pub. 1825); Traherne: *Centuries of Meditations*, pub. 1906; Defoe: *Robinson Crusoe*, 1719; Swift: *Gulliver's Travels*, 1726–7; Steele: *The Tatler*, 1709; Addison: *The Spectator*, 1711; Richardson: *Clarissa Harlowe*, 1748; Fielding: *Joseph Andrews*, 1742; Johnson: *Lives of the Poets*, 1779–81, *Rasselas*, 1759; Sterne: *Tristram Shandy*, 1759–65; Gray: *Letters, Journal in the Lakes*, 1765; Walpole: *Letters*, 1745–97 (pub. 1798, 1857); White: *Natural History of Selborne*, 1789; Goldsmith: *The Vicar of Wakefield*, 1762? pub. 1776, *The Citizen of the World*, 1762; Burke: *Reflections on the French Revolution*, 1790, *Impeachment of Warren Hastings*, 1788, *Thoughts on the Present Discontents*, 1770; Macpherson: *Fragments of Ancient Poetry*, 1760; Gibbon: *Decline and Fall of the Roman Empire*, 1776–88, *Autobiography*, pub. posthumously by Lord Sheffield; Boswell: *Life of Dr Johnson*, 1791; Scott: *Heart of Midlothian*, 1818, *Rob Roy*, 1817; Coleridge: *Biographia Literaria*, 1817, *Lectures on Shakespeare*, 1811–1812; Austen: *Pride and Prejudice*, 1813; Landor: *Pentameron*, 1837; Lamb: *Essays of Elia*, 1821–3, *On the Tragedies of Shakespeare* (*The Reflector*, 1811); Hazlitt: *Table Talk*, 1821–2, *Spirit of the Age*, 1825; Leigh Hunt: *The Indicator*, 1819–21; De Quincey: *Confessions of an English Opium-Eater*, 1821, *Reminiscences of the English Lake Poets* (*Edinburgh Review, c.* 1834), *Joan of Arc*, 1847; Carlyle: *Heroes and Hero-Worship*, 1838, *Sartor Resartus*, 1838, *Past and Present*, 1843; Macaulay: *Essays* (contributed to *Edinburgh Review*, 1834 and onwards); Gladstone: *On the Ancient Beliefs in a Future State* (*Indian Church Quarterly Review*, 1891); Gaskell: *Cranford*, 1851–3; Brown: *Horae Subsecivae*, 1858, 1861, 1882; Bright: *Speech* of 1854; Thackeray: *Esmond*, 1852; Dickens: *Nicholas Nickleby*, 1839, *David Copperfield*, 1849–50; Brontë: *Shirley*, 1848–9; Ruskin: *Sesame and Lilies*, 1865, *Stones of Venice*, 1851–3; Eliot: *Adam Bede*, 1859;

Kingsley: *Westward Ho!*, 1855; Arnold: *Essays on Criticism*, First Series, 1865; Meredith: *The Amazing Marriage*, 1895; Carroll: *Alice in Wonderland*, 1865; Morris: *Early Romances (Oxford and Cambridge Magazine*, 1856); Ritchie: *The Village on the Cliff*, 1867; Pater: *Marius the Epicurean*, 1885; Dobson: *Eighteenth Century Vignettes*, 1892; Hardy: *Far from the Madding Crowd*, 1874; Lang: *New and Old Letters to Dead Authors*, 1866; Jefferies: *The Open Air*, 1885; Stevenson: *Vailima Letters*, 1894; Macleod: *Collected Works*, vol. ii, *The Sin-Eater*, 1910 (first pub. 1896).

CONTENTS

xi

Contents

PAGE

Contents

Contents

Contents

BEDE (673–735)

I.—THE CONVERSION OF KING EDWIN

King Edwin is persuaded to believe by a vision which he had seen when he was in exile. (Before A.D. 625.)

THUS the aforesaid Pope Boniface wrote for the salvation of King Edwin and his nation. But a heavenly vision, which the Divine Mercy was pleased once to reveal to this king, when he was in banishment at the court of Redwald, king of the Angles, was of no little use in urging him to embrace and understand the doctrines of salvation. Paulinus, therefore, perceiving that it was a very difficult task to incline the king's lofty mind to the humility of the way of salvation, and to embrace the mystery of the cross of life, and at the same time using both exhortation with men and prayer to God, for his and his subjects' salvation; at length, as we may suppose, it was shown him in spirit what was the vision that had been formerly revealed to the king. Nor did he lose any time, but immediately admonished the king to perform the vow which he made, when he received the oracle, promising to put the same in execution, if he was delivered from the trouble he was at that time under, and should be advanced to the throne.

The vision was this. When Ethelfrid, his predecessor, was persecuting him, he for many years wandered in a private manner through several places and kingdoms, and at last came to Redwald, beseeching him to give him protection against the snares of his powerful persecutor. Redwald willingly admitted him, and promised to perform what he requested. But when Ethelfrid understood that he had appeared in that province, and that he and his companions were hospitably entertained by Redwald, he sent messengers to offer that king a great sum of money to murder him, but without effect. He sent a second and a third time, bidding more and more each time, and threatening to make war on him if he refused. Redwald, either terrified by his threats, or gained by his gifts, complied with his request, and promised either to kill Edwin, or to deliver him up to the ambassadors. This being observed by a trusty friend of his, he went into his chamber, where he was going to bed, for it was the first hour of the night; and calling him out, discovered what the king had promised to do with him, adding, " If, therefore, you think fit, I will this very hour conduct you out of this province, and lead you to a place where neither Redwald nor Ethelfrid shall ever find you." He answered, " I thank you for your good will, yet I cannot do what you propose, or be guilty of breaking the compact I have made with so great a king, when he has done me no harm, nor offered me any injury; but, on the contrary, if I must die, let it rather be by his hand than by that of any meaner person. For whither shall I now fly, when I have for so many years been a vagabond through all the provinces of Britain, to escape the hands of my enemies? " His friend being gone, Edwin remained alone without, and sitting with a heavy heart before the palace, began to be overwhelmed with many thoughts, not knowing what to do, or which way to turn himself.

When he had remained a long time in silence, brooding over his misfortunes in anguish of mind, he, on a sudden, in the dead of night, saw approaching a person, whose face and habit were equally strange, at which unexpected sight he was not a little frightened. The stranger coming close up, saluted him, and asked him, " Why he sat there alone and melancholy on a stone at that time, when all others were taking their rest, and were fast asleep? " Edwin, in his turn, asked, " What it was to him, whether he spent the night within doors or abroad? " The stranger, in reply, said, " Do not think that I am ignorant of the cause of your grief, your watching, and sitting alone without. For I know who you are, and why you grieve, and the evils which you fear will fall upon you. But tell me, what reward you will give the man that shall deliver you out of this anguish, and persuade Redwald neither to do you any harm himself, nor to deliver you up to be murdered by your enemies." Edwin replied, " That he would give that person all that he was able for so singular a favour." The other further added, " What if I also assure you, that you shall overcome your enemies, and surpass in power, not only all your own progenitors, but even all that have reigned before you over the English nation? " Edwin, encouraged by these questions, did not hesitate to promise that he would make a suitable return to him who should so highly oblige him. Then said the other, " But if he who foretells so much good as is to befall you, can also give you better advice for your life and salvation than any of your progenitors or kindred ever heard of, do you consent to submit to him, and to follow his wholesome counsel?" Edwin did not hesitate to promise that he would in all things follow the directions of that man who should deliver him from so many calamities, and raise him to a throne.

Having received this answer, the person that talked to him laid his hand on his head saying, "When this sign shall be given you, remember this present discourse that has passed between us, and do not delay the performance of what you now promise." Having uttered these words, he is said to have immediately vanished, that the king might understand it was not a man, but a spirit, that had appeared to him.

Whilst the royal youth still sat there alone, glad of the comfort he had received, but seriously considering who he was, or whence he came, that had so talked to him, his above-mentioned friend came to him, and saluting him with a pleasant countenance, "Rise," said he, "go in and compose yourself to sleep without fear; for the king's resolution is altered, and he designs to do you no harm, but rather to perform the promise which he made you; for when he had privately acquainted the queen with his intention of doing what I told you before, she dissuaded him from it, declaring it was unworthy of so great a king to sell his good friend in such distress for gold, and to sacrifice his honour, which is more valuable than all other ornaments, for the lucre of money." In short, the king did as he was advised, and not only refused to deliver up the banished man to his enemy's messengers, but assisted him to recover his kingdom. For as soon as the ambassadors were returned home, he raised a mighty army to make war on Ethelfrid; who, meeting him with much inferior forces (for Redwald had not given him time to gather all his power), was slain on the borders of the kingdom of Mercia, on the east side of the river that is called Idle. In this battle, Redwald's son, called Regnhere, was killed; and thus Edwin, pursuant to the oracle he had received, not only escaped the danger from the king his enemy, but, by his death, succeeded him in the throne.

King Edwin, therefore, delaying to receive the word of God at the preaching of Paulinus, and using for some time, as has been said, to sit several hours alone, and seriously to ponder with himself what he was to do, and what religion he was to follow, the man of God came to him, laid his right hand on his head, and asked, "Whether he knew that sign?" The king in a trembling condition, was ready to fall down at his feet, but he raised him up, and in a familiar manner said to him, "Behold by the help of God you have escaped the hands of the enemies whom you feared. Behold you have of his gift obtained the kingdom which you desired. Take heed not to delay that which you promised to perform; embrace the faith, and keep the precepts of Him who, delivering you from temporal adversity, has raised you to the honour of a temporal kingdom; and if, from this time forward, you shall be obedient to his will, which through me He signifies to you, He will not only deliver you from the everlasting torments of the wicked, but also make you partaker with Him of his eternal kingdom in heaven."

(*Ecclesiastical History.*)

II.—The Poet Cædmon

There was in the same monastery a brother, on whom the gift of writing verses was bestowed by Heaven. (A.D. 680.)

There was in this abbess's monastery a certain brother, particularly remarkable for the grace of God, who was wont to make pious and religious verses, so that whatever was interpreted to him out of Scripture, he soon after put the same into poetical expressions of much sweetness and humility, in English, which was his native language. By his verses the minds of many were often excited to despise the world, and to aspire to heaven. Others after him attempted, in the English nation, to compose religious poems, but none could ever compare with him, for he did not learn the art of poetry from men, but from God; for which reason he never could compose any trivial or vain poem, but only those which relate to religion suited his religious tongue; for having lived in a secular habit till he was well advanced in years, he had never learned anything of versifying; for which reason being sometimes at entertainments, when it was agreed for the sake of mirth that all present should sing in their turns, when he saw the instrument come towards him, he rose up from table and returned home.

Having done so at a certain time, and gone out of the house where the entertainment was, to the stable, where he had to take care of the horses that night, he there composed himself to rest at the proper time; a person appeared to him in his sleep, and saluting him by his name, said, " Cædmon, sing some song to me." He answered, " I cannot sing; for that was the reason why I left the entertainment, and retired to this place because I could not sing." The other who talked to him, replied, " However, you shall sing." " What shall I sing? " rejoined he. " Sing the beginning of created beings," said the other. Hereupon he presently began to sing verses to the praise of God, which he had never heard, the purport whereof was thus :—We are now to praise the Maker of the heavenly kingdom, the power of the Creator and His counsel, the deeds of the Father of glory. How He, being the eternal God, became the author of all miracles, who first, as almighty preserver of the human race, created heaven for the sons of men as the roof of the house, and next the earth. This is the sense, but not the words in order as he sang them in his sleep; for verses, though never so well composed, cannot be literally translated out of one language into another, without losing much of their beauty and loftiness. Awaking from his sleep, he remembered all that he had sung in his dream, and soon added much more to the same effect in verse worthy of the Deity.

In the morning he came to the steward, his superior, and having acquainted him with the gift he had received, was conducted to the abbess, by whom he was ordered, in the presence of many learned men, to tell his dream, and repeat the verses, that they might all give their judgment what it was, and whence his verse proceeded. They all concluded that heavenly grace had been conferred on him by our Lord. They expounded to him a passage in holy writ, either historical, or doctrinal, ordering him, if he could, to put the same into verse. Having undertaken it, he went away, and returning the next morning, gave it to them composed in most excellent verse; whereupon the abbess, embracing the grace of God in the man, instructed him to quit the secular habit, and take upon him the monastic life; which being accordingly done, she associated him to the rest of the brethren in her monastery, and ordered that he should be taught the whole series of sacred history. Thus Cædmon, keeping in mind all he heard, and as it were chewing the cud, converted the same into most harmonious verse; and sweetly repeating the same, made his masters in their turn his hearers. He sang the creation of the world, the origin of man, and all the history of Genesis : and made many verses on the departure of the children of Israel out of Egypt, and their entering into the land of promise, with many other histories from holy writ; the incarnation, passion, resurrection of our Lord, and His ascension into heaven; the coming of the Holy Ghost, and the preaching of the apostles; also the terror of future judgment, the horror of the pains of hell, and the delights of heaven; besides many more about the Divine benefits and judgments, by which he endeavoured to turn away all men from the love of vice, and to excite in them the love of, and application to, good actions; for he was a very religious man, humbly submissive to regular discipline but full of zeal against those who behaved themselves otherwise; for which reason he ended his life happily.

For when the time of his departure drew near, he laboured for the space of fourteen days under a bodily infirmity which seemed to prepare the way, yet so moderate that he could talk and walk the whole time. In his neighbourhood was the house to which those that were sick, and like shortly to die, were carried. He desired the person that attended him, in the evening, as the night came on in which he was to depart this life, to make ready a place there for him to take his rest. This person, wondering why he should desire it, because there was as yet no sign of his dying soon, did what he had ordered. He accordingly went there, and conversing pleasantly in a joyful manner with the rest that were in the house before, when it was past midnight, he asked them, whether they had the Eucharist there? They answered, " What need of the Eucharist? for you are not likely to die, since you talk so merrily with us, as if you were in perfect health."—" However," said he, " bring me the Eucharist." Having received the same into his hand, he asked, whether they were all in charity with him, and without any enmity or rancour? They answered, that they were all in perfect charity, and free from anger; and in their turn asked him, whether he was in the same mind towards them? He answered, " I am in charity, my children, with all the servants of God." Then strengthening himself with the heavenly viaticum, he prepared for the entrance into another life, and asked, how near the time was when the brothers were to be awakened to sing the nocturnal praises of our Lord? They answered, " It is not far off." Then he said, " Well, let us wait that hour;" and signing himself with the sign of the cross, he laid his head on the pillow, and falling into a slumber, ended his life so in silence.

Thus it came to pass, that as he had served God with a simple and pure mind, and undisturbed devotion, so he now departed to his presence, leaving the world by a quiet death; and that tongue, which had composed so many holy words in praise of the Creator, uttered its last words whilst he was in the act of signing himself with the cross, and recommending himself into his hands, and by what has been here said, he seems to have had foreknowledge of his death.

(*Ecclesiastical History.*)

THE ANGLO-SAXON CHRONICLE

I.—CYNEWULF AND CYNEHEARD

From the Winchester (Parker) Chronicle, 755

IN this year Cynewulf and the councillors of Wessex deprived Sigeberht of his kingdom for unlawful actions, with the exception of Hampshire; but this he kept until he slew the ealdorman who remained faithful to him longer than the rest. And Cynewulf frequently fought great battles against the Welsh; and after ruling thirty-one years he wished to expel a prince called Cyneheard; and Cyneheard was the brother of Sigeberht. And then he learnt that the king was visiting a mistress at Merton, with but a small retinue; and he surprised him there, and surrounded the bower before the men who were with the king became aware of him. And then the king perceived this, and he went to the door and then gallantly defended himself until he caught sight of the prince, and then rushed out on him and severely wounded him; and they all set on the king until they had slain him. And then from the woman's cries the king's thanes became aware of the disturbance, and whoever then was ready and quickest ran thither; and the prince offered each of them money and life, and none of them would accept it, but they went on fighting continuously until they all lay slain, except one Welsh hostage, and he was badly wounded. When in the morning the king's thanes who had been left behind heard that the king was slain, then they rode thither, and his ealdorman Osric and Wigfrith his thane and the men whom he had left behind, and found the prince in the residence where the king lay slain, and they had closed the gates upon themselves, and then they attacked. And then he offered them their own choice of money and land if they would grant him the kingdom, and they told them that kinsmen of theirs were with them who would not desert them; and then they replied that no kinsman was dearer to them than their lord, and they never would follow his slayer; and then they offered to let their kinsmen depart unharmed. And they replied that the same had been offered to their companions who had been with the king; then they said that they themselves did not care for this "any more than your comrades who were slain with the king." And they went on fighting around the gates until they penetrated inside and slew the prince and the men who were with him, all except one who was the ealdorman's godson, and he (the ealdorman) saved his life, and yet he (the godson) had been wounded many times.

II.—ALFRED AND GUTHRUM

From the Peterborough (Laud) Chronicle, 878 (877)

In this year the host went secretly in midwinter after Twelfth Night to Chippenham, and rode over Wessex and occupied it, and drove a great part of the inhabitants beyond the sea, and of the rest the greater part they reduced to submission, except Alfred the king, and he with a small company moved under difficulties through woods and into inaccessible places in marshes. And in the same winter a brother of Ivar and Halfdan was in Wessex, in Devon, and there he was slain and eight hundred men with him and forty men of his retinue; and there the banner which they called the Raven was captured. And the Easter after, king Alfred with a small company built a fortification at Athelney, and from that fortification, with that part of the men of Somerset nearest to it, he continued fighting against the host. Then in the seventh week after Easter he rode to *Ecgbrihtesstan*, to the east of Selwood, and came to meet him there all the men of Somerset and Wiltshire and that part of Hampshire which was on this side of the sea, and they received him warmly. And one day later he went from those camps to Iley Oak, and one day later to Edington; and there he fought against the entire host, and put it to flight, and rode after it up to the fortification, and laid siege there a fortnight, and then the host gave him hostages and solemn oaths that they would leave his kingdom, and promised in addition that their king would receive baptism, and fulfilled this promise. And three weeks later the king Guthrum came to him, one of thirty of the most honourable men in the host, at Aller which is near Athelney, where the king stood sponsor to him at baptism; and the ceremony of the removal of the baptismal fillet took place at Wedmore, and he was twelve days with the king, who greatly honoured him and his companions with riches.

III.—THE BUILDING OF THE LONG SHIPS

From the Winchester (Parker) Chronicle, 897 (896)

Then the following summer, in this year, the host dispersed, some to East Anglia, some to Northumbria, and those without stock got themselves ships, and sailed south across the sea to the Seine.

The host, by the mercy of God, had not altogether utterly

crushed the English people; but they were much more severely crushed during those three years by murrain and plague, most of all by the fact that many of the best of the king's servants in the land passed away during those three years: one of these was Swithwulf, bishop of Rochester, and Ceolmund, ealdorman in Kent, and Beorhtwulf, ealdorman in Essex, and Wulfred, ealdorman in Hampshire, and Ealhheard, bishop at Dorchester, and Eadwulf, the king's thane in Sussex, and Beornwulf, town-reeve in Winchester, and Ecgwulf, the king's marshal, and many others in addition to them, though I have named the most distinguished.

This same year the hosts in East Anglia and Northumbria greatly harassed Wessex along the south coast with predatory bands, most of all with the warships they had built many years before. Then king Alfred ordered warships to be built to meet the Danish ships: they were almost twice as long as the others, some had sixty oars, some more; they were both swifter, steadier, and with more freeboard than the others; they were built neither after the Frisian pattern nor after the Danish, but as it seemed to himself that they could be most serviceable. Then on one occasion the same year came six ships to the Isle of Wight and did much harm there, both in Devon and almost everywhere along the coast. Then the king ordered nine of the new ships to put out, and they blockaded the entrance from the open sea against their escape. Then the Danes sailed out with three ships against them, and three of their ships were beached on dry land at the upper end of the harbour, and the crews had gone off inland. Then the English seized two of the three ships at the entrance to the estuary, and slew the men, but the other escaped; in her also all but five were slain; and they escaped because the ships of the others were aground: they were also very awkwardly aground; three had gone aground on the side of the channel where the Danish ships were aground, and the others all on the other side, so that none of them could reach the others. But when the tide had ebbed many furlongs from the ships, the Danes went from the three ships to the other three which were stranded on their side, and then there they fought. There were slain Lucumon, the king's reeve, and Wulfheard the Frisian, and Æbbe the Frisian, and Æthelhere the Frisian, and Æthelfrith of the king's household, totalling sixty-two killed of English and Frisians, and one hundred and twenty of the Danes. The tide, however, came first to the Danish ships, before the Christians could push off theirs, and hence they rowed away out to sea. They were so sorely crippled that they were unable to row past Sussex, but there the sea cast two of them ashore; the men were led to the king at Winchester, and he had them hanged there. The men who were on the single ship reached East Anglia badly wounded. This same summer no less than twenty ships perished with all hands along the south coast. The same year Wulfric, the king's marshal, passed away: he had also been the Welsh reeve.

IV.—KING HAROLD, EARL TOSTIG, AND EARL WILLIAM

From the Abingdon Chronicle, 1066

Then meanwhile came Harold, the king of the English, with all his levies on the Sunday to Tadcaster and there set his ships in order; and on the Monday he marched through York. Harold, king of Norway, and earl Tostig and their force had gone from their ships beyond York to Stamford Bridge, for it had been expressly promised them that hostages would be brought to meet them there from the whole of the shire. Then Harold, king of the English, came upon them unawares beyond the bridge. They joined battle and fierce fighting went on until late in the day; and there Harold, king of Norway, was slain and earl Tostig and countless numbers of men with them, both English and Norwegians. The Norwegians fled from the English, but there was one Norwegian who stood firm against the English forces, so that they could not scale the bridge nor clinch victory. An Englishman shot with an arrow but to no avail, and another went under the bridge and stabbed him through under the coat of mail. Then Harold, king of the English, crossed the bridge and his levies went forward with him; and there made great slaughter of both Norwegians and Flemings: and Harold let the king's son, who was called Mundus [the "Elegant"], return to Norway with all the ships.

Then duke William sailed into Pevensey on the eve of Michaelmas [28 September]. As soon as his men were fit for service, they constructed a castle at Hastings. When king Harold was informed of this, he gathered together a great host, and came to oppose him at the grey apple tree and William came upon him unexpectedly before his army was set in order. Nevertheless the king fought against him most resolutely with those men who wished to stand by him, and there was great slaughter on both sides. King Harold was slain, and Leofwine his brother, and earl Gyrth his brother, and many good men. The French had possession of the place of slaughter, as God granted them because of the nation's sins. Archbishop Ealdred and the citizens of London wished to have prince Edgar for king, as was indeed his right by birth, and Edwin and Morcar promised that they would fight for him, but always when some initiative should have been shewn there was delay from day to day until matters went from bad to worse, as everything did in the end. This battle took place on the day of pope Calixtus [14 October].

V.—THE DEATH OF KING HENRY

From the Peterborough (Laud) Chronicle, 1138

At Lammas [1 August] of this year king Henry went overseas; and on the following day, while he lay asleep on board, the light of day was eclipsed over all lands, and the sun looked like a moon three nights old and there were stars around it at midday.

Then men were greatly astonished and terrified, and said that some important event should follow upon this; and so it did, for in that very year the king died in Normandy the day after St. Andrew's day [30 November]. Then at once this country was in eclipse, for every man who could was quick to rob his neighbour. Then his son and his friends took his body and brought it to England, and they buried him at Reading. He was a good man, and was held in great awe. In his days no man dared to wrong another. He made peace for man and beast. Whoever bore a burden of gold and silver, no man dared say to him aught but good. (From the version by G. N. Garmonsway.)

KING ALFRED (849–901)

I.—THE VOYAGE OF OTHERE

OTHERE said to his lord, King Alfred, that he dwelt furthest north of all the Northmen. He said that he dwelt in the land northwards along the Western Sea. He said, however, that that land stretches very far north from thence; but it is all waste except in a few places here and there where Finns dwell, hunting in winter, and in summer fishing in the sea. He said that at some time he tried to find out how far that land stretched to the north, and whether any man dwelt to the north of the waste. Then he went north along the land, and all the way for three days he had that waste land on the starboard and the open sea on the larboard. Then he was as far north as the whale fishers go. Then he went northwards as far as he could sail in three more days. Then the land bent eastwards, or the sea flowed in upon the land, he knew not which; but he knew that he awaited there a north-west wind and went eastward

along the land as far as he could sail in four days. Then he
had to wait for a due north wind, because the land there bent
to the south, or the sea flowed in upon the land, he knew not
which. Then he sailed due south along the land as far as he
could in five days. There went a great river up into the land.
Then they turned up the river because they dared not sail past
it for fear of hostility; for the land was all inhabited on the
other side of the river. Before this he had not found any inhabited land since he left his own home; but all the way there
had been waste land on the starboard, except for fishers and
fowlers and hunters, and they were all Finns; and on the larboard was always the open sea. The Permeans had cultivated
their land very well; but they dared not go there. But the
land of the Finns was all waste except where the hunters, fishers,
or fowlers dwelt.

The Permians told him many stories, both of their own land
and the lands which lay about them, but he did not know what
was true for he had not seen them himself. It seemed to him
that the Finns and the Permians spoke almost the same language. Besides for surveying the land, he went there chiefly
because of the walruses, for they have very fine bone in their
teeth (they brought some of the teeth to the king), and their
hide is very good for ships' ropes. The walrus is much smaller
than other whales, it is not more than seven ells long; but in
his own land is the best walrus-fishing; there they are forty-
eight ells long, and the biggest fifty; he said that he with five
others slew sixty of these in two days.

He was a very rich man in the possessions in which their
wealth consists, that is in deer.

He had, when he came to the king, six hundred tame deer
unsold. These deer are called reindeer; of these six were
decoy-deer; these are very precious among the Finns, because
they catch the wild deer with them. He was one of the chief
men in the land, though he had not more than twenty cattle
and twenty sheep and twenty swine; and the little that he
ploughed he ploughed with horses. But their wealth lies chiefly
in the tribute which the Finns pay them. That tribute consists
of deerskins, birds' feathers, and walrus bone, and of the ship's
ropes which are made of walrus hide, or of seal. Each man pays
according to his rank. The highest must pay the skins of fifteen
martens and five reindeer, and one bear's skin and ten measures
of feathers, and a tunic of bear or otter skin and two ropes; both
must be sixty ells long and made either of whale hide or of seal.

(From the Anglo-Saxon of Alfred's *Orosius*.)

GEOFFREY OF MONMOUTH (*c.* 1120)

I.—THE GRIEF OF LEAR

SOME long time after, when Lear began to wax more sluggish by reason of age, the aforesaid dukes, with whom and his two daughters he had divided Britain, rebelled against him and took away from him the realm and the kingly power which up to that time he had held right manfully and gloriously. Howbeit, concord was restored, and one of his sons-in-law, Maglaunus, duke of Albany, agreed to maintain him with threescore knights, so that he should not be without some semblance of state. But after that he had sojourned with his son-in-law two years, his daughter Goneril began to wax indignant at the number of his knights, who flung gibes at her servants for that their rations were not more plentiful. Whereupon, after speaking to her husband, she ordered her father to be content with a service of thirty knights and to dismiss the other thirty that he had. The king, taking his in dudgeon, left Maglaunus, and betook him to Henvin, duke of Cornwall, unto whom he had married his other daughter. Here, at first, he was received with honour, but a year had not passed before discord again rose betwixt those of the king's household and those of the duke's, insomuch as that Regan, waxing indignant, ordered her father to dismiss all his company save five knights only to do him service. Her father, beyond measure aggrieved thereat, returned once more to his eldest daughter, thinking to move her to pity and to persuade her to maintain himself and his retinue. Howbeit, she had never renounced her first indignation, but swore by all the gods of Heaven that never should he take up his abode with her save he contented himself with the service of a single knight and were quit of all the rest. Moreover, she upbraided the old man for that, having nothing of his own to give away, he should be minded to go about with such a retinue; so that finding she would not give way to his wishes one single tittle, he at last obeyed and remained content with one knight only, leaving the rest to go their way. But when the remembrance of his former dignity came back unto him, bearing witness to the misery of the estate to which he was now reduced, he began to bethink him of going to his youngest daughter oversea. Howbeit, he sore misdoubted that she would do nought for him, seeing that he had held her, as I have said, in such scanty honour in the matter of her marriage. Natheless, disdaining any longer to endure so mean a life, he betook him across the Channel into

Gaul. But when he found that two other princes were making the passage at the same time, and that he himself had been assigned but the third place, he brake forth into tears and sobbing, and cried aloud: "Ye destinies that do pursue your wonted way marked out by irrevocable decree, wherefore was it your will ever to uplift me to happiness so fleeting? For a keener grief it is to call to mind that lost happiness than to suffer the presence of the unhappiness that cometh after. For the memory of the days when in the midst of hundreds of thousands of warriors I went to batter down the walls of cities and to lay waste the provinces of mine enemies is more grievous unto me than the calamity that hath overtaken me in the mean- ness of mine estate, which hath incited them that but now were grovelling under my feet to desert my feebleness. O angry fortune! will the day ever come wherein I may requite the evil turn that hath thus driven forth the length of my days and my poverty? O Cordelia, my daughter, how true were the words wherein thou didst make answer unto me, when I did ask of thee how much thou didst love me! For thou saidst: 'So much as thou hast, so much art thou worth, and so much do I love thee.' So long, therefore, as I had that which was mine own to give, so long seemed I of worth unto them that were the lovers, not of myself but of my gifts. They loved me at times, but better loved they the presents I made unto them. Now that the presents are no longer forthcoming, they too have gone their ways. But with what face, O thou dearest of my children, shall I dare appear before thee? I who, wroth with thee for these thy words, was minded to marry thee less honourably than thy sisters, who, after all the kindnesses I have conferred upon them have allowed me to become an outcast and a beggar?"

Landing at last, his mind filled with these reflections and others of a like kind, he came to Karitia, where his daughter lived, and waiting without the city, sent a messenger to tell her into what indigence he had fallen, and to beseech his daughter's compassion inasmuch as he had neither food nor clothing. On hearing the tidings, Cordelia was much moved and wept bitterly. When she made inquiry how many armed men he had with him, the messenger told her that he had none save a single knight, who was waiting with him without the city. Then took she as much gold and silver as was needful and gave it unto the messenger, bidding him take her father to another city, where he should bathe him, clothe him, and nurse him, feigning that he was a sick man. She commanded also that he should have a retinue of forty knights well appointed and armed, and that then he should duly announce his arrival to Aganippus and herself. The messenger accordingly forthwith attended King Lear into another city, and hid him there in secret until that he had fully accomplished all that Cordelia had borne him on hand to do.

(History of the Kings of Britain.)

II.—THE CORONATION OF ARTHUR

When all at last were assembled in the city on the high day of the festival, the archbishops were conducted unto the palace to crown the king with the royal diadem. Dubric, therefore, upon whom the charge fell, for that the court was held within his diocese, was ready to celebrate the service. As soon as the king had been invested with the ensigns of kingship, he was led in right comely wise to the church of the metropolitan see, two archbishops supporting him, the one upon his right hand side the other upon his left. Four kings, moreover—to wit, those of Albany, Cornwall, and North and South Wales—went before him, bearing before him, as was their right, four golden swords. A company of clerics in holy orders of every degree went chanting music marvellous sweet in front. Of the other party, the archbishops and pontiffs led the queen, crowned with laurel and wearing her own ensigns, unto the church of the virgins dedicate. The four queens, moreover, of the four kings already mentioned, did bear before her according to wont and custom four white doves, and the ladies that were present did follow after her rejoicing greatly. At last, when the procession was over, so manifold was the music of the organs and so many were the hymns that were chanted in both churches, that the knights who were there scarce knew which church they should enter first for the exceeding sweetness of the harmonies in both. First into the one and then into the other they flocked in crowds, nor, had the whole day been given up to the celebration, would any have felt a moment's weariness thereof. And when the divine services had been celebrated in both churches, the king and queen put off their crowns, and doing on lighter robes of state, went to meat, he to his palace with the men, she to another palace with the women. For the Britons did observe the ancient custom of the Trojans, and were wont to celebrate their high festival days, the men with the men and the women with the women severally. And when all were set at table according as the rank of each did demand, Kay the seneschal in a doublet furred of ermines, and a thousand youths of full high degree in his company, all likewise clad in ermines, did serve the meats along with him. Of the other part, as many in doublets furred of vair did follow Bedevere the butler, and along with him did serve the drinks from the divers ewers into the manifold-fashioned cups. In the palace of the queen no less did numberless pages, clad in divers brave liveries, offer their services each after his office, the which were I to go about to describe I might draw out my history into an endless prolixity. For at that time was Britain exalted into so high a pitch of dignity as that it did surpass all other kingdoms in plenty of riches, in luxury of adornment, and in the courteous wit of them that dwelt therein. Whatsoever knight in the land was of renown for his prowess did wear his clothes and his arms all of one same colour. And the dames, no less witty, would apparel them in like manner in a single colour, nor would they deign have the love of none save he had thrice approved him in the wars. Wherefore at that time did dames wax chaste and knights the nobler for their love.

Refreshed by their banqueting, they go forth into the fields without the city, and sundry among them fall to playing at sundry manner games. Presently the knights engage in a game on horseback, making show of fighting a battle whilst the dames and damsels looking on from the top of the walls, for whose sake the courtly knights make believe to be fighting, do cheer them on for the sake of seeing the better sport. Others elsewhere spend the rest of the day in shooting arrows, some in tilting with spears, some in flinging heavy stones, some in putting the weight; others again in playing at the dice or in a diversity of other games, but all without wrangling; and whosoever had done best in his own game was presented by Arthur with a boon of price. And after the first three days had been spent on this wise, upon the fourth day all they that had done service in virtue of the office they held were summoned, and unto each was made grant of the honour of the office he held, in possession, earldom, to wit, of city or castle, archbishopric, bishopric, abbacy, or whatsoever else it might be.

(History of the Kings of Britain.)

THE NUNS' RULE (ANCRENE RIWLE) (*c.* 1220)

ASCRIBED TO RICHARD POORE, BISHOP OF SALISBURY, 1217–1229

I.—OF SPEECH

SPEAKING and tasting are both in the mouth, as sight is in the eyes; but we shall let tasting alone until we speak of your food, and treat, at present, of speaking, and thereafter of hearing, of both in common, in some measure, as they go together.

First of all, when you have to go to your parlour window, learn from your maid who it is that is come; for it may be some one whom you ought to shun; and, when you must needs go forth, make the sign of the cross carefully on your mouth, ears, and eyes, and on your breast also, and go forth in the fear of God to a priest. Say, first, " Confiteor," and then, " Benedicite," which he ought to say; hear his words and sit quite still, that, when he parteth from you, he may not know either good or evil of you, nor know anything either to praise or to blame in you. Some one is so learned and of such wise speech, that she would have him to know it, who sits and talks to him and gives him word for word, and becomes a preceptor, who should be an anchoress, and teaches him who is come to teach her; and would, by her own account, soon be celebrated and known among the wise. Known she is well; for, from the very circumstance that she thinketh herself to be reputed wise, he understands that she is a fool; for she hunteth after praise and catches reproach. For, at last, when he is gone away he will say, " This anchoress is a great talker." Eve, in Paradise, held a long conversation with the serpent, and told him all the lesson that God had taught her and Adam concerning the apple; and thus the fiend, by her talk, understood, at once, her weakness, and found out the way to ruin her. Our lady, Saint Mary, acted in a quite different manner. She told the angel no tale, but asked him briefly that which she wanted to know. Do you, my dear sisters, imitate our lady, and not the cackling Eve. Wherefore, let an anchoress, whatsoever she be, keep silence as much as ever she can and may. Let her not have the hen's nature. When the hen has laid, she must needs cackle. And what does she get by it? Straightway comes the chough and robs her of her eggs and devours all that of which she should have brought forth her live birds. And just so the wicked chough, the devil, beareth away from the cackling anchoresses, and swalloweth up, all the good they have brought forth, and which ought, as birds, to bear them up toward heaven, if it had not been cackled. The poor pedlar makes more noise to cry his soap than a rich mercer all his valuable wares. Of a spiritual man in whom you place confidence, as you may do, it is good that you ask counsel, and that he teach you a safe remedy against temptations; and in confession show him, if it will hear you, your greatest and vilest sins, that he may pity you, and out of compassion cry internally to Christ to have mercy upon you, and have you often in his mind and in his prayers. "But be aware and on your guard," saith our Lord, "for many come to you clothed in lambs' fleece, and are raging wolves." Believe secular men little, religious still less. Desire not too much their acquaintance. Eve spoke with the serpent without fear. Our lady was afraid of speaking with Gabriel.

II.—OF TRAFFIC AND OF DRESS

Ye shall not possess any beast, my dear sisters, except only a cat. An anchoress that hath cattle appears as Martha was, a better housewife than anchoress; nor can she in any wise be Mary, with peacefulness of heart. For then she must think of the cow's fodder, and of the herdsman's hire, flatter the heyward, defend herself when her cattle is shut up in the pinfold, and moreover pay the damage. Christ knoweth, it is an odious thing when people in the town complain of anchoresses' cattle. If, however, any one must needs have a cow, let her take care that she neither annoy nor harm any one, and that her own thoughts be not fixed thereon. An anchoress ought not to have any thing that draweth her heart outward. Carry ye on no traffic. An anchoress that is a buyer and seller selleth her soul to the chapman of hell. Do not take charge of other men's property in your house, nor of their cattle, nor their clothes, neither perceive under your care the church vestments, nor the chalice, unless force compel you, or great fear, for oftentimes much harm has come from such caretaking. Let no man sleep within your walls. If, however, great necessity should cause your house to be used, see that, as long as it is used, ye have therein with you a woman of unspotted life day and night.

Because no man seeth you, nor do ye see any man, ye may be well content with your clothes, be they white, be they black; only see that they be plain, and warm, and well made—skins well tawed; and have as many as you need, for bed and also for back.

Next your flesh ye shall wear no flaxen cloth, except it be of hards and of coarse canvas. Whoso will may have a stamin, and whoso will may be without it. Ye shall sleep in a garment and girt. Wear no iron, nor haircloth, nor hedgehog-skins; and do not beat yourselves therewith, nor with a scourge of leather thongs, nor leaded; and do not with holly nor with briars cause yourselves to bleed without leave of your confessor; and do not, at one time, use too many flagellations. Let your shoes be thick and warm. In summer ye are at liberty to go and to sit barefoot, and to wear hose without vamps, and whoso liketh may lie in them. A woman may well enough wear drawers of haircloth very well tied, with the strapples reaching down to her feet, laced tightly. If ye would dispense with wimples, have warm capes, and over them black veils. She who wishes to be seen, it is no great wonder though she adorn herself; but, in the eyes of God, she is more lovely who is unadorned outwardly for his sake. Have neither ring, nor brooch, nor ornamental girdle, nor gloves, nor any such thing that is not proper for you to have.

JOHN WYCLIFFE (1324–1384)
A Rule of Life

If thou be a lord, look thou live a rightful life in thine own person, both anent God and man, keeping the hests of God, doing the works of mercy, ruling well thy five wits, and doing reason and equity and good conscience to all men. The second time, govern well thy wife, thy children and thy homely men in God's law, and suffer no sin among them, neither in word nor in deed, up thy might, that they may be ensamples of holiness and righteousness to all other. For thou shalt be damned for their evil life and thine evil sufferance, but if thou amend it up thy might. The third time, govern well thy tenants, and maintain them in right and reason and be merciful to them in their rents and worldly merciments, and suffer not thy officers to do them wrong nor extortions, and chastise in good manner them that be rebel against God's hests and virtuous living, more than for rebellion against thine own cause or person. And hold with God's cause, and love, reward, praise, and cherish the true and virtuous of life, more than if they do only thine own profit and worship; and maintain truly, up thy cunning and might, God's law and true preachers thereof, and God's servants in rest and peace, for by this reason thou holdest thy lordship of God. And if thou failest of this, thou forfeitest against God in all thy lordship, in body and soul; principally if thou maintainest Antichrist's disciples in their errors against Christ's life and His teaching, for blindness and worldly friendship, and helpest to slander and pursue true men that teach Christ's Gospel and His life. And warn the people of their great sins, and of false priests and hypocrites that deceive Christian men, in faith and virtuous life, and worldly goods also.

If thou be a labourer, live in meekness, and truly and wilfully do thy labour; that if thy lord or thy master be an heathen man that by thy meekness and wilful and true service, he have not to murmur against thee, nor slander thy God nor Christendom.

And serve not to Christian lords with murmuring, nor only in their presence, but truly and wilfully in their absence, not only for worldly dread nor worldly reward, but for dread of God and good conscience, and for reward in heaven. For that God that putteth thee in such service wots what state is best for thee, and will reward thee more than all earthly lords may, if thou dost it truly and wilfully for His ordinance. And in all things beware of murmuring against God and His visitation, in great labour and long, and great sickness and other adversities, and beware of wrath, of cursing and *warying*, or banning of man or of beast. And ever keep patience and meekness and charity both to God and man. And thus each man in these three states oweth to live, to save himself and help other; and thus should good life, rest, peace, and charity be among Christian men, and they be saved, and heathen men soon converted, and God magnified greatly in all nations and sects that now despise Him and His law, for the wicked living of false Christian men.

SIR JOHN MANDEVILLE (b.   ?–d. 1372)

I.—THE ROYAL ESTATE OF PRESTER JOHN

THIS emperor, Prester John, possesses very extensive territory, and has many very noble cities and good towns in his realm, and many great and large isles. For all the country of India is divided into isles, by the great floods that come from Paradise, that separate all the land into many parts. And also in the sea he has full many isles. And the best city in the isle of Pentexoire is Nyse, a very royal city, noble and very rich. This Prester John has under him many kings, and many isles, and many divers people of divers conditions. And this land is full good and rich, but not so rich as the land of the great chan. For the merchants come not thither so commonly to buy merchandise as they do in the land of the great chan, for it is too far.

And on the other side, in the isle of Cathay, men find all things needful to man, cloths of gold, of silk, and spicery. And therefore, although men have them cheap in the isle of Prester John, they dread the long way and the great perils in the sea. For in many places of the sea are great rocks of stone of adamant (loadstone), which of its nature draws iron to it; and therefore there pass no ships that have either bonds or nails of iron in them; and if they do, anon the rocks of adamant draw them to them, that they may never go thence. I myself have seen afar in that sea, as though it had been a great isle full of trees and bushes, full of thorns and briers, in great plenty; and the shipmen told us that all that was of ships that were drawn thither by the adamants, for the iron that was in them. And of the rottenness and other things that were within the ships, grew such bushes, and thorns, and briers, and green grass, and such kinds of things; and of the masts and the sailyards, it seemed a great wood or a grove.

And such rocks are in many places thereabout. And therefore merchants dare not pass there, except they know well the passages, or unless they have good pilots. And also they dread the long way, and, therefore, they go to Cathay, because it is nearer; and yet it is not so nigh but men must travel by sea and land eleven or twelve months, from Genoa or from Venice, to Cathay. And yet is the land of Prester John more far, by many dreadful days' journey. And the merchants pass by the kingdom of Persia, and go to a city called Hermes, because Hermes the philosopher founded it. And after that they pass an arm of the sea, and then they go to another city called Golbache; and there they find merchandise, and as great abundance of parrots as men find here of geese. In that country is but little wheat or barley, and therefore they eat rice and honey, milk, cheese, and fruit.

This emperor, Prester John, takes always to wife the daughter of the great chan; and the great chan also in the same wise the daughter of Prester John. For they two are the greatest lords under the firmament.

In the land of Prester John are many divers things and many precious stones, so great and so large, that men make of them plates, dishes, cups, etc. And many other marvels are there, that it were too long to put in a book. But I will tell you of his principal isles, and of his estate, and of his law. This emperor Prester John is a Christian, and a great part of his country also; but they have not all the articles of our faith. They believe in the Father, Son, and Holy Ghost, and they are very devout and true to one another. And he has under him seventy-two provinces, and in every province is a king, all which kings are tributary to Prester John. And in his lordships are many great marvels, for in his country is the sea called the Gravelly Sea, which is all gravel and sand, without a drop of water; and it ebbs and flows in great waves, as other seas do, and it is never still. And no man can pass that sea with ships, and, therefore, no man knows what land is beyond that sea. And although it has no water, men find therein, and on the banks, very good fish, of different nature and shape from what is found in any other sea; and they are of very good taste, and delicious to eat.

Three days from that sea are great mountains, out of which runs a great river which comes from Paradise, and it is full of precious stones, without a drop of water, and it runs through the desert, on one side, so that it makes the Gravelly Sea where it ends. And that river runs only three days in the week, and brings with it great stones and the rocks also therewith, and that in great plenty. And when they are entered into the Gravelly Sea they are seen no more. And in those three days that that river runneth, no man dare enter into it, but in the other days men dare enter well enough. Beyond that river, more up towards the deserts, is a great plain all gravelly between the mountains; and in that plain, every day at sunrise, small trees begin to grow, and they grow till mid-day, bearing fruit; but no man dare take of that fruit, for it is a thing of fairie. And after mid-day they decrease and enter again into the earth, so that at sunset they appear no more; and so they do every day.

In that desert are many wild men, hideous to look on, and horned; and they speak nought, but grunt like pigs. And there is also great plenty of wild dogs. And there are many parrots, which speak of their own nature, and salute men that go through the deserts, and speak to them as plainly as though it were a man. And they that speak well have a large tongue, and have five toes upon each foot. And there are also others which have but three toes upon each foot, and they speak but little.

This emperor Prester John, when he goes to battle against any other lord, has no banners borne before him; but he has three large crosses of gold full of precious stones; and each cross is set in a chariot full richly arrayed. And to keep each cross are appointed ten thousand men of arms, and more than one hundred thousand footmen. And this number of people is independent of the chief army. And when he has no war, but rides with a private company, he has before him but one plain cross of wood, in remembrance that Jesus Christ suffered death upon a wooden cross. And they carry before him also a platter of gold full of earth, in token that his nobleness, and his might, and his flesh, shall turn to earth. And he has borne before him also a vessel of silver, full of noble jewels of gold and precious stones, in token of his lordship, nobility, and power. He dwells commonly in the city of Susa, and there is his principal palace, which is so rich and noble that no man can conceive it without seeing it.

(Travels.)

II.—THE PERILOUS VALLEY

Near that isle of Mistorak, upon the left side, nigh to the river of Pison, is a marvellous thing. There is a vale between the mountains which extends nearly four miles; and some call it the Enchanted Vale, some call it the Vale of Devils, and some the Perilous Vale. In that vale men hear oftentimes great tempests and thunders, and great murmurs and noises, day and night; and great noise as it were of tabors, and nakeres, and trumpets, as though it were of a great feast. This vale is all full of devils and has been always; and men say there that it is one of the entrances of hell. In that vale is great plenty of gold and silver; wherefore many misbelieving men, and many Christians also, oftentimes go in, to have of the treasure; but few return, especially of the misbelieving men, for they are anon strangled by the devils.

And in the centre of that vale, under a rock, is a head and the visage of a devil bodily, full horrible and dreadful to see, and it shows but the head to the shoulders. But there is no man in the world so bold, Christian or other, but he would be in dread to behold it, and he would feel almost dead with fear, so hideous is it to behold. For he looks at every man so sharply with dreadful eyes, that are ever moving and sparkling like fire, and changes and stirs so often in divers manners, with so horrible a countenance, that no man dare approach towards him. And from him issues smoke, and stink, and fire, and so much abomination that scarce any man may endure there. But the good Christians, that are stable in their faith, enter without peril; for they will first shrive them, and mark them with the sign of the holy cross, so that the fiends have no power over them. But although they are without peril, yet they are not without dread when they see the devils visibly and bodily all about them, that make full many divers assaults and menaces, in air and on earth, and terrify them with strokes of thunder-blasts and of tempests. And the greatest fear is that God will take vengeance then of that which men have misdone against His will.

And you shall understand that when my fellows and I were in this vale, we were in great thought whether we durst put our bodies in aventure, to go in or not, in the protection of God; and some of our fellows agreed to enter, and some not. So there were with us two worthy men, friars minors of Lombardy, who said that if any man would enter they would go in with us; and when they had said so, upon the gracious trust of God and of them, we heard mass, and every man was shriven and housled; and when we entered, fourteen persons, but at our going out we were but nine. And so we never knew whether our fellows were lost, or had turned back for fear; but we never saw them after. They were two men of Greece, and three of Spain. And our other fellows, that would not go in with us, went by another road to be before us; and so they were.

And thus we passed that Perilous Vale, and found therein gold and silver, and precious stones, and rich jewels, in great plenty, both here and there, as it seemed; but whether it was as it seemed I know not, for I touched none; because the devils are so subtle to make a thing to seem otherwise than it is, to deceive mankind; and therefore I touched none; and also because that I would not be put out of my devotion, for I was more devout then than ever I was before or after, and all for the dread of fiends that I saw in divers figures; and also for the great multitude of dead bodies that I saw there lying by the way, in all the vale, as though there had been a battle between two kings, and the mightiest of the country, and that the greater party had been discomfited and slain. And I believe that hardly should any country have so many people in it as lay slain in that vale, as it seemed to us, which was a hideous sight to see. And I marvelled much that there were so many, and the bodies all whole, without rotting; but I believe that fiends made them seem to be so fresh, without rotting. And many of them were in habits of Christian men; but I believe they were such as went in for covetousness of the treasure that was there, and had overmuch feebleness in faith; so that their hearts might not endure in the belief for dread. And therefore we were the more devout a great deal; and yet we were cast down and beaten down many times to the hard earth by winds, and thunders, and tempests; but evermore God of His grace helped us. And so we passed that Perilous Vale without peril, and without encumbrance, thanked be Almighty God!

(Travels.)

WILLIAM CAXTON (1422?–1491)

I.—THE FORM OF A KING

THE king must be thus made. For he must sit in a chair clothed in purple, crowned on his head, in his right hand a sceptre and in the left hand an apple of gold. For he is the most greatest and highest in dignity above all other and most worthy. And that is signified by the crown. For the glory of the people is the dignity of the king. And above all other the king ought to be replenished with virtues and of grace, and this signifieth the purple. For in like wise as robes of purple maketh fair and embellisheth the body, the same wise virtues maketh the soul. He ought alway think on the government of the Royaume and who hath the administration of justice. And this should be by himself principally. This signifieth the apple of gold that he holdeth in his left hand. And for as much as it appertaineth unto him to punish the rebels hath he the sceptre in his right hand. And for as much as misericord and truth conserve and keep the king in his throne therefore ought a king to be merciful and debonair.

(The Game and Play of Chess.)

II.—THE AUTHOR'S APOLOGY

When I remember that every man is bound by the commandment and counsel of the wise man to eschew sloth and idleness, which is mother and nourisher of vices, and ought to put myself unto virtuous occupation and business, then I, having no great charge of occupation, following the said counsel, took a French book and read therein many strange and marvellous histories wherein I had great pleasure and delight, as well for the novelty of the same as for the fair language of French, which was in prose so well and compendiously set and written, which methought I understood the sentence and substance of every matter. And for so much as this book was new and late made and drawn into French, and never had seen it in our English tongue, I thought in myself it should be a good business to translate it into our English to the end that it might be had as well in the realm of England as in other lands, and also for to pass therewith the time, and thus concluded in myself to begin this said work. And forthwith took pen and ink, and began boldly to run forth as blind Bayard, in this present work which is named the Recueil of the Trojan histories. And afterward when I remembered myself of my simpleness and unperfectness that I had in both languages, that is, to wit, in French and in English, for in France was I never, and was born and learned mine English in Kent in the Weald where, I doubt not, is spoken as broad and rude English as in any place of England, and have continued by the space of thirty years, for the most part in the countries of Brabant, Flanders, Holland, and Zeeland; and thus when all these things came before me after that I had made and written a five or six quires, I fell in despair of this work and purposed no more to have continued therein, and those quires laid apart, and in two years after laboured no more in this work. And was fully in will to have left it, till on a time it fortuned that the right high, excellent, and right-virtuous princess, my right redoubted lady, my lady Margaret, by the grace of God sister unto the king of England and of France, my sovereign lord—

duchess of Bourgoyne, of Lotryk, of Brabant, of Lymburgh, and of Luxembourg, countess of Flanders and Artois and of Bourgoyne, palatine of Hainault, of Holland, of Zeeland, and of Namur, marchioness of the holy empire, lady of Fries, of Salins, and of Mechlin—sent for me to speak with her good grace of divers matters. Among the which, I let her highness have knowledge of the aforesaid beginning of this work, which anon commanded me to show the said five or six quires to her said grace, and when she had seen them, anon she found a default in mine English, which she commanded me to amend, and moreover commanded me straitly to continue and make an end of the residue then not translated; whose dreadful com- mandment I durst in no wise disobey, because I am a servant unto her said grace, and receive of her yearly fee, and other many good and great benefits, and also hope many more to receive of her highness; but forthwith went and laboured in the said translation after my simple and poor cunning; also, nigh as I can, following mine author, meekly beseeching the bounteous highness of my said lady that of her benevolence list to accept and take in gree this simple and rude work here following. And if there be anything written or said to her pleasure, I shall think my labour well employed, and whereas there is default that she arette it to the simpleness of my cunning which is full small in this behalf, and require and pray all them that shall read this said work to correct it, and to hold me excused of the rude and simple translation.

(Recueil des Histoires de Troye.)

JOHN BOURCHIER LORD BERNERS (1467–1533)

FROISSART VISITS ENGLAND

TRUE it was that I, Sir John Froissart, had great affection to go and see the realm of England. . . . Many reasons moved me to make that voyage: one was, because in my youth I had been brought up in the court of the noble King Edward the Third, and of Queen Philippa his wife, and among their children and other barons of England, that as then were alive, in whom I found all nobleness, honour, largesse, and courtesy; therefore I desired to see the country, thinking thereby I should live much the longer, for I had not been there twenty-seven years before, and I thought, though I saw not those lords that I left alive there, yet at the least I should see their heirs, the which should do me much good to see, and also to justify the histories and matters that I had written of them. . . . I had engrossed in a fair book well enlumined all the matters of amours and moralities, that in four and twenty years before I had made and compiled, which greatly quickened my desire to go into England to see King Richard, who was son to the noble prince of Wales and of Aquitaine, for I had not seen this King Richard since he was christened in the cathedral church of Bourdeaux, at which time I was there, and thought to have gone with the prince the journey into Galicia in Spain; and when we were in the city of Aste, the prince sent me back into England to the queen his mother.

For these causes and other I had great desire to go into England to see the king and his uncles. Also I had this said fair book well covered with velvet garnished with clasps of silver and gilt, thereof to make a present to the king at my first coming to his presence; I had such desire to go this voyage that the pain and travail grieved me nothing. Thus provided of horses and other necessaries, I passed the sea at Calais, and came to Dover, the twelfth day of the month of July. When I came there I found no man of my knowledge, it was so long sith I had been in England, and the houses were all newly changed, and young children were become men and the women knew me not nor I them: so I abode half a day and all a night at Dover: it was on a Tuesday, and the next day by nine of the clock I came to Canterbury, to Saint Thomas's Shrine, and to the Tomb of the noble prince of Wales who is there interred right richly: there I heard mass, and made mine offering to the Holy Saint, and then dined at my lodging: and there I was informed how King Richard should be there the next day on pilgrimage, which was after his return out of Ireland where he had been the space of nine months or there about: the king had a devotion to visit St. Thomas's Shrine, and also because the prince his father was there buried. Then I thought to abide the king there, and so I did; and the next day the king came thither with a noble company of lords, ladies, and damoselles: and when I was among them they seemed to me all new folks, I knew no person: the time was sore changed in twenty-eight years, and with the king as then was none of his uncles; the duke of Lancaster was in Aquitaine, and the dukes of York and Gloucester were in other businesses, so that I was at the first all abashed, for if I had seen any ancient knight that had been with King Edward or with the prince I had been well recomforted and would have gone to him, but I could see none such. Then I demanded for a knight called Sir Richard Seury, whether he were alive or not?

and it was shewed me yes, but he was in London. Then I
thought to go to the lord Thomas Percy, great seneschal of
England, who was there with the king : so I acquainted me
with him, amd I found him right honourable and gracious, and
he offered to present me and my letters to the king, whereof
I was right joyful, for it behoved me to have some means to
bring me to the presence of such a prince as the king of England
was. He went to the king's chamber at which time the king
was gone to sleep, and so he shewed me, and bade me return to
my lodging, and come again, and so I did; and when I came
to the bishop's palace, I found the lord Thomas Percy ready to
ride to Ospring, and he counselled me to make as then no knowledge of my being here, but to follow the court; and he said
he would cause me ever to be well lodged, till the king should
be at the fair castle of Ledes in Kent. I ordered me after his
counsel and rode before to Ospring; and by adventure I was
lodged in a house where was lodged a gentle knight of England,
called Sir William Lisle; he was tarried there behind the king,
because he had pain in his head all the night before; he was
one of the king's privy chamber; and when he saw that I was
a stranger, and as he thought, of the Marchesse of France,
because of my language, we fell in acquaintance together; for
gentlemen of England are courteous, treatable, and glad of
acquaintance; then he demanded what I was, and what
business I had to do in those parts; I showed him a great part
of my coming thither, and all that the lord Thomas Percy had
said to me, and ordered me to do.

(*Translation of Froissart's Chronicles.*)

SIR THOMAS MALORY (*c.* 1470)

I.—SIR TRISTRAM AND LA BEALE ISOUD

*How Sir Tristram demanded La Beale Isoud for King Mark,
and how Sir Tristram and Isoud drank the Love Drink.*

THEN upon a day King Anguish asked Sir Tristram why
he asked not his boon, for whatsomever he had promised him
he should have it without fail. Sir, said Sir Tristram, now is it
time; this is all that I will desire, that ye will give me La Beale
Isoud, your daughter, not for myself, but for mine uncle, King
Mark, that shall have her to wife, for so have I promised him.
Alas, said the king, I had liefer than all the land that I have ye
would wed her yourself. Sir, an I did then I were shamed for
ever in this world, and false of my promise. Therefore, said

Sir Tristram, I pray you hold your promise that ye promised
me; for this is my desire, that ye will give me La Beale Isoud
to go with me into Cornwall for to be wedded to King Mark,
mine uncle. As for that, said King Anguish, ye shall have her
with you to do with her what it please you; that is for to say
if that ye list to wed her yourself, that is me liefest, and if ye will
give her unto King Mark, your uncle, that is in your choice.
So to make short conclusion, La Beale Isoud was made ready
to go with Sir Tristram, and Dame Bragwaine went with her
for her chief gentlewoman, with many other. Then the queen,
Isoud's mother, gave to her and Dame Bragwaine, her daughter's
gentlewoman, and unto Gouvernail, a drink, and charged them
that what day King Mark should wed, that same day they should
give him that drink, so that King Mark should drink to La Beale
Isoud, and then, said the queen, I undertake either shall love
other the days of their life. So this drink was given unto Dame
Bragwaine, and unto Gouvernail. And then anon Sir Tristram
took the sea, and La Beale Isoud; and when they were in their
cabin, it happed so that they were thirsty, and they saw a little
flacket of gold stand by them, and it seemed by the colour and
the taste that it was noble wine. Then Sir Tristram took the
flacket in his hand and said, Madam Isoud, here is the best
drink that ever ye drank, that Dame Bragwaine, your maiden,
and Gouvernail, my servant, have kept for themself. Then they
laughed and made good cheer, and either drank to other freely
and they thought never drink that ever they drank to other
was so sweet nor so good. But by that their drink was in their
bodies, they loved either other so well that never their love
departed for weal neither for woe. And thus it happed the
love first betwixt Sir Tristram and La Beale Isoud, the which
love never departed the days of their life.

(*Morte d'Arthur.*)

II.—THE SIEGE PERILOUS

*How the letters were found written in the Siege Perilous, and of
the marvellous adventure of the sword in a stone.*

Now, fair sir, said Sir Launcelot, will ye come with me unto
the court of King Arthur? Nay, said he, I will not go with you
as at this time. Then he departed from them and took his two
cousins with him, and so they came unto Camelot by the hour
of underne on Whitsunday. By that time the king and the
queen were gone to the minster to hear their service. Then
the king and the queen were passing glad of Sir Bors and Sir
Lionel, and so was all the fellowship. So when the king and all

the knights were come from service, the barons espied in the sieges of the Round Table all about, written with golden letters : Here ought to sit he, and he ought to sit here. And thus they went so long till that they came to the Siege Perilous, where they found letters newly written of gold which said : Four hundred winters and four and fifty accomplished after the passion of our Lord Jesu Christ ought this siege to be fulfilled. Then all they said : This is a marvellous thing and an adventurous. In the name of God, said Sir Launcelot; and then accounted the term of the writing from the birth of our Lord unto that day. It seemeth me, said Sir Launcelot, this siege ought to be fulfilled this same day, for this is the feast of Pentecost after the four hundred and four and fifty year; and if it would please all parties, I would none of these letters were seen this day, till he be come that ought to achieve this adventure. Then made they to ordain a cloth of silk, for to cover these letters in the Siege Perilous. Then the king bad haste unto dinner. Sir, said Sir Kay the steward, if ye go now to your meat ye shall break your old custom of your court, for ye have not used on this day to sit at your meat or that ye have seen some adventure. Ye say sooth, said the king, but I had so great joy of Sir Launcelot and of his cousins, which be come to the court whole and sound, so that I bethought me not of mine old custom. So, as they stood speaking, in came a squire and said unto the king : Sir, I bring unto you marvellous tidings. What be they? said the king. Sir, there is here beneath at the river a great stone which I saw fleet above the water, and therein I saw sticking a sword. The king said : I will see that marvel. So all the knights went with him, and when they came to the river they found there a stone fleeting, as it were of red marble, and therein stuck a fair rich sword, and in the pommel thereof were precious stones wrought with subtil letters of gold. Then the barons read the letters which said in this wise : Never shall man take me hence, but only he by whose side I ought to hang, and he shall be the best knight of the world. When the king had seen the letters, he said unto Sir Launcelot : Fair sir, this sword ought to be yours, for I am sure ye be the best knight of the world. Then Sir Launcelot answered full soberly : Certes, sir, it is not my sword; also, sir, wit ye well I have no hardiness to set my hand to it, for it longed not to hang by my side. Also, who that assayeth to take the sword and faileth of it, he shall receive a wound by that sword that he shall not be whole long after. And I will that ye wit that this same day shall the adventures of the Sangreal, that is called the Holy Vessel, begin.

How Sir Gawaine essayed to draw out the sword, and how an old man brought in Galahad.

Now, fair nephew, said the king unto Sir Gawaine, essay ye for my love. Sir, he said, save your good grace I shall not do that. Sir, said the king, essay to take the sword and at my commandment. Sir, said Gawaine, your commandment I will obey. And therewith he took up the sword by the handles, but he might not stir it. I thank you, said the king to Sir Gawaine. My lord Sir Gawaine, said Sir Launcelot, now wit ye well this sword shall touch you so sore that ye shall will ye had never set your hand thereto for the best castle of this realm. Sir, he said, I might not withsay mine uncle's will and commandment. But when the king heard this he repented it much, and said unto Sir Percivale that he should essay, for his love. And he said : Gladly, for to bear Sir Gawaine fellowship. And therewith he set his hand on the sword and drew it strongly, but he might not move it. Then were there more than durst be so hardy to set their hands thereto. Now may ye go to your dinner, said Sir Kay unto the king, for a marvellous adventure have ye seen. So the king and all went unto the court, and every knight knew his own place, and set him therein, and young men that were knights served them. So when they were served, and all sieges fulfilled save only the Siege Perilous, anon there befell a marvellous adventure, that all the doors and windows of the palace shut by themself. Not for then the hall was not greatly darked ; and therewith they abashed both one and other. Then King Arthur spake first and said : By God, fair fellows and lords, we have seen this day marvels, but or night I suppose we shall see greater marvels. In the meanwhile came in a good old man, and an ancient, clothed all in white, and there was no knight knew from whence he came. And with him he brought a young knight, both on foot, in red arms, without sword or shield, save a scabbard hanging by his side. And these words he said : Peace be with you, fair lords. Then the old man said unto Arthur : Sir, I bring here a young knight, the which is of king's lineage, and of the kindred of Joseph of Aramathie, whereby the marvels of this court, and of strange realms, shall be fully accomplished.

How the old man brought Galahad to the siege Perilous and set him therein, and how all the knights marvelled.

The king was right glad of his words, and said unto the good man : Sir, ye be right welcome, and the young knight with you. Then the old man made the young man to unarm him, and he was in a coat of red sendel, and bare a mantle upon his shoulder that was furred with ermine, and put that upon him. And the old knight said unto the young knight : Sir, follow me. And anon he led him unto the Siege Perilous, where beside sat Sir Launcelot; and the good man lift up the cloth, and found there letters that said thus : This is the siege of Galahad, the haut prince. Sir, said the old knight, wit ye well that place is yours. And then he set him down surely in that siege. And then he said to the old man : Sir, ye may now go your way, for well have ye done that ye were commanded to do ; and recommend me unto my grandsire, King Pelles, and unto my lord Petchere, and say them on my behalf, I shall come and see them as soon as ever I may. So the good man departed ; and there met him twenty noble squires, and so took their horses and went their way. Then all the knights of the Table Round marvelled greatly of Sir Galahad, that he durst sit there in that Siege Perilous, and was so tender of age ; and wist not from whence he came but only by God ; and said : This is he by whom the Sangreal shall be achieved, for there sat never none but he, but he were mischieved. Then Sir Launcelot beheld his son and had great joy of him. Then Bors told his fellows : Upon pain of my life this young knight shall come unto great worship. This noise was great in all the court, so that it came to the queen. Then she had marvel what knight it might be that durst adventure him to sit in the Siege Perilous. Many said unto the queen he resembled much unto Sir Launcelot. I may well suppose, said the queen, that Sir Launcelot begat him on King Pelles' daughter, by the which he was made to lie by, by enchantment, and his name is Galahad. I would fain see him, said the queen, for he must needs be a noble man, for so is his father that him begat, I report me unto all the Table Round. So when the meet was done that the king and all were arisen, the king yede unto the Siege Perilous and lift up the cloth, and found there the name of Galahad ; and then he showed it unto Sir Gawaine, and said : Fair nephew, now have we among us Sir Galahad, the good knight that shall worship us all ; and upon pain of my life he shall achieve the Sangreal, right as Sir Launcelot had done us to understand. Then came King Arthur unto Galahad and said : Sir, ye be welcome, for ye shall move many good knights to the quest of the Sangreal, and ye shall achieve that never knights might bring to an end. Then the king took him by the hand, and went down from the palace to shew Galahad the adventures of the stone.

(*Morte d'Arthur*.)

III.—THE PASSING OF ARTHUR

How King Arthur commanded to cast his sword Excalibur into the water, and how he was delivered to ladies in a barge.

Ah, Sir Launcelot, said King Arthur, this day have I sore missed thee : alas, that ever I was against thee, for now have I my death, whereof Sir Gawaine me warned in my dream Then Sir Lucan took up the king the one part, and Sir Bedivere the other part, and in the lifting the king swooned; and Sir Lucan fell in a swoon with the lift, that the part of his guts fell out of his body, and therewith the noble knight's heart brast. And when the king awoke, he beheld Sir Lucan, how he lay foaming at the mouth, and part of his guts lay at his feet. Alas, said the king, this is to me a full heavy sight, to see this noble duke so die for my sake, for he would have holpen me, that had more need of help than I. Alas, he would not complain him, his heart was so set to help me : now Jesu have mercy upon his soul ! Then Sir Bedivere wept for the death of his brother. Leave this mourning and weeping, said the king, for all this will not avail me, for wit thou well an I might live myself, the death of Sir Lucan would grieve me evermore; but my time hieth fast, said the king. Therefore, said Arthur unto Sir Bedivere, take thou Excalibur, my good sword, and go with it to yonder water side, and when thou comest there I charge thee throw my sword in that water, and come again and tell me what thou there seest. My lord, said Bedivere, your commandment shall be done, and lightly bring you word again. So Sir Bedivere departed, and by the way he beheld that noble sword, that the pommel and the half was all of precious stones; and then he said to himself : If I throw this rich sword in the water, thereof shall never come good, but harm and loss. And then Sir Bedivere hid Excalibur under a tree. And so, as soon as he might, he came again unto the king, and said he had been at the water; and had thrown the sword in the water. What saw thou there? said the king. Sir, he said, I saw nothing but waves and winds. That is untruly said of thee, said the king, therefore go thou lightly again, and do my commandment; as thou art to me lief and dear, spare not, but throw it in. Then Sir Bedivere returned again, and took the sword in his hand; and then him thought sin and shame to throw away that noble sword, and so efte he hid the sword, and returned again, and told to the king that he had been at the water, and done his commandment. What saw thou there? said the king. Sir, he said, I saw nothing but the waters wappe and waves wanne. Ah, traitor untrue, said

King Arthur, now hast thou betrayed me twice. Who would have weened that, thou that hast been to me so lief and dear? And thou art named a noble knight, and would betray me for the richness of the sword. But now go again lightly, for thy long tarrying putteth me in great jeopardy of my life, for I have taken cold. And but if thou do now as I bid thee, if ever I may see thee, I shall slay thee with mine own hands; for thou wouldst for my rich sword see me dead. Then Sir Bedivere departed, and went to the sword, and lightly took it up, and went to the water side; and there he bound the girdle about the hilts, and then he threw the sword as far into the water as he might; and there came an arm and an hand above the water and met it, and caught it, and so shook it thrice and brandished, and then vanished away the hand with the sword in the water. So Sir Bedivere came again to the king, and told him what he saw. Alas, said the king, help me hence, for I dread me I have tarried over long. Then Sir Bedivere took the king upon his back, and so went with him to that water side. And when they were at the water side, even fast by the back hoved a little barge with many fair ladies in it, and among them all was a queen, and all they had black hoods, and all they wept and shrieked when they saw King Arthur. Now put me into the barge, said the king. And so he did softly; and there received him three queens with great mourning; and so they set him down, and in one of their laps, King Arthur laid his head. And then that queen said: Ah, dear brother, why have ye tarried so long from me? alas, this wound on your head hath caught over-much cold. And so then they rowed from the land, and Sir Bedivere beheld all those ladies go from him. Then Sir Bedivere cried: Ah, my lord Arthur, what shall become of me, now ye go from me and leave me here alone among mine enemies? Comfort thyself, said the king, and do as well as thou mayest, for in me is no trust for to trust in; for I will into the vale of Avillion to heal me of my grievous wound: and if thou hear never more of me, pray for my soul. But ever the queens and ladies wept and shrieked, that it was pity to hear. And as soon as Sir Bedivere had lost sight of the barge, he wept and wailed, and so took the forest; and so he went all that night, and in the morning he was ware betwixt two holts hoar, of a chapel and an hermitage.

(Morte d'Arthur.)

SIR THOMAS MORE (1478–1535)
I.—OF JEWELS AND WEALTH

I NEVER saw a clearer instance of the different impressions that different customs make on people, than I observed in the ambassadors of the Anemolians who came to Amaurot when I was there : and because they came to treat of affairs of great consequence, the deputies from the several towns had met to wait for their coming. The ambassadors of the nations that lie near Utopia, knowing their customs, and that fine clothes are in no esteem among them; that silk is despised, and gold is a badge of infamy, use to come very modestly clothed; but the Anemolians that lay more remote, and so had little commerce with them, when they understood that they were coarsely clothed, and all in the same manner, they took it for granted that they had none of those fine things among them of which they made no use; and they being a vainglorious, rather than a wise people, resolved to set themselves out with so much pomp, that they should look like gods, and so strike the eyes of the poor Utopians with their splendour. Thus three ambassadors made their entry with an hundred attendants, that were all clad in garments of different colours, and the greater part in silk; the ambassadors themselves, who were of the nobility of their country, were in cloth of gold, and adorned with massy chains, ear-rings, and rings of gold : their caps were covered with bracelets set full of pearls and other gems : in a word, they were set out with all those things, that among the Utopians were either the badges of slavery, the marks of infamy, or children's rattles. It was not unpleasant to see on the one side how they looked big, when they compared their rich habits with the plain clothes of the Utopians, who were come out in great numbers to see them make their entry : and on the other side, to observe how much they were mistaken in the impression which they hoped this pomp would have made on them : it appeared so ridiculous a show to all that had never stirred out of their country, and so had not seen the customs of other nations, that though they paid some reverence to those that were the most meanly clad, as if they had been the ambassadors, yet when they saw the ambassadors, themselves so full of gold chains, they looking upon them as slaves, made them no reverence at all. You might have seen their children, who were grown up to that bigness, that they had thrown away their jewels, call to their mothers, and push them gently, and cry out, See that great fool that wears pearls and gems, as if he were yet a child. And their mothers answered them in good earnest, Hold your peace, this is, I believe, one of the ambassador's fools. Others censured the fashion of their chains, and observed that they were of no use, for they were too slight to bind their slaves, who would easily break them; and they saw them hang so loose about them, that they reckoned they could easily throw them away, and so get from them. But after the ambassadors had stayed a day among them, and saw so vast a quantity of gold in their houses, which was as much despised by them, as it was esteemed in other nations, and that there was more gold and silver in the chains and fetters of one slave, than all their ornaments amounted to, their plumes fell, and they were ashamed of all that glory for which they had formerly valued themselves, and so laid it aside : to which they were the more determined, when upon their engaging into some free discourse with the Utopians, they discovered their sense of such things, and their other customs. The Utopians wonder how any man should be so much taken with the glaring doubtful lustre of a jewel or stone, that can look up to a star, or to the sun himself; or how any should value himself, because his cloth is made of a finer thread : for how fine soever that thread may be, it was once no better than the fleece of a sheep, and that sheep was a sheep still for all its wearing it. They wonder much to hear, that gold, which in itself is so useless a thing, should be everywhere so much esteemed, that even men for whom it was made, and by whom it has its value, should yet be thought of less value than it is : so that a man of lead, who has no more sense than a log of wood, and is as bad as he is foolish, should have many wise and good men serving him, only because he has a great heap of that metal; and if it should so happen, that by some accident, or trick of law, (which does sometimes produce as great changes as chance itself) all this wealth should pass from the master to the meanest varlet of his whole family, he himself would very soon become one of his servants, as if he were a thing that belonged to his wealth, and so were bound to follow its fortune. But they do much more admire and detest their folly, who when they see a rich man, though they neither owe him anything, nor are in any sort obnoxious to him, yet merely because he is rich, they give him little less than Divine honours; even though they know him to be so covetous and base-minded that notwithstanding all his wealth, he will not part with one farthing of it to them as long as he lives.

(Utopia.)

II.—Of Fools, and of Law and Magistrates

They take great pleasure in fools, and as it is thought a base and unbecoming thing to use them ill, so they do not think it amiss for people to divert themselves with their folly : and they think this is a great advantage to the fools themselves : for if men were so sullen and severe, as not at all to please themselves with their ridiculous behaviour, and foolish sayings, which is all that they can do to recommend themselves to others, it could not be expected that they would be so well looked to, nor so tenderly used as they must otherwise be. If any man should reproach another for his being misshaped or imperfect in any part of his body, it would not at all be thought a reflection on the person that were so treated, but it would be accounted a very unworthy thing for him that had upbraided another with that which he could not help. It is thought a sign of a sluggish and sordid mind, not to preserve carefully one's natural beauty; but it is likewise an infamous thing among them to use paint or fard. And they all see that no beauty recommends a wife so much to her husband, as the probity of her life, and her obedience : for as some few are catched and held only by beauty, so all people are held by the other excellencies which charm all the world.

As they fright men from committing crimes by punishments, so they invite them to the love of virtue, by public honours : therefore they erect statues in honour to the memories of such worthy men as have deserved well of their country, and set these in their market-places, both to perpetuate the remembrance of their actions, and to be an incitement to their posterity to follow their example.

If any man aspires to any office, he is sure never to compass it : they live all easily together, for none of the magistrates are either insolent or cruel to the people; but they affect rather to be called fathers, and by being really so, they well deserve that name; and the people pay them all the marks of honour the more freely, because none are exacted of them. The prince himself has no distinction either of garments, or of a crown; but is only known by a sheaf of corn that is carried before him, as the high priest is also known by the wax light that is carried before him.

They have but few laws, and such is their constitution, that they need not many. They do very much condemn other nations whose laws, together with the commentaries on them, swell up to so many volumes; for they think it is an unreasonable thing to oblige men to obey a body of laws, that are both of such a bulk, and so dark, that they cannot be read or understood by every one of the subjects.

They have no lawyers among them, for they consider them as a sort of people whose profession it is to disguise matters, as well as to wrest laws; and therefore they think it is much better that every man should plead his own cause, and trust it to the judge, as well as in other places the client does it to a counsellor. By this means they both cut off many delays, and find out truth more certainly: for after the parties have laid open the merits of their cause, without those artifices which lawyers are apt to suggest, the judge examines the whole matter, and supports the simplicity of such well-meaning persons, whom otherwise crafty men would be sure to run down: and thus they avoid those evils, which appear very remarkably among all those nations that labour under a vast load of laws. Every one of them is skilled in their law, for as it is a very short study, so the plainest meaning of which words are capable, is always the sense of their laws. And they argue thus: All laws are promulgated for this end, that every man may know his duty; and therefore the plainest and most obvious sense of the words is that which must be put on them; since a more refined exposition cannot be easily comprehended, and laws become thereby useless to the greater part of mankind, who need most the direction of them: for to them it is all one not to make a law at all, and to couch it in such terms, that without a quick apprehension, and much study, a man cannot find out the true meaning of it; and the generality of mankind are both so dull, and so much employed in their several trades, that they have neither the leisure nor the capacity requisite for such an inquiry.

Some of their neighbours, who are masters of their own liberties, having long ago, by the assistance of the Utopians, shaken off the yoke of tyranny; and being much taken with those virtues that they observe among them, have come to them, and desired that they would send magistrates among them to govern them; some changing them every year, and others every five years. At the end of their government, they bring them back to Utopia, with great expressions of honour and esteem, and carry away others to govern in their stead. In this they seem to have fallen upon a very good expedient for their own happiness and safety: for since the good or ill condition of a nation depends so much upon their magistrates, they could not have made a better choice, than by pitching on men whom no advantages can bias; for wealth is of no use to them, since they must go so soon back to their own country; and they, being strangers among them, are not engaged in any of their heats or animosities : and it is certain, that when public judicatories are swayed, either by partial affections, or by avarice, there must follow upon it a dissolution of all justice, which is the chief sinew of society.

The Utopians call those nations that come and ask magistrates from them, neighbours; but they call those to whom they have been more particularly assisting, friends. And whereas all other nations are perpetually either making leagues, or breaking them, they never enter into any alliance with any other state. They think leagues are useless things, and reckon, that if the common ties of human nature do not knit men together, the faith of promises will have no great effect on them : and they are the more confirmed in this, by that which they see among the nations round about them, who are no strict observers of leagues and treaties. We know how religiously they are observed in Europe; more particularly where the Christian doctrine is received, among whom they are sacred and inviolable. Which is partly owing to the justice and goodness of the princes themselves, and partly to their reverence that they pay to the popes: who as they are most religious observers of their own promises, so they exhort all other princes to perform theirs; and when fainter methods do not prevail, they compel them to it by the severity of the pastoral censure; and think that it would be the most indecent thing possible, if men who are particularly designed by the title of the Faithful, should not religiously keep the faith of their treaties. But in that new-found world, which is not more distant from us in situation, that it is disagreeing from us in their manners, and course of life, there is no trusting to leagues, even though they were made with all the pomp of the most sacred ceremonies that is possible : on the contrary, they are the sooner broken for that, some slight pretence being found in the words of the treaties, which are contrived in such ambiguous terms, and that on design, that they can never be so strictly bound, but they will always find some loop-hole to escape at; and so they break both their leagues and their faith. And this is done with that impudence, that those very men who value themselves on having suggested these advices to their princes, would yet, with a haughty scorn, declaim against such craft, or to speak plainer, such fraud and deceit, if they found private men make use of it in their bargains; and would readily say, that they deserved to be hanged for it.

By this means it is, that all sort of justice passes in the world, but for a low-spirited and vulgar virtue, which is far below the dignity of royal greatness. Or at least, there are two sorts of justice set up : the one is mean, and creeps on the ground, and therefore becomes none but the baser sort of men, and so must be kept in severely by many restraints, that it may not break out beyond the bounds that are set to it. The other is, the peculiar virtue of princes, which as it is more majestic than that which becomes the rabble, so takes a freer compass ; and lawful or unlawful, are only measured by pleasure and interest. These practices among the princes that lie about Utopia, who make so little account of their faith, seem to be the reasons that determine them to engage in no confederacies : perhaps they would change their mind if they lived among us : but yet though treaties were more religiously observed, they would still dislike the custom of making them; since the world has taken up a false maxim upon it, as if there were no tie of Nature knitting one nation to another, that are only separated perhaps by a mountain, or a river, and that all were born in a state of hostility, and so might lawfully do all that mischief to their neighbours, against which there is no provision made by treaties : and that when treaties are made, they do not cut off the enmity, or restrain the licence of preying upon one another, if by the unskilfulness of wording them, there are no effectual provisos made against them. They on the other hand judge, that no man is to be esteemed our enemy that has never injured us; and that the partnership of the human nature, that is among all men, is instead of a league. And that kindness and good nature unite men more effectually, and more forcibly than any agreements whatsoever ; since thereby the engagements of men's hearts become stronger, than anything can be to which a few words can bind them.

(*Utopia*.)

HUGH LATIMER (1485–1555)

London

NOWE what shall we saye of these ryche citizens of London? what shall I saye of them? Shal I call them proud men of London, malicious men of London, mercylesse men of London. No, no, I may not saye so, they will be offended wyth me than. Yet must I speake. For is there not reygning in London, as much pride, as much covetousness, as much crueltie, as much opprission, as much supersticion, as was in Nebo? Yes, I thynke and muche more to. Therfore I saye, repente O London. Repente, repente. Thou heareste thy faults tolde the, amend them, amend them. I thinke if Nebo had had the preachynge

yat thou haste they would have converted. And you rulers
and officers be wise and circumspect; loke to your charge and
see you do your duties and rather be glad to amend your yll
livyng then to be angrye when you are warned or tolde of your
faulte. What a do was there made in London at a certain
man because he sayd, and in dede at that time on a just cause :
Burgesses, quod he, nay butterflies. Lorde what a do there
was for yat worde. And yet would God they were no worse
than butterflies. Butterflies do but theyre nature, the butterflye is not covetouse, is not gredye of other mens goodes, is
not ful of envye and hatered, is not malicious, is not cruel, is
not mercilesse. The butterflye gloriethe not in hyr oun dedes,
nor preferreth the tradicions of men before Gods worde; it
committeth not idolatry nor worshyppeth false goddes. But
London cannot abyde to be rebuked, suche is the nature of man.
If they be prycked, they wyll kycke. If they be rubbed on the
gale, they wil wynce. But yet they wyll not amende theyr
faultes, they wyl not be yl spoken of. But howe shal I speke
wel of them. If you could be contente to receyve and folowe
the worde of God and favoure good preachers, if you coude
bear to be tolde of youre faultes, if you could amende when you
heare of them : if you woulde be gladde to reforme that is
amisse : if I mighte se anie suche inclinacion in you, that leave
to be mercilesse and begynne to be charytable I would then hope
wel of you. But London was never so yll as it is now. In
tymes past men were full of pytie and compassion but nowe there
is no pitie, for in London their brother shal die in the streetes
fro colde, he shall lye sycke at theyr doore betwene stocke and
stocke—I can not tel what to call it—and peryshe there for hunger. Was there any more unmercifulness in Nebo? I thynke
not. In tymes paste when any ryche man dyed in London,
they were wonte to healp the pore scholers of the universitye
wyth exhibition. When any man dyed they woulde bequeth
greate summes of money towarde the releve of the pore. When
I was a scholer in Cambrydge my selfe, I harde verye good reporte
of London and knewe manie that had releve of the rytche men
of London, but nowe I can heare no such good reporte, and yet
I inquyre of it, and herken for it, but nowe charitie is waxed
colde, none helpeth the scholer nor yet the pore. And in those
dayes what dyd they whan they helped the scholers? Many
they maynteyned and gave them livynges that were verye
papists and professed the popes doctrine and nowe that the
knowledge of Gods word is brought to lyght, and many earnestelye
studye and laboure to set it forth now almost no man healpeth

to maynteyne them. Oh London, London, repente repente, for I thynke God is more displeased wyth London than ever he was with the citie of Nebo. Repente, therefor, repent London, and remember that the same God liveth nowe yat punyshed Nebo, even the same God and none other, and he wyl punyshe synne as well nowe as he dyd then, and he wyl punishe the iniquitie of London as well as he did then of Nebo. Amende therefore and ye that be prelatis loke well to your office, for right preletynge is busye labourynge and not lordyng. Therefore preache and teache and let your ploughe be doynge, ye lordes I saye that live lyke loyterers, loke well to your office, the plough is your office and charge.

(*A Sermon on the Plough.*)

WILLIAM TYNDALE (1495?-1536).

LOWLINESS OF HEART

BROTHER JACOB, beloved in my heart! there liveth not in whom I have so good hope and trust, and in whom my heart rejoiceth, and my soul comforteth herself, as in you; not the thousandth part so much for your learning, and what other gifts else you have, as because you will creep alow by the ground, and walk in those things that the conscience may feel, and not in the imaginations of the brain; in fear, and not in boldness; in open necessary things, and not to pronounce or define of hid secrets, or things that neither help nor hinder, whether it be so or no: in unity, and not in seditious opinions: insomuch that if you be sure you know, yet in things that may abide leisure, you will defer, and say (till others agree with you), "Methinks the text requireth this sense or understanding." Yea and if you be sure that if your part be good, and another hold the contrary, yet if it be a thing that maketh no matter, you will laugh and let it pass, and refer the thing to other men, and stick you stiff and stubbornly in earnest and necessary things. And I trust you be persuaded even so of me: for I call God to record against the day we shall all appear before our Lord Jesus, to give a reckoning of our doings, that I never altered one syllable of God's word against my conscience, nor would this day, if all that is in the earth, whether it be pleasure, honour, or riches, might be given me. Moreover I take God to record to my conscience, that I desire of God to myself in this world no more than that without which I cannot keep his laws. Finally if there were in me any gift that could help at hand, and aid you if need required, I promise you I would not be far off, and commit the end to God. My soul is not faint though my body be weary. But God hath made me evil favoured in this world, and without grace in the sight of men, speechless and rude, dull and slow witted; your part shall be to supply what lacketh in me; remembering that as lowliness of heart shall make you high with God, even so meekness of words shall make you to sink into the hearts of men. Nature giveth age authority, but meekness is the glory of youth, and giveth them honour.

(Letter to Frith.)

SIR THOMAS ELYOT (1499?–1546)

LESSONS FROM HOMER AND VIRGIL

I COULDE reherce diuers other poetis whiche for mater and eloquence be very necessary, but I feare me to be to longe from noble Homere : from whom as from a fountaine proceded all eloquence and lernyng. For in his bokes be contained, and moste perfectly expressed, nat only the documents marciall and discipline of armes, but also incomparable wisedomes, and instructions for politike gouernaunce of people : with the worthy commendation and laude of noble princis : where with the reders shall be so all inflamed, that they most feruently shall desire and coueite, by the imitation of their vertues, to acquire semblable glorie. For the whiche occasion, Aristotel, moost sharpest witted and excellent lerned Philosopher, as sone as he had receiued Alexander from kynge Philip his father, he before any other thynge taught hym the moost noble warkes of Homere : wherin Alexander founde suche swetenes and frute, that euer after he had Homere nat onely with hym in all this iournayes, but also laide hym under his pillowe whan he went to reste : and often tymes wolde purposely wake some houres of the nyght, to take as it were his passe tyme with that mooste noble poete.

For by the redinge of his warke called *Iliados*, where the assembly of the most noble grekes agayne Troy is recited with theyr affaires, he gathered courage and strength agayne his ennemies, wysdome, and eloquence, for consultations, and persuations to his people and army. And by the other warke called *Odissea*, whiche recounteth the sondry aduentures of the wise Ulisses, he, by the example of Ulisses, apprehended many noble vertues, and also lerned to eskape the fraude and deceitfull imaginations of sondry and subtile crafty wittes. Also there shall he lerne to enserche and perceiue the maners and conditions of them that be his familiars, siftinge out (as I mought say) the best from the warst, wherby he may surely committe his affaires, and truste to euery persone after his vertues. Therfore I nowe conclude that there is no lesson for a yonge gentil man to be compared with Homere, if he be playnly and substancially expouned and declared by the mayster.

Nat withstandinge, for as moche as the saide warkes be very longe, and do require therfore a great time to be all lerned and kanned, some latine autour wolde be therwith myxte, and specially Virgile; whiche, in his warke called *Eneidos*, is most lyke to Homere, and all moste the same Homere in latine. Also, by the ioynynge to gether of those autours, the one shall be the better understande by the other. And veruly (as I before saide) none one autour serueth to so diuers witts as doth Virgile. For there is nat that affect or desire, wherto any childes fantasie is disposed, but in some of Virgils warkes may be founden matter therto apte and propise.

For what thinge can be more familiar than his bucolikes? nor no warke so nighe approcheth to the commune daliaunce and maners of children, and the praty controuersies of the simple shepeherdes, therin contained, wonderfully rejoyceth the childe that hereth hit well declared, as I knowe by myne owne experience. In his Georgikes lorde what plesant varietie there is : the diuers graynes, herbes, and flowers that be there described, that, reding therin, hit semeth to a man to be in a delectable gardeine or paradise. What ploughe man knoweth so moche of husbandry as there is expressed ? who, delitynge in good horsis, shall nat be therto more enflamed, reding there of the bredyng, chesinge, and kepyng, of them ? In the declaration whereof Virgile leaueth farre behynde hym all breders, hakneymen, and skosers.

Is there any astronomer that more exactly setteth out the ordre and course of the celestiall bodies : or that more truely dothe deuine in his pronostications of the tymes of the yere, in their qualities, with the future astate of all thinges prouided by husbandry, than Virgile doth recite in that warke ?

If the childe haue a delite in huntyng, what pleasure shall he take of the fable of Aristeus : semblably in the huntynge of Dido and Eneas, whiche is discriued moste elegantly in his boke of Eneidos. If he haue pleasure in wrastling, rennyng, or other lyke exercise, where shall he se any more plesant esbatementes, than that whiche was done by Eurealus and other troyans, whiche accompanyed Eneas ? If he take solace in hearynge minstrelles, what minstrell may be compared to Jopas, whiche sange before Dido and Eneas? or to blinde Demodocus, that played and sange moste swetely at the dyner, that the kynge Alcinous made to Ulisses : whose dities and melodie excelled as farre the songes of our minstrelles, as Homere and Virgile excelle all other poetes.

If he be more desirous, (as the most parte of children be,) to here thinges marueilous and exquisite, whiche hath in it a visage of some things incredible, wherat shall be more wonder, than whan he shall beholde Eneas folowe Sibille in to helle? What shal he more drede, than the terrible visages of Cerberous, Gorgon, Megera, and other furies and monstrous? Howe shall he abhorre tyranny, fraude, and auarice, whan he doth se the paynes of duke Theseus, Prometheus, Sisiphus, and such other tourmented for their dissolute and vicious lyuyng? Howe glad soone after shall he be, whan he shall beholde, in the pleasant feldes of Elisius, the soules of noble princes and capitaines which, for their vertue, and labours in aduancing the publike weales of their countrayes, do lyue eternally in pleasure inexplicable. And in the laste bokes of Eneidos shall he finde matter to ministre to hym audacite, valiaunt courage, and policie, to take and susteyne noble enterprises, if any shall be nedefull for the assailynge of his enemies.

(The Governour.)

ROGER ASCHAM (1515–1568)

I.—PASTIME AND LEARNING

YET some will say, that children of nature love pastime, and mislike learning : because, in their kinde, the one is easie and pleasant, the other hard and werisome : which is an opinion not so true as some men weene : For, the matter lieth not so much in the disposition of them that be yong, as in the order and manner of bringing up, by them that be old, nor yet in the difference of learning and pastime. For, beate a child, if he daunce not well, and cherish him though he learne not well, ye shall have him unwilling to go to daunce, and glad to go to his booke. Knocke him always, when he draweth his shaft ill, and favour him again though he fault at his booke, ye shall have him verie loth to be in the field, and verie willing to be in the schole. Yea, I saie more, and not of myselfe, but by the judgment of those, from whom few wise men will gladly dissent, that if ever the nature of man be given at any tyme more than other, to receive goodness, it is in innocencie of yong yeares, before that experience of evill have taken roote in him. For the pure cleane witte of a sweete yong babe, is like the newest wax, most hable to receive the best and fayrest printing : and like a new bright silver dishe never occupied, to receive and kepe cleane, anie good thyng that is put into it.

(*Scholemaster.*)

II.—LADY JANE GREY

Before I went into Germanie, I came to Brodegate in Leicester-shire to take my leave of that noble Ladie Jane Grey, to whom I was exceding moch beholdinge. Hir parentes, the Duke and Duches, with all the houshold, Gentlemen and Gentlewomen, were hunting in the Parke : I founde her, in her Chamber, readinge Phædon Platonis in Greeke, and that with as moche delite, as som gentlemen would read a merie tale in Bocase. After salutation, and deutie done, with som other taulke, I asked hir, whie she would lose such pastime in the Parke? Smiling she answered me : I wisse all their sport in the Parke is but a shadoe to that pleasure that I find in Plato : Alas, good folke, they never felt, what trewe pleasure ment. And howe came you Madame, quoth I, to this deepe knowledge of pleasure, and what did chieflie allure you unto it : seeing, not many women, but verie fewe men have attained thereunto. I will tell you, quoth she, and tell you a troth, which perchance ye will mervell at. One of the greatest benefites, that ever God gave me, is, that he sent me so sharpe and severe Parentes, and so gentle a scholemaster. For when I am in presence either of father or mother, whether I speake, kepe silence, sit, stand, or go, eate, drinke, be merie, or sad, be sowyng, plaiyng, dauncing, or doing anie thing els, I must do it as it were, even in such weight, mesure, and number, even so perfitelie, as God made the world, or else I am so sharplie taunted, so cruellie threatened, yea presentlie some tymes, with pinches, nippes, and bobbes, and other waies, which I will not name, for the honor I bear them, so without measure misordered, that I thinke my selfe in hell, till tyme cum, that I must go to M. Elmer, who teacheth me so gentlie, so pleasantly, with soch faire allurements to learning that I thinke all the tyme nothing, whiles I am with him. And when I am called from him, I fall on weeping, because whatsoever I do else, but learning, is ful of grief, trouble, feare, and whole misliking unto me : and thus my booke, hath bene so moch my pleasure, and bringeth dayly to me more pleasure and more, that in respect of it, all other pleasures, in very deede, be but trifles and troubles unto me. I remember this talk gladly, both because it is so worthy of memorie, and because also, it was the last talke that ever I had, and the last tyme, that ever I saw that noble and worthie Ladie.

(Scholemaster.)

III.—QUEEN ELIZABETH

It is your shame, (I speake to you all, you yong Ientlemen of England) that one mayde should go beyond you all, in excellencie of learnyng, and knowledge of divers tonges. Pointe forth six of the best given Gentlemen of this Court, and all they together shew not so much good will, spend not so much tyme, bestow not so many houres, dayly, orderly, and constantly, for the increase of learning and knowledge, as doth the Queenes Majestie her selfe. Yea I beleve, that beside her perfit redines, in Latin, Italian, French, and Spanish, she readeth here now at Windsore more Greeke every day, than some Prebendarie of this chirch doth read Latin in a whole weeke. And that which is most praise worthie of all, within the walles of her privie chamber, she hath obteyned that excellencie of learnyng, to understand, speake, and write, both wittely with head, and faire with hand, as scarce one or two rare wittes in both the Universities have in many years reached unto. Amongest all the benefites yet God hath blessed me with all, next the knowledge of Christes true Religion, I counte this the greatest, that it pleased God to call me, to be one poore minister in settyng forward these excellent giftes of learnyng in this most excellent Prince. Whose onely example, if the rest of our nobilitie would folow, than might England be, for learnyng and wisedome in nobilitie, a spectacle to all the world beside.

(Scholemaster.)

RAPHAEL HOLINSHED (1515?-1580?)

I.—THE WEIRD SISTERS

It fortuned as Makbeth and Banquho journeyed towards Fores, where the king then lay, they went sporting by the way together without other company save only themselves, passing through the woods and fields, when suddenly in the middest of a laund, there met them three women in strange and wild apparel, resembling creatures of the elder world, whom when they attentively beheld, wondering much at the sight, the first of them spake and said : " All hail Makbeth, thane of Glammis ! "

(for he had lately entered into that office by the death of his
father Sinell). The second of them said : " Hail Makbeth,
thane of Cawdor ! " But the third said : " All hail Makbeth,
that hereafter shall be king of Scotland ! "

Then Banquho : " What manner of women (saith he) are you
that seem so little favourable unto me, whereas to my fellow
here, besides high offices, ye assign also the kingdom, appointing
forth nothing for me at all ? " " Yes," (saith the first of them,)
" we promise greater benefits unto thee than unto him ; for
he shall reign indeed, but with an unlucky end ; neither shall
he leave any issue behind him to succeed in his place, when
certainly thou shalt not reign at all, but of thee those shall be
born which shall govern the Scottish kingdom by long order
of continual descent." Herewith the foresaid women vanished
immediately out of their sight. This was reputed at the first
but some vain fantastical illusion by Makbeth and Banquho,
insomuch that Banquho would call Makbeth in jest, King of
Scotland ; and Makbeth again would call him in sport likewise,
father of many kings. But afterwards the common opinion was,
that these women were either the weird sisters, that is (as ye
would say) the goddesses of destiny, or else some nymphs or
fairies, indued with knowledge of prophecie by their necro-
mantical science, because everything came to pass as they had
spoken.

(Chronicle of England and Scotland.)

II.—THE MURDER OF THE LITTLE PRINCES

Upon this page's words King Richard arose and came out
into the pallet chamber, on which he found in bed Sir James
and Sir Thomas Tirrells, of person like, and brethren in blood,
but nothing akin in conditions.

Then said the king merrily to them : " What, sirs, be ye
in bed so soon ? " and, calling up Sir James, brake to him
secretly his mind in this mischievous matter. In which he
found him nothing strange. Wherefore on the morrow he sent
him to Brackenbury with a letter, by which he was commanded
to deliver Sir James all the keys of the Tower for one night, to
the end he might accomplish the king's pleasure in such things
as he had given him commandment. After which letter delivered,
and the keys received, Sir James appointed the night next
ensuing to destroy them, devising before and preparing the
means. The prince (as soon as the Protector left that name and
took himself as King) had it showed unto him that he should not
reign, but his uncle should have the crown. At which word the

prince sore abashed began to sigh, and said : " Alas, I would my uncle would let me have my life yet, though I lose my kingdom."

Then he that told him the tale, used him with good words, and put him in the best comfort he could. But forthwith was the prince and his brother both shut up, and all other removed from them, only one (called Black Will or William Slaughter) excepted, set to serve them and see them sure. After which time the prince never tied his points nor aught wrought of himself, but, with that young babe his brother, lingered with thought and heaviness, until this traitorous death delivered them of that wretchedness. For Sir James Tirrell devised that they should be murdered in their beds. To the execution thereof he appointed Miles Forrest one of the four that kept them, a fellow fleshed in murder before time. To him he joined one John Dighton, his own horse-keeper, a big, broad, square, and strong knave.

Then all the other being removed from them, this Miles Forrest and John Dighton, about midnight (the seely children lying in their beds) came to the chamber, and suddenly lapping them up among the clothes, so too bewrapped them and entangled them, keeping down by force the feather bed and pillows hard unto their mouths, that within a while, smothered and stifled, their breath failing, they gave up to God their innocent souls into the joys of Heaven, leaving to the tormentors their bodies dead in the bed. Which after that the wretches perceived, first by the struggling with the pains of death, and after long lying still to be thoroughly dead, they laid their bodies naked out upon the bed, and fetched Sir James to see them ; which upon the sight of them caused those murderers to bury them at the stair-foot meetly deep in the ground, under a great heap of stones. Then rode Sir James in great haste to King Richard, and showed him all the manner of the murder ; who gave him great thanks, and (as some say) there made him knight. But he allowed not as I have heard the burying in so vile a corner, saying that he would have them buried in a better place, because they were a king's sons. Lo, the honourable courage of a king ! Whereupon they say that a priest of Sir Robert Brackenbury's took up the bodies again and secretly enterred them in such a place as by the occasion of his death which only knew it, could never since come to light.

(Chronicle of England and Scotland.)

SIR THOMAS NORTH (1535?–1601?)

THE DEATH OF CÆSAR

CERTAINLY destiny may easier be foreseen than avoided, considering the strange and wonderful signs that were said to be seen before Cæsar's death. For, touching the fires in the element, and spirits running up and down in the night, and also the solitary birds to be seen at noondays sitting in the great market-place, are not all these signs perhaps worth the noting, in such a wonderful chance as happened? But Strabo the philosopher writeth, that divers men were seen going up and down in fire: and furthermore, that there was a slave of the soldiers that did cast a marvellous burning flame out of his hand, insomuch as they that saw it thought he had been burnt; but when the fire was out, it was found he had no hurt. Cæsar self also doing sacrifice unto the gods, found that one of the beasts which was sacrificed had no heart: and that was a strange thing in nature, how a beast could live without a heart. Furthermore there was a certain soothsayer that had given Cæsar warning long time afore, to take heed of the day of the Ides of March, (which is the fifteenth of the month), for on that day he should be in great danger. That day being come, Cæsar going unto the Senate-house, and speaking merrily unto the soothsayer, told him " the Ides of March be come: " " So they be," softly answered the soothsayer, " but yet are they not past." And the very day before, Cæsar, supping with Marcus Lepidus, sealed certain letters, as he was wont to do, at the board: so, talk falling out amongst them, reasoning what death was best, he preventing their opinions, cried out aloud, " Death unlooked for." Then going to bed the same night, as his manner was, all the windows and doors of his chamber flying open, the noise awoke him, and made him afraid when he saw such light: but more, when he heard his wife Calpurnia, being fast asleep, weep and sigh, and put forth many fumbling lamentable speeches: for she dreamed that Cæsar was slain, and that she had him in her arms. Others also do deny that she had any such dream, as amongst other, Titus Livius writeth that it was in this sort: the Senate having set upon the top of Cæsar's house, for an ornament and setting forth of the same, a certain pinnacle, Calpurnia dreamed that she saw it broken down, and that she thought she lamented and wept for it. Insomuch that, Cæsar rising in the morning, she prayed him, if it were possible, not to go out of the doors that day, but to adjourn the session of the

Senate until another day. And if that he made no reckoning
of her dream, yet that he would search further of the soothsayers
by their sacrifices, to know what should happen him that day.
Thereby it seemed that Cæsar likewise did fear or suspect somewhat, because his wife Calpurnia until that time was never
given to any fear and superstition: and that then he saw her so
troubled in mind with this dream she had. But much more
afterwards, when the soothsayers having sacrificed many beasts
one after another, told him that none did like them: then he
determined to send Antonius to adjourn the session of the Senate.

But in the mean time came Decius Brutus, surnamed Albinus,
in whom Cæsar put such confidence, that in his last will and
testament he had appointed him to be his next heir, and yet
was of the conspiracy with Cassius and Brutus: he, fearing that
if Cæsar did adjourn the session that day, the conspiracy
would be betrayed, laughed at the soothsayers, and reproved
Cæsar, saying, " that he gave the Senate occasion to mislike
with him, and that they might think he mocked them, considering that by his commandment they were assembled, and
that they were ready willingly to grant him all things, and to
proclaim him king of all his provinces of the Empire of Rome
out of Italy, and that he should wear his diadem in all other
places both by sea and land. And furthermore, that if any man
should tell them from him they should depart for that present
time, and return again when Calpurnia should have better
dreams, what would his enemies and ill-willers say, and how
could they like of his friend's words? And who could persuade
them otherwise, but that they would think his dominion a
slavery unto them and tyrannical in himself? And yet if it
be so," said he, " that you utterly mislike of this day, it is better
that you go yourself in person, and, saluting the Senate, to
dismiss them till another time." Therewithal he took Cæsar
by the hand, and brought him out of his house. Cæsar was not
gone far from his house, but a bondman, a stranger, did what he
could to speak with him: and when he saw he was put back by
the great press and multitude of people that followed him, he
went straight into his house, and put himself into Calpurnia's
hands, to be kept till Cæsar came back again, telling her that he
had greater matters to impart unto him. And one Artemidorus
also, born in the isle of Cnidos, a doctor of rhetoric in the Greek
tongue, who by means of his profession was very familiar with
certain of Brutus' confederates, and therefore knew the most
part of all their practices against Cæsar, came and brought him
a little bill, written with his own hand, of all that he meant to

tell him. He, marking how Cæsar received all the supplications
that were offered him, and that he gave them straight to his
men that were about him, pressed nearer to him, and said :
"Cæsar, read this memorial to yourself, and that quickly, for
they be matters of great weight, and touch you nearly." Cæsar
took it of him, but could never read it, though he many times
attempted it, for the number of people that did salute him :
but holding it still in his hand, keeping it to himself, went on
withal into the Senate-house. Howbeit others are of opinion,
that it was some man else that gave him that memorial, and not
Artemidorus, who did what he could all the way as he went to
give it Cæsar, but he was always repulsed by the people. For
these things, they may seem to come by chance ; but the place
where the murder was prepared, and where the Senate were
assembled, and where also there stood up an image of Pompey
dedicated by himself amongst other ornaments which he gave
unto the theatre, all these were manifest proofs, that it was
the ordinance of some god that made this treason to be executed,
specially in that very place. It is also reported, that Cassius
(though otherwise he did favour the doctrine of Epicurus)
beholding the image of Pompey, before they entered into the
action of their traitorous enterprise, he did softly call upon it
to aid him : but the instant danger of the present time, taking
away his former reason, did suddenly put him into a furious
passion, and made him like a man half besides himself. Now
Antonius, that was a faithful friend to Cæsar, and a valiant
man besides of his hands, him Decius Brutus Albinus entertained
out of the Senate-house, having begun a long tale of set purpose.
So Cæsar coming into the house, all the Senate stood up on the
feet to do him honour. Then part of Brutus' company and
confederates stood round about Cæsar's chair, and part of them
also came towards him, as though they made suit with Metellus
Cimber, to call home his brother again from banishment : and
thus prosecuting still their suit, they followed Cæsar till he was
set in his chair. Who denying their petitions, and being offended
with them one after another, because the more they were denied
the more they pressed upon him and were the earnester with
him, Metellus at length, taking his gown with both his hands,
pulled it over his neck, which was the sign given the confederates
to set upon him. Then Casca, behind him, strake him in the
neck with his sword ; howbeit the wound was not great nor
mortal, because it seemed the fear of such a devilish attempt did
amaze him and take his strength from him, that he killed him
not at the first blow. But Cæsar, turning straight unto him,

caught hold of his sword and held it hard; and they both cried out, Cæsar in Latin : " O vile traitor Casca, what doest thou ? " and Casca, in Greek, to his brother : " Brother, help me." At the beginning of this stir they that were present, not knowing of the conspiracy, were so amazed with the horrible sight they saw, they had no power to fly, neither to help him, nor so much as once to make an outcry. They on the other side that had conspired his death compassed him in on every side with their swords drawn in their hands, that Cæsar turned him no where but he was stricken at by some, and still had naked swords in his face, and was hackled and mangled among them, as a wild beast taken of hunters. For it was agreed among them that every man should give him a wound, because all their part should be in this murder : and then Brutus himself gave him one wound about his middle. Men report also, that Cæsar did still defend himself against the rest, running every way with his body : but when he saw Brutus with his sword drawn in his hand, then he pulled his gown over his head, and made no more resistance, and was driven either casually or purposely, by the counsel of the conspirators, against the base whereupon Pompey's image stood, which ran all of a gore-blood till he was slain. Thus it seemed that the image took just revenge of Pompey's enemy, being thrown down on the ground at his feet, and yielding up the ghost there, for the number of wounds he had upon him. For it is reported, that he had three and twenty wounds upon his body : and divers of the conspirators did hurt themselves striking one body with so many blows.

(*Plutarch's Life of Cæsar.*)

RICHARD HAKLUYT (1552 ?–1616)

I.—DRAKE AND THE INDIANS

WHEREIN our General having satisfied them, they returned with glad tidings to their king, who marched to us with a princely majesty, the people crying continually after their manner; and as they drew near unto us, so did they strive to behave themselves in their actions with comeliness. In the fore-front was a man of a goodly personage, who bare the sceptre or mace before the king; whereupon hanged two crowns, a less and a bigger, with three chains of a marvellous length. The crowns were made of knit work, wrought artificially with feathers of divers colours. The chains were made of a bony substance, and few be the persons among them that are admitted to wear them; and of that number also the persons are stinted, as some ten, some twelve, etc. Next unto him which bare the sceptre, was the king himself, with his guard about his person, clad with coney skins, and other skins. After them followed the naked common sort of people, every one having his face painted, some with white, some with black, and other colours, and having in their hands one thing or another for a present. Not so much as their children, but they also brought their presents.

In the meantime our General gathered his men together, and marched within his fenced place, making, against their approaching, a very warlike show. They being trooped together in their order, and a general salutation being made, there was presently a general silence. Then he that bare the sceptre before the king, being informed by another, whom they assigned to that office, with a manly and lofty voice proclaimed that which the other spake to him in secret, continuing half an hour. Which ended and a general *Amen*, as it were, given, the king with the whole number of men and women, the children excepted, came down without any weapon; who, descending to the foot of the hill, set themselves in order. In coming towards our bulwarks and tents, the sceptre-bearer began a song, observing his measures in a dance, and that with a stately countenance; whom the king with his guard, and every degree of persons, following, did in like manner sing and dance, saving only the women, which danced and kept silence. The General permitted them to enter within our bulwark, where they continued their song and dance a reasonable time. When they had satisfied themselves, they made signs to our General to sit down; to whom the king and divers others made several orations, or rather supplications, that he would take their province and kingdom into his hand, and become their king, making signs that they would resign unto him their right and title of the whole land, and become his subjects. In which, to persuade us the better, the king and the rest, with one consent, and with great reverence, joyfully singing a song, did set the crown upon his head, enriched his neck with all their chains, and offered him many other things, honouring him by the name of *Hioh*, adding thereunto, as it seemed, a sign of triumph; which thing our General thought not meet to reject, because he knew not what honour and profit it might be to our country. Wherefore in the name, and to the use of her Majesty, he took the sceptre, crown, and dignity of the said country into his hands, wishing that the riches and treasure thereof might so conveniently be transported to the enriching of her kingdom at home, as it aboundeth in the same.

(*Voyages*.)

II.—THE ESQUIMAUX

These people I judge to be a kind of *Tartar*, or rather a kind of *Samoed*, of the same sort and condition of life that the Samoeds be to the north-eastwards beyond Muscovy. Who are called Samoeds, which is as much to say, in the Muscovy tongue, as " eaters of themselves "; and so the Russians, their borderers, do name them. And by late conference with a friend of mine, with whom I did sometime travel in the parts of Muscovy, who hath great experience of those Samoeds and people of the north-east, I find that in all their manner of living, those people of the north-east and these of the north-west are like. They are of the colour of a ripe olive, which how it may come to pass, being born in so cold a climate, I refer to the judgment of others; for they are naturally born children of the same colour and complexion that all the Americans are, which dwell under the equinoctial line.

They are men very active and nimble. They are a strong people and very warlike, for in our sight upon the tops of the hills they would often muster themselves, and, after the manner of a skirmish, trace their ground very nimbly, and manage their bows and darts with great dexterity. They go clad in coats made of the skins of beasts, as of seals, deer, bears, foxes, and hares. They have also some garments of feathers, being made of the cases of fowls, finely sewed and compact together. Of all which sorts we brought home with us into England, which we found in their tents. In summer they use to wear the hairy side of their coats outward, and sometime go naked for too much heat. And in winter, as by signs they have declared, they wear four or five fold upon their bodies with the hair, for warmth, turned inwards. Hereby it appeareth, that the air there is not indifferent, but either it is fervent hot or else extreme cold, and far more excessive in both qualities than the reason of the climate should yield; for there it is colder, being under 62 degrees in latitude, than it is at Wardhouse, in the voyage to St. Nicholas in Muscovy, being at above 72 degrees in latitude. The reason hereof perhaps may be, that this *Meta Incognita* is much frequented and vexed with eastern and north-eastern winds, which from the sea and ice bringeth often an intolerable cold air, which was also the cause that this year our Straits were so long shut up with so great store of ice. But there is hope and likelihood, that further within the Straits it will be more constant and temperate weather.

These people are in nature very subtle and sharp-witted,

ready to conceive our meaning by signs, and to make answer well to be understood again. And if they have not seen the thing whereof you ask them, they will wink, or cover their eyes with their hands, as who would say, it hath been hid from their sight. If they understand you not whereof you ask them, they will stop their ears. They will teach us the names of each thing in their language which we desire to learn, and are apt to learn anything of us. They delight in music above measure, and will keep time and stroke to any tune which you shall sing, both with their voice, head, hand, and feet, and will sing the same tune aptly after you. They will row with our oars in our boats, and keep a true stroke with our mariners, and seem to take great delight therein. They live in caves of the earth, and hunt for their dinners or prey, even as the bear or other wild beasts do. They eat raw flesh and fish, and refuse no meat, howsoever it be stinking. They are desperate in their fight, sullen of nature, and ravenous in their manner of feeding. Their sullen and desperate nature doth herein manifestly appear, that a company of them being environed by our men on the top of a high cliff, so that they could by no means escape our hands, finding themselves in this case distressed, chose to cast themselves headlong down the rocks into the sea, and so be bruised and drowned, rather than to yield themselves to our men's mercies.

For their weapons to offend their enemies or kill their prey withal, they have darts, slings, bows, and arrows headed with sharp stones, bones, and some with iron. They are exceeding friendly and kind-hearted one to the other, and mourn greatly at the loss or harm of their fellows; and express their grief of mind, when they part one from another, with a mournful song and dirges. They are very shamefaced . . . and very chaste in the manner of their living. For when the man, which we brought from thence into England the last voyage, should put off his coat . . . he would not suffer the woman to be present, but put her forth of his cabin. And in all the space of two or three months, while the man lived in company of the woman, there was never anything seen or perceived between them, more than might have passed between brother and sister. But the woman was in all things very serviceable for the man, attending him carefully when he was sick; and he likewise in all the meats which they did eat together, would carve unto her of the sweetest, fattest, and best morsels they had. They wondered much at all our things, and were afraid of our horses and other beasts out of measure. They began to grow more civil, familiar, pleasant, and docible amongst us in very short time.

They have boats made of leather, and covered clean over, saving one place in the middle to sit in, planked within with timber; and they use to row therein with one oar, more swiftly a great deal then we in our boats can do with twenty. They have one sort of greater boats wherein they can carry above twenty persons; and have a mast with a sail thereon, which sail is made of thin skins or bladders, sewed together with the sinews of fishes. They are good fishermen, and in their small boats, being disguised with their coats of seals' skins, they deceive the fish, who take them rather for their fellow seals, than for deceiving men. They are good markmen. With their dart or arrow they will commonly kill a duck, or any other fowl, in the head, and commonly in the eye. When they shoot at a great fish with any of their darts, they use to tie a bladder thereunto, whereby they may the better find them again; and the fish, not able to carry it so easily away, for that the bladder doth buoy the dart, will at length be weary, and die therewith. They use to traffic and exchange their commodities with some other people, of whom they have such things as their miserable country and ignorance of art to make, denieth them to have; as bars of iron, heads of iron for their darts, needles made four-square, certain buttons of copper, which they use to wear upon their foreheads for ornament, as our ladies in the Court of England do use great pearl. Also they have made signs unto us, that they have seen gold, and such bright plates of metals, which are used for ornaments amongst some people with whom they have conference. We found also in their tents a Guinea-bean of red colour, the which doth usually grow in the hot countries; whereby it appeareth they trade with other nations which dwell far off, or else themselves are great travellers.

(*Voyages.*)

SIR WALTER RALEIGH (1552?–1618)
On Death

For the rest if we seek a reason of the succession and continuance of this boundless ambition in mortal men, we may add to that which hath been already said, that the Kings and Princes of the world have always laid before them the actions, but not the ends of those great Ones which preceded them. They are always transported with the glory of the one, but they never mind the misery of the others, till they find the experience in themselves. They neglect the advice of God, while they enjoy life, or hope it; but they follow the counsel of Death upon his first approach. It is he that puts into man all the wisdom of the world, without speaking a word, which God with all the words of His law, promises, or threats, doth not infuse. Death, which hateth and destroyeth man, is believed; God, which hath made him and loves him, is always deferred: " I have considered," saith Solomon, " all the works that are under the sun, and, behold, all is vanity and vexation of spirit; " but who believes it till Death tells it us? It was Death which opening the conscience of Charles the Fifth made him enjoin his son Philip to restore Navarre; and King Francis the First of France, to command that justice should be done upon the murderers of the Protestants in Merindol and Cabrières, which till then he neglected. It is therefore Death alone that can suddenly make man to know himself. He tells the proud and insolent that they are but abjects, and humbles them at the instant, makes them cry, complain, and repent, yea even to hate their forepast happiness. He takes the account of the rich, and proves him a beggar, a naked beggar, which hath interest in nothing but in the gravel that fills his mouth. He holds a glass before the eyes of the most beautiful, and makes them see therein their deformity and rottenness, and they acknowledge it.

O eloquent, just, and mighty Death! whom none could advise thou hast perswaded; what none have dared thou hast done; and whom all the world hath flattered, thou only hast cast out of the world and despised; thou hast drawn together all the far-stretched greatness, all the pride, cruelty, and ambition of man, and covered it all over with these two narrow words, Hic jacet!

(History of the World.)

RICHARD HOOKER (1554?–1600)

PERFECTION OF KNOWLEDGE IN THE SOUL OF MAN

IN the matter of knowledge, there is between the Angels of God and the children of men this difference. Angels already have full and complete knowledge in the highest degree that can be imparted unto them; men, if we view them in their spring, are at the first without understanding or knowledge at all. Nevertheless from this utter vacuity they grow by degrees, till they come at length to be even as the Angels themselves are. That which agreeth to the one now, the other shall attain unto in the end; they are not so far disjoined and severed, but that they come at length to meet. The soul of man being therefore at the first as a book, wherein nothing is and yet all things may be imprinted; we are to search by what steps and degrees it riseth unto perfection of knowledge.

Unto that which hath been already set down concerning natural agents this we must add, that albeit therein we have comprised as well creatures living as void of life, if they be in degree of nature beneath men; nevertheless a difference we must observe between those natural agents that work altogether unwittingly, and those which have though weak yet some understanding what they do, as fishes, fowls, and beasts have. Beasts are in sensible capacity as ripe even as men themselves, perhaps more ripe. For as stones, though in dignity of nature inferior unto plants, yet exceed them in firmness of strength or durability of being; and plants, though beneath the excellency of creatures endued with sense, yet exceed them in the faculty of vegetation and of fertility: so beasts, though otherwise behind men, may notwithstanding in actions of sense and fancy go beyond them; because the endeavours of nature, when it hath a higher perfection to seek, are in lower the more remiss, not esteeming thereof so much as those things do, which have no better proposed unto them.

The soul of man therefore being capable of a more divine perfection, hath (besides the faculties of growing unto sensible knowledge which is common unto us with beasts) a further ability, whereof in them there is no shew at all, the ability of reaching higher than unto sensible things. Till we grow to some ripeness of years, the soul of man doth only store itself with conceits of things of inferior and more open quality, which afterwards do serve as instruments unto that which is greater; in the meanwhile above the reach of meaner creatures it ascendeth not. When once it comprehendeth any thing above this, as the differences of time, affirmations, negations, and contradictions in speech, we then count it to have some use of natural reason. Whereunto if afterwards there might be added the right helps of true art and learning (which helps, I must plainly confess, this age of the world, carrying the name of a learned age, doth neither much know nor greatly regard), there would undoubtedly be almost as great difference in maturity of judgment between men therewith inured, and that which now men are, as between men that are now and innocents. Which speech if any condemn, as being hyperbolical, let them consider but this one thing. No art is at the first finding out so perfect as industry may after make it. Yet the very first man that to any purpose knew the way we speak of and followed it, hath alone thereby performed more very near in all parts of natural knowledge, than sithence in any one part thereof the whole world besides hath done.

(*Ecclesiastical Polity.*)

JOHN LYLY (1554?–1600)

CONSTANCY

THEN Fidus I appeal in this case to thy honesty which shall determine of mine honour. Wouldest thou have me inconstant to my old friend, and faithful to a new? Knowest thou not that as the almond tree beareth most fruit when he is old, so love hath greatest faith when it groweth in age. It falleth out in love as it doth in vines, for the young vines bring the most wine, but the old the best: So tender love maketh great show of blossoms, but tried love bringeth forth sweetest juice.

And yet I will say thus much, not to add courage to thy attempts, that I have taken as great delight in thy company as ever I did in any's (my Thirsus only excepted) which was the cause that oftentimes I would either by questions move thee to talk, or by quarrels incense thee to choler, perceiving in thee a wit answerable to my desire, which I thought throughly to wet by some discourse. But wert thou in comeliness Alexander, and my Thirsus, Thersites, wert thou Ulysses, he Midas, thou Crœsus, he Codrus, I would not forsake him to have thee: no not if I might thereby prolong thy life, or save mine own, so fast a root hath true love taken in my heart, that the more it is digged at the deeper it groweth, the oftener it is cut the less it bleedeth, and the more it is loaden the better it beareth. . . . For as Amulins, the cunning painter, so portrayed Minerva, that which way soever one cast his eye, she always beheld him: so hath Cupid so exquisitely drawn the image of Thirsus in my heart, that what way soever I glance, me thinketh he looketh steadfastly upon me, insomuch that when I have seen any to gaze on my beauty (simple God wot though it be) I have wished to have the eyes of Augustus Cæsar to dim their sights with the sharp and scorching beams. . . . Consider with thyself, Fidus, that a fair woman without constancy, is not unlike unto a green tree without fruit, resembling the counterfeit that Praxiteles made for Flora, before the which if one stood directly, it seemed to weep, if on the left side to laugh, if on the other side to sleep: whereby he noted the light behaviour of her, which could not in one constant shadow be set down.

(*Euphues, His England.*)

SIR PHILIP SIDNEY (1554–1586)

LYRIC AND HEROIC POESIE

Is it the lyric that most displeaseth, who with his tuned lyre and well-accorded voice, giveth praise, the reward of virtue, to virtuous acts? who giveth moral precepts and natural problems? who sometimes raiseth up his voice to the height of the heavens, in singing the lauds of the immortal God? Certainly, I must confess mine own barbarousness; I never heard the old song of Percy and Douglas, that I found not my heart moved more than with a trumpet;[1] and yet it is sung but by some blind crowder, with no rougher voice than rude style; which being so evil apparelled in the dust and cobweb of that uncivil age, what would it work, trimmed in the gorgeous eloquence of Pindar? In Hungary I have seen it the manner at all feasts, and all other such-like meetings, to have songs of their ancestors' valour, which that right soldier-like nation think one of the chiefest kindlers of brave courage. The incomparable Lacedæmonians did not only carry that kind of music ever with them to the field, but even at home, as such songs were made, so were they all content to be singers of them; when the lusty men were to tell what they did, the old men what they had done, and the young what they would do. And where a man may say that Pindar many times praiseth highly victories of small moment, rather matters of sport than virtue; as it may be answered, it was the fault of the poet, and not of the poetry, so, indeed, the chief fault was in the time and custom of the Greeks, who set those toys at so high a price, that Philip of Macedon reckoned a horse-race won at Olympus among his three fearful felicities. But as the inimitable Pindar often did, so is that kind most capable, and most fit, to awake the thoughts from the sleep of idleness, to embrace honourable enterprises.

There rests the heroical,[2] whose very name, I think, should daunt all backbiters. For by what conceit can a tongue be directed to speak evil of that which draweth with him no less champions than Achilles, Cyrus, Æneas, Turus, Tydeus, Rinaldo? who doth not only teach and move to truth, but teacheth and moveth to the most high and excellent truth : who maketh magnanimity and justice shine through all misty fearfulness and foggy desires? who, if the saying of Plato and Tully be true, that who could see virtue, would be wonderfully ravished with

---

[1] *The old song of Percy and Douglas,* Chevy Chase in its first form.
[2] *Or the Heroic ?*

the love of her beauty; this man setteth her out to make her more lovely, in her holiday apparel, to the eye of any that will deign not to disdain until they understand. But if any thing be already said in the defence of sweet poetry, all concurreth to the maintaining the heroical, which is not only a kind, but the best and most accomplished kind, of poetry. For, as the image of each action stirreth and instructeth the mind, so the lofty image of such worthies most inflameth the mind with desire to be worthy, and informs with counsel how to be worthy. Only let Æneas be worn in the tablet of your memory, how he governeth himself in the ruin of his country; in the preserving his old father, and carrying away his religious ceremonies; in obeying God's commandments, to leave Dido, though not only passionate kindness, but even the human consideration of virtuous gratefulness, would have craved other of him; how in storms, how in sports, how in war, how in peace, how a fugitive, how victorious, how besieged, how besieging, how to strangers, how to allies, how to enemies; how to his own, lastly, how in his inward self, and how in his outward government; and I think, in a mind most prejudiced with a prejudicating humour, he will be found in excellency fruitful. Yea, as Horace saith, "Melius Chrysippo et Crantore:"[1] but, truly, I imagine it falleth out with these poet-whippers as with some good women who often are sick, but in faith they cannot tell where. So the name of poetry is odious to them, but neither his cause nor effects, neither the sum that contains him, nor the particularities descending from him, give any fast handle to their carping dispraise.

(*A Defence of Poesie.*)

THOMAS LODGE (1558?–1625)

I.—GANIMEDE AND ROSADER

Of all proud birds the eagle pleaseth Jove,
Of pretie fowles kind Venus likes the dove,
Of trees Minerva doth the olive love,
    Of all sweet nimphs I honour Rosalynd.

Of all her gifts her wisedome pleaseth most,
Of all her graces vertue she doth boast:
For all these gifts my life and joy is lost,
    If Rosalynde prove cruell and unkind.

IN these and such-like passions Rosader did every day eternize the name of his Rosalynd; and this day especially when Aliena

---

[1] Epistles I. ii. 4. Better than Chrysippus and Crantor. They were both philosophers, Chrysippus a subtle stoic, Crantor the first commentator upon Plato.

and Ganimede (inforced by the heat of the sun to seeke for shelter) by good fortune arrived in that place, where this amorous forrester registred his melancholy passions. They saw the sodaine change of his looks, his folded armes, his passionate sighes : they heard him often abruptly cal on Rosalynd, who (poore soule) was as hotly burned as himselfe, but that shee shrouded her paines in the cinders of honorable modesty. Whereupon (gessing him to be in love, and according to the nature of their sexe being pittifull in that behalfe) they sodainly brake off his melancholy by theyr approach, and Ganimede shooke him out of his dumps thus.

What newes, forrester? hast thou wounded some deere, and lost him in the fall? Care not man for so small a losse : thy fees was but the skinne, the shoulder, and the horns : tis hunters lucke to ayme faire and misse; and a woodmans fortune to strike and yet go without the game.

Thou art beyond the marke Ganimede (quoth Aliena) : his passions are greater, and his sighs discovers more losse : perhaps in traversing these thickets, he hath seene some beautifull nimph, and is growne amorous. It may be so (quoth Ganimede) for here he hath newly ingraven some sonnet : come, and see the discourse of the forresters poems. Reading the sonnet over, and hearing him name Rosalynde, Aliena lookt on Ganimede and laught, and Ganimede looking backe on the forrester, and seeing it was Rosader, blusht; yet thinking to shrowd all under her pages apparell, she boldly returned to Rosader, and began thus.

I pray thee tell me, forrester, what is this Rosalynd for whom thou pinest away in such passions? Is shee some nymph that wayts upon Dianaes traine, whose chastitie thou hast deciphred in such epethites? Or is she some shepherdesse that hants these playnes whose beautie hath so bewitched thy fancie, whose name thou shaddowest in covert under the figure of Rosalynd, as Ovid did Julia under the name of Corinna? or say mee forsooth, is it that Rosalynde, of whome wee shepheards have heard talke, shee, forrester, that is the daughter of Gerismond, that once was king, and now an outlawe in the forrest of Arden? At this Rosader fecht a deepe sigh, and sayde, It is she, O gentle swayne, it is she : the saint it is whom I serve, that goddesse at whose shrine I doe bend all my devotions : the most fayrest of all faires, the phenix of all the sexe, and the puritie of all earthly perfection. And why (gentle forrester) if shee be so beautifull, and thou so amorous, is there such a disagreement in thy thoughts? Happily she resembleth the rose, that is sweete, but full of prickles? or the serpent regius that hath scales as glorious as the sunne, and a breath as infectious as the aconitum is deadly? So thy Rosalynd may be most amiable, and yet unkind; full of favour and yet froward, coy without wit, and disdainfull without reason.

Oh, Shepheard (quoth Rosader), knewest thou her personage, graced with the excellence of all perfection, beeing a harbour wherein the graces shrowd their vertues, thou wouldest not breath out such blasphemy against the beauteous Rosalind. She is a diamond, bright, but not hard, yet of most chast operation : a pearle so orient, that it can be stained with no blemish : a rose without prickles, and a princesse absolute, as well in beauty as in vertue. But I, unhappy I, have let mine eye soare with the eagle against so bright a sun, that I am quite blind : I have with Apollo enamoured myself of a Daphne, not (as she) disdainful, but farre more chast than Daphne : I have with Ixion laide my love on Juno, and shall (I feare) embrace nought but a clowde. Ah, Shepheard, I have reacht at a starre, my desires have mounted above my degree, and my thoughts above my fortunes. I being a peasant, have ventured to gaze on a princesse, whose honors are too high to vouchsafe such base loves.

Why, forrester, quoth Ganimede, comfort thy selfe : be blyth and frolike man. Love sowseth as low as she soareth high : Cupid shootes at a ragge assoon as at a roabe; and Venus eye that was so curious, sparkled favour on pole-footed Vulcan. Feare not, man, womens lookes are not tied to dignities feathers, nor make they curious esteeme where the stone is found, but what is the vertue. Feare not, forrester : faint heart never woone faire ladye. But where lives Rosalynde now? at the court?

Oh no, quoth Rosader, she lives I knowe not where, and that is my sorrow, banished by Toresmond, and that is my hell : for might I but finde her sacred personage, and plead before the bar of her pitie the plaint of my passions, hope telles me shee would grace me with some favour, and that would suffice as a recompence of all my former miseries.

(Rosalynde.)

II.—Morning in Arden

The sunne was no sooner stept from the bed of Aurora, but Aliena was wakened by Ganimede, who restlesse all night, had tossed in her passions, saying it was then time to go to the field to unfold their sheepe. Aliena (that spied where the hare was by the hounds, and could see day at a little hole) thought to be pleasaunt with her Ganimede, and therefore replied thus: "What,

wanton; the sun is but new up, and as yet Iris riches lies folded
in the bosome of Flora : Phœbus hath not dried up the pearled
dew, and so long Coridon hath taught me it is not fitte to lead
the sheepe abroad, least the deaw being unwholesome, they get
the rot : but now see I the old proverbe true, he is in hast whom
the devill drives, and where love prickes forward, there is no
worse death then delay. Ah, my good page, is there fancie
in thine eye, and passions in thy heart? What, hast thou wrapt
love in thy looks, and sette all thy thoughts on fire by affection?
I tell thee, it is a flame as harde to be quencht as that of Aetna.
But nature must have her course : womens eies have faculty
attractive like the jeat, and retentive like the diamond : they
dally in the delight of faire objects, til gazing on the panthers
beautiful skin, repenting experience tel them he hath a devouring
paunch. Come on (quoth Ganimede) this sermon of yours is
but a subtiltie to lie stil a bed, because either you think the
morning cold, or els I being gone, you would steale a nappe
this shift carried no paulme, and therefore up and away. And
for Love, let me alone : Ile whip him away with nettles, and set
disdaine as a charme to withstande his forces; and therefore
looke you to your selfe : be not too bold, for Venus can make
you bend, nor too coy, for Cupid hath a piercing dart, that will
make you crie *peccavi*. And that is it (quoth Aliena) that hath
raised you so earlie this morning. And with that she slipt on
her peticoat, and start up; and assoone as she had made her
ready, and taken her breakfast, away goe these two with their
bagge and bottles to the field, in more pleasant content of mynd
then ever they were in the court of Torismond.

(*Rosalynde.*)

ROBERT GREENE (1560?-1592)

"An Upstart Crow"

If woeful experience may move you, gentlemen, to beware,
or unheard-of wretchedness entreat you to take heed, I doubt
not but you will look back with sorrow on your time past, and
endeavour with repentance to spend that which is to come.
. . . Base-minded men all three of you, if by my misery ye be
not warned; for unto none of you (like me) sought those burs to
cleave, those puppets I mean that speak from our mouths,
those antics garnished in our colours. Is it not strange that I
to whom they all have been beholden—shall (were ye in that
case that I am now) be both of them at once forsaken? Yes,
thrust them not : for there is an upstart crow beautified with our

feathers, that with his *tiger's heart wrapped in a player's hide,*
supposes he is as well able to bombast out a blank verse as the
best of you; and being an absolute *Johannes factotum,* is in his
own conceit the only *Shake-scene* in a country. Oh, that I
might entreat your rare wits to be employed in more profitable
courses, and let these apes imitate your past excellence, and never
more acquaint them with your admired inventions! I know
the best husband of you all will never prove an usurer, and the
kindest of them all will never prove a kind nurse: yet, whilst
you may, seek you better masters; for it is pity men of such
rare wits should be subject to the pleasures of such rude grooms.

In this I might insert two more, that both have writ against
these buckram gentlemen; but let their own work serve to
witness against their own wickedness, if they persevere to maintain any more such peasants. For other new-comers, I leave
them to the mercy of these painted monsters, who (I doubt not)
will drive the best minded to despise them; for the rest, it skills
not though they make a jest at them.

But now return I again to you three, knowing my misery
is to you no news; and let me heartily entreat you to be warned
by my harms. Delight not (as I have done) in irreligious
oaths; for from the blasphemer's house a curse shall not depart.
Despise drunkenness, which wasteth the wit, and making men
all equal unto beasts. Fly lust as the deathsman of the soul,
and defile not the temple of the Holy Ghost. Abhor those
epicures whose loose life hath made religion loathsome to your
ears: and when they soothe you with terms of mastership,
remember *Robert Greene,* whom they have so often flattered,
perishes now for want of comfort. Remember, gentlemen,
your lives are like so many light tapers, that are with care
delivered to all of you to maintain; these with wind-puffed
wrath may be extinguished, which drunkenness put out, which
negligence let fall; for man's time of itself is not so short, but it
is more shortened by sin. The fire of my light is now at the last
snuff, and the want of wherewith to sustain it, there is no
substance for life to feed on. Trust not them (I beseech ye),
to such weak stays; for they are as changeable in mind as in
many attires. Well, my hand is tired, and I am forced to leave
where I would begin; for a whole book cannot contain their
wrongs, which I am forced to knit up in some few lines of words:

Desirous that you should live, though himself be dying,

ROBERT GREENE.

(*A Groat's Worth of Wit bought with a Million of Repentance.*)

FRANCIS BACON, VISCOUNT ST. ALBANS (1561–1626)

I.—OF DEATH

MEN fear death, as children fear to go in the dark : and as that natural fear in children is increased with tales, so is the other. Certainly, the contemplation of death, as the wages of sin, and passage to another world, is holy, and religious; but the fear of it, as a tribute due unto nature, is weak. Yet in religious meditations, there is sometimes mixture of vanity, and of superstition. You shall read, in some of the friars' books of mortification, that a man should think with himself what the pain is, if he have but his finger's end pressed, or tortured; and thereby imagine what the pains of death are, when the whole body is corrupted and dissolved; when many times death passeth with less pain than the torture of a limb : for the most vital parts are not the quickest of sense. And by him, that spake only as a philosopher, and natural man, it was well said : *Pompa mortis magis terret, quàm mors ipsa.* Groans and convulsions, and a discoloured face, and friends weeping, and blacks, and obsequies, and the like, show death terrible. It is worthy the observing, that there is no passion in the mind of man so weak, but it mates, and masters, the fear of death : and therefore death is no such terrible enemy, when a man hath so many attendants, about him, that can win the combat of him. Revenge triumphs over death; love slights it; honour aspireth to it; grief flieth to it; fear pre-occupateth it; nay, we read, after Otho the Emperor had slain himself, pity (which is the tenderest of affections) provoked many to die, out of mere compassion to their sovereign, and as the truest sort of followers. Nay, Seneca adds niceness and satiety : *Cogita quam diu eadem feceris ; mori velle, non tantum fortis, aut miser, sed etiam fastidiosus potest.* A man would die, though he were neither valiant, nor miserable, only upon a weariness to do the same thing, so oft over and over. It is no less worthy to observe, how little alteration, in good spirits, the approaches of death make; for they appear to be the same men, till the last instant. Augustus Cæsar died in a compliment : *Livia, conjugii nostri memor, vive et vale.* Tiberius in dissimulation; as Tacitus saith of him : *Jam Tiberium vires, et corpus, non dissimulatio, deserebant.* Vespasian in a jest, sitting upon the stool : *Ut puto Deus fio.* Galba with a sentence : *Feri, si ex re sit populi Romani ;* holding forth his neck. Septimius Severus in despatch : *Adeste, si quid mihi restat agendum.* And the like. Certainly, the Stoics bestowed too much cost upon death, and by their great preparations made it appear more fearful. Better saith he : *Qui finem vitæ extremum inter munera ponat naturæ.* It is as natural to die, as to be born; and to a little infant, perhaps, the one is as painful as the other. He that dies in an earnest pursuit is like one that is wounded in hot blood; who, for the time, scarce feels the hurt; and therefore, a mind fixed, and bent upon somewhat that is good, doth avert the dolours of death : but above all, believe it, the sweetest canticle is, *Nunc dimittis ;* when a man hath obtained worthy ends, and expectations. Death hath this also; that it openeth the gate to good fame, and extinguisheth envy.

—*Extinctus amabitur idem.*

(*Essays.*)

II.—OF FRIENDSHIP

It had been hard for him that spake it, to have put more truth and untruth together, in a few words, than in that speech : " Whosoever is delighted in solitude is either a wild beast, or a god." For it is most true, that a natural and secret hatred, and aversation towards society, in any man, hath somewhat of the savage beast ; but it is most untrue, that it should have any character, at all, of the divine nature; except it proceed, not out of a pleasure in solitude, but out of a love and desire to sequester a man's self for a higher conversation : such as is found to have been falsely and feignedly in some of the heathen ; as Epimenides the Candian, Numa the Roman, Empedocles the Sicilian, and Apollonius of Tyana ; and truly and really, in divers of the ancient hermits, and holy fathers of the Church. But little do men perceive what solitude is and how far it extendeth. For a crowd is not company ; and faces are but a gallery of pictures ; and talk but a tinkling cymbal, where there is no love. The Latin adage meeteth with it a little : *Magna civitas, magna solitudo ;* because in a great town friends are scattered; so that there is not that fellowship, for the most part, which is in less neighbourhoods. But we may go further, and affirm most truly, that it is a mere and miserable solitude, to want true friends ; without which the world is but a wilderness : and even in this sense also of solitude, whosoever in the frame of his nature and affections is unfit for friendship, he taketh it of the beast, and not from humanity.

A principal fruit of friendship is the ease and discharge of the fullness and swellings of the heart, which passions of all kinds do cause and induce. We know diseases of stoppings, and suffocations, are the most dangerous in the body; and it is not much otherwise in the mind : you may take sarza to open the liver; steel to open the spleen; flower of sulphur for the lungs; castoreum for the brain; but no receipt openeth the heart, but a true friend; to whom you may impart griefs, joys, fears, hopes, suspicions, counsels, and whatsoever lieth upon the heart, to oppress it, in a kind of civil shrift or confession.

It is a strange thing to observe, how high a rate great kings and monarchs, do set upon this fruit of friendship, whereof we speak : so great, as they purchase it, many times, at the hazard of their own safety, and greatness. For princes, in regard of the distance of their fortune, from that of their subjects and servants, cannot gather this fruit; except (to make themselves capable thereof) they raise some persons, to be as it were companions, and almost equals to themselves, which many times sorteth to inconvenience. The modern languages give unto such persons the name of favourites, or privadoes; as if it were matter of grace, or conversation. But the Roman name attaineth the true use, and cause thereof; naming them *participes curarum ;* for it is that which tieth the knot. And we see plainly, that this hath been done, not by weak and passionate princes only, but by the wisest, and most politic that ever reigned; who have oftentimes joined to themselves some of their servants; whom both themselves have called friends; and allowed others likewise to call them in the same manner; using the word which is received between private men.

L. Sylla, when he commanded Rome, raised Pompey (after surnamed the Great) to that height, that Pompey vaunted himself for Sylla's overmatch. For when he had carried the consulship for a friend of his, against the pursuit of Sylla, and that Sylla did a little resent thereat, and began to speak great, Pompey turned upon him again, and in effect bade him be quiet; "for that more men adored the sun rising, than the sun setting." With Julius Cæsar, Decimus Brutus had obtained that interest, as he set him down, in his testament, for heir in remainder, after his nephew. And this was the man that had power with him to draw him forth to his death. For when Cæsar would have discharged the senate, in regard of some ill presages, and specially a dream of Calpurnia, this man lifted him gently by the arm, out of his chair, telling him, he hoped he would not dismiss the senate, till his wife had dreamed a better dream. And it seemeth, his favour was so great, as Antonius in a letter, which is recited verbatim, in one of Cicero's Philippics, calleth him *venefica,* witch; as if he had enchanted Cæsar. Augustus raised Agrippa (though of mean birth) to that height, as when

he consulted with Mæcenas, about the marriage of his daughter
Julia, Mæcenas took the liberty to tell him : " That he must
either marry his daughter to Agrippa, or take away his life,
there was no third way, he had made him so great." With
Tiberius Cæsar, Sejanus had ascended to that height, as they
two were termed and reckoned as a pair of friends. Tiberius
in a letter to him saith : *Hæc pro amicitiâ nostrâ non occultavi.*
And the whole senate dedicated an altar to friendship, as to a
goddess, in respect of the great dearness of friendship between
them two. The like or more was between Septimius Severus,
and Plautianus. For he forced his eldest son to marry the
daughter of Plautianus ; and would often maintain Plautianus,
in doing affronts to his son : and did write also in a letter to the
senate, by these words : " I love the man so well, as I wish he may
overlive me." Now if these princes had been as a Trajan, or a
Marcus Aurelius, a man might have thought that this had proceeded of an abundant goodness of nature ; but being men so wise,
of such strength and severity of mind, and so extreme lovers of
themselves, as all these were ; it proveth most plainly, that they
found their own felicity (though as great as ever happened to
mortal men) but as a half-piece, except they might have a friend
to make it entire : and yet, which is more, they were princes
that had wives, sons, nephews ; and yet all these could not
supply the comfort of friendship.

It is not to be forgotten, what Commineus observeth, of his
first master Duke Charles the Hardy ; namely, that he would
communicate his secrets with none ; and, least of all, those
secrets which troubled him most. Whereupon he goeth on,
and saith, that towards his latter time : " That closeness did
impair, and a little perish his understanding." Surely Commineus
might have made the same judgment also, if it had pleased him,
of his second master Louis the Eleventh, whose closeness was
indeed his tormentor. The parable of Pythagoras is dark, but
true : *Cor ne edito* (" Eat not the heart "). Certainly, if a
man would give it a hard phrase, those that want friends to
open themselves unto are cannibals of their own hearts. But
one thing is most admirable, (wherewith I will conclude this
firstfruit of friendship,) which is, that this communicating of
a man's self to his friend, works two contrary effects ; for it
redoubleth joys, and cutteth griefs in halves. For there is no
man, that imparteth his joys to his friend, but he joyeth the more ;
and no man, that imparteth his griefs to his friend, but he
grieveth the less. So that it is, in truth of operation upon a
man's mind, of like virtue as the alchemists use to attribute

to their stone for man's body; that it worketh all contrary effects, but still to the good, and benefit of nature. But yet, without praying in aid of alchemists, there is a manifest image of this in the ordinary course of nature. For in bodies union strengtheneth and cherisheth any natural action; and, on the other side, weakeneth and dulleth any violent impression: and even so is it of minds.

The second fruit of friendship is healthful and sovereign for the understanding, as the first is for the affections. For friendship maketh indeed a fair day in the affections, from storm and tempests: but it maketh daylight in the understanding, out of darkness and confusion of thoughts. Neither is this to be understood only of faithful counsel, which a man receiveth from his friend; but before you come to that, certain it is that whosoever hath his mind fraught with many thoughts, his wits and understanding do clarify and break up, in the communicating and discoursing with another: he tosseth his thoughts more easily; he marshalleth them more orderly; he seeth how they look when they are turned into words; finally, he waxeth wiser then himself; and that more by an hour's discourse, than by a day's meditation. It was well said by Themistocles to the King of Persia: "That speech was like cloth of Arras, opened, and put abroad; whereby the imagery doth appear in figure; whereas, in thought, they lie but as in packs." Neither is this second fruit of friendship, in opening the understanding, restrained only to such friends as are able to give a man counsel, (they indeed are best) but even, without that, a man learneth of himself, and bringeth his own thoughts to light, and whetteth his wits as against a stone, which itself cuts not. In a word, a man were better relate himself to a statue, or picture, than to suffer his thoughts to pass in smother.

Add now, to make this second fruit of friendship complete, that other point, which lieth more open, and falleth within vulgar observation; which is faithful counsel from a friend. Heraclitus saith well, in one of his enigmas: "Dry light is ever the best." And certain it is, that the light that a man receiveth by counsel from another, is drier, and purer, than that which cometh from his own understanding and judgment; which is ever infused and drenched in his affections and customs. So as there is as much difference between the counsel that a friend giveth, and that a man giveth himself, as there is between the counsel of a friend, and of a flatterer. For there is no such flatterer as is a man's self; and there is no such remedy, against flattery of a man's self, as the liberty of a friend. Counsel is of two sorts; the one concerning manners, the other concerning business. For the first, the best preservative to keep the mind in health is the faithful admonition of a friend. The calling of a man's self to a strict account is a medicine sometime too piercing and corrosive. Reading good books of morality is a little flat, and dead. Observing our faults in others is sometimes improper for our case. But the best receipt (best, I say, to work, and best to take) is the admonition of a friend. It is a strange thing to behold, what gross errors, and extreme absurdities, many (especially of the greater sort) do commit, for want of a friend, to tell them of them; to the great damage, both of their fame and fortune. For, as St. James saith, they are as men, "that look sometimes into a glass, and presently forget their own shape, and favour." As for business, a man may think, if he will, that two eyes see no more than one; or that a gamester seeth always more than a looker-on; or that a man in anger is as wise as he that said over the four-and-twenty letters; or that a musket may be shot off as well upon the arm, as upon a rest; and such other fond and high imaginations, to think himself all in all. But when all is done, the help of good counsel is that which setteth business straight. And if any man think that he will take counsel, but it shall be by pieces; asking counsel in one business of one man, and in another business of another man; it is well, (that is to say, better perhaps than if he asked none at all;) but he runneth two dangers: one, that he shall not be faithfully counselled; for it is a rare thing, except it be from a perfect and entire friend, to have counsel given, but such as shall be bowed and crooked to some ends, which he hath that giveth it. The other, that he shall have counsel given, hurtful and unsafe, (though with good meaning,) and mixed, partly of mischief, and partly of remedy: even as if you would call a physician, that is thought good, for the cure of the disease you complain of, but is unacquainted with your body; and therefore, may put you in way for a present cure, but overthroweth your health in some other kind; and so cure the disease, and kill the patient. But a friend, that is wholly acquainted with a man's estate, will beware by furthering any present business how he dasheth upon other inconvenience. And therefore, rest not upon scattered counsels; they will rather distract, and mislead, than settle and direct.

After these two noble fruits of friendship, (peace in the affections, and support of the judgment,) followeth the last fruit; which is like the pomegranate, full of many kernels; I mean aid, and bearing a part, in all actions, and occasions. Here the best way to represent to life the manifold use of friendship is to cast and see how many things there are which a man cannot do himself; and then it will appear, that it was a sparing speech of the ancients to say " That a friend is another himself : " for that a friend is far more than himself. Men have their time, and die many times in desire of some things which they principally take to heart; the bestowing of a child, the finishing of a work, or the like. If a man have a true friend, he may rest almost secure that the care of those things will continue after him. So that a man hath as it were two lives in his desires. A man hath a body, and that body is confined to a place; but where friendship is, all offices of life are as it were granted to him, and his deputy. For he may exercise them by his friend. How many things are there which a man cannot, with any face or comeliness, say or do himself? A man can scarce allege his own merits with modesty, much less extol them : a man cannot sometimes brook to supplicate or beg : and a number of the like. But all these things are graceful in a friend's mouth, which are blushing in a man's own. So again, a man's person hath many proper relations, which he cannot put off. A man cannot speak to his son, but as a father; to his wife, but as a husband; to his enemy, but upon terms : whereas a friend may speak, as the case requires, and not as it sorteth with the person. But to enumerate these things were endless : I have given the rule, where a man cannot fitly play his own part : if he have not a friend, he may quit the stage.

(*Essays.*)

III.—OF BUILDING

Houses are built to live in, and not to look on : therefore let use be preferred before uniformity; except where both may be had. Leave the goodly fabrics of houses, for beauty alone, to the enchanted palaces of the poets : who build them with small coast. He that builds a fair house, upon an ill seat, committeth himself to prison. Neither do I reckon it an ill seat, only, where the air is unwholesome; but likewise where the air is unequal; as you shall see many fine seats, set upon a knap of ground, environed with higher hills round about it : whereby the heat of the sun is pent in, and the wind gathereth as in troughs; so as you shall have, and that suddenly, as great diversity of heat and cold, as if you dwelt in several places. Neither is it ill air only, that maketh an ill seat, but ill ways, ill markets; and, if you will consult with Momus, ill neighbours. I speak not of many more : want of water; want of wood, shade, and shelter; want of fruitfulness, and mixture of grounds of several natures; want of prospect; want of level grounds; want of places, at some near distance, for sports of hunting, hawking, and races; too near the sea, too remote; having the commodity of navigable rivers, of the discommodity of their overflowing; too far off from great cities, which may hinder business; or too near them, which lurcheth all provisions, and maketh everything dear: where a man hath a great living laid together, and where he is scanted: all which, as it is impossible, perhaps, to find together, so it is good to know them, and think of them, that a man may take as many as he can: and if he have several dwellings that he sort them so, that what he wanteth in the one, he may find in the other. Lucullus answered Pompey well; who when he saw his stately galleries, and rooms, so large and lightsome, in one of his houses, said: "Surely, an excellent place for summer, but how do you in winter?" Lucullus answered: "Why do you not think me as wise, as some fowls are, that ever change their abode towards the winter?"

To pass from the seat to the house itself; we will do as Cicero doth, in the orator's art; who writes books *De Oratore*, and a book he entitles *Orator :* whereof the former delivers the precepts of the art; and the latter the perfection. We will therefore describe a princely palace, making a brief model thereof. For it is strange to see, now in Europe, such huge buildings as the Vatican, and Escurial, and some others be, and yet scarce a very fair room in them.

First, therefore, I say, you cannot have a perfect palace, except you have two several sides; a side for the banquet, as is spoken of in the book of Hester; and a side for the household: the one for feasts and triumphs, and the other for dwelling. I understand both these sides to be not only returns, but parts of the front; and to be uniform without, though severally partitioned within; and to be on both sides of a great and stately tower, in the midst of the front; that, as it were, joineth them together, on either hand. I would have on the side of the banquet, in front, one only goodly room, above stairs, of some forty feet high; and under it, a room, for a dressing or preparing place, at times of triumphs. On the other side, which is the household side, I wish it divided at the first, into a hall, and a chapel, (with a partition between;) both of good state, and bigness: and those not to go all the length, but to have, at the further end, a winter, and a summer parlour, both fair. And under these rooms, a fair and large cellar, sunk under ground: and likewise, some privie kitchens, with butteries, and pantries, and the like. As for the tower, I would have it two storeys, of eighteen feet high apiece, above the two wings; and a goodly leads upon the top, railed with statues interposed; and the same tower to be divided into rooms, as shall be thought fit. The stairs likewise, to the upper rooms, let them be upon a fair open newell, and finely railed in, with images of wood, cast into a brass colour: and a very fair landing-place at the top. But this to be, if you do not point any of the lower rooms for a dining-place of servants. For otherwise, you shall have the servants' dinner after you own: for the steam of it will come up as in a tunnel. And so much for the front. Only, I understand the height of the first stairs, to be sixteen feet, which is the height of the lower room.

Beyond this front is there to be a fair court, but three sides of it of a far lower building, than the front. And in all the four corners of that court, fair staircases, cast into turrets, on the outside, and not within the row of buildings themselves. But those towers are not to be of the height of the front; but rather proportionable to the lower building. Let the court not be paved, for that striketh up a great heat in summer, and much cold in winter. But only some side alleys, with a cross, and the quarters to graze, being kept shorn, but not too near shorn. The row of return, on the banquet side, let it be all stately galleries; in which galleries, let there be three, or five, fine cupolas in the length of it, placed at equal distance: and fine coloured windows of several works. On the household side, chambers of presence, and ordinary entertainments, with some bed-chambers; and let all three sides be a double house, without through lights, on the sides, that you may have rooms from the sun, both for forenoon, and afternoon. Cast it also, that you may have rooms both for summer, and winter: shady for summer, and warm for winter. You shall have sometimes fair houses, so full of glass, that one cannot tell where to become, to be out of the sun, or cold: for imbowed windows, I hold them of good use; (in cities indeed, upright do better, in respect of the uniformity towards the street;) for they be pretty retiring places for conference; and besides, they keep both the wind, and sun off: for that which would strike almost through the room, doth scarce pass the window. But let them be but few, four in the court, on the sides only.

Beyond this court, let there be an inward court of the same square, and height; which is to be environed with the garden, on all sides: and in the inside, cloistered on all sides, upon decent and beautiful arches, as high as the first storey. On the under storey, towards the garden, let it be turned to a grotto, or place of shade, or estivation. And only have opening and windows towards the garden; and be level upon the floor, no whit sunk under ground, to avoid all dampishness. And let there be a fountain, or some fair work of statues, in the midst of this court; and to be paved as the other court was. These buildings to be for privie lodgings, on both sides; and the end, for privie galleries. Whereof, you must foresee, that one of them be for an infirmary, if the prince, or any special person should be sick, with chambers, bed-chamber, antecamera, and recamera, joining to it. This upon the second storey. Upon the ground storey, a fair gallery open, upon pillars: and upon the third storey likewise, an open gallery upon pillars, to take the prospect, and freshness of the garden. At both corners of the further side, by way of return, let there be two delicate or rich cabinets, daintily paved, richly hanged, glazed with crystalline glass, and a rich cupola in the midst; and all other elegancy that may be thought upon. In the upper gallery too I wish that there may be, if the place will yield it, some fountains running, in divers places, from the wall, with some fine avoidances. And thus much, for the model of the palace: save that you must have, before you come to the front, three courts. A green court plain, with a wall about it: a second court of the same, but more garnished, with little turrets, or rather embellishments, upon the wall: and a third court, to make a square with the front, but not to be built, nor yet enclosed with a naked wall, but enclosed with tarrasses, leaded aloft, and fairly garnished, on the three sides; and cloistered on the inside, with pillars, and not with arches below. As for offices, let them stand at distance, with some low galleries, to pass from them to the palace itself.

(*Essays.*)

IV.—THE ISLAND IN THE SOUTH SEA

We sailed from Peru, (where we had continued for the space of one whole year,) for China and Japan, by the South Sea; taking with us victuals for twelve months; and had good winds from the east, though soft and weak, for five months' space, and more. But then the wind came about, and settled in the west for many days, so as we could make little or no way, and were sometimes in purpose to turn back. But then again there arose strong and great winds from the south, with a point east; which carried us up (for all that we could do) towards the north; by which time our victuals failed us, though we had made good spare of them. So that finding ourselves, in the midst of the greatest wilderness

of waters in the world, without victuals, we gave ourselves for
lost men, and prepared for death. Yet we did lift up our hearts
and voices to God above, who "showeth his wonders in the
deep," beseeching him of his mercy, that as in the beginning he
discovered the face of the deep, and brought forth dry land; so
he would now discover land to us, that we might not perish.
And it came to pass that, the next day about evening, we saw
within a kenning before us, towards the north, as it were thick
clouds, which did put us in some hope of land; knowing how that
part of the South Sea was utterly unknown; and might have
islands, or continents, that hitherto were not come to light.
Wherefore we bent our course thither, where we saw the appearance of land, all that night; and in the dawning of the next day,
we might plainly discern that it was a land; flat to our sight,
and full of boscage; which made it show the more dark. And
after an hour and a half's sailing, we entered into a good haven,
being the port of a fair city; not great indeed, but well built,
and that gave a pleasant view from the sea: and we thinking
every minute long, till we were on land, came close to the shore
and offered to land. But straightways we saw divers of the
people, with batons in their hands, (as it were) forbidding us
to land; yet without any cries or fierceness, but only as warning
us off, by signs that they made. Whereupon being not a little
discomforted, we were advising with ourselves, what we should
do. During which time, there made forth to us a small boat,
with about eight persons in it; whereof one of them had in his
hand a tipstaff of a yellow cane, tipped at both ends with blue,
who came aboard our ship, without any show of distrust at
all. And when he saw one of our number present himself somewhat afore the rest, he drew forth a little scroll of parchment,
(somewhat yellower than our parchment, and shining like
the leaves of writing-tables, but otherwise soft and flexible,)
and delivered it to our foremost man. In which scroll were
written, in ancient Hebrew, and in ancient Greek, and in good
Latin of the school, and in Spanish, these words : " Land ye not,
none of you; and provide to be gone, from this coast, within
sixteen days, except you have further time given you. Meanwhile, if you want fresh water, or victual, or help for your sick, or
that your ship needeth repair, write down your wants, and you
shall have that, which belongeth to mercy." This scroll was
signed with a stamp of cherubim's wings, not spread, but hanging
downwards; and by them a cross. This being delivered, the
officer returned, and left only a servant with us to receive our
answer. Consulting hereupon amongst ourselves, we were

much perplexed. The denial of landing, and hasty warning us away, troubled us much; on the other side, to find that the people had languages, and were so full of humanity, did comfort us not a little. And above all, the sign of the cross to that instrument was to us a great rejoicing, and as it were a certain presage of good. Our answer was in the Spanish tongue: " That for our ship, it was well; for we had rather met with calms, and contrary winds, than any tempests. For our sick, they were many, and in very ill case; so that if they were not permitted to land, they ran danger of their lives." Our other wants we set down in particular, adding " that we had some little store of merchandise, which if it pleased them to deal for, it might supply our wants, without being chargeable unto them." We offered some reward in pistolets unto the servant, and a piece of crimson velvet to be presented to the officer; but the servant took them not, nor would scarce look upon them; and so left us, and went back in another little boat, which was sent for him.

About three hours after we had despatched our answer, there came towards us a person (as it seemed) of place. He had on him a gown with wide sleeves, of a kind of water-camlet, of an excellent azure colour, far more glossy than ours: his under-apparel was green; and so was his hat, being in the form of a turban, daintily made, and not so huge as the Turkish turbans; and the locks of his hair came down below the brims of it. A reverend man was he to behold. He came in a boat, gilt in some part of it, with four persons more only in that boat; and was followed by another boat, wherein were some twenty. When he was come within a flight-shot of our ship, signs were made to us, that we should send forth some to meet him upon the water: which we presently did in our ship's boat, sending the principal man amongst us save one, and four of our number with him. When we were come within six yards of their boat, they called to us to stay, and not to approach further; which we did. And thereupon the man, whom I before described, stood up, and with a loud voice, in Spanish, asked: " Are ye Christians ? " We answered: " We were;" fearing the less because of the cross we had seen in the subscription. At which answer the said person lifted up his right hand towards heaven and drew it softly to his mouth, (which is the gesture they use when they thank God;) and then said: " If ye will swear, (all of you,) by the merits of the Saviour, that ye are no pirates; nor have shed blood lawfully, or unlawfully, within forty days past; you may have license to come on land." We said: " We were all ready to take that oath." Whereupon one of those that were with him, being (as it seemed) a notary, made an entry of this act. Which done, another of the attendants of the great person, who was with him in the same boat, after his lord had spoken a little to him, said aloud : " My lord would have you know, that it is not of pride, or greatness, that he cometh not aboard your ship; but for that, in your answer, you declare that you have many sick amongst you, he was warned by the conservator of health, of the city, that he should keep a distance." We bowed ourselves towards him, and answered : " We were his humble servants; and accounted for great honour, and singular humanity, towards us, that which was already done; but hoped well, that the nature of the sickness of our men, was not infectious." So he returned; and awhile after came the notary to us aboard our ship; holding in his hand a fruit of that country, like an orange, but of colour between orange-tawny and scarlet; which cast a most excellent odour. He used it (as it seemeth) for a preservative against infection. He gave us our oath : " By the name of Jesus, and his merits : " and after told us, that the next day, by six of the clock, in the morning, we should be sent to, and brought to the Strangers' House, (so he called it,) where we should be accommodated of things, both for our whole, and for our sick. So he left us; and when we offered him some pistolets, he smiling said : " He must not be twice paid, for one labour : " meaning (as I take it) that he had salary sufficient of the state for his service. For (as I after learned) they call an officer, that taketh rewards, " twice-paid."

(*New Atlantis.*)

THOMAS DEKKER (1570?–1641?)

I.—SLEEP

FOR do but consider what an excellent thing sleep is : it is so inestimable a jewel, that, if a tyrant would give his crown for an hour's slumber, it cannot be bought : of so beautiful a shape is it, that, though a man lie with an empress, his heart cannot be at quiet till he leaves her embracements to be at rest with the other : yea, so greatly indebted are we to this kinsman of death, that we owe the better tributary half of our life to him; and there's good cause why we should do so, for sleep is that golden chain that ties health and our bodies together. Who complains of want, of wounds, of cares, of great men's oppressions, of captivity, whilst he sleepeth? Beggars in their beds take as much pleasure as kings. Can we therefore surfeit on this delicate ambrosia? Can we drink too much of that, whereof to taste too little tumbles us into a churchyard; and to use it but indifferently throws us into Bedlam? No, no! Look upon Endymion, the Moon's minion, who slept threescore and fifteen years; and was not a hair the worse for it.

(*The Gull's Hornbook.*)

II.—THE GALLANT IN PAUL'S WALKS

Now for your venturing into the walk. Be circumspect and wary what pillar you come in at; and take heed in any case, as you love the reputation of your honour, that you avoid the serving-man's log, and approach not within five fathoms of that pillar; but bend your course directly in the middle line, that the whole body of the church may appear to be yours; where, in view of all, you may publish your suit in what manner you affect most, either with the slide of your cloak from the one shoulder—and then you must, as 'twere in anger, suddenly snatch at the middle of the inside, if it be taffeta at the least, and so by that means your costly lining is betrayed; or else by the pretty advantage of compliment. But one note by the way do I especially woo you to, the neglect of which makes many of our gallants cheap and ordinary, that by no means you be seen above four turns; but in the fifth make yourself away, either in some of the sempsters' shops, the new tobacco-office, or amongst the booksellers, where, if you cannot read, exercise your smoke, and inquire who has writ against this divine weed, etc. For this withdrawing yourself a little will much benefit your suit, which else, by too long walking, would be stale to the whole spectators : but howsoever, if Paul's jacks be once up with their elbows, and quarrelling to strike eleven; as soon as ever the clock has parted them, and ended the fray with his hammer, let not the Duke's gallery contain you any longer, but pass away apace in open view : in which departure, if by chance you either encounter, or aloof off throw your inquisitive eye upon any knight or squire, being your familar, salute him not by his name of *Sir such a one*, or so; but call him *Ned*, or *Jack*, etc. This will set off your estimation with great men : and if—though there be a dozen companies between you, 'tis the better—he call aloud to you, for that's most genteel, to know where he shall find you at two o'clock; tell him at such an ordinary, or such; and be sure to name those that are dearest, and whither none but your gallants resort. After dinner you may appear again, having translated yourself out of your English cloth cloak into a light Turkey grogram, if you have that happiness of shifting; and then be seen, for a turn or two, to correct your teeth with some quill or silver instrument, and to cleanse your gums with a wrought handkercher: it skills not whether you dined, or no—that's best known to your stomach—or in what place you dined; though it were with cheese, of your own mother's making, in your chamber or study.

(The Gull's Hornbook.)

III.—THE BEHAVIOUR OF A POET IN AN ORDINARY

If you be a poet, and come into the ordinary (though it can be no great glory to be an ordinary poet), order yourself thus. Observe no man; doff not cap to that gentleman to-day at dinner, to whom, not two nights since, you were beholden for a supper; but, after a turn or two in the room, take occasion, pulling out your gloves, to have some epigram, or satire, or sonnet fastened in one of them, that may, as it were unwittingly to you, offer itself to the gentlemen; they will presently desire it; but, without much conjuration from them, and a pretty kind of counterfeit loathness in yourself, do not read it; and, though it be none of your own, swear you made it. Marry, if you chance to get into your hands any witty thing of another man's that is somewhat better; I would counsel you then, if demand be made who composed it, you may say: "Faith, a learned gentleman, a very worthy friend." And this seeming to lay it on another man will be counted either modesty in you, or a sign that you are not ambitious of praise; or else that you dare not take it upon you, for fear of the sharpness it carries with it. Besides, it will add much to your fame to let your tongue walk faster than your teeth, though you be never so hungry: and, rather than you should sit like a dumb cox-comb, to repeat by heart either some verses of your own, or of any other man's, stretching even very good lines upon the rack of censure; though it be against all law, honesty, or conscience: it may chance save you the price of your ordinary, and beget you other supplements. Marry, I would further entreat our poet to be in league with the mistress of the ordinary; because from her, upon condition that he will but rime knights and young gentlemen to her house, and maintain the table in good fooling, he may easily make up his mouth at her cost, *gratis.*

(The Gull's Hornbook.)

THE ENGLISH BIBLE, AUTHORIZED VERSION
(1611)

I.—CHRIST AND HIS CHURCH

I AM the rose of Sharon, and the lily of the valleys. As the lily among thorns, so is my love among the daughters. As the apple tree among the trees of the wood, so is my beloved among the sons. I sat down under his shadow with great delight and his fruit was sweet to my taste. He brought me to the banqueting house, and his banner over me was love. Stay me with flagons, comfort me with apples : for I am sick of love. His left hand is under my head and his right hand doth embrace me. I charge you, O ye daughters of Jerusalem, by the roes, and by the hinds of the field, that ye stir not up nor awake my love, till he please.

The voice of my beloved ! behold, he cometh leaping upon the mountains, skipping upon the hills. My beloved is like a roe or a young hart : behold, he standeth behind our wall, he looketh forth at the windows, shewing himself through the lattice. My beloved spake and said unto me, Rise up, my loved, my fair one, and come away. For, lo, the winter is past, the rain is over and gone; the flowers appear on the earth; the time of the singing of birds is come, and the voice of the turtle is heard in our land; the fig tree putteth forth her green figs, and the wines with the tender grape give a good smell. Arise, my love, my fair one, and come away. O my dove, that art in the clefts of the rock, in the secret places of the stairs, let me see thy countenance, let me hear thy voice; for sweet is thy voice, and thy countenance is comely. Take us the foxes, the little foxes, that spoil the vines : for our vines have tender grapes. My beloved is mine and I am his : he feedeth among the lilies. Until the day break, and the shadows flee away, turn, my beloved, and be thou like a roe or a young hart upon the mountains of Bether.

(*The Song of Solomon, Chap. II.*)

II.—THE VOICE OF THE PROPHET

Comfort ye, comfort ye my people, saith your God. Speak ye comfortably to Jerusalem, and cry unto her, that her warfare is accomplished, that her iniquity is pardoned : for she hath received of the Lord's hand double for all her sins.

The voice of him that crieth in the wilderness, Prepare ye the way of the Lord, make straight in the desert a highway for our God. Every valley shall be exalted and every mountain and hill shall be made low : and the crooked shall be made straight, and the rough places plain : and the glory of the Lord shall be revealed, and all flesh shall see it together : for the mouth of the Lord hath spoken it.

The voice said, Cry. And he said, What shall I cry? All flesh is grass, and all the goodliness thereof is as the flower of the field : The grass withereth, the flower fadeth : because the spirit of the Lord bloweth upon it : surely the people is grass.

The grass withereth, the flower fadeth : but the word of our God shall stand for ever.

O Zion, that bringest good tidings, get thee up into the high mountain; O Jerusalem, that bringest good tidings, lift up thy voice with strength; lift it up, be not afraid; say unto the cities of Judah, Behold your God ! Behold the Lord God will come with strong hand, and his arm shall rule for him : behold, his reward is with him, and his work before him. He shall feed his flock like a shepherd : he shall gather the lambs with his arm, and carry them in his bosom, and shall gently lead those that are with young.

(Isaiah, Chap. XL.)

III.—CHARITY

Though I speak with the tongues of men and of angels, and have not charity, I am become as sounding brass or a tinkling cymbal. And though I have the gift of prophecy, and understand all mysteries and all knowledge; and though I have all faith, so that I could remove mountains, and have not charity, I am nothing. And though I bestow all my goods to feed the poor, and though I give my body to be burned, and have not charity it profiteth me nothing. Charity suffereth long and is kind; charity envieth not; charity vaunteth not itself, is not puffed up, doth not behave itself unseemly, seeketh not her own, is not easily provoked, thinketh no evil; rejoiceth not in iniquity, but rejoiceth in the truth; beareth all things, believeth all things, hopeth all things, endureth all things. Charity never faileth : but whether there be prophecies they shall fail; whether there be tongues they shall cease; whether there be knowledge it shall vanish away. For we know in part and we prophesy in part. But when that which is perfect is come, then that which is in part shall be done away. When I was a child, I spake as a child, I understood as a child, I thought as a child : but when I became a man, I put away childish things. For now we see through a glass, darkly; but then face to face : now I know in part; but then shall I know even as also I am known. And now abideth faith, hope, charity, these three; but the greatest of these is charity.

(*First Epistle to the Corinthians, Chap. XIII.*)

SIR THOMAS OVERBURY (1581–1613)

I.—A FAIR AND HAPPY MILKMAID

A FAIR and happy milkmaid is a country wench that is so far from making herself beautiful by art, that one look of hers is able to put all face-physic out of countenance. She knows a fair look is but a dumb orator to commend virtue, therefore minds it not. All her excellences stand in her so silently, as if they had stolen upon her without her knowledge. The lining of her apparel, which is herself, is far better than outsides of tissue; for though she be not arrayed in the spoil of the silkworm, she is decked in innocency, a far better wearing. She doth not, with lying long abed, spoil both her complexion and conditions; Nature hath taught her, too, immoderate sleep is rust to the soul; she rises therefore with chanticleer, her dame's cock, and at night makes the lamb her curfew. In milking a cow, and straining the teats through her fingers, it seems that so sweet a milk-press makes the milk the whiter or sweeter; for never came almond-glove, or aromatic ointment on her palm to taint it. The golden ears of corn fall and kiss her feet when she reaps them, as if they wished to be bound and led prisoners by the same hand that felled them. Her breath is her own, which scents all the year long of June, like a new-made haycock. She makes her hand hard with labour, and her heart soft with pity; and when winter's evenings fall early (sitting at her merry wheel) she sings a defiance to the giddy wheel of fortune. She doth all things with so sweet a grace, it seems ignorance will not suffer her to do ill, being her mind is to do well. She bestows her year's wages at next fair, and in choosing her garments, counts no bravery in the world like decency. The garden and beehive are all her physic and surgery, and she lives the longer for it. She dares go alone and unfold sheep in the night, and fears no manner of ill, because she means none; yet, to say truth, she is never alone, but is still accompanied with old songs, honest thoughts, and prayers, but short ones; yet they have their efficacy, in that they are not palled with ensuing idle cogitations. Lastly, her dreams are so chaste, that she dare tell them; only a Friday's dream is all her superstition; that she conceals for fear of anger.

Thus lives she, and all her care is, she may die in the spring-time, to have store of flowers stuck upon her winding-sheet.

(Characters.)

II.—AN AFFECTATE TRAVELLER

IS a speaking fashion; he hath taken pains to be ridiculous, and hath seen more than he had perceived. His attire speaks *French* or *Italian*, and his gait cries, *Behold me*. He censures all things by countenances, and shrugs, and speaks his own language with shame and lisping: he will choke, rather than confess beer good drink; and his pick-tooth is a main part of his behaviour. He chooseth rather to be counted a spy than not a politician; and maintains his reputation by naming great men familiarly. He chooseth rather to tell lies, than not wonders, and talks with men singly: his discourse sounds big, but means nothing; and his boy is bound to admire him how-soever. He comes still from great personages, but goes with mean. He takes occasion to show jewels given him in regard of his virtue, that were bought at S. Martin's; and not long after having with a mountebank's method pronounced them worth thousands, impawneth them for a few shillings. Upon festival days he goes to court, and salutes without resaluting: at night in an ordinary he canvasseth the business in hand, and seems as conversant with all intents and plots as if he begot them. His extraordinary account of men is, first to tell them the ends of all matters of consequence, and then to borrow money of them; he offereth courtesies, to show them, rather than himself, humble. He disdains all things above his reach, and preferreth all countries before his own. He imputeth his want and poverty to the ignorance of the time, not his own unworthiness; and concludes his discourse with half a period, or a word, and leaves the rest to imagination. In a word, his religion is fashion, and both body and soul are governed by fame; he loves most voices above truth.

(Characters.)

THOMAS HOBBES (1588–1679)
IMAGINATION

THE decay of sense in men waking is not the decay of the motion made in sense, but an obscuring of it in such manner as the light of the sun obscureth the light of the stars, which stars do no less exercise their virtue, by which they are visible, in the day than in the night. But because amongst many strokes which our eyes, ears, and other organs, receive from external bodies, the predominant only is sensible; therefore, the light of the sun being predominant, we are not affected with the action of the stars. And any object being removed from our eyes, though the impression it made in us remain, yet other objects more present succeeding and working on us, the imagination of the past is obscured and made weak, as the voice of a man is in the noise of the day. From whence it followeth that the longer the time is, after the sight or sense of any object, the weaker is the imagination. For the continual change of man's body destroys in time the parts which in sense were moved; so that distance of time, and of place, hath one and the same effect in us. For as at a great distance of place that which we look at appears dim and without distinction of the smaller parts, and as voices grow weak and inarticulate, so also after great distance of time our imagination of the past is weak; and we lose, for example, of cities we have seen many particular streets, and of actions many particular circumstances. This " decaying sense," when we would express the thing itself, I mean " fancy " itself, we call " imagination," as I said before; but when we would express the decay, and signify that the sense is fading, old, and past, it is called " memory." So that imagination and memory are but one thing, which for divers considerations hath divers names.

The imaginations of them that sleep are those we call " dreams." And these also, as also all other imaginations, have been before, either totally or by parcels, in the sense. And, because in sense, the brain and nerves, which are the necessary organs of sense, are so benumbed in sleep as not easily to be moved by the action of external objects, there can happen in sleep no imagination, and therefore no dream, but what proceeds from the agitation of the inward parts of man's body; which inward parts, for the connection they have with the brain and other organs, when they be distempered, do keep the same in motion; whereby the imaginations there formerly made appear as if a man were waking; saving that the organs of sense being now benumbed, so as there is no new object which can master and obscure them with a more vigorous impression, a dream must needs be more clear in this silence of sense than our waking thoughts. And hence it cometh to pass that it is a hard matter, and by many thought impossible, to distinguish exactly between sense and dreaming. For my part, when I consider that in dreams I do not often nor constantly think of the same persons, places, objects, and actions, that I do waking, nor remember so long a train of coherent thoughts, dreaming, as at other times, and because waking I often observe the absurdity of dreams, but never dream of the absurdities of my waking thoughts, I am well satisfied, that, being awake, I know I dream not, though when I dream I think myself awake.

The most difficult discerning of a man's dream from his waking thoughts is, then, when by some accident we observe not that we have slept : which is easy to happen to a man full of fearful thoughts, and whose conscience is much troubled, and that sleepeth without the circumstances of going to bed or putting off his clothes, as one that noddeth in a chair. For he that taketh pains, and industriously lays himself to sleep, in case any uncouth and exorbitant fancy come unto him, cannot easily think it other than a dream. We read of Marcus Brutus (one that had his life given him by Julius Cæsar, and was also his favourite, and notwithstanding murdered him) how at Philippi, the night before he gave battle to Augustus Cæsar, he saw a fearful apparition, which is commonly related by historians as a vision; but, considering the circumstances, one may easily judge to have been but a short dream. For, sitting in his tent, pensive and troubled with the horror of his rash act, it was not hard for him, slumbering in the cold, to dream of that which most affrighted him; which fear, as by degrees it made him wake, so also it must needs make the apparition by degrees to vanish; and, having no assurance that he slept, he could have no cause to think it a dream or anything but a vision. And this is no very rare accident; for even they that be perfectly awake, if they be timorous and superstitious, possessed with fearful tales, and alone in the dark, are subject to the like fancies, and believe they see spirits and dead men's ghosts walking in church-yards; whereas it is either their fancy only, or else the knavery of such persons as make use of such superstitious fear to pass disguised in the night to places they would not be known to haunt.

From this ignorance of how to distinguish dreams and other strong fancies from vision and sense, did arise the greatest part of the religion of the Gentiles in time past, that worshipped satyrs, fawns, nymphs, and the like; and nowadays the opinion that rude people have of fairies, ghosts, and goblins, and of the power of witches. For as for witches, I think not that their witchcraft is any real power; but yet that they are justly punished for the false belief they have that they can do such mischief, joined with their purpose to do it if they can; their trade being nearer to a new religion than to a craft or science. And for fairies and walking ghosts, the opinion of them has, I think, been on purpose either taught, or not confuted, to keep in credit the use of exorcism, of crosses, of holy water, and other such inventions of ghostly men. Nevertheless there is no doubt but God can make unnatural apparitions; but that He does it so often as men need to fear such things more than they fear the stay or change of the course of nature, which He also can stay and change, is no point of Christian faith. But evil men, under pretext that God can do anything, are so bold as to say anything when it serves their turn, though they think it untrue; it is the part of a wise man to believe them no farther than right reason makes that which they say appear credible. If this superstitious fear of spirits were taken away, and with it prognostics from dreams, false prophecies, and many other things depending thereon, by which crafty ambitious persons abuse the simple people, men would be much more fitted than they are for civil obedience.

And this ought to be the work of the schools; but they rather nourish such doctrine. For, not knowing what imagination or the senses are, what they receive they teach : some saying that imaginations rise of themselves and have no cause; others that they rise most commonly from the will, and that good thoughts are blown (inspired) into a man by God, and evil thoughts by the devil; or that good thoughts are poured (infused) into a man by God, and evil ones by the devil. Some say the senses receive the species of things, and deliver them to the common sense, and the common sense delivers them over to the fancy, and the fancy to the memory, and the memory to the judgment, like handing of things from one to another, with many words making nothing understood.

The imagination that is raised in man, or any other creature indued with the faculty of imagining, by words or other voluntary signs, is that we generally call " understanding," and is common to man and beast. For a dog by custom will understand the call or the rating of his master; and so will many other beasts. That understanding which is peculiar to man is the understanding not only his will but his conceptions and thoughts, by the sequel and contexture of the names of things into affirmations, negations, and other forms of speech; and of this kind of understanding I shall speak hereafter.

(Leviathan.)

IZAAK WALTON (1593–1683)
I.—COUNTRY SCENTS AND OLD-FASHIONED SONGS

Piscator. Nay, stay a little, good scholar. I caught my last Trout with a worm; now I will put on a minnow, and try a quarter of an hour about yonder trees for another; and so, walk towards our lodging. Look you, scholar, thereabout we shall have a bite presently, or not at all. Have with you, Sir: o' my word, I have hold of him. Oh! it is a great logger-headed Chub; come, hang him upon that willow twig, and let's be going. But turn out of the way a little, good scholar! toward yonder, high honeysuckle hedge; there we'll sit and sing, whilst this shower falls so gently upon the teeming earth, and gives yet a sweeter smell to the lovely flowers that adorn these verdant meadows.

Look! under that broad beech-tree I sat down, when I was last this way a-fishing; and the birds in the adjoining grove seemed to have a friendly contention with an echo, whose dead voice seemed to live in a hollow tree near to the brow of that primrose hill. There I sat viewing the silver streams glide silently towards their centre, the tempestuous sea; yet sometimes opposed by rugged roots and pebble-stones, which broke their waves, and turned them into foam; and sometimes I beguiled time by viewing the harmless lambs; some leaping securely in the cool shade, whilst others sported themselves in the cheerful sun; and saw others craving comfort from the swollen udders of their bleating dams. As I thus sat, these and other sights had so fully possest my soul with content that I thought, as the poet has happily exprest it—

> "I was for that time lifted above earth;
> And possest joys not promised in my birth."

As I left this place, and entered into the next field, a second pleasure entertained me; 'twas a handsome milkmaid, that had not yet attained so much age and wisdom as to load her mind with any fears of many things that will never be, as too many men often do; but she cast away all care, and sung like a nightingale. Her voice was good, and the ditty fitted for it; it was that smooth song which was made by Kit Marlow, now at least fifty years ago; and the milkmaid's mother sung an answer to it, which was made by Sir Walter Raleigh, in his younger days. They were old-fashioned poetry, but choicely good; I think much better than the strong lines that are now in fashion in this critical age. Look yonder! on my word, yonder, they both be a-milking again. I will give her the Chub, and persuade them to sing those two songs to us.

"God speed you, good woman! I have been a-fishing; and am going to Bleak Hall to my bed; and having caught more fish than will sup myself and my friend, I will bestow this upon you and your daughter, for I use to sell none.

Milk-woman. Marry! God requite you, Sir, and we'll eat it cheerfully. And if you come this way a-fishing two months hence, a grace of God! I'll give you a syllabub of new verjuice, in a new-made haycock, for it. And my Maudlin shall sing you one of her best ballads; for she and I both love all anglers, they be such honest, civil, quiet men. In the meantime, will you drink a draught of red cow's milk? You shall have it freely.

Piscator. No, thank you; but, I pray, do us a courtesy that shall stand you and your daughter in nothing, and yet we will think ourselves still something in your debt: it is but to sing us a song that was sung by your daughter when I last passed over this meadow, about eight or nine days since.

Milk-woman. What song was it, I pray? Was it, "Come, Shepherds, deck your herds"? or "As at noon Dulcina rested"? or "Phillida flouts me"? or "Chevy Chace"? or "Johnny Armstrong"? or "Troy Town"?

Piscator. No, it is none of those; it is a song that your daughter sung the first part, and you sung the answer to it.

Milk-woman. O, I know it now. I learned the first part in my golden age, when I was about the age of my poor daughter; and the latter part, which indeed fits me best now, but two or three years ago, when the cares of the world began to take hold of me: but you shall, God willing, hear them both; and sung as well as we can, for we both love anglers. Come, Maudlin, sing the first part to the gentlemen, with a merry heart; and I'll sing the second, when you have done.

(*The Compleat Angler.*)

II.—Content and Angling

Venator. Well sung, master; this day's fortune and pleasure, and this night's company and song, do all make me more and more in love with angling. Gentlemen, my master left me alone for an hour this day; and I verily believe he retired himself from talking with me that he might be so perfect in this song; was it not, master?

Piscator. Yes, indeed, for it is many years since I learned it; and having forgotten a part of it, I was forced to patch it up by the help of mine own invention, who am not excellent at poetry, as my part of the song may testify; but of that I will say no more, lest you should think I mean, by discommending it, to beg your commendations of it. And therefore, without replications, let's hear your catch scholar; which I hope will be a good one, for you are both musical and have a good fancy to boot.

Venator. Marry, and that you shall; and as freely as I would have my honest master tell me some more secrets of fish and fishing, as we walk and fish towards London to-morrow. But, master, first let me tell you, that very hour which you were absent from me, I sat down under a willow-tree by the water-side, and considered what you had told me of the owner of that pleasant meadow in which you then left me; that he had a plentiful estate, and not a heart to think so; that he had at this time many law-suits depending, and that they both damped his mirth and took up so much of his time and thoughts, that he himself had not leisure to take the sweet content that I, who pretended no title to them, took in his fields: for I could there sit quietly; and looking on the water, see some fishes sport themselves in the silver streams, others leaping at flies of several shapes and colours; looking on the hills, I could behold them spotted with woods and groves; looking down the meadows, could see, here a boy gathering lilies and lady-smocks, and there a girl cropping culverkeys and cow-slips, all to make garlands suitable to this present month of May: these, and many other field flowers so perfumed the air, that I thought that very meadow like that field in Sicily of which Diodorus speaks, where the perfumes arising from the place make all dogs that hunt in it to fall off, and to lose their hottest scent. I say, as I thus sat, joying in my own happy condition, and pitying this poor rich man that owned this and many other pleasant groves and meadows about me, I did thankfully remember what my Saviour said, that the meek possess the earth; or rather, they enjoy what the others possess and enjoy not; for anglers and meek, quiet-spirited men are free from those high, those restless thoughts, which corrode the sweets of life; and they, and they only, can say, as the poet has happily expressed it—

> " Hail ! blest estate of lowliness ;
>   Happy enjoyments of such minds
> As, rich in self-contentedness,
>   Can, like the reeds, in roughest winds,
> By yielding make that blow but small
> At which proud oaks and cedars fall."

Gentlemen, these were a part of the thoughts that then possessed me. And I there made a conversion of a piece of an old catch, and added more to it, fitting them to be sung by us anglers.

Come, master, you can sing well; you must sing a part of it as it is in this paper—

> "Man's life is but vain; for 'tis subject to pain,
>   And sorrow, and short as a bubble;
> 'Tis a hodge-podge of business, and money, and care,
>   And care, and money, and trouble.
>
> But we'll take no care when the weather proves fair;
>   Nor will we vex now though it rain;
> We'll banish all sorrow, and sing till to-morrow,
>   And angle, and angle again."

(The Compleat Angler.)

III.—George Herbert at Bemerton

The third day after he was made Rector of Bemerton, and had changed his sword and silk clothes into a canonical coat, he returned so habited with his friend Mr. Woodnot to Bainton; and immediately after he had seen and saluted his wife, he said to her: "You are now a Minister's wife, and must now so far forget your father's house, as not to claim a precedence of any of your parishioners; for you are to know, that a Priest's wife can challenge no precedence or place, but that which she purchases by her obliging humility; and I am sure, places so purchased do best become them. And let me tell you, that I am so good a Herald, as to assure you that this is truth." And she was so meek a wife, as to assure him, " it was no vexing news to her, and that he should see her observe it with a willing cheerfulness." And, indeed, her unforced humility, that humility that was in her so original, as to be born with her, made her so happy as to do so; and her doings so begot her an unfeigned love, and a serviceable respect from all that conversed with her; and this love followed her in all places, as inseparably as shadows follow substances in sunshine.

It was not many days before he returned back to Bemerton, to view the church, and repair the chancel: and indeed to rebuild almost the parts of his house, which was fallen down, or decayed by reason of his predecessor's living at a better Parsonage-house; namely, at Minal, sixteen or twenty miles from this place. At which time of Mr. Herbert's coming alone to Bemerton, there came to him a poor old woman, with an intent to acquaint him with her necessitous condition, as also with some troubles of her mind: but after she had spoke some few words to him, she was surprised with a fear, and that begot a shortness of breath, so that her spirits and speech failed her; which he perceiving did so compassionate her, and was so humble, that he took her by the hand, and said : " Speak, good mother; be not afraid to speak to me; for I am a man that will hear you with patience; and will relieve your necessities too if I be able : and this I will do willingly; and, therefore, mother, be not afraid to acquaint me with what you desire." After which comfortable speech he again took her by the hand, made her sit down by him, and understanding she was of his parish, he told her " he would be acquainted with her, and take her into his care." And having with patience heard and understood her wants—and it is some relief for a poor body to be but heard with patience—he, like a Christian clergyman, comforted her by his meek behaviour and counsel : but because that cost him nothing, he relieved her with money too, and so sent her home with a cheerful heart, praising God and praying for him. Thus worthy, and like David's blessed men, thus lowly, was Mr. George Herbert in his own eyes, and thus lovely in the eyes of others.

(Life of Herbert.)

JOHN EARLE (1601 ?–1665)

I.—A CHILD

is a man in a small letter, yet the best copy of Adam before he tasted of Eve, or the Apple; and he is happy whose small practice in the world can only write this character. He is Nature's fresh picture newly drawn in oil, which time and much handling dims and defaces. His soul is yet a white paper unscribbled with observations of the world, wherewith at length it becomes a blurred note-book. He is purely happy, because he knows no evil, nor hath made means by sin to be acquainted with misery. He arrives not at the mischief of being wise, nor endures evils to come by foreseeing them. He kisses and loves all, and when the smart of the rod is past, smiles on his beater. Nature and his parents alike dandle him, and tice him on with a bait of sugar to a draught of wormwood. He plays yet, like a young prentice the first day, and is not come to his task of melancholy. His hardest labour is his tongue, as if he were loath to use so deceitful an organ; and he is best company with it when he can but prattle. We laugh at his foolish sports, but his game is our earnest; and his drums, rattles and hobby horses but the emblems and mockings of man's business. His father hath writ him as his own little story, wherein he reads those days of his life that he cannot remember; and sighs to see what innocence he has outlived. The elder he grows he is a stair lower from God; and like his first father much worse in his breeches. He is the Christian's example and the old man's relapse : the one imitates his pureness, and the other falls into his simplicity. Could he put off his body with his little coat, he had got eternity without a burthen, and exchanged but one heaven for another.

(Micro-Cosmographie.)

II.—A PLAIN COUNTRY FELLOW

A plain country fellow is one that manures his ground well, but lets himself lie fallow and untilled. He has reason enough to do his business, and not enough to be idle or melancholy. He seems to have the judgment of Nebuchednezzar : for his conversation is among beasts, and his talons none of the shortest, only he eats not grass because he loves not sallets. His hand guides the plough, and the plough his thoughts, and his ditch and landmark is the very mound of his meditations. He expostulates with his oxen very understandingly, and speaks Gee and Ree better than English. His mind is not much distracted with objects : but if a good fat cow come in his way, he stands dumb and astonisht, and though his haste be never so great, will fix here half an hour's contemplation. His habitation is some poor thatcht roof, distinguisht from his barn by the loop-holes that let out smoak, which the rain had long since washt thorow, but for the double seeling of bacon on the inside, which has hung there from his grandsire's time, and is yet to make rashers for posterity. His dinner is his other work, for he sweats at it as much as at his labour; he is a terrible fastner on a piece of beef, and you may hope to stave the guard off sooner. His religion is a part of his copyhold, which he takes from his landlord, and refers it wholly to his discretion. Yet if he give him leave, he is a good Christian to his power; that is, comes to church in his best clothes, and sits there with his neighbours, where he is capable only of two prayers, for rains and fair weather. He apprehends God's blessings only in a good year or a fat pasture, and never praises him but on good ground. Sunday he esteems a day to make merry in, and thinks a bagpipe as essential to it as evening prayer, where he walks very solemnly after service with his hands coupled behind him, and censures the dancing of his parish. His compliment with his neighbour is a good thump on the back; and his salutation commonly some blunt curse. He thinks nothing to be vices but pride and ill husbandry, for which he will gravely dissuade youth, and has some thrifty hobnail proverbs to clout his discourse. He is a niggard all the week except only market-day, where if his corn sell well, he thinks he may be drunk with a good conscience. He is sensible of no calamity but the burning of a stack of corn or the overflowing of a meadow, and thinks Noah's flood the greatest plague that ever was, not because it drowned the world, but spoiled the grass. For Death he is never troubled, and if he get in but his harvest before, let it come when it will he cares not.

(Micro-Cosmographie.)

SIR THOMAS BROWNE (1605–1682)
I.—OF HIMSELF

Now for my life, it is a miracle of thirty years, which to relate, were not a History, but a piece of Poetry, and would sound to common ears like a Fable. For the World, I count it not an Inn, but an Hospital; and a place not to live, but to dye in. The world that I regard is my self; it is the Microcosm of my own frame that I cast mine eye on; for the other, I use it but like my Globe, and turn it round sometimes for my recreation. Men that look upon my outside, perusing only my condition and Fortunes, do err in my Altitude; for I am above Atlas his shoulders. The earth is a point not only in respect of the Heavens above us, but of that heavenly and celestial part within us; that mass of Flesh that circumscribes me, limits not my mind : that surface that tells the Heavens it hath an end, cannot persuade me I have any : I take my circle to be above three hundred and sixty; though the number of the Ark do measure my body, it comprehendeth not my mind : whilst I study to find how I am a Microcosm, or little World, I find myself something more than the great. There is surely a piece of Divinity in us, something that was before the Elements, and owes no homage unto the Sun. Nature tells me I am the Image of GOD, as well as Scripture : he that understands not thus much, hath not his introduction or first lesson, and is yet to begin the Alphabet of man. Let me not injure the felicity of others, if I say I am as happy as any : *Ruat cælum, fiat voluntas Tua*, salveth all; so that whatsoever happens, it is but what our daily prayers desire. In brief, I am content; and what should Providence add more? Surely this is it we call Happiness, and this do I enjoy; with this I am happy in a dream, and as content to enjoy a happiness in a fancy, as others in a more apparent truth and realty. There is surely a neerer apprehension of any thing that delights us in our dreams, than in our waked senses : without this I were unhappy; for my awaked judgment discontents me, ever whispering unto me, that I am from my friend ; but my friendly dreams in the night requite me, and make me think I am within his arms. I thank GOD for my happy dreams, as I do for my good rest ; for there is a satisfaction in them unto reasonable desires, and such as can be content with a fit of happiness : and surely it is not a melancholy conceit to think we are all asleep in this World, and that the conceits of this life are as meer dreams to those of the next ; as the Phantasms of the night, to the conceits of the day. There is an equal delusion in both, and the one doth but seem to be the embleme or picture of the other : we are somewhat more than our selves in our sleeps, and the slumber of the body seems to be but the waking of the soul. It is the ligation of sense, but the liberty of reason; and our waking conceptions do not match the Fancies of our sleeps. At my Nativity my Ascendant was the watery sign of Scorpius ; I was born in the Planetary hour of Saturn, and I think I have a piece of that Leaden Planet in me. I am no way facetious, nor disposed for the mirth and galliardize of company ; yet in one dream I can compose a whole Comedy, behold the action, apprehend the jests, and laugh my self awake at the conceits thereof. Were my memory as faithful as my reason is then fruitful, I would never study but in my dreams ; and this time also would I chuse for my devotions : but our grosser memories have then so little hold of our abstracted understandings, that they forget the story, and can only relate to our awaked souls, a confused and broken tale of that that hath passed. Aristotle, who hath written a singular Tract *Of Sleep*, hath not, methinks, throughly defined it ; nor yet Galen, though he seem to have corrected it ; for those Noctambuloes and night-walkers, though in their sleep, do yet injoy the action of their senses. We must therefore say that there is something in us that is not in the jurisdiction of Morpheus ; and that those abstracted and ecstatick souls do walk about in their own corps, as spirits with the bodies they assume, wherein they seem to hear, see, and feel, though indeed the Organs are destitute of sense, and their natures of those faculties that should inform them. Thus it is observed, that men sometimes, upon the hour of their departure, do speak and reason above themselves ; for then the soul, beginning to be freed from the ligaments of the body begins to reason like her self, and to discourse in a strain above mortality.

We term sleep a death ; and yet it is waking that kills us,

and destroys those spirits that are the house of life. 'Tis indeed a part of life that best expresseth death; for every man truely lives, so long as he acts his nature, or some way makes good the faculties of himself. Themistocles, therefore, that slew his Soldier in his sleep, was a merciful Executioner: 'tis a kind of punishment the mildness of no laws hath invented: I wonder the fancy of Lucan and Seneca did not discover it. It is that death by which we may be literally said to dye daily; a death which Adam dyed before his mortality; a death whereby we live a middle and moderating point between life and death: in fine, so like death, I dare not trust it without my prayers, and an half adieu unto the World, and take my farewel in a Colloquy with GOD.

(Religio Medici.)

II.—IMMORTALITY

Oblivion is not to be hired. The greater part must be content to be as though they had not been, to be found in the register of God, not in the record of man. Twenty-seven names make up the first story, and the recorded names ever since contain not one living century. The number of the dead long exceedeth all that shall live. The night of time far surpasseth the day, and who knows when was the equinox? Every hour adds unto that current arithmetick, which scarce stands one moment. And since death must be the *Lucina* of life, and even Pagans could doubt, whether thus to live were to die; since our longest sun sets at right descensions, and makes but winter arches, and therefore it cannot be long before we lie down in darkness, and have our light in ashes; since the brother of death daily haunts us with dying mementos, and time that grows old in itself, bids us hope no long duration;—diuturnity is a dream and folly of expectation.

Darkness and light divide the course of time, and oblivion shares with memory a great part even of our living beings; we slightly remember our felicities, and the smartest strokes of affliction leave but short smart upon us. Sense endureth no extremities, and sorrows destroy us or themselves. To weep into stones are fables. Afflictions induce callosities; miseries are slippery, or fall like snow upon us, which notwithstanding is no unhappy stupidity. To be ignorant of evils to come, and forgetful of evils past, is a merciful provision in nature, whereby we digest the mixture of our few and evil days, and, our delivered senses not relapsing into cutting remembrances, our sorrows are not kept raw by the edge of repetitions. A great part of antiquity contented their hopes of subsistency with a transmigration of their souls—a good way to continue their memories, while having the advantage of plural successions, they could not but act something remarkable, in such variety of beings and enjoying the fame of their passed selves, make accumulation of glory unto their last durations. Others, rather than be lost in the uncomfortable night of nothing, were content to recede into the common being, and make one particle of the public soul of all things, which was no more than to return into their unknown and divine original again. Egyptian ingenuity was more unsatisfied, contriving their bodies in sweet consistencies, to attend the return of their souls. But all was vanity, feeding the wind, and folly. The Egyptian mummies, which Cambyses or time hath spared, avarice now consumeth. Mummy is become merchandise, Mizraim cures wounds, and Pharaoh is sold for balsams.

In vain do individuals hope for immortality, or any patent from oblivion, in preservations below the moon; men have been deceived even in their flatteries above the sun, and studied conceits to perpetuate their names in heaven. The various cosmography of that part hath already varied the names of contrived constellations; Nimrod is lost in Orion, and Osyris in the Dog-star. While we look for incorruption in the heavens, we find they are but like the earth;—durable in their main bodies, alterable in their parts; whereof, beside comets and new stars, perspectives begin to tell tales, and the spots that wander about the sun, with Phaeton's favour, would make clear conviction.

There is nothing strictly immortal, but immortality. Whatever hath no beginning, may be confident of no end (all others have a dependent being and within the reach of destruction); which is the peculiar of that necessary Essence that cannot destroy itself; and the highest strain of omnipotency, to be so powerfully constituted as not to suffer even from the power of itself. But the sufficiency of Christian immortality frustrates all earthly glory, and the quality of either state after death, makes a folly of posthumous memory. God who can only destroy our souls, and hath assured our resurrection, either of our bodies or names hath directly promised no duration. Wherein there is so much of chance, that the boldest expectants have found unhappy frustration; and to hold long subsistence, seems but a scape in oblivion. But man is a noble animal, splendid in ashes, and pompous in the grave, solemnizing nativities and deaths with equal lustre, nor omitting ceremonies of bravery in the infamy of his nature.

Life is a pure flame, and we live by an invisible sun within us. A small fire sufficeth for life, great flames seemed too little after death, while men vainly affected precious pyres, and to burn like Sardanapalus; but the wisdom of funeral laws found the folly of prodigal blazes, and reduced undoing fires unto the rule of sober obsequies, wherein few could be so mean as not to provide wood, pitch, a mourner, and an urn.

Five languages secured not the epitaph of Gordianus. The man of God lives longer without a tomb, than any by one, invisibly interred by angels, and adjudged to obscurity, though not without some marks directing human discovery. Enoch and Elias, without either tomb or burial, in an anomalous state of being, are the great examples of perpetuity, in their long and living memory, in strict account being still on this side death, and having a late part yet to act upon this stage of earth. If in the decretory term of the world, we shall not all die but be changed, according to received translation, the last day will make but few graves; at least quick resurrections will anticipate lasting sepultures. Some graves will be opened before they be quite closed, and Lazarus be no wonder. When many that feared to die, shall groan that they can die but once, the dismal state is the second and living death, when life puts despair on the damned; when men shall wish the coverings of mountains, not of monuments, and annihilations shall be courted.

While some have studied monuments, others have studiously declined them, and some have been so vainly boisterous, that they durst not acknowledge their graves; wherein Alaricus seems most subtle, who had a river turned to hide his bones at the bottom. Even Sylla, that thought himself safe in his urn, could not prevent revenging tongues, and stones thrown at his monument. Happy are they whom privacy makes innocent, who deal so with men in this world, that they are not afraid to meet them in the next; who, when they die, make no commotion among the dead, and are not touched with that poetical taunt of Isaiah.

Pyramids, arches, obelisks, were but the irregularities of vain-glory, and wild enormities of ancient magnanimity. But the most magnanimous resolution rests in the Christian religion, which trampleth upon pride, and sits on the neck of ambition, humbly pursuing that infallible perpetuity, unto which all others must diminish their diameters, and be poorly seen in angles of contingency,

Pious spirits who passed their days in raptures of futurity, made little more of this world, than the world that was before it, while they lay obscure in the chaos of pre-ordination, and night of their fore-beings. And if any have been so happy as truly to understand Christian annihilation, ecstasies, exolution, liquefaction, transformation, the kiss of the spouse, gustation of God, and ingression into the divine shadow, they have already had an handsome anticipation of heaven; the glory of the world is surely over, and the earth in ashes unto them.

To subsist in lasting monuments, to live in their productions, to exist in their names and predicament of chimæras, was large satisfaction unto old expectations, and made one part of their Elysiums. But all this is nothing in the metaphysicks of true belief. To live indeed, is to be again ourselves, which being not only an hope, but an evidence in noble believers, 'tis all one to lie in St. Innocents' church-yard, as in the sands of Egypt. Ready to be any thing, in the ecstasy of being ever, and as content with six foot as the *moles* of Adrianus.

(Urn Burial.)

THOMAS FULLER (1608–1661)

I.—OF JESTING

HARMLESS mirth is the best cordial against the consumption of the spirits : wherefore jesting is not unlawful if it trespasseth not in quantity, quality, or season.

1. *It is good to make a jest, but not to make a trade of jesting.* The Earl of Leicester, knowing that Queen Elizabeth was much delighted to see a gentleman dance well, brought the master of the dancing school to dance before her. " Pish," said the Queen, " it is his profession, I will not see him." She liked it not where it was a master quality, but where it attended on other perfections. The same may we say of jesting.

2. *Jest not with the two-edged sword of God's Word.* Will nothing please thee to wash thy hands in, but the font, or to drink healths in, but the church chalice ? And know the whole art is learnt at the first admission, and profane jests will come without calling. If in the troublesome days of King Edward the Fourth, a citizen in Cheapside was executed as a traitor for saying he would make his son heir to the Crown, though he only meant his own house, having a crown for the sign; more dangerous it is to wit-wanton it with the majesty of God. Wherefore, if without thine intention, and against thy will, by chance medley thou hittest Scripture in ordinary discourse, yet fly to the city of refuge and pray to God to forgive thee.

3. *Wanton jests make fools laugh, and wise men frown.* Seeing we are civilized Englishmen, let us not be naked savages in our talk. Such rotten speeches are worst in withered age, when men run after that sin in their words which flieth from them in the deed.

4. *Let not thy jests, like mummy, be made of dead men's flesh.* Abuse not any that are departed; for to wrong their memories is to rob their ghosts of their winding-sheets.

5. *Scoff not at the natural defects of any which are not in their power to amend.* Oh, it is cruelty to beat a cripple with his own crutches! Neither flout any for his profession, if honest, though poor and painful. Mock not a cobbler for his black thumbs.

6. *He that relates another man's wicked jests with delight adopts them to be his own.* Purge them therefore from their poison. If the profaneness may be severed from the wit, it is like a lamprey; take out the string in the back, it may make good meat. But if the staple conceit consists in profaneness, then it is a viper, all poison, and meddle not with it.

7. *He that will lose his friend for a jest, deserves to die a beggar by the bargain.* Yet some think their conceits, like mustard, not good except they bite. We read that all those who were born in England the year after the beginning of the great mortality 1349 wanted their four cheek-teeth. Such let thy jests be, that may not grind the credit of thy friend, and make not jests so long till thou becomest one.

8. *No time to break jests when the heart-strings are about to be broken.* No more showing of wit when the head is to be cut off, like that dying man, who, when the priest coming to him to give him extreme unction, asked of him where his feet were, answered, "At the end of my legs." But at such a time jests are unmannerly *crepitus ingenii.* And let those take heed who end here with Democritus, that they begin not with Heraclitus hereafter.

(The Holy and Profane State.)

II.—Geoffrey Chaucer

His father was a vintner in London; and I have heard his arms quarrelled at, being argent and gules strangely contrived, and hard to be blazoned. Some more wits have made it the dashing of white and red wine (the parents of our ordinary claret), as nicking his father's profession. But were Chaucer alive, he would justify his own arms in the face of all his opposers, being not so devoted to the Muses, but he was also a son of Mars. He was the prince of English poets; married the daughter of Pain Roëc, king of arms in France, and sister to the wife of John of Gaunt, king of Castile.

He was a great refiner and illuminer of our English tongue; and, if he left it so bad, how much worse did he find it ! Witness Leland thus praising him :

> " Prædicat Algerum merito Florentia Dantem,
> Italia et numeros tota, Petrarche, tuos.
> Anglia Chaucerum veneratur nostra Poëtam,
> Cui Veneres debet patria lingua suas."

> " Of Alger Dante Florence doth justly boast,
> Of Petrarch brags all the Italian coast.
> England doth poet Chaucer reverence,
> To whom our language owes its eloquence."

Indeed, Verstegan, a learned antiquary, condemns him for spoiling the purity of the English tongue by the mixture of so many French and Latin words. But he who mingles wine with water, though he destroys the nature of water, improves the quality thereof.

I find this Chaucer fined in the Temple two shillings for striking a Franciscan friar in Fleet Street; and it seems his hands ever after itched to be revenged, and have his penny-worth's out of them, so tickling religious orders with his tales, and yet so pinching them with his truths, that friars, in reading his books, know not how to dispose their faces betwixt crying and laughing. He lies buried in the south aisle of St. Peter's, Westminster; and since hath got the company of Spenser and Drayton, a pair royal of poets, enough almost to make passengers' feet to move metrically, who go over the place where so much poetical dust is interred.

(Church History of Britain.)

JOHN MILTON (1608–1674)

I.—A POET'S AMBITION.

FOR although a poet, soaring in the high reason of his fancies, with his garland and singing robes about him, might, without apology, speak more of himself than I mean to do; yet for me sitting here below in the cool element of prose, a mortal thing among many readers of no empyreal conceit, to venture and divulge unusual things of myself, I shall petition to the gentler sort, it may not be envy to me. I must say, therefore, that after I had for my first years, by the ceaseless diligence and care of my father—whom God recompense !—been exercised to the tongues, and some sciences, as my age would suffer, by sundry masters and teachers both at home and at the schools, it was found that whether aught was imposed me by them that had the overlooking, or betaken to of mine own choice in English or other tongue, prosing or versing, but chiefly by this latter, the style, by certain vital signs it had, was likely to live. But much latelier in the private academies of Italy, whither I was favoured to resort, perceiving that some trifles which I had in memory, composed at under twenty or thereabout—for the manner is, that every one must give some proof of his wit and reading there,— met with acceptance above what was looked for; and other things, which I had shifted in scarcity of books and conveniences to patch up amongst them, were received with written encomiums, which the Italian is not forward to bestow on men of this side the Alps; I began thus far to assent both to them and divers of my friends here at home, and not less to an inward prompting which now grew daily upon me, that by labour and intense study, which I take to be my portion in this life, joined with the strong propensity of nature, I might perhaps leave something so written to aftertimes, as they should not willingly let it die. These thoughts at once possessed me, and these other; that if I were certain to write as men buy leases, for three lives and downward, there ought no regard be sooner had than to God's glory, by the honour and instruction of my country. For which cause, and not only for that I knew it would be hard to arrive at the second rank among the Latins, I applied myself to that resolution, which Ariosto followed against the persuasions of Bembo, to fix all the industry and art I could unite to the adorning of my native tongue; not to make verbal curiosities the end—that were a toilsome vanity,—but to be an interpreter and relater of the best and sagest things among mine own citizens throughout this island in the mother dialect. That what the greatest and choicest wits of Athens, Rome, or modern Italy, and those Hebrews of old did for their country, I, in my proportion, with this over and above, of being a Christian, might do for mine; not caring to be once named abroad, though perhaps I could attain to that, but content with these British islands as my world; whose fortune hath hitherto been, that if the Athenians, as some say, made their small deeds great and renowned by their eloquent writers, England hath had her noble achievements made small by the unskilful handling of monks and mechanics.

Time serves not now, and perhaps I might seem too profuse, to give any certain account of what the mind at home, in the spacious circuits of her musing, hath liberty to propose to herself, though of highest hope and hardest attempting; whether that epic form whereof the two poems of Homer, and those other two of Virgil and Tasso, are a diffuse, and the book of Job a brief model : or whether the rules of Aristotle herein are strictly to be kept, or nature to be followed, which in them that know art and use judgment is no transgression but an enriching of art : and lastly, what king or knight before the Conquest might be chosen, in whom to lay the pattern of a Christian hero.   And as Tasso gave to a prince of Italy his choice whether he would command him to write of Godfrey's expedition against the Infidels, or Belisarius against the Goths, or Charlemain against the Lombards; if to the instinct of nature and the emboldening of art aught may be trusted, and that there be nothing adverse in our climate or the fate of this age, it haply would be no rashness, from an equal diligence and inclination, to present the like offer in our own ancient stories; or whether those dramatic constitutions wherein Sophocles and Euripides reign shall be found more doctrinal and exemplary to a nation.   The Scripture also affords us a divine pastoral drama in the Song of Solomon, consisting of two persons and a double chorus, as Origen rightly judges.   And the Apocalypse of St. John is the majestic image of a high and stately tragedy, shutting up and intermingling her solemn scenes and acts with a sevenfold chorus of hallelujahs and harping symphonies : and this my opinion the grave authority of Pareus, commenting that book, is sufficient to confirm.   Or if occasion shall lead, to imitate those magnific odes and hymns, wherein Pindarus and Callimachus are in most things worthy, some others in their frame judicious, in their matter most an end faulty.   But those frequent songs throughout the Law and Prophets beyond all these, not in their divine argument alone, but in the very critical art of composition, may be easily made appear over all the kinds of lyric poesy to be incomparable.   These abilities, wheresoever they be found, are the inspired gift of God, rarely bestowed, but yet to some—though most abuse—in every nation; and are of power, beside the office of a pulpit, to imbreed and cherish in a great people the seeds of virtue and public civility, to allay the perturbations of the mind, and set the affections in right tune; to celebrate in glorious and lofty hymns the throne and equipage of God's Almightiness, and what He works, and what He suffers to be wrought with high providence in His Church : to sing victorious agonies of martyrs and saints, the deeds and triumphs of just and pious nations, doing valiantly through faith against the enemies of Christ; to deplore the general relapses of kingdoms and states from justice and God's true worship. Lastly, whatsoever in religion is holy and sublime, in virtue amiable or grave, whatsoever hath passion or admiration in all the changes of that which is called fortune from without, or the wily subtleties and refluxes of man's thoughts from within; all these things with a solid and treatable smoothness to paint out and describe. Teaching over the whole book of sanctity and virtue, through all the instances of example, with such delight to those especially of soft and delicious temper, who will not so much as look upon Truth herself, unless they see her elegantly dressed; that whereas the paths of honesty and good life appear now rugged and difficult, though they be indeed easy and pleasant, they will appear to all men both easy and pleasant, though they were rugged and difficult indeed.

(The Reason of Church Government.)

II.—A NOBLE AND PUISSANT NATION.

For as in a body when the blood is fresh, the spirits pure and vigorous, not only to vital but to rational faculties, and those in the acutest and the pertest operations of wit and subtlety, it argues in what good plight and constitution the body is; so when the cheerfulness of the people is so sprightly up, as that it has not only wherewith to guard well its own freedom and safety, but to spare, and to bestow upon the solidest and sublimest points of controversy and new invention, it betokens us not degenerated, nor drooping to a fatal decay, by casting off the old and wrinkled skin of corruption to outlive these pangs and wax young again, entering the glorious ways of truth and prosperous virtue, destined to become great and honourable in these latter ages. Methinks I see in my mind a noble and puissant nation rousing herself like a strong man after sleep, and shaking her invincible locks. Methinks I see her as an eagle mewing her mighty youth, and kindling her undazzled eyes at the full midday beam; purging and unscaling her long-abused sight at the fountain itself of heavenly radiance; while the whole noise of timorous and flocking birds, with those also that love the twilight, flutter about, amazed at what she means, and in their envious gabble would prognosticate a year of sects and schisms.

(Areopagitica.)

III.—OF TRUTH

Truth indeed came once into the world with her Divine Master, and was a perfect shape most glorious to look on: but when he ascended, and his apostles after him were laid asleep, then straight arose a wicked race of deceivers, who, as that story goes of the Egyptian Typhon with his conspirators, how they dealt with the good Osiris, took the virgin Truth, hewed her lovely form into a thousand pieces, and scattered them to the four winds. From that time ever since, the sad friends of Truth, such as durst appear, imitating the careful search that Isis made for the mangled body of Osiris, went up and down gathering up limb by limb still as they could find them. We have not yet found them all, Lord and Commons, nor ever shall do, till her Master's second coming; he shall bring together every joint and member, and shall mould them into an immortal feature of loveliness and perfection. Suffer not these licensing prohibitions to stand at every place of opportunity forbidding and disturbing them that continue seeking, that continue to do our obsequies to the torn body of our martyred saint.

We boast our light; but if we look not wisely on the sun itself, it smites us into darkness. Who can discern those planets that are oft combust, and those stars of brightest magnitude that rise and set with the sun, until the opposite motion of their orbs bring them to such a place in the firmament where they may be seen evening or morning? The light which we have gained was given us, not to be ever staring on, but by it to discover onward things more remote from our knowledge. It is not the unfrocking of a priest, the unmitring of a bishop, and the removing him from off the Presbyterian shoulders, that will make us a happy nation. No; if other things as great in the Church, and in the rule of life both economical and political be not looked into and reformed, we have looked so long upon the blaze that Zuinglius and Calvin have beaconed up to us that we are stark blind.

There be who perpetually complain of schisms and sects, and make it such a calamity that any man dissents from their maxims. It is their own pride and ignorance which causes the disturbing, who neither will hear with meekness nor can convince, yet all must be suppressed which is not found in their Syntagma. They are the troublers, they are the dividers of unity, who neglect and permit not others to unite those dissevered pieces, which are yet wanting to the body of Truth. To be still searching what we know not by what we know, still closing up truth to truth as we find it (for all her body is homogeneal, and proportional), this is the golden rule in theology as well as in arithmetic, and makes up the best harmony in a

Church; not the forced and outward union of cold, and neutral, and inwardly divided minds.

Lord and Commons of England! consider what nation it is whereof ye are, and whereof ye are the governors: a nation not slow and dull, but of a quick, ingenious, and piercing spirit; acute to invent, subtile and sinewy to discourse, not beneath the reach of any point the highest that human capacity can soar to. Therefore the studies of learning in her deepest sciences have been so ancient and so eminent among us, that writers of good antiquity and able judgment have been persuaded that even the school of Pythagoras and the Persian wisdom took beginning from the old philosophy of this island. And that wise and civil Roman, Julius Agricola, who governed once here for Cæsar, preferred the natural wits of Britain before the laboured studies of the French.

(*Areopagitica.*)

IV.—HIMSELF A TRUE POEM

And long it was not after when I was confirmed in this opinion, that he who would not be frustrate of his hope to write well hereafter in laudable things, ought himself to be a true poem; that is, a composition and pattern of the best and honourablest things; not presuming to sing high praises of heroic men, or famous cities, unless he have in himself the experience and the practice of all that which is praiseworthy. . . . Next (for hear me out now, readers), that I may tell ye whither my young feet wandered; I betook me among those lofty fables and romances, which recount in solemn cantos the deeds of knighthood founded by our victorious kings, and from hence had in renown over all Christendom. There I read it in the oath of every knight that he should defend to the expense of his best blood, or of his life if it so befell him, the honour and chastity of virgin or matron; from whence even then I learned what a noble virtue chastity sure must be, to the defence of which so many worthies, by such a dear adventure of themselves, had sworn. . . . Thus from the laureate fraternity of poets, riper years and the ceaseless round of study and reading led me to the shady spaces of philosophy; but chiefly to the divine volumes of Plato, and his equal Xenophon: where, if I should tell ye what I learnt of chastity and love, I mean that which is truly so, whose charming cup is only virtue, which she bears in her hand to those who are worthy (the rest are cheated with a thick intoxicating potion, which a certain sorceress, the abuser of love's name, carries about); and how the first and chiefest office of love begins and ends in the soul producing those happy twins of her divine generation, knowledge and virtue.

(*Apology for Smectymnus*.)

EDWARD HYDE, EARL OF CLARENDON
(1609–1674)

I.—ESCAPE OF CHARLES II

MR. LANE had a niece, or very near kinswoman, who was married to a gentleman, one Mr. Norton, a person of eight or nine hundred pounds per annum, who lived within four or five miles of Bristol, which was at least four or five days' journey from the place where the King then was, but a place most to be wished for the King to be in, because he did not only know all that country very well, but knew many persons also, to whom in an extraordinary case, he durst make himself known. It was hereupon resolved, that Mrs. Lane should visit this cousin, who was known to be of good affections; and that she should ride behind the King, who was fitted with clothes and boots for such a service; and that a servant of her father's, in his livery, should wait upon her. A good house was easily pitched upon for the first night's lodging; where Wilmot had notice given him to meet. And in this equipage the King began his journey; the colonel keeping him company at a distance, with a hawk upon his fist, and two or three spaniels; which, where there were any fields at hand, warranted him to ride out of the way, keeping his company still in his eye, and not seeming to be of it. In this manner they came to their first night's lodging; and they need not now contrive to come to their journey's end about the close of the evening, for it was in the month of October far advanced, that the long journeys they made could not be dispatched sooner. Here the Lord Wilmot found them; and their journeys being then adjusted, he was instructed where he should be every night : so they were seldom seen together in the journey, and rarely lodged in the same house at night. In this manner the colonel hawked two or three days, till he had brought them within less than a day's journey of Mr. Norton's house; and then he gave his hawk to the Lord Wilmot; who continued the journey in the same exercise.

There was great care taken when they came to any house, that the King might be presently carried into some chamber; Mrs. Lane declaring, " that he was a neighbour's son, whom his father had lent her to ride before her, in hope that he would the sooner recover from a quartan ague, with which he had been miserably afflicted, and was not yet free." And by this artifice she caused a good bed to be still provided for him, and the best meat to be sent; which she often carried herself, to hinder others from doing it. There was no resting in any place till they came to Mr. Norton's, nor any thing extraordinary that happened in the way, save that they met many people every day in the way, who were very well known to the King; and the day that they went to Mr. Norton's, they were necessarily to ride quite through the city of Bristol; a place, and people, the King had been so well acquainted with, that he could not but send his eyes abroad to view the great alterations which had been made there, after his departure from thence : and when he rode near the place where the great fort had stood, he could not forbear putting his horse out of the way, and rode with his mistress behind him round about it.

They came to Mr. Norton's house sooner than usual, and it being on a holiday, they saw many people about a bowling-green that was before the door; and the first man the King saw was a chaplain of his own, who was allied to the gentleman of the house, and was sitting upon the rails to see how the bowlers played. William, by which name the King went, walked with his horse into the stable, until his mistress could provide for his retreat. Mrs. Lane was very welcome to her cousin, and was presently conducted to her chamber; where she no sooner was, than she lamented the condition of " a good youth, who came with her, and whom she had borrowed of his father to ride before her, who was very sick, being newly recovered of an ague ; " and desired her cousin, " that a chamber might be provided for him, and a good fire made : for that he would go early to bed, and was not fit to be below stairs." A pretty little chamber was presently made ready, and a fire prepared, and a boy sent into the stable to call William, and to show him his chamber; who was very glad to be there, freed from so much company as was below. Mrs. Lane was put to find some excuse for making a visit at that time of the year, and so many days' journey from her father, and where she had never been before, though the mistress of the house and she had been bred together, and friends as well as kindred. She pretended, " that she was, after a little rest, to go into Dorsetshire to another friend." When it was supper-time, there being broth brought to the table, Mrs. Lane filled a little dish, and desired the butler, who waited at the table, " to carry that dish of porridge to William, and to tell him that he should have some meat sent to him presently." The butler carried the porridge into the chamber, with a napkin, and spoon, and bread, and spoke kindly to the young man; who was willing to be eating.

The butler, looking narrowly upon him, fell upon his knees, and with tears told him, "he was glad to see His Majesty." The King was infinitely surprised, yet recollected himself enough to laugh at the man, and to ask him "what he meant?" The man had been falconer to Sir Thomas Jermyn, and made it appear that he knew well enough to whom he spoke, repeating some particulars, which the King had not forgot. Whereupon the King conjured him "not to speak of what he knew, so much as to his master, though he believed him a very honest man." The fellow promised, and faithfully kept his word; and the King was the better waited upon during the time of his abode there.

Dr. Georges, the King's chaplain, being a gentleman of a good family near that place, and allied to Mr. Norton, supped with them; and, being a man of a cheerful conversation, asked Mrs. Lane many questions concerning William, of whom he saw she was so careful by sending up meat to him, "how long his ague had been gone? and whether he had purged since it left him?" and the like; to which she gave such answers as occurred. The doctor, from the final prevalence of the parliament, had, as many others of that function had done declined his profession, and pretended to study physic. As soon as supper was done, out of good nature, and without telling anybody, he went to see William. The King saw him coming into the chamber, and withdrew to the inside of the bed, that he might be farthest from the candle; and the doctor came, and sat down by him, felt his pulse, and asked him many questions, which he answered in as few words as was possible, and expressing great inclination to go to his bed; to which the doctor left him, and went to Mrs. Lane, and told her "that he had been with William, and that he would do well;" and advised her what she should do if his ague returned. The next morning the doctor went away, so that the King saw him no more, of which he was right glad. The next day the Lord Wilmot came to the house with his hawk, to see Mrs. Lane, and so conferred with William; who was to consider what he was to do. They thought it necessary to rest some days, till they were informed what port lay most convenient for them, and what person lived nearest to it, upon whose fidelity they might rely: and the King gave him directions to inquire after some persons, and some other particulars, of which when he should be fully in-

structed, he should return again to him. In the meantime
Wilmot lodged at a house not far from Mr. Norton's, to which
he had been recommended.

After some days' stay here, and communication between the
King and the Lord Wilmot by letters, the King came to know
that Colonel Francis Windham lived within little more than a
day's journey of the place where he was; of which he was very
glad; for besides the inclination he had to his eldest brother,
whose wife had been his nurse, this gentleman had behaved
himself very well during the war, and had been governor of
Dunstar Castle, where the King had lodged when he was in
the west. After the end of the war, and when all other places
were surrendered in that county, he likewise surrendered that,
upon fair conditions, and made his peace, and afterwards
married a wife with a competent fortune, and lived quietly,
without any suspicion of having lessened his affection towards
the King.

The King sent Wilmot to him, and acquainted him where
he was, and "that he would gladly speak with him." It was
not hard for him to choose a good place where to meet, and
thereupon the day was appointed. After the King had taken
his leave of Mrs. Lane, who remained with her cousin Norton,
the King, and the Lord Wilmot, met the colonel; and, in the
way, he encountered in a town, through which they passed,
Mr. Kirton, a servant of the King's, who well knew the Lord
Wilmot, who had no other disguise than the hawk, but took
no notice of him nor suspected the King to be there; yet that
day made the King more wary of having him in his company
upon the way. At the place of meeting they rested only one
night, and then the King went to the colonel's house; where
he rested many days, whilst the colonel projected at what
place the King might embark, and how they might procure a
vessel to be ready there; which was not easy to find; there being
so great caution in all the ports, and so great a fear possessing
those who were honest, that it was hard to procure any vessel
that was outward bound to take in any passenger.

(*History of the Rebellion.*)

II.—CHARACTER OF LORD FALKLAND

He had a courage of the most clear and keen temper, and
so far from fear, that he was not without appetite of danger;
and therefore, upon any occasion of action, he always engaged
his person in those troops, which he thought, by the forwardness of the commanders, to be most like to be farthest engaged;

and in all such encounters, he had about him a strange cheerfulness and companiableness, without at all affecting the
execution that was then principally to be attended, in which
he took no delight, but took pains to prevent it, where it was
not, by resistance, necessary; insomuch that at Edgehill, when
the enemy was routed, he was like to have incurred great peril,
by interposing to save those who had thrown away their arms,
and against whom it may be, others were more fierce for their
having thrown them away; insomuch as a man might think
he came into the field only out of curiosity to see the face of
danger, and charity to prevent the shedding of blood. Yet in
his natural inclination he acknowledged he was addicted to the
profession of a soldier; and shortly after he came to his fortune,
and before he came to age, he went into the Low Countries, with
a resolution of procuring command and to give himself up to
it, from which he was converted by the complete inactivity
of that summer; and so he returned into England, and shortly
after entered upon that vehement course of study we mentioned
before, till the first alarum from the north; and then again he
made ready for the field, and though he received some repulse
at the command of a troop of horse, of which he had a promise,
he went a volunteer with the Earl of Essex.

From the entrance into this unnatural war, his natural
cheerfulness and vivacity grew clouded, and a kind of sadness
and dejection of spirit stole upon him, which he had never been
used to; yet being one of those who believed that one battle
would end all differences, and that there would be so great a
victory on one side, that the other would be compelled to
submit to any conditions from the victor (which supposition
and conclusion generally sunk in to the minds of most men,
and prevented the looking after many advantages that might
have been laid hold of), he resisted those indispositions, *et in
luctu, bellum inter remedia erat.*

But after the king's return from Brentford, and the furious
resolution of the two houses not to admit any treaty for peace,
those indispositions, which had not before touched him, grew
into a perfect habit of uncheerfulness; and he, who had been
so perfectly unreserved and affable to all men, that his face and
countenance was always present and vacant to his company,
and held any cloudiness and less pleasantness of his visage a
kind of rudeness or uncivility, became on a sudden less communicable; and thence, very sad, pale and exceedingly affected
with the spleen. In his clothes and habit, which he had intended before always with more neatness, and industry, and

expense than is usual to so great a mind, he was not now only incurious, but too negligent; and in his reception of suitors, and the necessary or casual addresses to his place, so quick and sharp and severe, that there wanted not some men (who were strangers to his nature and disposition), who believed him proud and imperious, from which no mortal man was ever more free.

The truth is, that as he was of a most incomparable gentleness, application, and even demissiveness and submission to good and worthy and entire men, so he was naturally (which could not but be more evident in his place, which objected him to another conversation and admixture than his own election had done), *adversus malos injucundus :* and was so ill a dissembler of his dislike and disinclination to all men, that it was not possible for such not to discern it. There was once in the House of Commons, such a declared acceptance of the good service an eminent member had done to them, and, as they said, to the whole kingdom, that it was moved, he being present, "that the Speaker might, in the name of the whole house, give him thanks; and then, that every member might, as testimony of his particular acknowlededgment, stir or move his hat towards him," the which (though not ordered) when very many did, the Lord Falkland (who believed the service itself not to be of that moment, and that an honourable and generous person could not have stooped to it for any recompense), instead of moving his hat, stretched both his arms out and clasped his hands together upon the crown of his hat and held it close down to his head, that all men might see how odious that flattery was to him, and the very approbation of the person, though at that time most popular.

When there was any overture or hope of peace he would be more erect and vigorous, and exceedingly solicitous to press anything which he thought might promote it, and sitting among his friends often, after a deep silence and frequent sighs, would, with a shrill and sad accent, ingeminate the word *Peace, Peace ;* and would passionately profess, "that the very agony of the war, and the view of the calamities and desolation the kingdom did and must endure, took his sleep from him, and would shortly break his heart." This made some think, or pretend to think, "that he was so much enamoured on peace, that he would have been glad the king should have bought it at any price "; which was a most unreasonable calumny; as if a man, that was himself the most punctual and precise in every circumstance that might reflect upon conscience or honour, could have wished the king to have committed a trespass against either. And yet this senseless scandal made some impression on him, or at least he used it for an excuse of the daringness of his spirit; for at the leaguer before Gloucester, when his friends passionately reprehended him for exposing his person unnecessarily to danger (as he delighted to visit the trenches, and nearest approaches, and to discover what the enemy did), as being so much beside the duty of his place, that it might be understood against it, he would say merrily, " that his office could not take away the privileges of his age; and a secretary in war might be present at the greatest secret of danger "; but withal alleged seriously, " that it concerned him to be more active in enterprises of hazard, than other men; that all might see that his impatiency for peace proceeded not from pusillanimity or fear to adventure his own person."

In the morning after the battle, as always upon action, he was very cheerful, and put himself into the first rank of Lord Byron's regiment, who was then advancing upon the enemy, who had lined the hedges of both sides with musketeers; from whence he was shot with a musket in the lower part of the belly, and in the instant falling from his horse, his body was not found till the next morning; till when, there was some hope he might have been a prisoner; though his nearest friends, who knew his temper, received small comfort from that imagination. Thus fell that incomparable young man, in the four and thirtieth year of his age, having so much dispatched the business of life that the oldest rarely attain to that immense knowledge, and the youngest enter not into the world with more innocence; whosoever leads such a life, need not care upon how short warning it be taken from him.

(History of the Rebellion.)

JEREMY TAYLOR (1613-1667)
I.—On Prayer

THE first thing that hinders the prayer of a good man from obtaining its effects is a violent anger, and a violent storm in the spirit of him that prays. For anger sets the house on fire, and all the spirits are busy upon trouble, and intend propulsion, defence, displeasure, or revenge; it is a short madness, and an eternal enemy to discourse, and sober counsels, and fair conversation; it intends its own object with all the earnestness of perception, or activity of design, and a quicker motion of a

too warm and distempered blood; it is a fever in the heart, and
a calenture in the head, and a fire in the face, and a sword in
the hand, and a fury all over; and therefore can never suffer
a man to be in a disposition to pray. For prayer is an action
and a state of intercourse and desire exactly contrary to this
character of anger. Prayer is an action of likeness to the
Holy Ghost, the Spirit of gentleness and dove-like simplicity;
an imitation of the holy Jesus, whose spirit is meek up to the
greatness of the biggest example, and a conformity to God;
whose anger is always just, and marches slowly, and is without
transportation, and often hindered, and never hasty, and is full
of mercy : prayer is the peace of our spirit, the stillness of our
thoughts, the evenness of recollection; the seat of meditation,
the rest of our cares, and the calm of our tempest; prayer is
the issue of a quiet mind, of untroubled thoughts, it is the
daughter of charity, and the sister of meekness; and he that
prays to God with an angry, that is, with a troubled and dis-
composed spirit, is like him that retires into a battle to meditate,
and sets up his closet in the out-quarters of an army, and
chooses a frontier garrison to be wise in. Anger is a perfect
alienation of the mind from prayer, and therefore is contrary
to that attention which presents our prayers in a right line to
God. For so have I seen a lark rising from his bed of grass,
and soaring upwards, singing as he rises, and hopes to get to
heaven, and climb above the clouds; but the poor bird was
beaten back with the loud sighings of an eastern wind, and his
motion made irregular and unconstant, descending more at
every breath of the tempest, than it could recover by the
libration and frequent weighing of its wings; till the little
creature was forced to sit down and pant, and stay till the
storm was over; and then it made a prosperous flight, and
did rise and sing, as if it had learned music and motion from
an angel as he passed sometimes through the air about his
ministries here below : so is the prayer of a good man. . . .

(*Works.*)

II.—Spiritual Arts of Lengthening our Days

Neither must we think that the life of a man begins when
he can feed himself, or walk alone, when he can fight or beget
his like; for so he is contemporary with a camel or a cow : but
he is first a man, when he comes to a certain steady use of
reason, according to his proportion; and when that is, all the
world of men cannot tell precisely. Some are called *at age* at
fourteen, some at one-and-twenty, some never; but all men

late enough, for the life of a man comes upon him slowly and insensibly. But as when the sun approaches towards the gates of the morning, he first opens a little eye of heaven, and sends away the spirits of darkness, and gives light to a cock, and calls up the lark to matins, and by and by gilds the fringes of a cloud, and peeps over the eastern hills, thrusting out his golden horns, like those which decked the brows of *Moses* when he was forced to wear a veil, because himself had seen the face of God; and still while a man tells the story, the sun gets up higher, till he shews a fair face and a full light, and then he shines one whole day, under a cloud often, and sometimes weeping great and little showers, and sets quickly: so is a man's reason and his life. He first begins to perceive himself, to see or taste, making little reflections upon his actions of sense, and can discourse of flies and dogs, shells and play, horses and liberty: but when he is strong enough to enter into arts and little institutions, he is at first entertained with trifles and impertinent things, not because he needs them, but because his understanding is no bigger, and little images of things are laid before him, like a cock-boat to a whale, only to play withal: but before a man comes to be wise, he is half dead with gouts and consumption, with catarrhs and aches, with sore eyes and a worn-out body. So that if we must not reckon the life of a man but by the accounts of his reason, he is long before his soul be dressed: and he is not to be called a man without a wise and an adorned soul, a soul at least furnished with what is necessary towards his well-being: but by that time his soul is thus furnished, his body is decayed; and then you can hardly reckon him to be alive, when his body is possessed by so many degrees of death.

But there is yet another arrest. At first he wants strength of body, and then he wants the use of reason, and when that is come, it is ten to one but he stops by the impediments of vice, and wants the strength of the *spirit;* and we know that *body*, and *soul*, and *spirit*, are the constituent parts of every christian man. And now let us consider what that thing is which we call *years of discretion*. The young man is past his tutors, and arrived at the bondage of a caitiff spirit; he is run from discipline, and is let loose to passion; the man by this time hath wit enough to choose his vice, to act his lust, to court his mistress, to talk confidently, and ignorantly, and perpetually. To despise his betters, to deny nothing to his appetite, to do things that when he is indeed a man he must for ever be ashamed of: for this is all the discretion that most men shew in the first stage of their manhood; they can discern good from evil; and they prove their skill by leaving all that is good; and wallowing in the evils of folly and an unbridled appetite. And by this time the young man hath contracted vicious habits, and is a beast in manners, and therefore it will not be fitting to reckon the beginning of his life; he is a fool in his understanding, and that is a sad death; and he is dead in trespasses and sins, and that is a sadder; so that he hath no life but a natural, the life of a beast, or a tree; in all other capacities he is dead; he neither hath the intellectual nor the spiritual life, neither the life of a man nor of a Christian; and this sad truth lasts too long. For old age seizes upon most men while they still retain the minds of boys and vicious youth, doing actions from principles of great folly and a mighty ignorance, admiring things useless and hurtful, and filling up all the dimensions of their abode with businesses of empty affairs, being at leisure to attend no virtue. They cannot pray, because they are busy, and because they are passionate. They cannot communicate, because they have quarrels and intrigues of perplexed causes, complicated hostilities, and things of the world; and therefore they cannot attend to the things of God : little considering that they must find a time to die in, when death comes they must be at leisure for that. Such men are like sailors loosing from a port, and tossed immediately with a perpetual tempest, lasting till their cordage crack, and either they sink or return back again to the same place : they did not make a voyage, though they were long at sea. The business and impertinent affairs of most men steal all their time, and they are restless in a foolish motion : but this is not the progress of a man; he is no farther advanced in the course of a life, though he reckon many years; for still his soul is childish and trifling, like an untaught boy.

(*Holy Dying.*)

ABRAHAM COWLEY (1618–1667)

I.—OF SOLITUDE

Nunquam minus solus, quam cum solus, is now become a very vulgar saying. Every man, and almost every boy, for these seventeen hundred years has had it in his mouth. But it was at first spoken by the excellent Scipio, who was without question a most eloquent and witty person, as well as the most wise, most worthy, most happy, and the greatest of all mankind. His meaning no doubt was this : that he found more satisfaction to his mind, and more improvement of it by solitude than by company; and to show that he spoke not this loosely or out of vanity, after he had made Rome mistress of almost the whole world, he retired himself from it by a voluntary exile, and at a private house in the middle of a wood near Linternum passed the remainder of his glorious life no less gloriously. This house Seneca went to see so long after with great veneration, and, among other things, describes his bath to have been of so mean a structure that now, says he, the basest of the people would despise them, and cry out, "Poor Scipio understood not how to live." What an authority is here for the credit of retreat! and happy had it been for Hannibal if adversity could have taught him as much wisdom as was learnt by Scipio from the highest prosperities. This would be no wonder if it were as truly as it is colourably and wittily said by Monsieur de Montaigne, that ambition itself might teach us to love solitude: there is nothing does so much hate to have companions. It is true, it loves to have its elbows free, it detests to have company on either side, but it delights above all things in a train behind, ay, and ushers too, before it. But the greater part of men are so far from the opinion of that noble Roman, that if they chance at any time to be without company they are like a becalmed ship; they never move but by the wind of other men's breath, and have no oars of their own to steer withal. It is very fantastical and contradictory in human nature that men should love themselves above all the rest of the world and yet never endure to be with themselves. When they are in love with a mistress, all others persons are importunate and burdensome to them. *Tecum vivere amem, tecum obeam lubens,* "They would live and die with her alone."

> *Sic ego secretis possum benè vivere silvis*
> *Quà nulla humano sit via trita pede,*
> *Tu mihi curarum requies, tu nocte vel atrâ*
> *Lumen, et in solis tu mihi turba locis.*

> With thee for ever I in woods could rest,
> Where never human foot the ground has pressed
> Thou from all shades the darkness canst exclude,
> And from a desert banish solitude.

And yet our dear self is so wearisome to us that we can scarcely support its conversation for an hour together. This is such an odd temper of mind as Catullus expresses towards one of his mistresses, whom we may suppose to have been of a very unsociable humour.

> *Odi et Amo, qua nam id faciam ratione requiris ?*
> *Nescio, sed fieri sentio, et excrucior.*

I hate, and yet I love thee too ;
How can that be ? I know not how ;
Only that so it is I know,
And feel with torment that 'tis so.

It is a deplorable condition this, and drives a man sometimes
to pitiful shifts in seeking how to avoid himself.

The truth of the matter is, that neither he who is a fop in
the world is a fit man to be alone, nor he who has set his heart
much upon the world, though he has ever so much understanding ; so that solitude can be well fitted and set right but upon
a very few persons. They must have enough knowledge of the
world to see the vanity of it, and enough virtue to despise all
vanity ; if the mind be possessed with any lust or passions, a
man had better be in a fair than in a wood alone. They may,
like petty thieves, cheat us perhaps, and pick our pockets in
the midst of company, but like robbers, they use [1] to strip and
bind, or murder us when they catch us alone. This is but to
retreat from men, and fall into the hands of devils. It is like
the punishment of parricides among the Romans, to be sewed
into a bag with an ape, a dog, and a serpent. The first work,
therefore, that a man must do to make himself capable of the
good of solitude is the very eradication of all lusts, for how is
it possible for a man to enjoy himself while his affections are
tied to things without himself ? In the second place, he must
learn the art and get the habit of thinking ; for this too, no less
than well speaking, depends upon much practice ; and cogitation
is the thing which distinguishes the solitude of a god from a
wild beast. Now because the soul of man is not by its own
nature or observation furnished with sufficient materials to
work upon ; it is necessary for it to have continual resource to
learning and books for fresh supplies, so that the solitary life
will grow indigent, and be ready to starve without them ; but
if once we be thoroughly engaged in the love of letters, instead
of being wearied with the length of any day, we shall only
complain of the shortness of our whole life.

O vita, stulto longa, sapienti brevis !
O life, long to the fool, short to the wise !

The First Minister of State has not so much business in
public as a wise man has in private ; if the one have little leisure
to be alone, the other has less leisure to be in company ; the
one has but part of the affairs of one nation, the other all the
works of God and nature under his consideration. There is

[1] Are wont.

no saying shocks me so much as that which I hear very often, "That a man does not know how to pass his time." It would have been but ill spoken by Methuselah in the nine hundred and sixty-ninth year of his life, so far it is from us, who have not time enough to attain to the utmost perfection of any part of any science, to have cause to complain that we are forced to be idle for want of work. But this you will say is work only for the learned, others are not capable either of the employments or the divertisements that arise from letters. I know they are not, and therefore cannot much recommend solitude to a man totally illiterate. But if any man be so unlearned as to want entertainment of the little intervals of accidental solitude, which frequently occur in almost all conditions (except the very meanest of the people, who have business enough in the necessary provisions for life), it is truly a great shame both to his parents and himself; for a very small portion of any ingenious art will stop up all those gaps of our time, either music, or painting, or designing, or chemistry, or history, or gardening, or twenty other things, will do it usefully and pleasantly; and if he happen to set his affections upon poetry (which I do not advise him too immoderately) that will overdo it; no wood will be thick enough to hide him from the importunities of company or business, which would abstract him from his beloved.

(Essays.)

II.—OF AGRICULTURE

As for the necessity of this art, it is evident enough, since this can live without all others, and no one other without this. This is like speech, without which the society of men cannot be preserved; the others like figures and tropes of speech which serve only to adorn it. Many nations have lived, and some do still, without any art but this; not so elegantly, I confess, but still they live; and almost all the other arts which are here practised are beholding to them for most of their materials. The innocence of this life is in the next thing for which I commend it, and if husbandmen preserve not that, they are much to blame, for no men are so free from the temptations of iniquity. They live by what they can get by industry from the earth, and others by what they can catch by craft from men. They live upon an estate given them by their mother, and others upon an estate cheated from their brethren. They live like sheep and kine, by the allowances of Nature, and others like wolves and foxes by the acquisition of rapine; and, I hope, I may affirm (without any offence to the great) that sheep and kine are very useful, and that wolves and foxes are pernicious creatures. They are, without dispute, of all men the most quiet and least apt to be inflamed to the disturbance of the commonwealth; their manner of life inclines them, and interest binds them, to love peace. In our late mad and miserable civil wars, all other trades, even to the meanest, set forth whole troops, and raised up some great commanders, who became famous and mighty for the mischiefs they had done. But I do not remember the name of any one husbandman who had so considerable a share in the twenty years' ruin of his country, as to deserve the curses of his countrymen; and if great delights be joined with so much innocence, I think it is ill done of men not to take them here where they are so tame and ready at hand, rather than hunt for them in courts and cities, where they are so wild and the chase so troublesome and dangerous.

We are here among the vast and noble scenes of Nature; we are there among the pitiful shifts of policy. We walk here in the light and open ways of the divine bounty; we grope there in the dark and confused labyrinths of human malice. Our senses are here feasted with the clear and genuine taste of their objects, which are all sophisticated there, and for the most part overwhelmed with their contraries. Here is harmless and cheap plenty, there guilty and expenseful luxury.

I shall only instance in one delight more, the most natural and best natured of all others, a perpetual companion of the husbandman: and that is, the satisfaction of looking round about him, and seeing nothing but the effects and improvements of his own art and diligence; to be always gathering of some fruits of it, and at the same time to behold others ripening, and others budding; to see all his fields and gardens covered with the beauteous creatures of his own industry; and to see, like God, that all his works are good.

The antiquity of his art is certainly not to be contested by any other. The three first men in the world were a gardener, a ploughman, and a grazier; and if any man object that the second of these was a murderer, I desire he would consider, that as soon as he was so, he quitted our profession and turned builder. It is for this reason, I suppose, that Ecclesiasticus forbids us to hate husbandry; because, says he, the Most High has created it. We were all born to this art, and taught by Nature to nourish our bodies by the same earth out of which they were made, and to which they must return and pay at last for their sustenance.

Behold the original and primitive nobility of all those great persons who are too proud now not only to till the ground, but almost to tread upon it. We may talk what we please of lilies and lions rampant, and spread eagles in fields d'or or d'argent; but if heraldry were guided by reason, a plough in a field arable would be the most noble and ancient arms.

All these considerations make me fall into the wonder and complaint of Columella, how it should come to pass that all arts or sciences (for the dispute, which is an art and which is a science does not belong to the curiosity of us husbandmen), metaphysic, physic, morality, mathematics, logic, rhetoric, etc., which are all, I grant, good and useful faculties, except only metaphysic, which I do not know whether it be anything or no, but even vaulting, fencing, dancing, attiring, cookery, carving, and such-like vanities, should all have public schools and masters; and yet that we should never see or hear of any man who took upon him the profession of teaching this so pleasant, so virtuous, so profitable, so honourable, so necessary art.

A man would think when he's in serious humour, that it were but a vain, irrational, and ridiculous thing for a great company of men and women to run up and down in a room together, in a hundred several postures and figures, to no purpose, and with no design; and therefore dancing was invented first, and only practised anciently, in the ceremonies of the heathen religion, which consisted all in mummery and madness; the latter being the chief glory of the worship, and accounted divine inspiration. This, I say, a severe man would think, though I dare not determine so far against so customary a part now of good breeding. And yet, who is there among our gentry that does not entertain a dancing master for his children as soon as they are able to walk? But did ever any father provide a tutor for his son to instruct him betimes in the nature and improvements of that land which he intended to leave him? That is at least a superfluity, and this a defect in our manner of education; and therefore I could wish, but cannot in these times much hope to see it, that one college in each university were erected, and appropriated to this study, as well as there are to medicine and the civil law. There would be no need of making a body of scholars and fellows, with certain endowments, as in other colleges; it would suffice if, after the manner of Halls in Oxford, there were only four professors constituted (for it would be too much work for only one master, or principal, as they call him there) to teach these four parts of it. First, aration, and all things relating to it. Secondly, pasturage; thirdly, gardens, orchards, vineyards.

and woods; fourthly, all parts of rural economy, which would contain the government of bees, swine, poultry, decoys, ponds, etc., and all that which Varro calls *Villaticas Pastiones*, together with the sports of the field, which ought not to be looked upon only as pleasures, but as parts of housekeeping, and the domestical conservation and uses of all that is brought in by industry abroad. The business of these professors should not be, as is commonly practised in other arts, only to read pompous and superficial lectures out of Virgil's *Georgics*, Pliny, Varro, or Columella, but to instruct their pupils in the whole method and course of this study, which might be run through perhaps with diligence in a year or two; and the continual succession of scholars upon a moderate taxation for their diet, lodging, and learning, would be a sufficient constant revenue for maintenance of the house and the professors, who should be men not chosen for the ostentation of critical literature, but for solid and experimental knowledge of the things they teach such men; so industrious and public spirited as I conceive Mr. Hartlib to be, if the gentleman be yet alive. But it is needless to speak further of my thoughts of this design, unless the present disposition of the age allowed more probability of bringing it into execution. What I have further to say of the country life shall be borrowed from the poets, who were always the most faithfull and affectionate friends to it.

(Essays.)

JOHN EVELYN (1620–1706)

I.—The Great Fire

1666, *2nd Sept.*—This fatal night, about ten, began that deplorable fire near Fish Street, in London.

3rd.—The fire continuing, after dinner I took coach with my wife and son, and went to the Bank-side in Southwark, where we beheld that dismal spectacle, the whole city in dreadful flames near the water-side; all the houses from the bridge, all Thames Street, and upwards towards Cheapside, down to the Three Cranes, were now consumed.

The fire having continued all this night, (if I may call that night which was as light as day for ten miles round about, after a dreadful manner,) when conspiring with a fierce eastern wind in a very dry season; I went on foot to the same place, and saw the whole south part of the city burning from Cheapside to the Thames, and all along Cornhill, (for it kindled back against the wind as well as forward,) Tower Street, Fenchurch Street, Gracechurch Street, and so along to Bainard's Castle,

and was now taking hold of St. Paul's Church, to which the
scaffolds contributed exceedingly. The conflagration was so
universal, and the people so astonished, that from the beginning, I know not by what despondency or fate, they hardly
stirred to quench it; so that there was nothing heard or seen
but crying out and lamentation, running about like distracted
creatures, without at all attempting to save even their goods;
such a strange consternation there was upon them so as it
burned both in breadth and length, the churches, public halls,
exchange, hospitals, monuments, and ornaments, leaping after
a prodigious manner from house to house, and street to street,
at great distances one from the other; for the heat, with a long
set of fair and warm weather, had even ignited the air and
prepared the materials to conceive the fire, which devoured
after an incredible manner, houses, furniture, and everything.
Here we saw the Thames covered with good floating, all the
barges and boats laden with what some had time and courage
to save, as, on the other, the carts, etc., carrying out to the
fields, which for many miles were strewed with movables of
all sorts, and tents erecting to shelter both people and what
goods they could get away. Oh, the miserable and calamitous
spectacle ! such as haply the world had not seen the like since
the foundation of it, nor be outdone till the universal conflagration. All the sky was of a fiery aspect, like the top of a
burning oven, the light seen above forty miles round about
for many nights. God grant my eyes may never behold the
like, now seeing above 10,000 houses all in one flame : the noise,
and cracking, and thunder of the impetuous flames, the shrieking
of women and children, the hurry of people, the fall of towers,
houses, and churches was like an hideous storm, and the air all
about so hot and inflamed, that at last one was not able to
approach it; so that they were forced to stand still and let the
flames burn on, which they did for near two miles in length
and one in breadth. The clouds of smoke were dismal, and
reached, upon computation, near fifty miles in length. Thus
I left it this afternoon burning, a resemblance of Sodom, or the
last day. It forcibly called to my mind that passage—*non
enim hic habemus stabilem civitatem.* London was, but is no more !

4*th.*—The burning still rages, and it has now gotten as far
as the Inner Temple, all Fleet Street, the Old Bailey, Ludgate
Hill, Warwick Lane, Newgate, Paul's Chain, Watling Street,
now flaming, and most of it reduced to ashes; the stones of
Paul's flew like granados, the melting lead running down the
streets in a stream, and the very pavements glowing with fiery

redness, so as no horse nor man was able to tread on them, and the demolition had stopped all the passages, so that no help could be applied. The eastern wind still more impetuously drove the flames forward. Nothing but the almighty power of God was able to stop them, for vain was the help of man.

5th.—It crossed towards Whitehall; oh, the confusion there was then at that court! It pleased his majesty to command me among the rest to look after the quenching of Fetter Lane end, to preserve, if possible, that part of Holborn, whilst the rest of the gentlemen took their several posts, (for now they began to bestir themselves, and not till now, who hitherto had stood as men intoxicated, with their hands across,) and began to consider that nothing was likely to put a stop, but the blowing up of so many houses as might make a wider gap than any had yet been made by the ordinary method of pulling them down with engines; this some stout seamen proposed early enough to have saved nearly the whole city, but this some tenacious and avaricious men, aldermen, etc., would not permit, because their houses must have been of the first. It was therefore now commanded to be practised, and my concern being particularly for the hospital of St. Bartholomew, near Smithfield, where I had many wounded and sick men, made me the more diligent to promote it, nor was my care for the Savoy less. It now pleased God, by abating the wind, and by the industry of the people, infusing a new spirit into them, that the fury of it began sensibly to abate about noon, so as it came no farther than the Temple westward, nor than the entrance of Smithfield north; but continued all this day and night so impetuous towards Cripplegate and the Tower, as made us all despair. It also broke out again in the Temple, but the courage of the multitude persisting, and many houses being blown up, such gaps and desolations were soon made, as with the former three days' consumption, the back fire did not so vehemently urge upon the rest as formerly. There was yet no standing near the burning and glowing ruins by near a furlong's space.

The coal and wood wharfs, and magazines of oil, rosin, etc., did infinite mischief, so as the invective which a little before I had dedicated to his majesty and published, giving warning what might probably be the issue of suffering those shops to be in the city, was looked on as a prophecy.

The poor inhabitants were dispersed about St. George's Fields and Moorfields, as far as Highgate, and several miles in circle, some tents, some under miserable huts and hovels, many without a rag, or any necessary utensils, bed, or board; who, from delicateness, riches, and easy accommodations in stately and well-furnished houses, were now reduced to extremest misery and poverty.

In this calamitous condition I returned with a sad heart to my house, blessing and adoring the mercy of God to me and mine, who in the midst of all this ruin was like Lot, in my little Zoar, safe and sound.

(Diary.)

II.—THE DEATH OF MR. PEPYS

26th May, 1703.—This day died Mr. Samuel Pepys, a very worthy, industrious and curious person, none in England exceeding him in knowledge of the Navy, in which he had passed through all the most considerable offices, Clerk of the Acts and Secretary of the Admiralty, all which he performed with great integrity. When King James II went out of England, he laid down his office, and would serve no more, but withdrawing himself from all public affairs, he lived at Clapham with his partner Mr. Hewer, formerly his clerk, in a very noble house and sweet place, where he enjoyed the fruit of his labours in great prosperity. He was universally belov'd, hospitable, generous, learned in many things, skill'd in music, a very great cherisher of learned men of whom he had the conversation. His library and collection of other curiosities were of the most considerable, the models of ships especially. Besides what he published of an Account of the Navy, as he found and left it, he had four divers years under his hand the History of the Navy, or Navalia, as he called it; but how far advanced, and what will follow of his, is left, I suppose, to his sister's son Mr. Jackson, a young gentleman whom Mr. Pepys had educated in all sorts of useful learning, sending to travel abroad, from whence he returned with extraordinary accomplishments and worthy to be heir. Mr. Pepys had been for near forty years so much my particular friend, that Mr. Jackson sent me complete mourning desiring me to be one to hold up the pall at his magnificent obsequies, but my indisposition hinder'd me from doing him this last office.

(Diary.)

JOHN BUNYAN (1628–1688)

I.—THE FIGHT WITH APOLLYON

THEN Apollyon straddled quite over the whole breadth of the way, and said "I am void of fear in this matter, prepare thyself to die, for I swear by my infernal den that thou shalt go no further, here will I spill thy soul"; and with that, he threw a flaming dart at his breast, but Christian had a shield in his hand, with which he caught it, and so prevented the danger of that. Then did Christian draw, for he saw 'twas time to bestir him; and Apollyon as fast made at him, throwing darts as thick as hail; by the which, notwithstanding all that Christian could do to avoid it, Apollyon wounded him in his head, his hand and foot; this made Christian give a little back: Apollyon therefore followed his work amain, and Christian again took courage, and resisted as manfully as he could. This sore combat lasted for above half a day, even till Christian was almost quite spent. For you must know that Christian by reason of his wounds, must needs grow weaker and weaker.

Then Apollyon espying his opportunity, began to gather up close to Christian, and wrestling with him, gave him a dreadful fall; and with that Christian's sword flew out of his hand. Then said Apollyon, "I am sure of thee now"; and with that, he had almost pressed him to death, so that Christian began to despair of life. But as God would have it, while Apollyon was fetching of his last blow, thereby to make a full end of this good man, Christian nimbly reached out his hand for his sword, and caught it, saying, "Rejoice not against me, O mine enemy! when I fall, I shall arise"; and with that, gave him a deadly thrust, which made him give back, as one that had received his mortal wound: Christian perceiving that, made at him again, saying, "Nay, in all these things we are more than conquerors, through Him that loved us." And with that, Apollyon spread forth his dragon's wings, and sped him away, that Christian saw him no more.

In this combat no man can imagine, unless he had seen and heard as I did, what yelling, and hideous roaring Apollyon made all the time of the fight, he spake like a dragon: and on the other side, what sighs and groans brast from Christian's heart. I never saw him all the while give so much as one pleasant look, till he perceived he had wounded Apollyon with his two edged sword, then indeed he did smile, and look upward: but 'twas the dreadfullest sight that ever I saw.

So when the battle was over, Christian said, "I will here give thanks to Him that hath delivered me out of the mouth of the lion; to him that did help me against Apollyon": and so he did, saying,

"Great Beelzebub, the captain of this fiend,
Designed my ruin; therefore to this end

He sent him harnessed out, and he with rage
That hellish was, did fiercely me engage:
But blessèd Michael helpèd me, and I,
By dint of sword, did quickly make him fly:
Therefore to him let me give lasting praise,
And thank and bless his holy name always."

Then there came to him an hand, with some of the leaves of the tree of life, the which Christian took, and applied to the wounds that he had received in the battle, and was healed immediately. He also sat down in that place to eat bread, and to drink of the bottle that was given him a little before; so being refreshed, he addressed himself to his journey, with his sword drawn in his hand, for he said, "I know not but some other enemy may be at hand." But he met with no other affront from Apollyon quite through this valley.

(*The Pilgrim's Progress.*)

II.—The Trial of Christian and Faithful

Then proclamation was made, that they that had aught to say for their lord the king against the prisoner at the bar, should forthwith appear and give in their evidence. So there came in three witnesses, to wit, *Envy*, *Superstition*, and *Pickthank*. They were then asked if they knew the prisoner at the bar; and what they had to say for their lord the king against him.

Then stood forth *Envy*, and said to this effect: My Lord, I have known this man a long time, and will attest upon my oath before this honourable bench that he is——

Judge. Hold! Give him his oath. (So they sware him.) Then he said—

Envy. My Lord, this man, notwithstanding his plausible name, is one of the vilest men in our country. He neither regardeth prince nor people, law nor custom; but doth all that he can to possess all men with certain of his disloyal notions, which he in the general calls principles of faith and holiness. And, in particular, I heard him once myself affirm that Christianity and the customs of our town of *Vanity* were diametrically opposite, and could not be reconciled. By which saying, my Lord, he doth at once not only condemn all our laudable doings, but us in the doing of them.

Judge. Then did the Judge say to him, Hast thou any more to say?

Envy. My Lord, I could say much more, only I would not be tedious to the court. Yet, if need be, when the other gentlemen have given in their evidence, rather than anything shall be wanting that will despatch him, I will enlarge my testimony against him. So he was bid to stand by.

Then they called *Superstition,* and bid him look upon the prisoner. They also asked, what he could say for their lord the king against him. Then they sware him; so he began.

Super. My Lord, I have no great acquaintance with this man, nor do I desire to have further knowledge of him; however, this I know, that he is a very pestilent fellow, from some discourse that, the other day, I had with him in this town; for then, talking with him, I heard him say, that our religion was nought, and such by which a man could by no means please God. Which sayings of his, my Lord, your Lordship very well knows, what necessarily thence will follow, to wit, that we do still worship in vain, are yet in our sins, and finally shall be damned; and this is that which I have to say.

Then was *Pickthank* sworn, and bid say what he knew in behalf of their lord the king, against the prisoner at the bar.

Pick. My Lord, and you gentlemen all,—This fellow I have known of a long time, and have heard him speak things that ought not to be spoke; for he hath railed on our noble prince *Beelzebub,* and hath spoken contemptibly of his honourable friends, whose names are the Lord *Old Man,* the Lord *Carnal Delight,* the Lord *Luxurious,* the Lord *Desire of Vain Glory,* my old Lord *Lechery,* Sir *Having Greedy,* with all the rest of our nobility; and he hath said, moreover, That if all men were of his mind, if possible, there is not one of these noblemen should have any longer a being in this town. Besides, he hath not been afraid to rail on you, my Lord, who are now appointed to be his judge, calling you an ungodly villain, with many other such like vilifying terms, with which he hath bespattered most of the gentry of our town.

When this *Pickthank* had told his tale, the Judge directed his speech to the prisoner at the bar, saying, Thou runagate, heretic, and traitor, hast thou heard what these honest gentlemen have witnessed against thee?

Faith. May I speak a few words in my own defence?

Judge. Sirrah! sirrah! thou deservest to live no longer, but to be slain immediately upon the place; yet, that all men may see our gentleness towards thee, let us hear what thou, vile runagate, hast to say.

Faith. 1. I say, then, in answer to what Mr. *Envy* hath spoken, I never said aught but this, That what rule, or laws, or customs, or people, were flat against the Word of God, are diametrically opposite to Christianity. If I have said amiss in this, convince me of my error, and I am ready here before you to make my recantation.

2. As to the second, to wit, Mr. *Superstition*, and his charge against me, I said only this, That in the worship of God there is required a Divine faith; but there can be no Divine faith without a Divine revelation of the will of God. Therefore, whatever is thrust into the worship of God that is not agreeable to Divine revelation, cannot be done but by a human faith, which faith will not be profitable to eternal life.

3. As to what Mr. *Pickthank* hath said, I say (avoiding terms, as that I am said to rail, and the like) that the prince of this town, with all the rabblement, his attendants, by this gentleman named, are more fit for a being in hell, than in this town and country : and so, the Lord have mercy upon me !

Then the Judge called to the jury (who all this while stood by, to hear and observe) : Gentlemen of the jury, you see this man about whom so great an uproar hath been made in this town. You have also heard what these worthy gentlemen have witnessed against him. Also you have heard his reply and confession. It lieth now in your breasts to hang him or save his life; but yet I think meet to instruct you into our law.

There was an Act made in the days of Pharaoh the Great, servant to our prince, that lest those of a contrary religion should multiply and grow too strong for him, their males should be thrown into the river. There was also an Act made in the days of Nebuchadnezzar the Great, another of his servants, that whosoever would not fall down and worship his golden image, should be thrown into a fiery furnace. There was also an Act made in the days of Darius, that whoso, for some time, called upon any god but him, should be cast into the lions' den. Now the substance of these laws this rebel has broken, not only in thought, (which is not to be borne,) but also in word and deed, which must therefore needs be intolerable.

For that of Pharaoh, his law was made upon a supposition, to prevent mischief, no crime being yet apparent; but here is a crime apparent. For the second and third, you see he disputeth against our religion; and for the treason he hath confessed, he deserveth to die the death.

Then went the jury out, whose names were, Mr. *Blind-man*, Mr. *No-good*, Mr. *Malice*, Mr. *Love-lust*, Mr. *Live-loose*, Mr. *Heady*, Mr. *High-mind*, Mr. *Enmity*, Mr. *Liar*, Mr. *Cruelty*, Mr. *Hate-light*, and Mr. *Implacable ;* who every one gave in his private verdict against him among themselves, and afterwards unani-

mously concluded to bring him in guilty before the Judge.
And first, among themselves, Mr. *Blind-man*, the foreman,
said, I see clearly that this man is a heretic. Then said Mr.
No-good, Away with such a fellow from the earth. Ay, said
Mr. *Malice*, for I hate the very looks of him. Then said Mr.
Love-lust, I could never endure him. Nor I, said Mr. *Live-loose*,
for he would always be condemning my way. Hang him, hang
him, said Mr. *Heady*. A sorry scrub, said Mr. *High-mind*. My
heart riseth against him, said Mr. *Enmity*. He is a rogue, said
Mr. *Liar*. Hanging is too good for him, said Mr. *Cruelty*. Let
us despatch him out of the way, said Mr. *Hate-light*. Then
said Mr. *Implacable*, Might I have all the world given me, I
could not be reconciled to him; therefore, let us forthwith bring
him in guilty of death. And so they did; therefore he was
presently condemned to be had from the place where he was
to the place from whence he came, and there to be put to the
most cruel death that could be invented.

They, therefore, brought him out, to do with him according
to their law; and, first, they scourged him, then they buffeted
him, then they lanced his flesh with knives; after that, they
stoned him with stones, then pricked him with their swords;
and, last of all, they burned him to ashes at the stake. Thus
came *Faithful* to his end.

Now I saw that there stood behind the multitude a chariot
and a couple of horses, waiting for *Faithful*, who (so soon as
his adversaries had despatched him) was taken up into it, and
straightway was carried up through the clouds, with sound of
trumpet, the nearest way to the *Celestial Gate*.

> " Brave *Faithful*, bravely done in word and deed ;
> Judge, witnesses, and jury have, instead
> Of overcoming thee, but shewn their rage :
> When they are dead, thou'lt live from age to age."

But as for *Christian*, he had some respite, and was remanded
back to prison. So he there remained for a space; but He
that overrules all things, having the power of their rage in his
own hand, so wrought it about, that *Christian* for that time
escaped them, and went his way.

(The Pilgrim's Progress.)

III.—The Summons

After this it was noised abroad, that Mr. Valiant-for-Truth
was taken with a summons by the same post as the other ; and
had this for a token that the summons was true, " That his
pitcher was broken at the fountain " (Ec. xii. 6). When he

understood it, he called for his friends, and told them of it. Then said he, I am going to my Father's, and though with great difficulty I am got hither, yet now I do not repent me of all the trouble I have been at to arrive where I am. My sword I give to him that shall succeed me in my pilgrimage, and my courage and skill to him that can get it. My marks and scars I carry with me, to be a witness for me, that I have fought his battles who now will be my rewarder. When the day that he must go hence was come, many accompanied him to the river side, into which as he went he said, " Death, where is thy sting ? " And as he went down deeper, he said, " Grave, where is thy victory ? " So he passed over, and all the trumpets sounded for him on the other side.

(*The Pilgrim's Progress, Part II.*)

SIR WILLIAM TEMPLE (1628–1699)

I.—MOOR PARK GARDEN

THE perfectest figure of a garden I ever saw, either at home or abroad, was that of Moor Park, in Hertfordshire, when I knew it, about thirty years ago. It was made by the Countess of Bedford, esteemed among the greatest wits of her time, and celebrated by Doctor Donne : and with very great care, excellent contrivance, and much cost; but greater sums may be thrown away without effect or honour, if there want sense in proportion to money, or if nature be not followed; which I take to be the great rule in this, and perhaps in everything else, as far as the conduct not only of our lives, but our governments. And whether the greatest of mortal men should attempt the forcing of nature may best be judged by observing how seldom God Almighty does it Himself, by so few, true and undisputed miracles, as we see or hear of in the world. For my own part, I know not three wiser precepts for the conduct either of princes or private men, than—

> " Servare modum, finemque tueri
> Naturamque sequi."

Because I take the garden I have named to have been in all kinds the most beautiful and perfect, at least in the figure and disposition, that I have ever seen, I will describe it for a model to those that meet with such a situation, and are above the regards of common expense. It lies on the side of a hill (upon which the house stands), but not very steep. The length of the house, where the best rooms and of most use or pleasure are, lies upon the breadth of the garden; the great parlour

opens into the middle of a terrace gravel walk that lies even
with it, and which may be, as I remember, about three hundred
paces long, and broad in proportion; the border set with standard
laurels, and at large distances, which have the beauty of orange-
trees out of flower and fruit: from this walk are three descents
by many stone steps, in the middle and at each end, into a
very large parterre.   This is divided into quarters by gravel
walks, and adorned by two fountains and eight statues in the
several quarters; at the end of the terrace walk are two summer-
houses, and the sides of the parterre are ranged with two large
cloisters, open to the garden, upon arches of stone, and ending
with two other summer-houses even with the cloisters, which
are paved with stone, and designed for walks of shade, there
being none other in the whole parterre.   Over these two cloisters
are two terraces covered with lead and fenced with balusters;
and the passage into these airy walks is out of the two summer-
houses, at the end of the first terrace walk.   The cloister facing
the south is covered with vines, and would have been proper for
an orange-house, and the other for myrtles, or other more
common greens; and had, I doubt not, been cast for that purpose, if this piece of gardening had been then in as much vogue
as it is now.

From the middle of the parterre is a descent by many steps
flying on each side of a grotto that lies between them (covered
with lead, and flat) into the lower garden, which is all fruit-
trees ranged about the several quarters of a wilderness, which
is very shady; the walks here are all green, the grotto embel-
lished with figures of shell rock-work, fountains and water-works.
If the hill had not ended with the lower garden, and the wall
were not bounded by a common way that goes through the
park, they might have added a third quarter of all greens; but
this want is supplied by a garden on the other side the house,
which is all of that sort, very wild, shady, and adorned with
rough rock-work and fountains.

This was Moor Park, when I was acquainted with it, and
the sweetest place, I think, that I have ever seen in my life,
either before or since, at home or abroad; what it is now, I can
give little account, having passed through several hands that
have made great changes in gardens as well as houses; but the
remembrance of what it was is too pleasant ever to forget,
and therefore I do not believe to have mistaken the figure of
it, which may serve for a pattern to the best gardens of our
manner, and that are most proper for our country and climate.

(*Essays.*)

II.—Of Poetry

Whether it be that the fierceness of the Gothic humours, or noise of their perpetual wars, frighted it away, or that the unequal mixture of the modern languages would not bear it; certain it is that the great heights and excellency both of poetry and music fell with the Roman learning and empire, and have never since recovered the admiration and applauses that before attended them : yet, such as they are among us, they must be confessed to be the softest and sweetest, the most general and most innocent amusements of common time and life. They still find room in the courts of princes and the cottages of shepherds : they serve to revive and animate the dead calm of poor or idle lives, and to allay or divert the violent passions and perturbations of the greatest and the busiest men. And both these effects are of equal use to human life : for the mind of man is like the sea which is neither agreeable to the beholder nor the voyager in a calm or in a storm, but is so to both when a little agitated by gentle gales ; and so the mind when moved by soft and easy passions and affections. I know very well, that many, who pretend to be wise by the forms of being grave, are apt to despise both poetry and music as toys and trifles too light for the use or entertainment of serious men : but whoever find themselves wholly insensible to these charms would, I think, do well to keep their own counsel, for fear of reproaching their own temper, and bringing the goodness of their natures, if not of their understandings, into question : it may be thought at least an ill sign, if not an ill constitution, since some of the fathers went so far, as to esteem the love of music a sign of predestination, as a thing divine, and reserved for the felicities of heaven itself. While this world lasts, I doubt not but the pleasure and requests of these two entertainments will do so too : and happy those that content themselves with these, or any other so easy and so innocent, and do not trouble the world or other men, because they cannot be quiet themselves, though nobody hurts them !

When all is done, human life is, at the greatest and best, but like a froward child, that must be played with and humoured a little to keep it quiet till it falls asleep, and then the care is over.

(*Essays.*)

JOHN DRYDEN (1631–1700)

I.—Shakspeare, Beaumont and Fletcher, Ben Johnson

" To begin, then, with Shakspeare. He was the man who of all modern, and perhaps ancient poets, had the largest and most comprehensive soul. All the images of nature were still present to him, and he drew them, not laboriously, but luckily; when he describes any thing, you more than see it, you feel it too. Those who accuse him to have wanted learning, give him the greater commendation : he was naturally learned ; he needed not the spectacles of books to read nature ; he looked inwards, and found her there. I cannot say he is every where alike ; were he so, I should do him injury to compare him with the greatest of mankind. He is many times flat, insipid ; his comick wit degenerating into clenches, his serious swelling into bombast. But he is always great, when some great occasion is presented to him ; no man can say he ever had a fit subject for his wit, and did not then raise himself as high above the rest of poets :

> *Quantum lenta solent inter viburna cupressi.*

The consideration of this made Mr. Hales of Eaton say, that there was no subject of which any poet ever writ, but he would produce it much better done in Shakspeare; and however others are now generally preferred before him, yet the age wherein he lived, which had contemporaries with him Fletcher and Johnson, never equalled them to him in their esteem : and in the last king's court, when Ben's reputation was at highest, Sir John Suckling, and with him the greater part of the courtiers, set our Shakspeare far above him.

" Beaumont and Fletcher, of whom I am next to speak, had, with the advantage of Shakspeare's wit, which was their precedent, great natural gifts, improved by study : Beaumont especially being so accurate a judge of plays, that Ben Johnson, while he lived, submitted all his writings to his censure, and, 'tis thought, used his judgment in correcting, if not contriving, all his plots. What value he had for him, appears by the verses he writ to him ; and therefore I need speak no farther of it. The first play that brought Fletcher and him in esteem was their *Philaster :* for before that, they had written two or three very unsuccessfully, as the like is reported of Ben Johnson, before he writ *Every Man in his Humour.* Their plots were generally more regular than Shakspeare's, especially those which were made before Beaumont's death ; and they understood and imitated the conversation of gentlemen much better ; whose wild debaucheries, and quickness of wit in reparties, no poet before them could paint as they have done. Humour, which Ben Johnson derived from particular persons, they made it not their business to describe : they represented all the passions very lively, but above all, love. I am apt to believe the English

language in them arrived to its highest perfection : what words
have since been taken in, are rather superfluous than ornamental. Their plays are now the most pleasant and frequent
entertainments of the stage ; two of theirs being acted through
the year for one of Shakspeare's or Johnson's : the reason is,
because there is a certain gaiety in their comedies, and pathos
in their more serious plays, which suits generally with all men's
humours. Shakspeare's language is likewise a little obsolete,
and Ben Johnson's wit comes short of theirs.

" As for Johnson, to whose character I am now arrived, if
we look upon him while he was himself, (for his last plays were
but his dotages,) I think him the most learned and judicious
writer which any theatre ever had. He was a most severe
judge of himself, as well as others. One cannot say he wanted
wit, but rather that he was frugal of it. In his works you find
little to retrench or alter. Wit, and language, and humour
also in some measure, we had before him ; but something of art
was wanting to the drama, till he came. He managed his
strength to more advantage than any who preceded him. You
seldom find him making love in any of his scenes, or endeavouring to move the passions ; his genius was too sullen and saturnine
to do it gracefully, especially when he knew he came after those
who had performed both to such an height. Humour was his
proper sphere ; and in that he delighted most to represent
mechanick people. He was deeply conversant in the ancients,
both Greek and Latin, and he borrowed boldly from them :
there is scarce a poet or historian among the Roman authors
of those times whom he has not translated in *Sejanus* and
Catiline. But he has done his robberies so openly, that one
may see he fears not to be taxed by any law. He invades
authors like a monarch ; and what would be theft in other
poets, is only victory in him. With the spoils of these writers
he so represents old Rome to us, in its rites, ceremonies, and
customs, that if one of their poets had written either of his
tragedies, we had seen less of it than in him. If there was any
fault in his language, 'twas that he weaved it too closely and
laboriously, in his comedies especially : perhaps too, he did
a little too much romanize our tongue, leaving the words which
he translated almost as much Latin as he found them : wherein,
though he learnedly followed their language, he did not
enough comply with the idiom of ours. If I would compare
him with Shakspeare, I must acknowledge him the more correct
poet, but Shakspeare the greater wit. Shakspeare was the
Homer, or father of our dramatick poets ; Johnson was the

Virgil, the pattern of elaborate writing; I admire him, but I love Shakspeare.

(Essay of Dramatic Poesy.)

II.—The Father of English Poetry

As Chaucer is the father of English poetry, so I hold him in the same degree of veneration as the Grecians held Homer, or the Romans Virgil : he is a perpetual fountain of good sense ; learned in all the sciences ; and therefore speaks properly on all subjects ; as he knew what to say, so he knows also when to leave off.   He must have been a man of a most wonderful comprehensive nature, because, as it has been truly observed of him, he has taken into the compass of his *Canterbury Tales* the various manners and humours (as we now call them) of the whole English nation, in his age.   Not a single character has escaped him.   All his pilgrims are severally distinguished from each other ; and not only in their inclinations, but in their very physiognomies and persons.   Baptista Porta could not have described their natures better than by the marks which the poet gives them.   The matter and manner of their tales and of their telling are so suited to their different educations, humours and callings, that each of them would be improper in any other mouth.   Even the grave and serious characters are distinguished by their several sorts of gravity : their discourses are such as belong to their age, their calling, and their breeding ; such as are becoming of them, and of them only.   Some of his persons are vicious, and some virtuous ; some are unlearned, and some are learned.   Even the ribaldry of the low characters is different : the Reeve, the Miller, and the Cook are several men, and distinguished from each other, as much as the mincing Lady Prioress and the broad-speaking gap-toothed Wife of Bath. But enough of this : there is such a variety of game springing up before me, that I am distracted in my choice, and know not which to follow.   'Tis sufficient to say, according to the proverb, that here is God's plenty.   We have our forefathers and great-granddames all before us, as they were in Chaucer's days ; their general characters are still remaining in mankind, and even in England, though they are called by other names than those of Monks and Friars, and Canons, and Lady Abbesses, and Nuns : for mankind is ever the same, and nothing lost out of nature, though everything is altered. . . .

(Preface to the Fables.)

SAMUEL PEPYS (1633–1703)

I.—His Coach

Nov. 30th.—My wife, after dinner, went the first time abroad
in her coach, calling on Roger Pepys, and visiting Mrs. Creed,
and my cozen Turner. Thus ended this month, with very
good content, but most expenseful to my purse on things of
pleasure, having furnished my wife's closet and the best
chamber, and a coach and horses, that ever I knew in the world;
and I am put into the greatest condition of outward state that
ever I was in, or hoped ever to be, or desired: and this at a
time when we do daily expect great changes in this Office;
and by all reports we must, all of us, turn out. But my eyes
are come to that condition that I am not able to work; and
therefore that, and my wife's desire, make me have no manner
of trouble in my thoughts about it. So God do his will in it!

Dec. 3rd.—Mr. Wren gives me but small hopes of the favour
I hoped to get for Mr. Steventon, Will's uncle, of having leave,
being upon the point of death, to surrender his place, which do
trouble me, but I will do what I can. To the Office, Sir Jer.
Smith with me; who is a silly, prating, talking man; but he
tells me what he hears,—that Holmes and Spragg now rule
all with the Duke of Buckingham, as to sea-business, and will
be great men: but he do prophesy what will be the fruit of it;
so I do. So to the Office, where we sat all the morning; and
at noon home to dinner, and then abroad again, with my wife,
to the Duke of York's playhouse, and saw "The Unfortunate
Lovers;" a mean play, I think, but some parts very good, and
excellently acted. We sat under the boxes, and saw the fine
ladies; among others, my Lady Kerneguy, who is most devil-
ishly painted. And so home, it being mighty pleasure to go
alone with my poor wife, in a coach of our own, to a play, and
makes us appear mighty great, I think, in the world; at least,
greater than ever I could, or my friends for me, have once
expected; or, I think, than ever any of my family ever yet
lived, in my memory, but my cozen Pepys in Salisbury Court.

(*The Diary.*)

II.—Visit to Epsom

July 14th. (Lord's day.)—Up, and my wife, a little before
four, and to make us ready; and by and by Mrs. Turner came
to us, by agreement, and she and I staid talking below, while
my wife dressed herself, which vexed me that she was so long
about it, keeping us till past five o'clock before she was ready.

She ready; and, taking some bottles of wine, and beer, and some cold fowle with us into the coach, we took coach and four horses, which I had provided last night, and so away. A very fine day, and so towards Epsom, talking all the way pleasantly, and particularly of the pride and ignorance of Mrs. Lowther, in having of her train carried up. The country very fine, only the way very dusty. To Epsom, by eight o'clock, to the well; where much company, and I drank the water: they did not, but I did drink four pints. And to the towne, to the King's Head; and hear that my Lord Buckhurst and Nelly are lodged at the next house, and Sir Charles Sedley with them: and keep a merry house. Poor girl! I pity her; but more the loss of her at the King's house. W. Hewer rode with us, and I left him and the women, and myself walked to church, where few people to what I expected, and none I knew, but all the Houblons, brothers, and them after sermon I did salute, and walk with towards my inne. James did tell me that I was the only happy man of the Navy, of whom, he says, during all this freedom the people have taken to speaking treason, he hath not heard one bad word of me, which is a great joy to me; for I hear the same of others, but do know that I have deserved as well as most. We parted to meet anon, and I to my women into a better room, which the people of the house borrowed for us, and there to a good dinner, and were merry, and Pembleton come to us, who happened to be in the house, and there talked and were merry. After dinner, he gone, we all lay down, the day being wonderful hot, to sleep, and each of us took a good nap, and then rose; and here Tom Wilson come to see me, and sat and talked an hour; and I perceive he hath been much acquainted with Dr. Fuller (Tom) and Dr. Pierson, and several of the great cavalier parsons during the late troubles; and I was glad to hear him talk of them, which he did very ingenuously, and very much of Dr. Fuller's art of memory, which he did tell me several instances of. By and by he parted, and we took coach and to take the ayre, there being a fine breeze abroad; and I carried them to the well, and there filled some bottles of water to carry home with me; and there I talked with the two women that farm the well, at £12 per annum, of the lord of the manor. Mr. Evelyn [1] with his lady, and also my Lord George Barkeley's lady, and their fine daughter, that the King of France liked so well,

---

[1] This was probably Richard Evelyn, of Woodcote Park, near Epsom, and his wife Elizabeth, daughter and heir of George Mynne, Esq., of Horton in Epsom, both of which places belonged to her.

and did dance so rich in jewells before the King at the ball I was at, at our Court, last winter, and also their son, a Knight of the Bath, were at church this morning. Here W. Hewer's horse broke loose, and we had the sport to see him taken again. Then I carried them to see my cozen Pepys's house, and 'light, and walked round about it, and they like it, as indeed it deserves, very well, and is a pretty place; and then I walked them to the wood hard by, and there got them in the thickets till they had lost themselves, and I could not find the way into any of the walks in the wood, which indeed are very pleasant, if I could have found them. At last got out of the wood again; and I, by leaping down the little bank, coming out of the wood, did sprain my right foot, which brought me great present pain, but presently, with walking, it went away for the present, and so the women and W. Hewer and I walked upon the Downes, where a flock of sheep was; and the most pleasant and innocent sight that ever I saw in my life. We found a shepherd and his little boy reading, far from any houses or sight of people, the Bible to him; so I made the boy read to me, which he did, with the forced tone that children do usually read, that was mighty pretty, and then I did give him something, and went to the father, and talked with him; and I find he had been a servant in my cozen Pepys's house, and told me what was become of their old servants. He did content himself mightily in my liking his boy's reading, and did bless God for him, the most like one of the old patriarchs that ever I saw in my life, and it brought those thoughts of the old age of the world in my mind for two or three days after. We took notice of his woolen knit stockings of two colours mixed, and of his shoes shod with iron, both at the toe and heels, and with great nails in the soles of his feet, which was mighty pretty: and, taking notice of them, why, says the poor man, the downes, you see, are full of stones, and we are faine to shoe ourselves thus; and these, says he, will make the stones fly till they ring before me. I did give the poor man something, for which he was mighty thankful, and I tried to cast stones with his horne crooke. He values his dog mightily, that would turn a sheep any way which he would have him, when he goes to fold them : told me there was about eighteen score sheep in his flock, and that he hath four shillings a week the year round for keeping of them : and Mrs. Turner, in the common fields here, did gather one of the prettiest nosegays that ever I saw in my life. So to our coach, and through Mr. Minnes's wood, and looked upon Mr. Evelyn's house; and so over the common, and through Epsom towne to our inne in the way stopping a poor woman with her milk-pail, and in one of my gilt tumblers, did drink our bellyfulls of milk, better than any creame; and so to our inne, and there had a dish of creame, but it was sour, and so had no pleasure in it; and so paid our reckoning, and took coach, it being about seven at night, and passed and saw the people walking with their wives and children to take the ayre, and we set out for home, the sun by and by going down, and we in the cool of the evening all the way with much pleasure home, talking and pleasing ourselves with the pleasures of this day's work. Mrs. Turner mightily pleased with my resolution, which, I tell her, is never to keep a country-house, but to keep a coach, and with my wife on the Saturday to go sometimes for a day to this place, and then quit to another place; and there is more variety and as little charge, and no trouble, as there is in a country-house. Anon it grew dark, and we had the pleasure to see several glow-wormes, which was mighty pretty, but my foot begins more and more to pain me, which Mrs. Turner, by keeping her warm hand upon it, did much ease; but so that when we come home, which was just at eleven at night, I was not able to walk from the lane's end to my house without being helped. So to bed, and there had a cere-cloth laid to my foot, but in great pain all night long.

(*The Diary.*)

III.—THE FIRE

Sept. 2nd. (Lord's day.)—Some of our maids sitting up late last night to get things ready against our feast to-day, Jane called us up about three in the morning, to tell us of a great fire they saw in the City. So I rose, and slipped on my night-gown, and went to her window; and thought it to be on the back-side of Marke-lane at the farthest; but, being unused to such fires as followed, I thought it far enough off; and so went to bed again, and to sleep. About seven rose again to dress myself, and there looked out at the window, and saw the fire not so much as it was, and further off. So to my closet to set things to rights, after yesterday's cleaning. By and by Jane comes and tells me that she hears that above 300 houses have been burned down to-night by the fire we saw, and that it is now burning down all Fish Street, by London Bridge. So I made myself ready presently, and walked to the Tower; and there got up upon one of the high places, Sir J. Robinson's little son going up with me; and there I did see the houses at that

end of the bridge all on fire, and an infinite great fire on this
and the other side the end of the bridge; which, among other
people, did trouble me for poor little Michell and our Sarah on
the bridge. So down, with my heart full of trouble, to the
Lieutenant of the Tower, who tells me that it begun this
morning in the King's baker's house in Pudding-lane, and
that it hath burned down St. Magnus's Church and most part
of Fish Street already. So I down to the water-side, and
there got a boat, and through bridge, and there saw a lamentable fire. Poor Michell's house, as far as the Old Swan, already
burned that way, and the fire running further, that, in a very
little time, it got as far as the Steele-yard, while I was there.
Every body endeavouring to remove their goods, and flinging
into the river, or bringing them into lighters that lay off;
poor people staying in their houses as long as till the very fire
touched them, and then running into boats, or clambering
from one pair of stairs, by the waterside, to another. And,
among other things, the poor pigeons, I perceive, were loth
to leave their houses, but hovered about the windows and
balconys, till they burned their wings, and fell down. Having
staid, and in an hour's time seen the fire rage every way; and
nobody, to my sight, endeavouring to quench it, but to remove
their goods, and leave all to the fire; and, having seen it get as
far as the Steele-yard, and the wind mighty high, and driving
it into the City; and everything, after so long a drought,
proving combustible, even the very stones of churches; and,
among other things, the poor steeple [1] by which pretty Mrs.
—— lives, and whereof my old schoolfellow Elborough is
parson, taken fire in the very top, and there burned till it fell
down; I to White Hall, with a gentleman with me, who desired
to go off from the Tower, to see the fire, in my boat; and
there up to the King's closet in the Chapel, where people come
about me, and I did give them an account dismayed them
all, and word was carried in to the King. So I was called
for, and did tell the King and Duke of York what I saw; and
that, unless his Majesty did command houses to be pulled
down, nothing could stop the fire. They seemed much troubled,
and the King commanded me to go to my Lord Mayor [2] from
him, and command him to spare no houses, but to pull down
before the fire every way. The Duke of York bid me tell
him, that if he would have any more soldiers, he shall; and
so did my Lord Arlington afterwards, as a great secret. Here

---

[1] St. Lawrence Poultney, of which Thomas Elborough was curate.
[2] Sir Thomas Bludworth.

meeting with Captain Cocke, I in his coach, which he lent me, and Creed with me to Paul's; and there walked along Watling Street, as well as I could, every creature coming away loaden with goods to save, and, here and there, sick people carried away in beds. Extraordinary good goods carried in carts and on backs. At last met my Lord Mayor in Canning Street, like a man spent, with a handkercher about his neck. To the King's message, he cried, like a fainting woman, " Lord ! what can I do? I am spent : people will not obey me. I have been pulling down houses; but the fire overtakes us faster than we can do it." That he needed no more soldiers; and that, for himself, he must go and refresh himself, having been up all night. So he left me, and I him, and walked home; seeing people all almost distracted, and no manner of means used to quench the fire. The houses, too, so very thick thereabouts, and full of matter for burning, as pitch and tar, in Thames Street; and warehouses of oyle, and wines, and brandy, and other things. Here I saw Mr. Isaac Houblon, the handsome man, prettily dressed and dirty at his door at Dowgate, receiving some of his brother's things, whose houses were on fire; and, as he says, have been removed twice already; and he doubts, as it soon proved, that they must be, in a little time, removed from his house also, which was a sad consideration. And to see the churches all filling with goods by people who themselves should have been quietly there at this time. By this time, it was about twelve o'clock; and so home, and there find my guests, who were Mr. Wood and his wife Barbary Shelden, and also Mr. Moone : she mighty fine, and her husband, for aught I see, a likely man. But Mr. Moone's design and mine, which was to look over my closet, and please him with the sight thereof, which he hath long desired, was wholly disappointed; for we were in great trouble and disturbance at this fire, not knowing what to think of it. However, we had an extraordinary good dinner, and as merry as at this time we could be. While at dinner, Mrs. Batelier come to enquire after Mr. Woolfe and Stanes, who, it seems, are related to them, whose houses in Fish Street are all burned, and they in a sad condition. She would not stay in the fright. Soon as dined, I and Moone away, and walked through the City, the streets full of nothing but people; and horses and carts loaden with goods, ready to run over one another, and removing goods from one burned house to another. They now removing out of Canning Street, which received goods in the morning, into Lumbard Street, and further : and, among others, I now saw my little goldsmith Stokes,[1] receiving some friend's goods, whose house itself was burned the day after. We parted at Paul's; he home, and I to Paul's Wharf, where I had appointed a boat to attend me, and took in Mr. Carcasse and his brother, whom I met in the street, and carried them below and above bridge too. And again to see the fire, which was now got further, both below and above, and no likelihood of stopping it. Met with the King and Duke of York in their barge, and with them to Queenhithe, and there called Sir Richard Browne to them. Their order was only to pull down houses apace, and so below bridge at the water-side; but this little was or could be done, the fire coming upon them so fast. Good hopes there was of stopping it at the Three Cranes above, and at Buttulph's Wharf below bridge, if care be used; but the wind carries it into the City, so as we know not, by the water-side, what it do there. River full of lighters and boats taking in goods, and good goods swimming in the water; and only I observed that hardly one lighter or boat in three that had the goods of a house in, but there was a pair of Virginalls in it. Having seen as much as I could now, I away to White Hall by appointment, and there walked to St. James's Park; and there met my wife, and Creed, and Wood, and his wife, and walked to my boat; and there upon the water again, and to the fire up and down, it still encreasing, and the wind great. So near the fire as we could for smoke; and all over the Thames, with one's faces in the wind, you were almost burned with a shower of fire-drops. This is very true: so as houses were burned by these drops and flakes of fire, three or four, nay, five or six houses, one from another. When we could endure no more upon the water, we to a little alehouse on the Bankside, over against the Three Cranes, and there staid till it was dark, almost, and saw the fire grow; and, as it grew darker, appeared more and more; and in corners and upon steeples, and between churches and houses, as far as we could see up the hill of the City, in a most horrid, malicious, bloody flame, not like the fine flame of an ordinary fire. Barbary and her husband away before us. We staid till, it being darkish, we saw the fire as only one entire arch of fire from this to the other side the bridge, and in a bow up the hill for an arch of above a mile long: it made me weep to see it. The churches, houses, and all on fire, and flaming at once; and a horrid noise the flames made, and the cracking of houses at their ruine. So home with a sad heart, and there find every body discoursing and lamenting the

[1] Humphrey Stocks, at the Black Horse in Lombard Street.

fire; and poor Tom Hater come with some few of his goods saved out of his house, which was burned upon Fish Street Hill. I invited him to lie at my house, and did receive his goods; but was deceived in his lying there, the news coming every moment of the growth of the fire; so as we were forced to begin to pack up our own goods, and prepare for their removal; and did by moonshine, it being brave, dry, and moonshine and warm weather, carry much of my goods into the garden; and Mr. Hater and I did remove my money and iron chests into my cellar, as thinking that the safest place. And got my bags of gold into my office, ready to carry away, and my chief papers of accounts also there, and my tallies into a box by themselves. So great was our fear, as Sir W. Batten hath carts come out of the country to fetch away his goods this night. We did put Mr. Hater, poor man! to bed a little; but he got but very little rest, so much noise being in my house, taking down of goods.

(*The Diary.*)

THOMAS TRAHERNE (1636?–1674)

THE WORLD SEEN BY A CHILD

THE corn was orient and immortal wheat, which never should be reaped, nor was ever sown. I thought it had stood from everlasting to everlasting. The dust and stones of the street were as precious as gold : the gates were the end of the world. The green trees when I saw them first through one of the gates transported and ravished me, their sweetness and unusual beauty made my heart to leap, and almost mad with ecstasy, they were such strange and wonderful things. The men ! O what venerable and reverend creatures did the aged seem ! Immortal Cherubims ! And young men glittering and sparkling Angels, and maids strange seraphic pieces of life and beauty ! Boys and girls tumbling in the street, and playing, were moving jewels. I knew not that they were born or should die; but all things abided eternally as they were in their proper places. Eternity was manifest in the Light of the Day, and something infinite behind everything, appeared : which talked with my expectation and moved my desire. The city seemed to stand in Eden, or to be built in Heaven. The streets were mine, the temple was mine, the people were mine, their clothes and gold and silver were mine, as much as their sparkling eyes, fair skins and ruddy faces. The skies were mine, and so were the sun and moon and stars, and all the world was mine; and

I the only spectator and enjoyer of it. I knew no churlish proprieties, nor bounds, nor divisions : but all proprieties [1] and divisions were mine : all treasures and the possessors of them. So that with much ado I was corrupted, and made to learn the dirty devices of this world. Which now I unlearn, and become, as it were, a little child again that I may enter into the Kingdom of God.

(Centuries of Meditations.)

DANIEL DEFOE (1661-1731)

I.—A FOOTPRINT

It happened one day, about noon, going towards my boat, I was exceedingly surprised with the print of a man's naked foot on the shore, which was very plain to be seen in the sand. I stood like one thunderstruck, or as if I had seen an apparition. I listened, I looked round me, I could hear nothing, nor see anything. I went up to a rising ground, to look farther. I went up the shore, and down the shore, but it was all one; I could see no other impression but that one. I went to it again to see if there were any more, and to observe if it might not be my fancy; but there was no room for that, for there was exactly the very print of a foot—toes, heel, and every part of a foot. How it came thither I knew not, nor could in the least imagine. But after innumerable fluttering thoughts, like a man perfectly confused and out of myself, I came home to my fortification, not feeling, as we say, the ground I went on, but terrified to the last degree, looking behind me at every two or three steps, mistaking every bush and tree, and fancying every stump at a distance to be a man; nor is it possible to describe how many various shapes affrighted imagination represented things to me in, how many wild ideas were found every moment in my fancy, and what strange unaccountable whimsies came into my thoughts, by the way.

When I came to my castle, for so I think I called it ever after this, I fled into it like one pursued. Whether I went over by the ladder, as first contrived, or went in at the hole in the rock, which I called a door, I cannot remember; no, nor could I remember the next morning, for never frighted hare fled to cover, or fox to earth, with more terror of mind than I to this retreat.

I slept none that night. The farther I was from the occasion

[1] This word is used here and elsewhere in its original sense, where we should now say "properties."

so that I began to starve for provision; for I had little or nothing within doors but some barley-cakes and water. Then I knew that my goats wanted to be milked too, which usually was my evening diversion; and the poor creatures were in great pain and inconvenience for want of it; and, indeed, it almost spoiled some of them, and almost dried up their milk.

Heartening myself, therefore, with the belief that this was nothing but the print of one of my own feet, and so I might be truly said to start at my own shadow, I began to go abroad again, and went to my country house to milk my flock. But to see with what fear I went forward, how often I looked behind me, how I was ready, every now and then, to lay down my basket, and run for my life, it would have made any one have thought I was haunted with an evil conscience, or that I had lately been most terribly frighted; and so, indeed, I had.

(Robinson Crusoe.)

JONATHAN SWIFT (1667-1745)

I.—THE INHABITANTS OF LILLIPUT

ALTHOUGH I intend to leave the description of this empire to a particular treatise, yet in the mean time I am content to gratify the curious reader with some general ideas. As the common size of the natives is somewhat under six inches high, so there is an exact proportion in all other animals, as well as plants and trees: for instance, the tallest horses and oxen are between four and five inches in height, the sheep an inch and a half, more or less: their geese about the bigness of a sparrow, and so the several gradations downwards till you come to the smallest, which, to my sight, were almost invisible; but nature had adapted the eyes of the Lilliputians to all objects proper for their view: they see with great exactness, but at no great distance. And to show the sharpness of their sight towards objects that are near, I have been much pleased with observing a cook pulling a lark, which was not so large as a common fly; and a young girl threading an invisible needle with invisible silk. Their tallest trees are about seven foot high: I mean some of those in the great royal park, the tops whereof I could but just reach with my fist clinched. The other vegetables are in the same proportion; but this I leave to the reader's imagination.

I shall say but little at present of their learning, which for many ages hath flourished in all its branches among them:

but their manner of writing is very peculiar, being neither from the left to the right, like the Europeans; nor from the right to the left, like the Arabians; nor from up to down, like the Chinese; nor from down to up, like the Cascagians; but aslant from one corner of the paper to the other, like ladies in England.

They bury their dead with their heads directly downwards, because they hold an opinion, that in eleven thousand moons they are all to rise again, in which period the earth (which they conceive to be flat) will turn upside down, and by this means they shall, at their resurrection, be found ready standing on their feet. The learned among them confess the absurdity of this doctrine, but the practice still continues, in compliance to the vulgar.

There are some laws and customs in this empire very peculiar; and if they were not so directly contrary to those of my own dear country, I should be tempted to say a little in their justification. It is only to be wished, that they were as well executed. The first I shall mention, relates to informers. All crimes against the state are punished here with the utmost severity; but if the person accused maketh his innocence plainly to appear upon his trial, the accuser is immediately put to an ignominious death; and out of his goods or lands, the innocent person is quadruply recompensed for the loss of his time, for the danger he underwent, for the hardship of his imprisonment, and for all the charges he hath been at in making his defence. Or, if that fund be deficient, it is largely supplied by the Crown. The Emperor does also confer on him some public mark of his favour, and proclamation is made of his innocence through the whole city.

And here it may perhaps divert the curious reader, to give some account of my domestic, and my manner of living in this country, during a residence of nine months and thirteen days. Having a head mechanically turned, and being likewise forced by necessity, I had made for myself a table and chair convenient enough, out of the largest trees in the royal park. Two hundred sempstresses were employed to make me shirts, and linen for my bed and table, all of the strongest and coarsest kind they could get; which, however, they were forced to quilt together in several folds, for the thickest was some degrees finer than lawn. Their linen is usually three inches wide, and three foot make a piece. The sempstresses took my measure as I lay on the ground, one standing at my neck, and another at my mid-leg, with a strong cord extended, that each held by the end, while the third measured the length of the cord with a rule of an inch long. Then they measured my right thumb, and desired no more; for by a mathematical computation, that twice round the thumb is once round the wrist, and so on to the neck and waist, and by the help of my old shirt, which I displayed on the ground before them for a pattern, they fitted me exactly. Three hundred tailors were employed in the same manner to make me clothes; but they had another contrivance for taking my measure. I kneeled down, and they raised a ladder from the ground to my neck; upon this ladder one of them mounted, and let fall a plumb-line from my collar to the floor, which just answered the length of my coat: but my waist and arms I measured myself. When my clothes were finished, which was done in my house, (for the largest of theirs would not have been able to hold them,) they looked like the patch-work made by the ladies in England, only that mine were all of a colour.

I had three hundred cooks to dress my victuals, in little convenient huts built about my house, where they and their families lived, and prepared me two dishes a-piece. I took up twenty waiters in my hand, and placed them on the table: an hundred more attended below on the ground, some with dishes of meat, and some with barrels of wine, and other liquors, slung on their shoulders; all which the waiters above drew up as I wanted, in a very ingenious manner, by certain cords, as we draw the bucket up a well in Europe. A dish of their meat was a good mouthful, and a barrel of their liquor a reasonable draught. Their mutton yields to ours, but their beef is excellent. I have had a sirloin so large, that I have been forced to make three bits of it; but this is rare. My servants were astonished to see me eat bones and all, as in our country we do the leg of a lark. Their geese and turkeys I usually eat at a mouthful, and I must confess they far exceed ours. Of their smaller fowl I could take up twenty or thirty at the end of my knife.

One day his Imperial Majesty, being informed of my way of living, desired that himself and his Royal Consort, with the young Princes of the blood of both sexes, might have the happiness (as he was pleased to call it) of dining with me. They came accordingly, and I placed them in chairs of state on my table, just over against me, with their guards about them. Flimnap, the Lord High Treasurer, attended there likewise with his white staff; and I observed he often looked on me with a sour countenance, which I would not seem to regard, but eat more than usual, in honour to my dear country, as well as to fill the court with admiration. I have some private reasons to believe, that this visit from his Majesty gave Flimnap an opportunity of doing me ill offices to his master. That minister had always been my secret enemy, though he outwardly caressed me more than was usual to the moroseness of his nature. He represented to the Emperor the low condition of his treasury; that he was forced to take up money at great discount; that exchequer bills would not circulate under nine per cent. below par; that in short I had cost his Majesty above a million and a half of *sprugs* (their greatest gold coin, about the bigness of a spangle); and upon the whole, that it would be advisable in the Emperor to take the first fair occasion of dismissing me.

(Gulliver's Travels.)

II.—The Learning of the Brobdingnagians

The learning of this people is very defective, consisting only in morality, history, poetry, and mathematics, wherein they must be allowed to excel. But the last of these is wholly applied to what may be useful in life, to the improvement of agriculture, and all mechanical arts; so that among us it would be little esteemed. And as to ideas, entities, abstractions, and transcendentals, I could never drive the least conception into their heads.

No law of that country must exceed in words the number of letters in their alphabet, which consists only in two and twenty. But, indeed, few of them extend even to that length. They are expressed in the most plain and simple terms, wherein those people are not mercurial enough to discover above one interpretation: and to write a comment upon any law is a capital crime. As to the decision of civil causes, or proceedings against criminals, their precedents are so few, that they have little reason to boast of any extraordinary skill in either.

They have had the art of printing, as well as the Chinese, time out of mind: but their libraries are not very large; for that of the King's, which is reckoned the biggest, doth not amount to above a thousand volumes, placed in a gallery of twelve hundred foot long, from whence I had liberty to borrow what books I pleased. The Queen's joiner had contrived in one of Glumdalclitch's rooms a kind of wooden machine five and twenty foot high, formed like a standing ladder; the steps were each fifty foot long. It was indeed a movable pair of stairs, the lowest end placed at ten foot distance from the wall of the chamber. The book I had a mind to read was put up leaning against the wall. I first mounted to the upper step of the ladder, and turning my face towards the book, began at the top of the page, and so walking to the right and left about eight or ten paces, according to the length of the lines, till I had gotten a little below the level of my eyes, and then descending gradually till I came to the bottom : after which I mounted again, and began the other page in the same manner, and so turned over the leaf, which I could easily do with both my hands, for it was as thick and stiff as a pasteboard, and in the largest folios not above eighteen or twenty foot long.

Their style is clear, masculine, and smooth, but not florid, for they avoid nothing more than multiplying unnecessary words, or using various expressions. I have perused many of their books, especially those in history and morality. Among the rest, I was much diverted with a little old treatise, which always lay in Glumdalclitch's bed-chamber, and belonged to her governess, a grave elderly gentlewoman, who dealt in writings of morality and devotion. The book treats of the weakness of human kind, and is in little esteem, except among the women and the vulgar. However, I was curious to see what an author of that country could say upon such a subject. This writer went through all the usual topics of European moralists, showing how diminutive, contemptible, and helpless an animal was man in his own nature; how unable to defend himself from the inclemencies of the air, or the fury of wild beasts : how much he was excelled by one creature in strength, by another in speed, by a third in foresight, by a fourth in industry. He added, that nature was degenerated in these latter declining ages of the world, and could now produce only small abortive births in comparison of those in ancient times. He said, it was very reasonable to think, not only that the species of men were originally much larger, but also, that there must have been giants in former ages, which, as it is asserted by history and tradition, so it hath been confirmed by huge bones and skulls casually dug up in several parts of the kingdom, far exceeding the common dwindled race of man in our days. He argued, that the very laws of nature absolutely required we should have been made in the beginning, of a size more large and robust, not so liable to destruction from every little accident of a tile falling from a house, or a stone cast from the hand of a boy, or of being drowned in a little brook. From this way of reasoning the author drew several moral applications useful in the conduct of life, but needless here to repeat. For my own part, I could not avoid reflecting how universally this talent was spread, of drawing lectures in morality, or indeed rather matter of discontent and repining, from the quarrels we raise with nature. And I believe, upon a strict enquiry, those quarrels might be shown as ill grounded among us, as they are among that people.

(*Gulliver's Travels.*)

SIR RICHARD STEELE (1672-1729)

I.—MR. BICKERSTAFF VISITS A FRIEND

THERE are several persons who have many pleasures and entertainments in their possession, which they do not enjoy. It is, therefore, a kind and good office to acquaint them with their own happiness, and turn their attention to such instances of their good fortune as they are apt to overlook. Persons in the married state often want such a monitor; and pine away their days, by looking upon the same condition in anguish and murmur, which carries with it in the opinion of others a complication of all the pleasures of life, and a retreat from its inquietudes.

I am led into this thought by a visit I made an old friend, who was formerly my school-fellow. He came to town last week with his family for the winter, and yesterday morning sent me word his wife expected me to dinner. I am, as it were, at home at that house, and every member of it knows me for their well-wisher. I cannot indeed express the pleasure it is, to be met by the children with so much joy as I am when I go thither. The boys and girls strive who shall come first, when they think it is I that am knocking at the door; and that child which loses the race to me runs back again to tell the father it is Mr. Bickerstaff. This day I was led in by a pretty girl, that we all thought must have forgotten me; for the family has been out of town these two years. Her knowing me again was a mighty subject with us, and took up our discourse at the first entrance. After which, they began to rally me upon a thousand little stories they heard in the country, about my marriage to one of my neighbour's daughters. Upon which the gentleman, my friend, said, " Nay, if Mr. Bickerstaff marries a child of any of his old companions, I hope mine shall have the preference; there is Mrs. Mary is now sixteen, and would make him as fine a widow as the best of them. But I know him too well; he is so enamoured with the very memory of those who flourished in our youth, that he will not so much as look upon the modern beauties. I remember, old gentleman, how often you went home in a day to refresh your countenance and dress when Teraminta reigned in your heart. As we came up in the coach, I repeated to my wife some of your verses on her." With such reflections on little passages which happened long ago, we passed our time, during a cheerful and elegant meal. After dinner, his lady left the room, as did also the children. As soon as we were alone, he took me by the hand. "Well, my good friend," says he, "I am heartily glad to see thee; I was afraid you would never have seen all the company that dined with you to-day again. Do not you think the good woman of the house a little altered since you followed her from the play-house, to find out who she was, for me?" I perceived a tear fall down his cheek as he spoke, which moved me not a little. But, to turn the discourse, I said, "She is not indeed quite that creature she was, when she returned me the letter I carried from you; and told me, ' she hoped, as I was a gentleman, I would be employed no more to trouble her, who had never offended me; but would be so much the gentleman's friend, as to dissuade him from a pursuit, which he could never succeed in.' You may remember, I thought her in earnest; and you were forced to employ your cousin Will, who made his sister get acquainted with her, for you. You cannot expect her to be for ever fifteen." "Fifteen!" replied my good friend: "Ah! you little understand, you that have lived a bachelor, how great, how exquisite a pleasure there is, in being really beloved! It is impossible, that the most beauteous face in nature should raise in me such pleasing ideas, as when I look upon that excellent woman. That fading in her countenance is chiefly caused by her watching with me in my fever. This was followed by a fit of sickness, which had like to have carried her off last winter. I tell you sincerely, I have so many obligations to her, that I cannot, with any sort of moderation, think of her present state of health. But as to what you say of fifteen, she gives me every day pleasures beyond what I ever knew in the possession of her beauty, when I was in the vigour of youth. Every moment of her life brings me fresh instances of her complacency to my inclinations, and her prudence in regard to my fortune. Her face is to me much more beautiful than when I first saw it; there is no decay in any feature, which I cannot trace, from the very instant it was occasioned by some anxious concern for my welfare and interests. Thus, at the same time, methinks, the love I conceived towards her for what she was, is heightened by my gratitude for what she is. The love of a wife is as much above the idle passion commonly called by that name, as the loud laughter of buffoons is inferior to the elegant mirth of gentlemen. Oh ! she is an inestimable jewel. In her examination of her household affairs, she shows a certain fearfulness to find a fault, which makes her servants obey her like children; and the meanest we have has an ingenuous shame for an offence, not always to be seen in children in other families. I speak freely to you, my old friend; ever since her sickness, things that gave me the quickest joy before, turn now to a certain anxiety. As the children play in the next room, I know the poor things by their steps, and am considering what they must do, should they lose their mother in their tender years. The pleasure I used to take in telling my boy stories of battles, and asking my girl questions about the disposal of her baby, and the gossiping of it, is turned into inward reflection and melancholy."

He would have gone on in this tender way, when the good lady entered, and with an inexpressible sweetness in her countenance told us, " she had been searching her closet for something very good, to treat such an old friend as I was." Her husband's eyes sparkled with pleasure at the cheerfulness of her countenance; and I saw all his fears vanish in an instant. The lady observing something in our looks which showed we had been more serious than ordinary, and seeing her husband receive her with great concern under a forced cheerfulness, immediately guessed at what we had been talking of; and applying herself to me, said, with a smile, " Mr. Bickerstaff, do not believe a word of what he tells you; I shall live still to have you for my second, as I have often promised you, unless he takes more care of himself than he has done since his coming to town. You must know, he tells me that he finds London is a much more healthy place than the country; for he sees several of his old acquaintance, and school-fellows are here, young fellows with fair full-bottomed periwigs. I could scarce keep him in this morning from going out open-breasted." My friend, who is always extremely delighted with her agreeable humour, made her sit down with us. She did it with that easiness which is peculiar to women of sense; and to keep up the good humour she had brought in with her, turned her raillery upon me. " Mr. Bickerstaff, you remember you followed me one night from the play-house; suppose you should carry me thither to-morrow night, and lead me into the front box." This put us into a long field of discourse about the beauties, who were mothers to the present, and shined in the boxes twenty years ago.

I told her " I was glad she had transferred so many of her charms, and I did not question but her eldest daughter was within half-a-year of being a toast."

We were pleasing ourselves with this fantastical preferment of the young lady, when on a sudden we were alarmed with the noise of a drum, and immediately entered my little godson to give me a point of war. His mother, between laughing and chiding, would have put him out of the room; but I would not part with him so. I found, upon conversation with him, though he was a little noisy in his mirth, that the child had excellent parts, and was a great master of all the learning on the other side eight years old. I perceived him a very great historian in Æsop's Fables : but he frankly declared to me his mind, " that he did not delight in that learning, because he did not believe they were true "; for which reason I found he had very much turned his studies, for about a twelvemonth past, into the lives and adventures of Don Belianis of Greece, Guy of Warwick, the Seven Champions, and other historians of that age. I could not but observe the satisfaction the father took in the forwardness of his son; and that these diversions might turn to some profit, I found the boy had made remarks, which might be of service to him during the course of his whole life. He would tell you the mismanagements of John Hicker-thrift, find fault with the passionate temper in Bevis of Southampton, and loved Saint George for being the champion of England; and by this means had his thoughts insensibly moulded into the notions of discretion, virtue, and honour. I was extolling his accomplishments, when the mother told me, " that the little girl who led me in this morning was in her way a better scholar than he. Betty," said she, " deals chiefly in fairies and sprights; and sometimes in a winter-night will terrify the maids with her accounts, until they are afraid to go up to bed."

I sat with them until it was very late, sometimes in merry, sometimes in serious discourse, with this particular pleasure, which gives the only true relish to all conversation, a sense that every one of us liked each other. I went home, considering the different conditions of a married life and that of a bachelor ; and I must confess it struck me with a secret concern, to reflect, that whenever I go off I shall leave no traces behind me. In this pensive mood I returned to my family; that is to say, to my maid, my dog, and my cat, who only can be the better or worse for what happens to me.

(*The Tatler.*)

II.—RECOLLECTIONS OF CHILDHOOD

There are those among mankind, who can enjoy no relish of their being, except the world is made acquainted with all that relates to them, and think everything lost that passes unobserved; but others find a solid delight in stealing by the crowd, and modelling their life after such a manner, as is as much above the approbation as the practice of the vulgar. Life being too short to give instances great enough of true friendship or good-will, some sages have thought it pious to preserve a certain reverence for the *manes* of their deceased friends; and have withdrawn themselves from the rest of the world at certain seasons, to commemorate in their own thoughts such of their acquaintance who have gone before them out of this life. And indeed, when we are advanced in years, there is not a more pleasing entertainment, than to recollect in a gloomy moment the many we have parted with, that have been dear and agreeable to us, and to cast a melancholy thought or two after those, with whom, perhaps, we have indulged ourselves in whole nights of mirth and jollity. With such inclinations in my heart I went to my closet yesterday in the evening, and resolved to be sorrowful; upon which occasion I could not but look with disdain upon myself, that though all the reasons which I had to lament the loss of many of my friends are now as forcible as at the moment of their departure, yet did not my heart swell with the same sorrow which I felt at the time; but I could, without tears, reflect upon many pleasing adventures I have had with some, who have long been blended with common earth. Though it is by the benefit of nature, that length of time thus blots out the violence of afflictions; yet, with tempers too much given to pleasure, it is almost necessary to revive the old places of grief in our memory; and ponder step by step on past life, to lead the mind into that sobriety of thought which poises the heart, and makes it beat with due time, without being quickened with desire, or retarded with despair, from its proper and equal motion. When we wind up a clock that is out of order, to make it go well for the future, we do not immediately set the hand to the present instant, but we make it strike the round of all its hours, before it can recover the regularity of its time. Such, thought I, shall be my method this evening; and since it is that day of the year which I dedicate to the memory of such in another life as I much delighted in when living, an hour or two shall be sacred to sorrow and their memory, while I run over all the melancholy circumstances of this kind which have occurred to me in my whole life.

The first sense of sorrow I ever knew was upon the death of my father, at which time I was not quite five years of age; but was rather amazed at what all the house meant, than possessed with a real understanding why nobody was willing to play with me. I remember I went into the room where his body lay, and my mother sat weeping alone by it. I had my battledore in my hand, and fell a-beating the coffin, and calling Papa; for, I know not how, I had some slight idea that he was locked up there. My mother catched me in her arms, and, transported beyond all patience of the silent grief she was before in, she almost smothered me in her embraces; and told me in a flood of tears, " Papa could not hear me, and would play with me no more, for they were going to put him under ground, whence he could never come to us again." She was a very beautiful woman, of a noble spirit, and there was a dignity in her grief amidst all the wildness of her transport; which, methought, struck me with an instinct of sorrow, that, before I was sensible of what it was to grieve, seized my very soul, and has made pity the weakness of my heart ever since. The mind in infancy is, methinks, like the body in embryo; and receives impressions so forcible, that they are as hard to be removed by reason, as any mark with which a child is born is to be taken away by any future application. Hence it is, that good-nature in me is no merit; but having been so frequently overwhelmed with her tears before I knew the cause of any affliction, or could draw defences from my own judgement, I imbibed commiseration, remorse, and an unmanly gentleness of mind, which has since ensnared me into ten thousand calamities; and from whence I can reap no advantage, except it be, that, in such a humour as I am now in, I can the better indulge myself in the softnesses of humanity, and enjoy that sweet anxiety which arises from the memory of past afflictions.

We, that are very old, are better able to remember things which befell us in our distant youth, than the passages of later days. For this reason it is, that the companions of my strong and vigorous years present themselves more immediately to me in this office of sorrow. Untimely and unhappy deaths are what we are most apt to lament; so little are we able to make it indifferent when a thing happens, though we know it must happen. Thus we groan under life, and bewail those who are relieved from it. Every object that returns to our imagination raises different passions, according to the circumstance of their departure. Who can have lived in an army, and in a serious hour reflect upon the many gay and agreeable men that might long have flourished in the arts of peace, and not join with the imprecations of the fatherless and widow on the tyrant to whose ambition they fell sacrifices? But gallant men, who are cut off by the sword, move rather our veneration than our pity; and we gather relief enough from their own contempt of death, to make that no evil, which was approached with so much cheerfulness, and attended with so much honour. But when we turn our thoughts from the great parts of life on such occasions, and instead of lamenting those who stood ready to give death to those from whom they had the fortune to receive it; I say, when we let our thoughts wander from such noble objects, and consider the havoc which is made among the tender and the innocent, pity enters with an unmixed softness, and possesses all our souls at once.

(The Tatler.)

JOSEPH ADDISON (1672–1719)

The Spectator, No. 112.—SIR ROGER AT CHURCH

I AM always very well pleased with a country Sunday; and think, if keeping holy the seventh day were only a human institution, it would be the best method that could have been thought of for the polishing and civilizing of mankind. It is certain the country-people would soon degenerate into a kind of savages and barbarians, were there not such frequent returns of a stated time, in which the whole village meet together with their best faces, and in their cleanliest habits, to converse with one another upon indifferent subjects, hear their duties explained to them, and join together in adoration of the Supreme Being. Sunday clears away the rust of the whole week, not only as it refreshes in their minds the notions of religion, but as it puts both the sexes upon appearing in their most agreeable forms, and exerting all such qualities as are apt to give them a figure in the eye of the village. A country-fellow distinguishes himself as much in the church-yard as a citizen does upon the Change, the whole parish-politics being generally discussed in that place either after sermon or before the bell rings.

My friend Sir Roger, being a good church-man, has beautified the inside of his church with several texts of his own choosing; he has likewise given a handsome pulpit-cloth, and railed in the communion-table at his own expense. He has often told me, that at his coming to his estate he found his parishioners very irregular; and that in order to make them kneel and join in the responses, he gave every one of them a hassoc and a Common Prayer Book; and at the same time employed an itinerant singing-master, who goes about the country for that purpose, to instruct them rightly in the tunes of the psalms; upon which they now very much value themselves, and indeed out-do most of the country churches that I have ever heard.

As Sir Roger is landlord to the whole congregation, he keeps them in very good order, and will suffer nobody to sleep in it besides himself; for if by chance he has been surprised into a short nap at sermon, upon recovering out of it he stands up and looks about him, and if he sees anybody else nodding, either wakes them himself, or sends his servant to them. Several other of the old knight's particularities break out upon these occasions : sometimes he will be lengthening out a verse in the singing-psalms, half a minute after the rest of the congregation have done with it; sometimes, when he is pleased with the matter of his devotion, he pronounces Amen three or four times to the same prayer; and sometimes stands up when everybody else is upon their knees, to count the congregation, or see if any of his tenants are missing.

I was yesterday very much surprised to hear my old friend, in the midst of the service, calling out to one John Matthews to mind what he was about, and not disturb the congregation. This John Matthews, it seems, is remarkable for being an idle fellow, and at that time was kicking his heels for his diversion. This authority of the knight, though exerted in that odd manner which accompanies him in all circumstances of life, has a very good effect upon the parish, who are not polite enough to see anything ridiculous in his behaviour; besides that the general good sense and worthiness of his character, make his friends observe these little singularities as foils that rather set off than blemish his good qualities.

As soon as the sermon is finished, nobody presumes to stir till Sir Roger is gone out of the church. The knight walks down from his seat in the chancel between a double row of his tenants, that stand bowing to him on each side; and every now and then he inquires how such an one's wife, or mother, or son, or father do, whom he does not see at church; which is understood as a secret reprimand to the person that is absent.

The chaplain has often told me, that upon a catechising-day, when Sir Roger has been pleased with a boy that answers well, he has ordered a Bible to be given him next day for his encouragement; and sometimes accompanies it with a flitch of bacon to his mother. Sir Roger has likewise added five pounds a year to the clerk's place; and that he may encourage the young fellows to make themselves perfect in the church-service, has promised, upon the death of the present incumbent, who is very old, to bestow it according to merit.

The fair understanding between Sir Roger and his chaplain, and their mutual concurrence in doing good, is the more remarkable, because the very next village is famous for the differences and contentions that rise between the parson and the 'squire, who live in a perpetual state of war. The parson is always at the 'squire, and the 'squire, to be revenged on the parson, never comes to church. The 'squire has made all his tenants atheists and tithe-stealers; while the parson instructs them every Sunday in the dignity of his order, and insinuates to them, almost in every sermon, that he is a better man than his patron. In short, matters are come to such an extremity, that the 'squire has not said his prayers either in public or private this half year; and that the parson threatens him, if he does not mend his manners, to pray for him in the face of the whole congregation.

Feuds of this nature, though too frequent in the country, are very fatal to the ordinary people; who are so used to be dazzled with riches, that they pay as much deference to the understanding of a man of an estate, as of a man of learning; and are very hardly brought to regard any truth, how important soever it may be, that is preached to them, when they know there are several men of five hundred a year who do not believe it.

(The Spectator.)

The Spectator, No. 69.—THE ROYAL EXCHANGE

There is no place in the town which I so much love to frequent as the Royal Exchange. It gives me a secret satisfaction, and, in some measure, gratifies my vanity, as I am an Englishman, to see so rich an assembly of countrymen and foreigners consulting together upon the private business of mankind, and making this metropolis a kind of emporium for the whole earth. I must confess I look upon high-change to be a great council, in which all considerable nations have their representatives. Factors in the trading world are what ambassadors are in the politic world; they negotiate affairs, conclude treaties, and maintain a good correspondence between those wealthy societies of men that are divided from one another by seas and oceans, or live on the different extremities of a continent.

I have often been pleased to hear disputes adjusted between an inhabitant of Japan and an alderman of London, or to see a subject of the Great Mogul entering into a league with one of the Czar of Muscovy. I am infinitely delighted in mixing with these several ministers of commerce, as they are distinguished by their different walks and different languages : sometimes I am justled among a body of Armenians; sometimes I am lost in a crowd of Jews; and sometimes make one in a group of Dutchmen. I am a Dane, Swede, or Frenchman at different times; or rather fancy myself like the old philosopher, who upon being asked what countryman he was, replied, that he was a citizen of the world.

Though I very frequently visit this busy multitude of people, I am known to nobody there but my friend Sir Andrew, who often smiles upon me as he sees me bustling in the crowd, but at the same time connives at my presence without taking any further notice of me. There is indeed a merchant of Egypt, who just knows me by sight, having formerly remitted me some money to Grand Cairo; but as I am not versed in the modern Coptic, our conferences go no further than a bow and a grimace.

This grand scene of business gives me an infinite variety of solid and substantial entertainments. As I am a great lover of mankind, my heart naturally overflows with pleasure at the sight of a prosperous and happy multitude, insomuch, that at many public solemnities I cannot forbear expressing my joy with tears that have stolen down my cheeks. For this reason I am wonderfully delighted to see such a body of men thriving in their own private fortunes, and at the same time promoting the public stock; or, in other words, raising estates for their own families, by bringing into their country whatever is wanting, and carrying out of it whatever is superfluous.

Nature seems to have taken a peculiar care to disseminate the blessings among the different regions of the world, with an eye to this mutual intercourse and traffic among mankind, that the natives of the several parts of the globe might have a kind of dependence upon one another, and be united together by this common interest. Almost every degree produces something peculiar to it. The food often grows in one country, and the sauce in another. The fruits of Portugal are corrected by the products of Barbadoes; the infusion of a China plant sweetened with the pith of an Indian cane. The Philippine Islands give a flavour to our European bowls. The single dress of a woman of quality is often the product of a hundred climates.

The muff and the fan come together from the different ends of the earth. The scarf is sent from the torrid zone, and the tippet from beneath the pole. The brocade petticoat rises out of the mines of Peru, and the diamond necklace out of the bowels of Indostan.

If we consider our own country in its natural prospect, without any of the benefits and advantages of commerce, what a barren, uncomfortable spot of earth falls to our share! Natural historians tell us, that no fruit grows originally among us besides hips and haws, acorns and pig-nuts, with other delicacies of the like nature; that our climate of itself, and without the assistance of art, can make no further advances towards a plum than to a sloe, and carries an apple to no greater a perfection than a crab: that our melons, our peaches, our figs, our apricots, and cherries, are strangers among us, imported in different ages, and naturalized in our English gardens; and that they would all degenerate and fall away into the trash of our own country, if they were wholly neglected by the planter, and left to the mercy of our sun and soil. Nor has traffic more enriched our vegetable world, than it has improved the whole face of nature among us. Our ships are laden with the harvest of every climate: our tables are stored with spices, and oils, and wines; our rooms are filled with pyramids of China, and adorned with the workmanship of Japan: our morning's draught comes to us from the remotest corners of the earth; we repair our bodies by the drugs of America, and repose ourselves under Indian canopies. My friend Sir Andrew calls the vineyards of France our gardens; the spice-islands our hot-beds; the Persians our silk-weavers, and the Chinese our potters. Nature indeed furnishes us with the bare necessaries of life, but traffic gives us a great variety of what is useful, and at the same time supplies us with everything that is convenient and ornamental. Nor is it the least part of this our happiness, that while we enjoy the remotest products of the north and south, we are free from those extremities of weather which give them birth; that our eyes are refreshed with the green fields of Britain, at the same time that our palates are feasted with fruits that rise between the tropics.

For these reasons there are not more useful members in a commonwealth than merchants. They knit mankind together in a mutual intercourse of good offices, distribute the gifts of nature, find work for the poor, and wealth to the rich, and magnificence to the great. Our English merchant converts the tin of his own country into gold, and exchanges his wool for rubies.

The Mahometans are clothed in our British manufacture, and the inhabitants of the frozen zone warmed with the fleeces of our sheep.

When I have been upon the Change, I have often fancied one of our old kings standing in person, where he is represented in effigy, and looking down upon the wealthy concourse of people with which that place is every day filled. In this case, how would he be surprised to hear all the languages of Europe spoken in this little spot of his former dominions, and to see so many private men, who in his time would have been the vassals of some powerful baron, negotiating like princes for greater sums of money than were formerly to be met with in the royal treasury! Trade, without enlarging the British territories, has given us a kind of additional empire: it has multiplied the number of the rich, made our landed estates infinitely more valuable than they were formerly, and added to them an accession of other estates as valuable as the lands themselves.

(The Spectator.)

The Spectator, No. 98.—THE HEAD-DRESS

There is not so variable a thing in nature as a lady's head-dress: within my own memory I have known it rise and fall above thirty degrees. About ten years ago it shot up to a very great height, insomuch that the female part of our species were much taller than the men. The women were of such an enormous stature, that " we appeared as grasshoppers before them : " at present the whole sex is in a manner dwarfed and shrunk into a race of beauties that seems almost another species. I remember several ladies, who were once very near seven foot high, that at present want some inches of five : how they came to be thus curtailed I cannot learn; whether the whole sex be at present under any penance which we know nothing of, or whether they have cast their head-dresses in order to surprise us with something in that kind which shall be entirely new; or whether some of the tallest of the sex, being too cunning for the rest, have contrived this method to make themselves appear sizeable, is still a secret; though I find most are of opinion, they are at present like trees new lopped and pruned, that will certainly sprout up and flourish with greater heads than before. For my own part, as I do not love to be insulted by women who are taller than myself, I admire the sex much more in their present humiliation, which has reduced them to their natural dimensions, than when they had extended their persons, and lengthened themselves out into formidable and gigantic figures. I am not for adding to the beautiful edifice of nature, nor for raising any whimsical superstructure upon her plans : I must, therefore, repeat it, that I am highly pleased with the coiffure now in fashion, and think it shows the good sense which at present very much reigns among the valuable part of the sex. One may observe, that women in all ages have taken more pains than men to adorn the outside of their heads; and, indeed, I very much admire, that those female architects, who raise such wonderful structures out of ribbons, lace, and wire, have not been recorded for their respective inventions. It is certain there have been as many orders in these kinds of building, as in those which have been made of marble : sometimes they rise in the shape of a pyramid, sometimes like a tower, and sometimes like a steeple. In Juvenal's time the building grew by several orders and stories, as he has very humorously described it—

> Tot premit ordinibus, tot adhuc compagibus altum
> Ædificat caput : Andromachen a fronte videbis ;
> Post minor est : aliam credas. — JUV.

But I do not remember, in any part of my reading, that the head-dress aspired to so great an extravagance as in the fourteenth century; when it was built up in a couple of cones or spires, which stood so excessively high on each side of the head, that a woman who was but a Pigmy without her head-dress, appeared like a Colossus upon putting it on. Monsieur Paradin says, " That these old-fashioned frontages rose an ell above the head; that they were pointed like steeples, and had long loose pieces of crape fastened to the tops of them, which are curiously fringed, and hung down their backs like streamers."

The women might possibly have carried this Gothic building much higher, had not a famous monk, Thomas Connecte by name, attacked it with great zeal and resolution. This holy man travelled from place to place to preach down this monstrous commode; and succeeded so well in it, that as the magicians sacrificed their books to the flames upon the preaching of an apostle, many of the women threw down their head-dresses in the middle of his sermon, and made a bonfire of them within sight of the pulpit. He was so renowned, as well for the sanctity of his life as his manner of preaching, that he had often a congregation of twenty thousand people; the men placing themselves on the one side of his pulpit, and the women on the other, that appeared (to use the similitude of an ingenious writer) like a forest of cedars with their heads reaching to the clouds. He so warmed and animated the people against this monstrous ornament, that it lay under a kind of persecution; and whenever it appeared in public, was pelted down by the rabble, who flung stones at the persons that wore it. But notwithstanding this prodigy vanished while the preacher was among them, it began to appear again some months after his departure; or, to tell it in Monsieur Paradin's own words, "The women, that, like snails in a fight, had drawn in their horns, shot them out again as soon as the danger was over." This extravagance of the women's head-dresses in that age is taken notice of by Monsieur D'Argentre in his *History of Bretagne*, and by other historians as well as the person I have here quoted.

It is usually observed, that a good reign is the only time for the making of laws against the exorbitance of power; in the same manner, an excessive head-dress may be attacked the most effectually when the fashion is against it. I do, therefore, recommend this paper to my female readers by way of prevention.

I would desire the fair sex to consider how impossible it is for them to add anything that can be ornamental to what is already the master-piece of nature. The head has the most beautiful appearance, as well as the highest station, in a human figure. Nature has laid out all her art in beautifying the face : she has touched it with vermilion, planted in it a double row of ivory, made it the seat of smiles and blushes, lighted it up and enlivened it with the brightness of the eyes, hung it on each side with curious organs of sense, given it airs and graces that cannot be described, and surrounded it with such a flowing shade of hair as sets all its beauties in the most agreeable light; in short, she seems to have designed the head as the cupola to the most glorious of her works; and when we load it with such a pile of supernumerary ornaments, we destroy the symmetry of the human figure, and foolishly contrive to call off the eye from great and real beauties, to childish gew-gaws, ribbons, and bone-lace.

(The Spectator.)

The Spectator, No. 159.—The Vision of Mirza

When I was at Grand Cairo I picked up several oriental manuscripts, which I have still by me. Among others I met with one entitled, *The Visions of Mirzah*, which I have read over with great pleasure. I intend to give it to the public when I have no other entertainment for them; and shall begin

with the first vision, which I have translated word for word
as follows—

"On the fifth day of the moon, which according to the custom
of my forefathers I always kept holy, after having washed myself,
and offered up my morning devotions, I ascended the high
hill of Bagdat, in order to pass the rest of the day in meditation
and prayer. As I was here airing myself on the tops of the
mountains, I fell into a profound contemplation on the vanity
of human life; and passing from one thought to another, surely,
said I, man is but a shadow and life a dream. Whilst I was thus
musing, I cast my eyes towards the summit of a rock that was
not far from me, where I discovered one in the habit of a shepherd, with a musical instrument in his hand. As I looked upon
him he applied it to his lips, and began to play upon it. The
sound of it was exceeding sweet, and wrought into a variety
of tunes that were inexpressibly melodious, and altogether
different from anything I had ever heard. They put me in
mind of those heavenly airs that are played to the departed
souls of good men upon their first arrival in paradise, to wear
out the impressions of their last agonies, and qualify them for
the pleasures of that happy place. My heart melted away in
secret raptures.

"I had often been told that the rock before me was the
haunt of a genius; and that several had been entertained with
music who had passed by it, but never heard that the musician
had before made himself visible. When he had raised my
thoughts, by those transporting airs which he played, to taste
the pleasures of his conversation, as I looked upon him like one
astonished, he beckoned to me, and by the waving of his hand
directed me to approach the place where he sat. I drew near
with that reverence which is due to a superior nature; and as
my heart was entirely subdued by the captivating strains
I had heard, I fell down at his feet and wept. The genius
smiled upon me with a look of compassion and affability that
familiarized him to my imagination, and at once dispelled all
the fears and apprehensions with which I approached him.
He lifted me from the ground, and taking me by the hand,
Mirzah, said he, I have heard thee in thy soliloquies, follow me.

"He then led me to the highest pinnacle of the rock, and
placed me on the top of it. Cast thy eyes eastward, said he,
and tell me what thou seest. I see, said I, a huge valley and
a prodigious tide of water rolling through it. The valley that
thou seest, said he, is the vale of misery, and the tide of water
that thou seest is part of the great tide of eternity. What

is the reason, said I, that the tide I see rises out of a thick mist at one end, and again loses itself in a thick mist at the other? What thou seest, says he, is that portion of eternity which is called time, measured out by the sun, and reaching from the beginning of the world to its consummation. Examine now, said he, this sea that is thus bounded with darkness at both ends, and tell me what thou discoverest in it. I see a bridge, said I, standing in the midst of the tide. The bridge thou seest, said he, is human life; consider it attentively. Upon a more leisurely survey of it, I found that it consisted of three-score and ten entire arches, with several broken arches, which added to those that were entire, made up the number about an hundred. As I was counting the arches the genius told me that this bridge consisted at first of a thousand arches; but that a great flood swept away the rest, and left the bridge in the ruinous condition I now beheld it. But tell me, further, said he, what thou discoverest on it. I see multitudes of people passing over it, said I, and a black cloud hanging on each end of it. As I looked more attentively, I saw several of the passengers dropping through the bridge, into the great tide that flowed underneath it; and upon further examination, perceived there were innumerable trap-doors that lay concealed in the bridge, which the passengers no sooner trod upon, but they fell through them into the tide and immediately disappeared. These hidden pit-falls were set very thick at the entrance of the bridge, so that throngs of people no sooner broke through the cloud, but many of them fell into them. They grew thinner towards the middle, but multiplied and lay closer together towards the end of the arches that were entire.

" There were indeed some persons, but their number was very small, that continued a kind of hobbling march on the broken arches, but fell through one after another, being quite tired and spent with so long a walk.

" I passed some time in the contemplation of this wonderful structure, and the great variety of objects which it presented. My heart was filled with a deep melancholy to see several dropping unexpectedly in the midst of mirth and jollity, and catching at everything that stood by them to save themselves. Some were looking up towards the heavens in a thoughtful posture, and in the midst of a speculation stumbled and fell out of sight. Multitudes were very busy in the pursuit of baubles that glittered in their eyes and danced before them, but often when they thought themselves within the reach of them, their footing failed and down they sunk. In this confusion of objects, I observed some with scimitars in their hands, and others with urinals, who ran to and fro upon the bridge, thrusting several persons upon trap-doors which did not seem to lie in their way, and which they might have escaped had they not been thus forced upon them.

"The genius seeing me indulge myself in this melancholy prospect, told me I had dwelt long enough upon it : take thine eyes off the bridge, said he, and tell me if thou seest anything thou dost not comprehend. Upon looking up, what mean, said I, those great flights of birds that are perpetually hovering about the bridge, and settling upon it from time to time? I see vultures, harpies, ravens, cormorants, and among many other feathered creatures, several little winged boys, that perch, in great numbers upon the middle arches. These, said the genius, are envy, avarice, superstition, despair, love, with the like cares and passions, that infect human life.

"I here fetched a deep sigh; alas, said I, man was made in vain! How is he given away to misery and mortality! tortured in life, and swallowed up in death! The genius, being moved with compassion towards me, bid me quit so uncomfortable a prospect. Look no more, said he, on man in the first stage of his existence, in his setting out for eternity; but cast thine eye on that thick mist into which the tide bears the several generations of mortals that fall into it. I directed my sight as I was ordered, and (whether or no the good genius strengthened it with any supernatural force, or dissipated part of the mist that was before too thick for the eye to penetrate) I saw the valley opening at the farther end, and spreading forth into an immense ocean, that had a huge rock of adamant running through the midst of it, and dividing it into two equal parts. The clouds still rested on one half of it, insomuch that I could discover nothing in it : but the other appeared to me a vast ocean planted with innumerable islands, that were covered with fruits and flowers, and interwoven with a thousand little shining seas that ran among them. I could see persons dressed in glorious habits with garlands upon their heads, passing among the trees, lying down by the sides of the fountains, or resting on beds of flowers; and could hear a confused harmony of singing birds, falling waters, human voices, and musical instruments. Gladness grew in me upon the discovery of so delightful a scene. I wished for the wings of an eagle, that I might fly away to those happy seats; but the genius told me there was no passage to them, except through the gates of death that I saw opening every moment upon the bridge. The islands, said he, that lie so fresh and green before thee, and with which the whole face of the ocean appears spotted as far as thou canst see, are more in number than the sands on the sea-shore; there are myriads of islands behind those which thou here discoverest, reaching farther than thine eye, or even thine imagination, can extend itself. These are the mansions of good men after death, who, according to the degree and kinds of virtue in which they excelled, are distributed among these several islands, which abound with pleasures of different kinds and degrees, suitable to the relishes and perfections of those who are settled in them: every island is a paradise, accommodated to its respective inhabitants. Are not these O Mirzah, habitations worth contending for? Does life appear miserable, that gives thee opportunities of earning such a reward? Is death to be feared, that will convey thee to so happy an existence? Think not man was made in vain, who has such an eternity reserved for him. I gazed with inexpressible pleasure on these happy islands. At length, said I, show me now, I beseech thee, the secrets that lie hid under those dark clouds which cover the ocean on the other side of the rock of adamant. The genius making me no answer, I turned about to address myself to him a second time, but I found that he had left me. I then turned again to the vision which I had been so long contemplating, but, instead of the rolling tide, the arched bridge, and the happy islands, I saw nothing but the long hollow valley of Bagdat, with oxen, sheep, and camels grazing upon the sides of it."

(*The Spectator.*)

SAMUEL RICHARDSON (1689–1761)
I.—Miss Clarissa Harlowe to Miss Howe

Friday, 3 o'clock.

My sister is but this moment gone from me. She came up all in a flame; which obliged me abruptly to lay down my pen; she ran to me—

O Spirit! said she, tapping my neck a little *too* hard. And is it come to this at last! Do you beat me, Bella?

Do you call this beating you? only tapping your shoulder thus, said she, tapping again more gently—this is what we expected it would come to—you want to be independent—my father has lived too long for you!

I was going to speak with vehemence; but she put her handkerchief before my mouth very rudely—you have done enough with your pen, mean listener as you are! But know that neither your independent scheme, nor any of your visiting ones will be granted you. Take your course, perverse one! Call in your rake to help you to an independence upon your parents, and a dependence upon him!—Do so!—Prepare this moment—resolve what you will take with you—to-morrow you go —depend upon it to-morrow you go!—No longer shall you stay here watching and creeping about to hearken to what people say.—'Tis determined, child!—you go to-morrow—my brother would have come up to tell you so; but I persuaded him to the contrary—for I know not what had become of you if he had. —Such a letter! such an insolent, such a conceited challenger! O thou vain creature! But prepare yourself, I say, to-morrow you go, my brother will accept of your bold challenge; but it must be personal: and at my Uncle Antony's—or perhaps at Mr. Solmes's——

Thus she ran on, almost foaming with passion; till, quite out of patience, I said, No more of your violence, Bella.—Had I known in what way you designed to come up, you should not have found my chamber-door open—talk to your servant in this manner. Unlike you, as I bless God I am, I am nevertheless your sister—and let me tell you that I won't go to-morrow, nor the next day, nor next day to that—except I am dragged away by violence.

What! not if your father or your mother command it—girl! said she, intending another word by her pause and manner before it came out.

Let it come to that, Bella; then I shall know what to say. But it shall be from their own mouths, if I do—not from yours, nor your Betty's.—And say another word to me in this manner, and be the consequence what it may I will force myself into their presence; and demand what I have done to be used thus!

Come along, child! Come along, Meekness—taking my hand, and leading me towards the door—Demand it of them now— you'll find both your despised parents together!—What!— does your heart fail you?—for I resisted being thus insolently offered to be led, and pulled my hand from her.

I want not to be led, said I; and since I can plead your invitation I will go: and was posting to the stairs accordingly in my passion—but she got between me and the door, and shut it.——

Let me first, bold one, said she, apprise them of your visit— for your own sake let me—for my brother is with them. But yet opening it again, seeing me shrink back—go, if you will!— why don't you go?—Why don't you go, Miss?—following me to my closet, whither I retired with my heart full, and pulled the sash-door after me; and could no longer hold in my tears.

Nor would I answer one word to her repeated aggravations, nor to her demands upon me to open the door (for the key was on the inside); nor so much as turn my head towards her, as she looked through the glass at me. And at last, which vexed her to the heart, I drew the silk curtain that she should not see me, and down she went muttering all the way.

Is not this usage enough to provoke a rashness never before thought of?

As it is but too probable that I may be hurried away to uncle's without being able to give you previous notice of it; I beg you that as soon as you shall hear of such a violence, you would send to the usual place, to take back such of your letters as may not have reached my hands, or to fetch any of mine that may be there.

May you, my dear, be always happy, prays your

CLARISSA HARLOWE.
(Clarissa Harlowe.)

II.—PORTRAIT OF HIMSELF

I go through the Park once or twice a week to my little retirement, but I will for a week together be in it every day three or four hours, at your command, till you tell me you have seen a person who answers to this description, namely short; rather plump than emaciated, notwithstanding his complaints; about five feet five inches; fair wig; lightish cloth coat, all black besides; one hand generally in his bosom, the other a cane in it, which he leans upon under the skirts of his coat usually, that it may imperceptibly serve him as a support when attacked by sudden tremors, or startings, and dizziness which too frequently attack him, but, thank God, not so often as formerly; looking directly fore-right, as passers-by would imagine, but observing all that stirs on either hand of him without moving his short neck; hardly ever turning back; of a light brown complexion; teeth not yet failing him; smoothish-faced and ruddy-cheeked; at some times looking to be about sixty-five; at other times much younger; a regular even pace, stealing away ground rather than seeming to rid it; a grey eye too often overclouded by mistiness from the head; by chance lively; very lively it will be if he have hope of seeing a lady whom he loves and honours; his eye always on the ladies; if they have very large hoops, he looks down and supercilious, and as if he would be thought wise, but perhaps the sillier for that; as he approaches a lady his eye is never fixed first upon her face, but upon her feet, and thence he raises it up pretty quickly for a dull eye; and one would think (if we thought him at all worthy of observation) that from her air and (the last beheld) her face, he sets her down in his mind as *so* or *so*, and then passes on to the next object he meets, only then looking back if he greatly likes or dislikes, as if he would see if the lady appear to be all of a piece, in the one light or in the other. Are these marks distinct enough, if you are resolved to keep all the advantages you set out with? And from this odd, this grotesque figure, think you, madam, that you have anything to apprehend? Anything that will not rather promote than check your mirth? I dare be bold to say (and allow it too) that you would rather see this figure than any other you ever saw, whenever you should find yourself graver than you wish to be.

(*Letter to Lady Bradshaigh.*)

HENRY FIELDING (1707-1754)

I.—Mr. Adams's Short Memory

Mr. Adams and Joseph were now ready to depart different ways, when an accident determined the former to return with his friend, which Tow-wouse, Barnabas, and the bookseller had not been able to do. This accident was, that those sermons, which the parson was travelling to London to publish, were, O my good reader! left behind; what he had mistaken for them in the saddlebags being no other than three shirts, a pair of shoes, and some other necessaries, which Mrs. Adams, who thought her husband would want shirts more than sermons on his journey, had carefully provided him.

This discovery was now luckily owing to the presence of Joseph at the opening the saddlebags; who, having heard his friend say he carried with him nine volumes of sermons, and not being of that sect of philosophers who can reduce all the matter of the world into a nutshell, seeing there was no room for them in the bags, where the parson had said they were deposited, had the curiosity to cry out, "Bless me, sir, where are your sermons?" The parson answered, "There there, child; there they are, under my shirts." Now it happened that he had taken forth his last shirt, and the vehicle remained visibly empty. "Sure, sir," says Joseph, "there is nothing in the bags." Upon which Adams, starting, and testifying some surprize, cried, "Hey! fie, fie upon it! they are not here sure enough. Ay, they are certainly left behind."

Joseph was greatly concerned at the uneasiness which he apprehended his friend must feel from this disappointment; he begged him to pursue his journey, and promised he would himself return with the books to him with the utmost expedition. " No, thank you, child," answered Adams; " it shall not be so. What would it avail me, to tarry in the great city, unless I had my discourses with me, which are *ut ita dicam*, the sole cause, the *aitia monotate* of my peregrination? No, child, as this accident hath happened, I am resolved to return back to my cure, together with you; which indeed my inclination sufficiently leads me to. This disappointment may perhaps be intended for my good." He concluded with a verse out of Theocritus, which signifies no more than that sometimes it rains, and sometimes the sun shines.

Joseph bowed with obedience and thankfulness for the inclination which the parson expressed of returning with him; and now the bill was called for, which, on examination, amounted within a shilling to the sum Mr. Adams had in his pocket. Perhaps the reader may wonder how he was able to produce a sufficient sum for so many days: that he may not be surprized, therefore, it cannot be unnecessary to acquaint him that he had borrowed a guinea of a servant belonging to the coach and six, who had been formerly one of his parishioners, and whose master, the owner of the coach, then lived within three miles of him; for so good was the credit of Mr. Adams, that even Mr. Peter, the Lady Booby's steward, would have lent him a guinea with very little security.

Mr. Adams discharged the bill, and they were both setting out, having agreed to ride and tie; a method of travelling much used by persons who have but one horse between them, and is thus performed. The two travellers set out together, one on horseback, the other on foot: now, as it generally happens that he on horseback outgoes him on foot, the custom is, that, when he arrives at the distance agreed on, he is to dismount, tie the horse to some gate, tree, post, or other thing, and then proceed on foot; when the other comes up to the horse he unties him, mounts, and gallops on, till, having passed by his fellow-traveller, he likewise arrives at the place of tying. And this is that method of travelling so much in use among our prudent ancestors, who knew that horses had mouths as well as legs, and that they could not use the latter without being at the expense of suffering the beasts themselves to use the former. This was the method in use in those days when, instead of a coach and six, a member of parliament's lady used to mount a pillion behind her husband; and a grave serjeant at law condescended to amble to Westminster on an easy pad, with his clerk kicking his heels behind him.

Adams was now gone some minutes, having insisted on Joseph's beginning the journey on horseback, and Joseph had his foot in the stirrup, when the hostler presented him a bill for the horse's board during his residence at the inn. Joseph said Mr. Adams had paid all; but this matter, being referred to Mr. Tow-wouse, was by him decided in favour of the hostler, and indeed with truth and justice; for this was a fresh instance of that shortness of memory which did not arise from want of parts, but that continual hurry in which parson Adams was always involved.

Joseph was now reduced to a dilemma which extremely puzzled him. The sum due for horse-meat was twelve shillings (for Adams, who had borrowed the beast of his clerk, had ordered him to be fed as well as they could feed him), and the cash in his pocket amounted to sixpence (for Adams had divided the last shilling with him). Now, though there have been some ingenious persons who have contrived to pay twelve shillings with sixpence, Joseph was not one of them. He had never contracted a debt in his life, and was consequently the less ready at an expedient to extricate himself. Tow-wouse was willing to give him credit till next time, to which Mrs. Tow-wouse would probably have consented (for such was Joseph's beauty, that it had made some impression even on that piece of flint which that good woman wore in her bosom by way of heart). Joseph would have found, therefore, very likely the passage free, had he not, when he honestly discovered the nakedness of his pockets, pulled out that little piece of gold which we have mentioned before. This caused Mrs. Tow-wouse's eyes to water; she told Joseph she did not conceive a man could want money whilst he had gold in his pocket. Joseph answered he had such a value for that little piece of gold, that he would not part with it for a hundred times the riches which the greatest esquire in the county was worth. "A pretty way, indeed," said Mrs. Tow-wouse, "to run in debt, and then refuse to part with your money, because you have a value for it! I never knew any piece of gold of more value than as many shillings as it would change for."— "Not to preserve my life from starving, nor to redeem it from a robber, would I part with this dear piece!" answered Joseph. "What," says Mrs. Tow-wouse, "I suppose it was given you by some vile trollop, some miss or other; if it had been the present of a virtuous woman, you would not have had such a value for it. My husband is a fool if he parts with the horse without being paid for him."—"No, no, I can't part with the horse, indeed, till I have the money," cried Tow-wouse. A resolution highly commended by a lawyer then in the yard, who declared Mr. Tow-wouse might justify the detainer.

As we cannot therefore at present get Mr. Joseph out of the inn, we shall leave him in it, and carry our reader on after parson Adams, who, his mind being perfectly at ease, fell into a contemplation on a passage in Æschylus, which entertained him for three miles together, without suffering him once to reflect on his fellow-traveller.

At length, having spun out his thread, and being now at the summit of a hill, he cast his eyes backwards, and wondered that he could not see any sign of Joseph. As he left him ready to mount the horse, he could not apprehend any mischief had happened, neither could he suspect that he missed his way, it being so broad and plain; the only reason which presented itself to him was, that he had met with an acquaintance who had prevailed with him to delay some time in discourse.

He therefore resolved to proceed slowly forwards, not doubting but that he should be shortly overtaken; and soon came to a large water, which, filling the whole road, he saw no method of passing unless by wading through, which he accordingly did up to his middle; but was no sooner got to the other side than he perceived, if he had looked over the hedge, he would have found a footpath capable of conducting him without wetting his shoes.

His surprize at Joseph's not coming up grew now very troublesome: he began to fear he knew not what; and as he determined to move no farther, and, if he did not shortly overtake him, to return back, he wished to find a house of public entertainment where he might dry his clothes and refresh himself with a pint; but, seeing no such (for no other reason than because he did not cast his eyes a hundred yards forwards), he sat himself down on a stile, and pulled out his Æschylus.

A fellow passing presently by, Adams asked him if he could direct him to an alehouse. The fellow, who had just left it, and perceived the house and sign to be within sight, thinking he had jeered him, and being of a morose temper, bade him follow his nose and be d—n'd. Adams told him he was a saucy jacknapes; upon which the fellow turned about angrily; but, perceiving Adams clench his fist, he thought proper to go on without taking any farther notice.

A horseman, following immediately after, and being asked the same question, answered, Friend, there is one within a stone's throw; I believe you may see it before you. Adams, lifting up his eyes, cried, I protest, and so there is; and, thanking his informer, proceeded directly to it.

(Joseph Andrews.)

II.—Discourse between the Poet and the Player

The poet, addressing the player, proceeded thus, " As I was saying " (for they had been at this discourse all the time of the engagement above-stairs), " the reason you have no good new plays is evident; it is from your discouragement of authors. Gentlemen will not write, sir, they will not write, without the expectation of fame or profit, or perhaps both. Plays are like trees, which will not grow without nourishment; but, like mushrooms, they shoot up spontaneously, as it were, in a rich soil. The muses, like vines, may be pruned, but not with a hatchet. The town, like a peevish child, knows not what it desires, and is always best pleased with a rattle. A farce-writer hath indeed some chance for success: but they have lost all taste for the sublime. Though I believe one reason of their depravity is the badness of the actors. If a man writes like an angel, sir, those fellows know not how to give a sentiment utterance."—" Not so fast," says the player: " the modern actors are as good at least as their authors, nay, they come nearer their illustrious predecessors; and I expect a Booth on the stage again, sooner than a Shakspear or an Otway; and indeed I may turn your observation against you, and with truth say, that the reason no authors are encouraged is because we have no good new plays."—" I have not affirmed the contrary," said the poet; " but I am surprized you grow so warm; you cannot imagine yourself interested in this dispute; I hope you have a better opinion of my taste than to apprehend I squinted at yourself. No, sir, if we had six such actors as you, we should soon rival the Bettertons and Sandfords of former times; for, without a compliment to you, I think it impossible for any one to have excelled you in most of your parts. Nay, it is solemn truth, and I have heard many, and all great judges, express as much; and, you will pardon me if I tell you, I think every time I have seen you lately you have constantly acquired some new excellence, like a snowball. You have deceived me in my estimation of perfection, and have outdone what I thought inimitable."— " You are as little interested," answered the player, " in what

I have said of other poets; for d—n me if there are not manly strokes, aye, whole scenes, in your last tragedy, which at least equal Shakspear. There is a delicacy of sentiment, a dignity of expression in it, which I will own many of our gentlemen did not do adequate justice to. To confess the truth, they are bad enough, and I pity an author who is present at the murder of his works."—"Nay, it is but seldom that it can happen," returned the poet; "the works of most modern authors, like dead-born children, cannot be murdered. It is such wretched half-begotten, half-writ, lifeless, spiritless, low, grovelling stuff, that I almost pity the actor who is obliged to get it by heart, which must be almost as difficult to remember as words in a language you don't understand."—"I am sure," said the player, "if the sentences have little meaning when they are writ, when they are spoken they have less. I know scarce one who ever lays an emphasis right, and much less adapts his action to his character. I have seen a tender lover in an attitude of fighting with his mistress, and a brave hero suing to his enemy with his sword in his hand. I don't care to abuse my profession, but rot me if in my heart I am not inclined to the poet's side."—"It is rather generous in you than just," said the poet; "and, though I hate to speak ill of any person's production,—nay, I never do it, nor will,— but yet, to do justice to the actors, what could Booth or Betterton have made of such horrible stuff as Fenton's Mariamne, Frowd's Philotas, or Mallet's Eurydice; or those low, dirty, last-dying-speeches, which a fellow in the city of Wapping, your Dillo or Lillo, what was his name, called tragedies?"—"Very well," says the player; "and pray what do you think of such fellows as Quin and Delane, or that face-making puppy young Cibber, that ill-looked dog Macklin, or that saucy slut Mrs. Clive? What work would they make with your Shakspears, Otways, and Lees? How would those harmonious lines of the last come from their tongues?—

> " '——No more; for I disdain
> All pomp when thou art by: far be the noise
> Of kings and crowns from us, whose gentle souls
> Our kinder fates have steer'd another way.
> Free as the forest birds we'll pair together,
> Without remem'ring who our fathers were:
> Fly to the arbours, grots, and flow'ry meads;
> There in soft murmurs interchange our souls;
> Together drink the crystal of the stream,
> Or taste the yellow fruit which autumn yields,
> And, when the golden evening calls us home,
> Wing to our downy nests, and sleep till morn.'

Or how would this disdain of Otway—

        'Who'd be that foolish sordid thing called man?'"

"Hold! hold! hold!" said the poet: "Do repeat that tender speech in the third act of my play which you made such a figure in."—"I would willingly," said the player, "but I have forgot it."—"Aye, you was not quite perfect enough in it when you played it," cries the poet, "or you would have had such an applause as was never given on the stage; an applause I was extremely concerned for your losing."—"Sure," says the player, "if I remember, that was hissed more than any passage in the whole play."—"Aye, your speaking it was hissed," said the poet.—"My speaking it!" said the player.—"I mean your not speaking it," said the poet. "You was out, and then they hissed."—"They hissed, and then I was out, if I remember," answered the player; "and I must say this for myself, that the whole audience allowed I did your part justice; so don't lay the damnation of your play to my account."—"I don't know what you mean by damnation," replied the poet.—"Why, you know it was acted but one night," cried the player.—"No," said the poet, "you and the whole town were enemies; the pit were all my enemies, fellows that would cut my throat, if the fear of hanging did not restrain them. All tailors, sir, all tailors."—"Why should the tailors be so angry with you?" cries the player. "I suppose you don't employ so many in making your clothes."—"I admit your jest," answered the poet; "but you remember the affair as well as myself; you know there was a party in the pit and upper-gallery that would not suffer it to be given out again; though much, aye infinitely, the majority, all the boxes in particular, were desirous of it; nay, most of the ladies swore they never would come to the house till it was acted again. Indeed, I must own their policy was good in not letting it be given out a second time: for the rascals knew if it had gone a second night it would have run fifty; for if ever there was distress in a tragedy,—I am not fond of my own performance; but if I should tell you what the best judges said of it—— Nor was it entirely owing to my enemies neither that it did not succeed on the stage as well as it hath since among the polite readers; for you can't say it had justice done it by the performers."— "I think," answered the player, "the performers did the distress of it justice; for I am sure we were in distress enough, who were pelted with oranges all the last act: we all imagined it would have been the last act of our lives."

The poet, whose fury was now raised, had just attempted to answer when they were interrupted, and an end put to their discourse.

(*Joseph Andrews.*)

SAMUEL JOHNSON (1709–1784)

I.—THE FATHER OF ENGLISH CRITICISM

DRYDEN may be properly considered as the father of English criticism, as the writer who first taught us to determine upon principles the merit of composition. Of our former poets, the greatest dramatist wrote without rules, conducted through life and nature by a genius that rarely misled, and rarely deserted him. Of the rest, those who knew the laws of propriety had neglected to teach them.

Two Arts of English Poetry were written in the days of Elizabeth by Webb and Puttenham, from which something might be learned, and a few hints had been given by Jonson and Cowley; but Dryden's *Essay on Dramatic Poetry* was the first regular and valuable treatise on the art of writing.

He who, having formed his opinions in the present age of English literature, turns back to peruse this dialogue, will not perhaps find much increase of knowledge, or much novelty of instruction; but he is to remember that critical principles were then in the hands of a few, who had gathered them partly from the ancients, and partly from the Italians and French. The structure of dramatic poems was then not generally understood. Audiences applauded by instinct; and poets perhaps often pleased by chance.

A writer who obtains his full purpose loses himself in his own lustre. Of an opinion which is no longer doubted, the evidence ceases to be examined. Of an art universally practised, the first teacher is forgotten. Learning once made popular is no longer learning; it has the appearance of something which we have bestowed upon ourselves, as the dew appears to rise from the field which it refreshes.

To judge rightly of an author, we must transport ourselves to his time, and examine what were the wants of his contemporaries, and what were his means of supplying them. That which is easy at one time was difficult at another. Dryden at least imported his science, and gave his country what it wanted before; or, rather, he imported only the materials, and manufactured them by his own skill.

The *Dialogue on the Drama* was one of his first essays of criticism, written when he was yet a timorous candidate for reputation, and therefore laboured with that diligence which, he might allow himself somewhat to remit, when his name gave sanction to his positions, and his awe of the public was abated, partly by custom, and partly by success. It will not be easy to find, in all the opulence of our language, a treatise so artfully variegated with successive representations of opposite probabilities, so enlivened with imagery, so brightened with illustrations. His portraits of the English dramatists are wrought with great spirit and diligence. The account of Shakspeare may stand as a perpetual model of encomiastic criticism; exact without minuteness, and lofty without exaggeration. The praise lavished by Longinus, on the attestation of the heroes of Marathon, by Demosthenes, fades away before it. In a few lines is exhibited a character, so extensive in its comprehension, and so curious in its limitations, that nothing can be added, diminished, or reformed; nor can the editors and admirers of Shakspeare, in all their emulation of reverence, boast of much more than of having diffused and paraphrased this epitome of excellence, of having changed Dryden's gold for baser metal, of lower value, though of greater bulk.

In this, and in all his other essays on the same subject, the criticism of Dryden is the criticism of a poet; not a dull collection of theorems, nor a rude detection of faults, which perhaps the censor was not able to have committed; but a gay and vigorous dissertation, where delight is mingled with instruction, and where the author proves his right of judgment by his power of performance.

The different manner and effect with which critical knowledge may be conveyed, was perhaps never more clearly exemplified than in the performances of Rymer and Dryden. It was said of a dispute between two mathematicians, " malim cum Scaligero errare, quam cum Clavio recte sapere;" that "it was more eligible to go wrong with one, than right with the other." A tendency of the same kind every mind must feel at the perusal of Dryden's prefaces and Rymer's discourses. With Dryden we are wandering in quest of Truth; whom we find, if we find her at all, dressed in the graces of elegance; and, if we miss her, the labour of the pursuit rewards itself; we are led only through fragrance and flowers. Rymer, without taking a nearer, takes a rougher way; every step is to be made through thorns and brambles; and Truth, if we meet her, appears repulsive by her mien, and ungraceful by her habit. Dryden's criticism has the majesty of a queen; Rymer's has the ferocity of a tyrant.

(*Life of Dryden.*)

II.—THE METAPHYSICAL POETS

The metaphysical poets were men of learning, and to show their learning was their whole endeavour : but, unluckily resolving to show it in rhyme, instead of writing poetry they only wrote verses, and very often such verses as stood the trial of the finger better than of the ear; for the modulation was so imperfect, that they were only found to be verses by counting the syllables.

If the father of criticism had rightly denominated poetry τέχνη μιμητικὴ, *an imitative art,* these writers will, without great wrong, lose their right to the name of poets; for they cannot be said to have imitated anything : they neither copied nature nor life; neither painted the forms of matter, nor represented the operations of intellect.

Those, however, who deny them to be poets, allow them to be wits. Dryden confesses of himself and his contemporaries, that they fall below Donne in wit; but maintains that they surpass him in poetry.

If wit be well described by Pope, as being " that which has been often thought, but was never before so well expressed," they certainly never attained, nor ever sought it; for they endeavoured to be singular in their thoughts, and were careless of their diction. But Pope's account of wit is undoubtedly erroneous : he depresses it below its natural dignity, and reduces it from strength of thought to happiness of language.

If by a more noble and more adequate conception, that be considered as wit which is at once natural and new, that which, though not obvious, is, upon its first production, acknowledged to be just; if it be that which he that never found it, wonders how he missed; to wit of this kind the metaphysical poets have seldom risen. Their thoughts are often new, but seldom natural; they are not obvious, but neither are they just; and the reader, far from wondering that he missed them, wonders more frequently by what perverseness of industry they were ever found.

But wit, abstracted from its effects upon the hearer, may be more rigorously and philosophically considered as a kind of *discordia concors ;* a combination of dissimilar images, or discovery of occult resemblances in things apparently unlike. Of wit, thus defined, they have more than enough. The most heterogeneous ideas are yoked by violence together; nature and art are ransacked for illustrations, comparisons, and allusions their learning instructs, and their subtilty surprises; but the reader commonly thinks his improvement dearly bought, and though he sometimes admires, is seldom pleased.

From this account of their compositions it will be readily inferred, that they were not successful in representing or moving the affections. As they were wholly employed on something unexpected and surprising, they had no regard to that uniformity of sentiment which enables us to conceive and to excite the pains and the pleasure of other minds : they never inquired what, on any occasion, they should have said or done ; but wrote rather as beholders than partakers of human nature ; as beings looking upon good and evil, impassive and at leisure ; as epicurean deities, making remarks on the actions of men, and the vicissitudes of life, without interest and without emotion. Their courtship was void of fondness, and their lamentation of sorrow. Their wish was only to say what they hoped had been never said before.

Nor was the sublime more within their reach than the pathetic ; for they never attempted that comprehension and expanse of thought which at once fills the whole mind, and of which the first effect is sudden astonishment, and the second rational admiration. Sublimity is produced by aggregation, and littleness by dispersion. Great thoughts are always general, and consist in positions not limited by exceptions, and in descriptions not descending to minuteness. It is with great propriety that subtlety, which in its original import means exility of particles, is taken in its metaphorical meaning for nicety of distinction. Those writers who lay on the watch for novelty, could have little hope of greatness ; for great things cannot have escaped former observation. Their attempts were always analytic ; they broke every image into fragments ; and could no more represent, by their slender conceits and laboured particularities, the prospects of nature, or the scenes of life, than he who dissects a sunbeam with a prism can exhibit the wide effulgence of a summer noon.

What they wanted, however, of the sublime they endeavoured to supply by hyperbole ; their amplifications had no limits ; they left not only reason but fancy behind them ; and produced combinations of confused magnificence, that not only could not be credited, but could not be imagined.

Yet great labour, directed by great abilities, is never wholly lost ; if they frequently threw away their wit upon false conceits, they likewise sometimes struck out unexpected truth ; if their conceits were far-fetched, they were often worth the carriage. To write on their plan, it was at least necessary to read and think. No man could be born a metaphysical poet, nor assume the dignity of a writer, by descriptions copied from descriptions, by imitations borrowed from imitations, by traditional imagery, and hereditary similes, by readiness of rhyme, and volubility of syllables.

In perusing the works of this race of authors, the mind is exercised either by recollection or inquiry; something already learned is to be retrieved, or something new is to be examined. If their greatness seldom elevates, their acuteness often surprises; if the imagination is not always gratified, at least the powers of reflection and comparison are employed; and in the mass of materials which ingenious absurdity has thrown together, genuine wit and useful knowledge may be sometimes found buried perhaps in grossness of expression, but useful to those who know their value; and such as, when they are expanded to perspicuity, and polished to elegance, may give lustre to works which have more propriety though less copiousness of sentiment.

This kind of writing, which was I believe, borrowed from Marino and his followers, had been recommended by the example of Donne, a man of very extensive and various knowledge and by Jonson, whose manner resembled that of Donne more in the ruggedness of his lines than in the cast of his sentiments.

When their reputation was high, they had undoubtedly more imitators than time has left behind. Their immediate successors, of whom any remembrance can be said to remain, were Suckling, Waller, Denham, Cowley, Clieveland, and Milton. Denham and Waller sought another way to fame, by improving the harmony of our members. Milton tried the metaphysic style only in his lines upon Hobson the carrier. Cowley adopted it, and excelled his predecessors, having as much sentiment and more music. Suckling neither improved versification, nor abounded in conceits. The fashionable style remained chiefly with Cowley; Suckling could not reach it, and Milton disdained it.

(Life of Cowley.)

III.—The Art of Flying

Among the artists that had been allured into the Happy Valley, to labour for the accommodation and pleasure of its inhabitants, was a man eminent for his knowledge of the mechanic powers, who had contrived many engines both of use and recreation. By a wheel which the stream turned, he forced the water into a tower, whence it was distributed to all the apartments of the palace. He erected a pavilion in the garden, around which he kept the air always cool by artificial showers. One of the groves, appropriated to the ladies, was ventilated by fans, to which the rivulets that ran through it gave a constant motion; and instruments of soft music were played at proper distances, of which some played by the impulse of the wind, and some by the power of the stream.

This artist was sometimes visited by Rasselas, who was pleased with every kind of knowledge, imagining that the time would come when all his acquisitions should be of use to him in the open world. He came one day to amuse himself in his usual manner, and found the master busy in building a sailing chariot. He saw that the design was practicable upon a level surface, and with expressions of great esteem solicited its completion.

The workman was pleased to find himself so much regarded by the Prince, and resolved to gain yet higher honours.

"Sir," said he, "you have seen but a small part of what the mechanic sciences can perform. I have been long of opinion that, instead of the tardy conveyance of ships and chariots, man might use the swifter migration of wings; that the fields of air are open to knowledge, and that only ignorance and idleness need crawl upon the ground."

This hint rekindled the Prince's desire of passing the mountains. Having seen what the mechanist had already performed, he was willing to fancy that he could do more; yet resolved to inquire further before he suffered hope to afflict him by disappointment.

"I am afraid," said he to the artist, "that your imagination prevails over your skill, and that you now tell me rather what you wish than what you know. Every animal has his element assigned him; the birds have the air, and man and beasts the earth."

"So," replied the mechanist, "fishes have the water, in which yet beasts can swim by nature and man by art. He that can swim needs not despair to fly; to swim is to fly in a grosser fluid, and to fly is to swim in a subtler. We are only to proportion our power of resistance to the different density of matter through which we are to pass. You will be necessarily upborne by the air if you can renew any impulse upon it faster than the air can recede from the pressure."

"But the exercise of swimming," said the Prince, "is very laborious; the strongest limbs are soon wearied. I am afraid the act of flying will be yet more violent; and wings will be of no great use unless we can fly further than we can swim."

"The labour of rising from the ground," said the artist, "will be great, as we see it in the heavier domestic fowls; but as we mount higher, the earth's attraction and the body's gravity will be gradually diminished, till we shall arrive at a region where the man shall float in the air without any tendency to fall; no care will then be necessary but to move forward, which the gentlest impulse will effect. You, sir, whose curiosity is so extensive, will easily conceive with what pleasure a philosopher, furnished with wings and hovering in the sky, would see the earth and all its inhabitants rolling beneath him, and presenting to him successively, by its diurnal motion, all the countries within the same parallel. How must it amuse the pendent spectator to see the moving scene of land and ocean, cities and deserts; to survey with equal security the marts of trade and the fields of battle; mountains infested by barbarians, and fruitful regions gladdened by plenty and lulled by peace. How easily shall we then trace the Nile through all his passages, pass over to distant regions, and examine the face of Nature from one extremity of the earth to the other."

" All this," said the Prince " is much to be desired, but I am afraid that no man will be able to breathe in these regions of speculation and tranquillity. I have been told that respiration is difficult upon lofty mountains; yet from these precipices, though so high as to produce great tenuity of air, it is very easy to fall; therefore I suspect that from any height where life can be supported, there may be danger of too quick descent."

" Nothing," replied the artist, " will ever be attempted if all possible objections must be first overcome. If you will favour my project, I will try the first flight at my own hazard. I have considered the structure of all volant animals, and find the folding continuity of the bat's wings most easily accommodated to the human form. Upon this model I shall begin my task to-morrow; and in a year expect to tower into the air beyond the malice and pursuit of man. But I will work only on this condition : that the art shall not be divulged, and that you shall not require me to make wings for any but ourselves."

" Why," said Rasselas, " should you envy others so great an advantage? All skill ought to be exerted for universal good; every man has owed much to others, and ought to repay the kindness that he has received."

" If men were all virtuous," returned the artist, " I should with great alacrity teach them to fly. But what would be the security of the good if the bad could at pleasure invade them from the sky? Against an army sailing through the clouds, neither walls, mountains, nor seas, could afford security. A flight of northern savages might hover in the wind, and light with irresistible violence upon the capital of a fruitful region. Even this valley, the retreat of princes, the abode of happiness, might be violated by the sudden descent of some of the naked nations that swarm on the coast of the southern sea ! "

The Prince promised secrecy, and waited for the performance, not wholly hopeless of success.

He visited the work from time to time, observed its progress, and remarked many ingenious contrivances to facilitate motion, and unite levity with strength. The artist was every day more certain that he should leave vultures and eagles behind him, and the contagion of his confidence seized upon the Prince. In a year the wings were finished ; and on a morning appointed the maker appeared, furnished for flight, on a little promontory : he waved his pinions a while to gather air, then leaped from his stand, and in an instant dropped into the lake. His wings, which were of no use in the air, sustained him in the water ; and the Prince drew him to land half dead with terror and vexation.

(Rasselas.)

LAURENCE STERNE (1713–1768)
I.—UNCLE TOBY ON HIS HOBBY-HORSE

WHEN a man gives himself up to the government of a ruling passion,—or, in other words, when his hobby-horse grows headstrong,——farewell cool reason and fair discretion !

My uncle *Toby's* wound was near well, and as soon as the surgeon recovered his surprise, and could get leave to say as much——he told him, 'twas just beginning to incarnate ; and that if no fresh exfoliation happened, which there was no sign of,—it would be dried up in five or six weeks. The sound of as many Olympiads, twelve hours before, would have conveyed an idea of shorter duration to my uncle *Toby's* mind.——The succession of his ideas was now rapid,—he burnt with impatience to put his design in execution ;——and so, without consulting farther with any soul living,—which, by the bye, I think is right, when you are predetermined to take no one soul's advice,——he privately ordered *Trim*, his man, to pack up a bundle of lint and dressings, and hire a chariot-and-four to be at the door exactly by twelve o'clock that day, when he knew my father would be upon 'Change.——So leaving a bank-note upon the table for the surgeon's care of him, and a letter of tender thanks for his brother's—he packed up his maps, his books of fortification, his instruments, etc., and by the help of a crutch on one side, and *Trim* on the other,——my uncle *Toby* embarked for *Shandy-Hall*.

The reason, or rather the rise of this sudden demigration was as follows :

The table in my uncle *Toby's* room, and at which, the night before this change happened, he was sitting with his maps, etc., about him—being somewhat of the smallest, for that infinity of great and small instruments of knowledge which usually lay crowded upon it—he had the accident, in reaching over for his tobacco-box, to throw down his compasses, and in stooping to take the compasses up, with his sleeve he threw down his case of instruments and snuffers;—and as the dice took a run against him, in his endeavouring to catch the snuffers in falling,——he thrust Monsieur *Blondell* off the table, and Count *de Pagan* o'top of him.

'Twas to no purpose for a man lame as my uncle *Toby* was, to think of redressing these evils by himself,—he rung his bell for his man *Trim ;*——*Trim*, quoth my uncle *Toby*, prithee see what confusion I have here been making—I must have some better contrivance, *Trim*.——Can'st thou take my rule, and measure the length and breadth of this table, and then go and bespeak me one as big again?——Yes, an' please your Honour, replied *Trim*, making a bow; but I hope your Honour will be soon well enough to get down to your country-seat, where,—as your Honour takes so much pleasure in fortification, we could manage this matter to a T.

I must here inform you, that this servant of my uncle *Toby's*, who went by the name of *Trim*, had been a corporal in my uncle's own company,—his real name was *James Butler*,—but having got the nick-name of *Trim* in the regiment, my uncle *Toby*, unless when he happened to be very angry with him, would never call him by any other name.

The poor fellow had been disabled for the service, by a wound on his left knee by a musket-bullet, at the battle of *Landen*, which was two years before the affair of *Namur ;*—and as the fellow was well-beloved in the regiment, and a handy fellow into the bargain, my uncle *Toby* took him for his servant; and of an excellent use was he, attending my uncle *Toby* in the camp and in his quarters as a valet, groom, barber, cook, sempster, and nurse; and indeed, from first to last, waited upon him and served him with great fidelity and affection.

My uncle *Toby* loved the man in return, and what attached him more to him still, was the similitude of their knowledge.—— For Corporal *Trim* (for so, for the future, I shall call him), by four years' occasional attention to his Master's discourse upon fortified towns, and the advantage of prying and peeping continually into his Master's plans, etc., exclusive and besides what he gain HOBBY-HORSICALLY, as a body-servant, *Non Hobby Horsical per se ;*——had become no mean proficient in the science; and was thought, by the cook and chamber-maid, to know as much of the nature of strong-holds as my uncle *Toby* himself.

I have but one more stroke to give to finish Corporal *Trim's* character,——and it is the only dark line in it.—The fellow loved to advise,—or rather to hear himself talk; his carriage, however, was so perfectly respectful, 'twas easy to keep him silent when you had 'him so; but set his tongue a-going,—you had no hold of him—he was voluble;—the eternal interlardings of *your Honour*, with the respectfulness of Corporal *Trim's* manner, interceding so strong in behalf of his elocution,—that though you might have been incommoded,——you could not well be angry. My uncle *Toby* was seldom either the one or the other with him,—or, at least, this fault, in *Trim*, broke no squares with them. My uncle *Toby*, as I said, loved the man;——and besides, as he ever looked upon a faithful servant,—but as an humble friend,—he could not bear to stop his mouth.——Such was Corporal *Trim*.

If I durst presume, continued *Trim*, to give your Honour my advice, and speak my opinion in this matter.—Thou art welcome, *Trim*, quoth my uncle *Toby*—speak,——speak what thou thinkest upon the subject, man, without fear. Why then, replied *Trim* (not hanging his ears and scratching his head like a country lout, but (stroking his hair back from his forehead, and standing erect as before his division,—I think, quoth *Trim*, advancing his left, which was his lame leg, a little forwards,—and pointing with his right hand open towards a map of *Dunkirk*, which was pinned against the hangings,——I think, quoth Corporal *Trim*, with humble submission to your Honour's better judgment,—— that these ravelins, bastions, curtains, and horn-works, make but a poor, contemptible, fiddle-faddle piece of work of it here upon paper, compared to what your Honour and I could make of it were we in the country by ourselves, and had but a rood, or a rood and a half of ground to do what we pleased with : As summer is coming on, continued *Trim*, your Honour might sit out of doors, and give me the nography—(Call it ichnography, quoth my uncle,)——of the town or citadel, your Honour was pleased to sit down before,—and I will be shot by your Honour upon the glacis of it, if I did not fortify it to your Honour's

mind——I dare say thou would'st, *Trim*, quoth my uncle.—
For if your Honour, continued the Corporal, could but mark
me the polygon, with its exact lines and angles—That I could
do very well, quoth my uncle.—I would begin with the fossé,
and if your Honour could tell me the proper depth and breadth
—I can to a hair's breadth, *Trim*, replied my uncle.—I would
throw out the earth upon this hand towards the town for the
scarp,—and on that hand towards the campaign for the counter-
scarp.—Very right, *Trim*, quoth my uncle *Toby* :——And
when I had sloped them to your mind,——an' please your
Honour, I would face the glacis, as the finest fortifications are
done in *Flanders*, with sods,——and as your Honour knows
they should be,—and I would make the walls and parapets
with sods too.—The best engineers call them gazons, *Trim*,
said my uncle *Toby*.——Whether they are gazons or sods, is
not much matter, replied *Trim* ; your Honour knows they are
ten times beyond a facing either of brick or stone.——I know
they are, *Trim*, in some respects,——quoth my uncle *Toby*,
nodding his head;—for a cannon-ball enters into the gazon,
right onwards, without bringing any rubbish down with it
which might fill the fossé (as was the case at *St. Nicolas's* gate),
and facilitate the passage over it.

Your Honour understands these matters, replied Corporal
Trim, better than any officer in his Majesty's service;——but
would your Honour please to let the bespeaking of the table
alone, and let us but go into the country, I would work under
your Honour's directions like a horse, and make fortifications
for you something like a tansy, with all their batteries, saps,
ditches, and palisadoes, that it should be worth all the world's
riding twenty miles to go and see it.

My uncle *Toby* blushed as red as scarlet as *Trim* went on;—
but it was not a blush of guilt,—of modesty,—or of anger,—it
was a blush of joy;—he was fired with Corporal *Trim's* project
and description.——*Trim !* said my uncle *Toby*, thou hast said
enough.—We might begin the campaign, continued *Trim*, on
the very day that his Majesty and the Allies take the field, and
demolish them town by town as fast as—*Trim*, quoth my uncle
Toby, say no more. Your Honour, continued *Trim*, might sit
in your arm-chair (pointing to it) this fine weather, giving me
your orders, and I would——Say no more, *Trim*, quoth my
uncle *Toby*——Besides, your Honour would get not only
pleasure and good pastime,—but good air, and good exercise,
and good health,—and your Honour's wound would be well
in a month. Thou hast said enough, *Trim*,—quoth my uncle

Toby (putting his hand into his breeches-pocket)——I like thy project mightily.—And if your Honour pleases, I'll this moment go and buy a pioneer's spade to take down with us, and I'll bespeak a shovel and a pick-axe, and a couple of——Say no more, *Trim*, quoth my uncle *Toby*, leaping up upon one leg, quite overcome with rapture,—and thrusting a guinea into *Trim's* hand,—*Trim*, said my uncle *Toby*, say no more;—but go down, *Trim*, this moment, my lad, and bring up my supper this instant.

Trim ran down and brought up his master's supper,——to no purpose :—*Trim's* plan of operation ran so in my uncle *Toby's* head, he could not taste it.—*Trim*, quoth my uncle *Toby*, get me to bed.—'Twas all one.—Corporal *Trim's* description had fired his imagination,—my uncle *Toby* could not shut his eyes.—The more he considered it, the more bewitching the scene appeared to him ;—so that, two full hours before day-light, he had come to a final determination, and had concerted the whole plan of his and Corporal *Trim's* decampment.

My uncle *Toby* had a little neat country-house of his own, in the village where my father's estate lay at *Shandy*, which had been left him by an old uncle, with a small estate of about one hundred pounds a-year. Behind this house, and contiguous to it, was a kitchen-garden of about half an acre ; and at the bottom of the garden, and cut off from it by a tall yew hedge, was a bowling-green, containing just about as much ground as Corporal *Trim* wished for ;—so that as *Trim* uttered the words, " A rood and a half of ground to do what they would with,"—this identical bowling-green instantly presented itself, and became curiously painted all at once, upon the retina of my uncle *Toby's* fancy ;—which was the physical cause of making him change colour, or at least of heightening his blush, to that immoderate degree I spoke of.

Never did lover post down to a beloved mistress with more heat and expectation, than my uncle *Toby* did, to enjoy this self-same thing in private ;—I say in private ; for it was sheltered from the house, as I told you, by a tall yew hedge, and was covered on the other three sides, from mortal sight, by rough holly and thick-set flowering shrubs :—so that the idea of not being seen, did not a little contribute to the idea of pleasure pre-conceived in my uncle *Toby's* mind.—Vain thought ! however thick it was planted about,——or private soever it might seem,—to think, dear uncle *Toby*, of enjoying a thing which took up a whole rood and a half of ground,——and not have it known !

How my uncle *Toby* and Corporal *Trim* managed this matter,

——with the history of their campaigns, which were no way barren of events,——may make no uninteresting under-plot in the epitasis and working-up of this drama.—At present the scene must drop,—and change for the parlour fire-side.

(*Tristram Shandy.*)

II.—The Poor Ass

——'Twas by a poor ass, who had just turned in with a couple of large panniers upon his back, to collect eleemosynary turnip-tops and cabbage-leaves; and stood dubious, with his two fore-feet on the inside of the threshold, and with his two hinder feet towards the street, as not knowing very well whether he was to go in or no.

Now, 'tis an animal (be in what hurry I may) I cannot bear to strike——there is a patient endurance of sufferings, wrote so unaffectedly in his looks and carriage, which pleads so mightily for him, that it always disarms me; and to that degree, that I do not like to speak unkindly to him : on the contrary, meet him where I will—whether in town or country—in cart or under panniers—whether in liberty or bondage——I have ever something civil to say to him on my part; and as one word begets another (if he has as little to do as I)——I generally fall into conversation with him; and surely never is my imagination so busy as in framing his responses from the etchings of his countenance—and where those carry me not deep enough——in flying from my own heart into his, and seeing what is natural for an ass to think—as well as a man, upon the occasion. In truth, it is the only creature of all the classes of beings below me, with whom I can do this : for parrots, jackdaws, etc.——I never exchange a word with them——nor with the apes, etc., for pretty near the same reason; they act by rote, as the others speak of it, and equally make me silent : nay my dog and my cat, though I value them both——(and for my dog he would speak if he could)—yet somehow or other, they neither of them possess the talents for conversation——I can make nothing of a discourse with them, beyond the *proposition*, the *reply*, and *rejoinder*, which terminated my father's and my mother's conversations, in his beds of justice——and those utter'd——there's an end of the dialogue——

—But with an ass, I can commune for ever.

Come, *Honesty!* said I,——seeing it was impracticable to pass betwixt him and the gate——art thou for coming in, or going out?

The ass twisted his head round to look up the street——

Well—replied I—we'll wait a minute for thy driver :
———He turned his head thoughtful about, and looked wistfully the opposite way——

I understand thee perfectly, answered I——If thou takest a wrong step in this affair, he will cudgel thee to death——Well! a minute is but a minute, and if it saves a fellow-creature a drubbing, it shall not be set down as ill spent.

He was eating the stem of an artichoke as this discourse went on, and in the little peevish contentions of nature betwixt hunger and unsavouriness, had dropt it out of his mouth half a dozen times, and pick'd it up again——God help thee, *Jack!* said I, thou hast a bitter breakfast on't—and many a bitter day's labour,—and many a bitter blow, I fear, for its wages—— 'tis all—all bitterness to thee, whatever life is to others.——And now thy mouth, if one knew the truth of it, is as bitter, I dare say, as soot—(for he had cast aside the stem) and thou hast not a friend perhaps in all this world, that will give thee a macaroon.——In saying this, I pull'd out a paper of 'em, which I had just purchased, and gave him one—and at this moment that I am telling it, my heart smites me, that there was more of pleasantry in the conceit, of seeing *how* an ass would eat a maca- roon——than of benevolence in giving him one, which presided in the act.

When the ass had eaten his macaroon, I press'd him to come in——the poor beast was heavy loaded——his legs seem'd to tremble under him——he hung rather backwards, and as I pull'd at his halter, it broke short in my hand——he look'd up pensive in my face—"Don't thrash me with it—but if you will, you may "——If I do, said I, I'll be d——d.

The word was but one-half of it pronounced, like the abbess of *Andoüillets'*—(so there was no sin in it)—when a person coming in, let fall a thundering bastinado upon the poor devil's crupper, which put an end to the ceremony.

(*Tristram Shandy.*)

THOMAS GRAY (1716–1771)

I.—THE GRANDE CHARTREUSE

IT is a fortnight since we set out hence, upon a little excursion to Geneva. We took the longest road which lies through Savoy, on purpose to see a famous monastery called the Grande Chartreuse, and had no reason to think our time lost. After having travelled seven days very slow—for we did not change horses, it being impossible for a chaise to go post in these roads—

we arrived at a little village among the mountains of Savoy, called Echelles; from thence we proceeded on horses, who are used to the way, to the mountain of the Chartreuse. It is six miles to the top; the road runs winding up it, commonly not six feet broad; on one hand is the rock, with woods of pine trees hanging overhead; on the other, a monstrous precipice, almost perpendicular, at the bottom of which rolls a torrent, that sometimes tumbling among the fragments of stone that have fallen from on high, and sometimes precipitating itself down vast descents with a noise like thunder, which is still made greater by the echo from the mountains on each side, concurs to form one of the most solemn, the most romantic, and the most astonishing scenes I ever beheld. Add to this the strange views made by the crags and cliffs on the other hand, the cascades that in many places throw themselves from the very summit down into the vale and the river below, and many other particulars impossible to describe, you will conclude we had no occasion to repent our pains. This place St. Bruno chose to retire to, and upon its very top founded the aforesaid convent, which is the superior of the whole order. When we came there, the two fathers who are commissioned to entertain strangers—for the rest must neither speak one to another, nor to any one else—received us very kindly and set before us a repast of dried fish, eggs, butter, and fruits, all excellent in their kind, and extremely neat. They pressed us to spend the night there, and to stay some days with them; but this we could not do, so they led us about their house, which is, you must think, like a little city, for there are a hundred fathers, besides three hundred servants, that make their clothes, grind their corn, press their wine, and do everything among themselves. The whole is quite orderly and simple; nothing of finery; but the wonderful decency and the strange situation, more than supply the place of it. In the evening we descended by the same way, passing through many clouds that were then forming themselves on the mountain's side.

(Letters.)

II.—To Grasmere

Bid farewell to Keswick and took the Ambleside road in a gloomy morning; wind east and afterwards north-east; about two miles from the town mounted an eminence called Castle Rigg, and the sun breaking out discovered the most beautiful view I have yet seen of the whole valley behind me, the two lakes, the river, the mountain, all in their glory! had almost a mind to have gone back again.   The road in some little patches is not completed, but good country road, through sound, but narrow and stony lanes, very safe in broad daylight.   This is the case about Cause-way foot, and among Naddle-fells to Lanthwaite.   The vale you go in has little breadth, the mountains are vast and rocky, the fields little and poor, and the inhabitants are now making hay, and see not the sun by two hours in a day so long as at Keswick.   Came to the foot of Helvellyn, along which runs an excellent road, looking down from a little height on Lee's water (called also Thirl-meer or Wibom-water), and soon descending on its margin.   The lake from its depth looks black (though really as clear as glass), and from the gloom of the vast crags, that scowl over it; it is narrow and about three miles long, resembling a river in its course; little shining torrents hurry down the rocks to join it, with not a bush to overshadow them, or cover their march : all is rock and loose stones up to the very brow, which lies so near your way, that not above half the height of Helvellyn can be seen.

Passed by the little chapel of Wibom, out of which the Sunday congregation were then issuing.   Past a beck near Dunmailraise and entered Westmorland a second time, now begin to see Helm-crag, distinguished from its rugged neighbours not so much by its height, as by the strange broken outline of its top, like some gigantic building demolished, and the stones that composed it flung across each other in wild confusion.   Just beyond it opens one of the sweetest landscapes that art ever attempted to imitate.   The bosom of the mountains, spreading here into a broad basin discovers in the midst Grasmere-water, its margin is hollowed into small bays with bold eminences : some of them rocks, some of soft turf that half conceal and vary the figure of the little lake they command.   From the shore a low promontory pushes itself far into the water, and on it stands a white village with the parish church rising in the midst of it, hanging enclosures, corn-fields and meadows green as an emerald, with their trees and hedges and cattle, fill up the whole space from the edge of the water.   Just opposite to you is a large farm-house, at the bottom of a steep smooth lawn embosomed in old woods, which climb half-way up the mountain's side, and discover above them a broken line of crags, that crown the scene.   Not a single red tile, no flaming gentleman's house, or garden walls break in upon the repose of this little unsuspected paradise, but all is peace, rusticity, and happy poverty in its neatest, most becoming attire.

(*Journal in the Lakes.*)

HORACE WALPOLE, EARL OF ORFORD (1717–1797)

I.—To Miss Hannah More

Strawberry Hill,
August 29, 1796.

You are not only the most beneficent but the most benevolent of human beings. Not content with being a perfect
saint yourself, which (forgive me for saying) does not always
imply prodigious compassion for others; not satisfied with
being the most disinterested, nay, the reverse of all patriots,
for you sacrifice your very slender fortune, not to improve it,
but to keep the poor honest instead of corrupting them; and
you write politics as simply, intelligibly, and unartfully, not as
cunningly as you can to mislead. Well, with all these giant
virtues, you can find room and time in your heart and occupa-
tions for harbouring and exercising what the French invented
and called *les petits morales*, which were to supply society with
filigrain duties, in the room of all the virtues, which they abol-
ished on their road to the adoption of philosophy and atheism.
Yes, though for ever busied in exercising services and charities
for individuals, or for whole bodies of people, you do not leave
a cranny empty into which you can slip a kindness. Your
enquiry after me to Miss Berry is so friendly that I cannot
trust solely to her thanking you for your letter, as I am sure
she will, having sent it to her as she is bathing in the sea at
Bognor Rocks; but I must with infinite gratitude give you a
brief account of myself—a very poor one indeed must I give.
Condemned as a cripple to my couch for the rest of my days I
doubt I am. Though perfectly healed, and even without a
scar, my leg is so weakened that I have not recovered the least
use of it, nor can move across my chamber unless lifted up and
held by two of my servants. This constitutes me totally a
prisoner. But why should I not be so? What business had
I to live to the brink of seventy-nine? And why should one
litter the world at that age? Then, I thank God, I have vast
blessings; I have preserved my eyes, ears, and teeth; I have no
pain left; and I would bet with any dormouse that it cannot
outsleep me. And when one can afford to pay for every relief,
comfort, or assistance that can be procured at fourscore, dares
one complain? Must not one reflect on the thousands of old
poor, who are suffering martyrdom, and have none of these
alleviations? Oh, my good friend, I must consider myself as
at my best; for if I drag on a little longer, can I expect to remain
even so tolerably? Nay, does the world present a pleasing

scene? Are not the devils escaped out of the swine, and over-
running the earth headlong?

What a theme for meditation, that the excellent humane
Louis Seize should have been prevented from saving himself
by that monster Drouet, and that that execrable wretch should
be saved even by those, some of whom one may suppose he
meditated to massacre; for at what does a Frenchman stop?
But I will quit this shocking subject, and for another reason too :
I omitted one of my losses, almost the use of my fingers : they
are so lame that I cannot write a dozen lines legibly, but am
forced to have recourse to my secretary. I will only reply by
a word or two to a question you seem to ask ; how I like Camilla?
I do not care to say how little. Alas ! she has reversed experience, which I have long thought reverses its own utility by coming
at the wrong end of our life when we do not want it. This
author knew the world and penetrated characters before she
had stepped over the threshold ; and now she has seen so much
of it, she has little or no insight at all : perhaps she apprehended
having seen too much, and kept the bags of foul air that she
brought from the Cave of Tempests too closely tied.

Adieu, thou who mightest be one of the cleverest of women
if thou didst not prefer being one of the best ! and when I say
one of the best, I have not engaged my vote for the second.—
Yours most gratefully.

(Letters.)

II.—STRAWBERRY HILL

*Twickenham,
June 8, 1747.*

You perceive by my date that I am got into a new camp, and
have left my tub at Windsor. It is a little plaything-house that I
got out of Mrs. Chevenix's shop, and is the prettiest bauble you
ever saw. It is set in enamelled meadows, with filigree hedges :

A small Euphrates through the piece is rolled,
And little finches wave their wings in gold.

Two delightful roads that you would call dusty, supply me continually with coaches and chaises ; barges as solemn as Barons
of the Exchequer move under my window ; Richmond Hill and
Ham walks bound my prospect ; but, thank God ! the Thames
is between me and the Duchess of Queensberry. Dowagers as
plenty as flounders inhabit all around, and Pope's ghost is just
now skimming under my window by a most poetical moonlight.
I have about land enough to keep such a farm as Noah's, when
he set up in the ark with a pair of each kind ; but my cottage

is rather cleaner than I believe his was after they had been cooped up together forty days. The Chevenixes had tricked it out for themselves : up two pair of stairs is what they call Mr. Chevenix's library, furnished with three maps, one shelf, a bust of Sir Isaac Newton, and a lame telescope without any glasses. Lord John Sackville predecessed me here, and instituted certain games called cricketalia, which have been celebrated this very evening in honour of him in a neighbouring meadow.

(Letters.)

GILBERT WHITE (1720–1793)
I.—SWALLOWS

IF ever I saw anything like actual migration, it was last Michaelmas Day. I was travelling, and out early in the morning; at first there was a vast fog, but, by the time that I was got seven or eight miles from home towards the coast, the sun broke out into a delicate warm day. We were then on a large heath or common, and I could discern, as the mist began to break away, great numbers of swallows (*hirundines rusticæ*) clustering on the stunted shrubs and bushes, as if they had roosted there all night. As soon as the air became clear and pleasant they were all on the wing at once; and, by a placid and easy flight, proceeded on southward towards the sea; after this I did not see any more flocks, only now and then a straggler.

I cannot agree with those persons that assert that the swallow kind disappear some and some gradually, as they come, for the bulk of them seem to withdraw at once; only some stragglers stay behind a long while, and do never, there is the greatest reason to believe, leave this island. Swallows seem to lay themselves up, and to come forth in a warm day, as bats do continually of a warm evening, after they have disappeared for weeks. For a very respectable gentleman assured me that, as he was walking with some friends under Merton Wall on a remarkably hot noon, either in the last week in December or the first week in January, he espied three or four swallows huddled together on the moulding of one of the windows of that college. I have frequently remarked that swallows are seen later at Oxford than elsewhere; is it owing to the vast massy buildings of that place, to the many waters round it, or to what else ?

When I used to rise in the morning last autumn, and see the swallows and martins clustering on the chimneys and thatch of the neighbouring cottages, I could not help being touched with a secret delight, mixed with some degree of mortification;

with delight, to observe how much ardour and punctuality those poor little birds obeyed the strong impulse towards migration, or hiding, imprinted on their minds by their great Creator; and with some degree of mortification when I reflected that, after all our pains and inquiries, we are yet not quite certain to what regions they do migrate, and are still farther embarrassed to find that some do not actually migrate at all.

(Natural History of Selborne.)

II.—THE GOAT-SUCKER

There is no bird, I believe, whose manners I have studied more than that of the *caprimulgus* (the goat-sucker), as it is a wonderful and curious creature; but I have always found that though sometimes it may chatter as it flies, as I know it does, yet in general it utters its jarring note sitting on a bough; and I have for many a half hour watched it as it sat with its under mandible quivering, and particularly this summer. It perches usually on a bare twig, with its head lower than its tail, in an attitude well expressed by your draughtsman in the folio *British Zoology*. This bird is most punctual in beginning its song exactly at the close of day—so exactly that I have known it strike up more than once or twice just at the report of the Portsmouth evening gun, which we can hear when the weather is still. It appears to me past all doubt that its notes are formed by organic impulse, by the powers of the parts of its windpipe formed for sound, just as cats purr. You will credit me, I hope, when I assure you that, as my neighbours were assembled in an hermitage on the side of a steep hill where we drink tea, one of these churn-owls came and settled on the cross of that little straw edifice and began to chatter, and continued his note for many minutes : and we were all struck with wonder to find that the organs of that little animal, when put in motion, gave a sensible vibration to the whole building ! This bird also sometimes makes a small squeak, repeated four or five times; and I have observed that to happen when the cock has been pursuing the hen in a toying way through the boughs of a tree.

(Natural History of Selborne.)

OLIVER GOLDSMITH (1728–1774)

I.—THE FAMILY OF WAKEFIELD

I WAS ever of opinion, that the honest man who married and brought up a large family, did more service than he who continued single and only talked of population. From this motive, I had scarcely taken orders a year, before I began to think

seriously of matrimony, and chose my wife, as she did her wed-
ding-gown, not for a fine glossy surface, but for such qualities
as would wear well. To do her justice, she was a good-natured
notable woman; and as for breeding, there were few country
ladies who could show more. She could read any English book
without much spelling; but for pickling, preserving, and cookery,
none could excel her. She prided herself also upon being an
excellent contriver in housekeeping; though I could never find
that we grew richer with all her contrivances.

However, we loved each other tenderly, and our fondness
increased as we grew old. There was in fact, nothing that
could make us angry with the world or each other. We had an
elegant house situated in a fine country, and a good neighbourhood. The year was spent in moral or rural amusements, in
visiting our rich neighbours, and relieving such as were poor.
We had no revolutions to fear, nor fatigues to undergo; all
our adventures were by the fire-side, and all our migrations
from the blue bed to the brown.

As we lived near the road, we often had the traveller or
stranger visit us to taste our gooseberry-wine, for which we
had great reputation; and I profess with the veracity of an
historian, that I never knew one of them find fault with it.
Our cousins too, even to the fortieth remove, all remembered
their affinity, without any help from the herald's office, and
came very frequently to see us. Some of them did us no great
honour by these claims of kindred; as we had the blind, the
maimed, and the halt amongst the number. However, my wife
always insisted that as they were the same flesh and blood
they should sit with us at the same table. So that if we had
not very rich, we generally had very happy friends about us;
for this remark will hold good through life, that the poorer the
guest, the better pleased he ever is with being treated; and as
some men gaze with admiration at the colours of a tulip, or the
wings of a butterfly, so I was by nature an admirer of happy
human faces. However, when any one of our relations was
found to be a person of very bad character, a troublesome guest,
or one we desired to get rid of, upon his leaving my house, I
ever took care to lend him a riding-coat, or a pair of boots, or
sometimes a horse of small value, and I always had the satisfaction of finding he never came back to return them. By
this the house was cleared of such as we did not like; but never
was the family of Wakefield known to turn the traveller or the
poor dependent out of doors.

Thus we lived several years in a state of much happiness,

not but that we sometimes had those little rubs which Providence sends to enhance the value of its favours. My orchard was often robbed by schoolboys, and my wife's custards plundered by the cats or the children. The 'Squire would sometimes fall asleep in the most pathetic parts of my sermon, or his lady return my wife's civilities at church with a mutilated courtesy. But we soon got over the uneasiness caused by such accidents, and usually in three or four days began to wonder how they vexed us.

My children, the offspring of temperance, as they were educated without softness, so they were at once well formed and healthy; my sons hardy and active, my daughters beautiful and blooming. When I stood in the midst of the little circle, which promised to be the supports of my declining age, I could not avoid repeating the famous story of Count Abensberg, who, in Henry II's progress through Germany, while other courtiers came with their treasures, brought his thirty-two children, and presented them to his sovereign as the most valuable offering he had to bestow. In this manner, though I had but six, I considered them as a very valuable present made to my country, and consequently looked upon it as my debtor. Our eldest son was named George, after his uncle, who left us ten thousand pounds. Our second child, a girl, I intended to call after her aunt Grissel; but my wife, who during her pregnancy had been reading romances, insisted upon her being called Olivia. In less than another year we had another daughter, and now I was determined that Grissel should be her name; but a rich relation taking a fancy to stand godmother, the girl was, by her directions, called Sophia; so that we had two romantic names in the family; but I solemnly protest I had no hand in it. Moses was our next, and after an interval of twelve years, we had two sons more.

It would be fruitless to deny my exultation when I saw my little ones about me; but the vanity and the satisfaction of my wife were even greater than mine. When our visitors would say, " Well, upon my word, Mrs. Primrose, you have the finest children in the whole country : "—" Ay, neighbour," she would answer, " they are as heaven made them, handsome enough, if they be good enough; for handsome is that handsome does." And then she would bid the girls hold up their heads; who, to conceal nothing, were certainly very handsome. Mere outside is so very trifling a circumstance with me, that I should scarcely have remembered to mention it, had it not been a general topic of conversation in the country. Olivia, now about eighteen, had that luxuriancy of beauty, with which painters generally draw Hebe; open, sprightly, and commanding. Sophia's features were not so striking at first, but often did more certain execution; for they were soft, modest, and alluring. The one vanquished by a single blow, the other by efforts successively repeated.

The temper of a woman is generally formed from the turn of her features, at least it was so with my daughters. Olivia wished for many lovers, Sophia to secure one. Olivia was often affected from too great a desire to please. Sophia even represt excellence, from her fears to offend. The one entertained me with her vivacity when I was gay, the other with her sense when I was serious. But these qualities were never carried to excess in either, and I have often seen them exchange characters for a whole day together. A suit of mourning has transformed my coquette into a prude, and a new set of ribbons has given her younger sister more than natural vivacity. My eldest son George was bred at Oxford, as I intended him for one of the learned professions. My second boy Moses, whom I designed for business, received a sort of miscellaneous education at home. But it is needless to attempt describing the particular characters of young people that had seen but very little of the world. In short, a family likeness prevailed through all, and properly speaking, they had but one character, that of being all equally generous, simple, and inoffensive.

(The Vicar of Wakefield.)

II.—FAMILY AMBITIONS

I now began to find, that all my long and painful lectures upon temperance, simplicity, and contentment, were entirely disregarded. The distinctions lately paid us by our betters awaked that pride which I had laid asleep, but not removed.— Our windows, again, as formerly, were filled with washes for the neck and face. The sun was dreaded as an enemy to the skin without doors, and the fire as a spoiler of the complexion within. —My wife observed that rising too early would hurt her daughter's eyes, that working after dinner would redden their noses, and she convinced me that the hands never looked so white as when they did nothing. Instead therefore of finishing George's shirts, we now had them new-modelling their old gauzes, or flourishing upon catgut. The poor Miss Flamboroughs, their former gay companions, were cast off as mean acquaintance, and the whole conversation ran upon high life and high-lived company, with pictures, taste, Shakspeare, and the musical glasses.

But we could have borne all this, had not a fortune-telling

gipsy come to raise us into perfect sublimity. The tawny sibyl no sooner appeared, than my girls came running to me for a shilling a-piece to cross her hand with silver. To say the truth I was tired of being always wise, and could not help gratifying their request, because I loved to see them happy. I gave each of them a shilling; though for the honour of the family it must be observed, that they never went without money themselves, as my wife always let them have a guinea each, to keep in their pockets, but with strict injunctions never to change it. After they had been closeted up with the fortune-teller for some time, I knew by their looks, upon their returning, that they had been promised something great.—" Well, my girls, how have you sped? Tell me, Livy, has the fortune-teller given thee a pennyworth? "—" I protest, Papa," says the girl, " I believe she deals with somebody that's not right; for she positively declared, that I am to be married to a 'Squire in less than a twelvemonth! "—" Well, now Sophy, my child," said I, " and what sort of a husband are you to have? "—" Sir," replied she, " I am to have a Lord soon after my sister has married the Squire."—" How," cried I, " is that all you are to have for your two shillings? Only a Lord and a 'Squire for two shillings! You fools, I could have promised you a Prince and a Nabob for half the money."

This curiosity of theirs, however, was attended with very serious effects : we now began to think ourselves designed by the stars to something exalted, and already anticipated our future grandeur.

It has been a thousand times observed, and I must observe it once more, that the hours we pass with happy prospects in view, are more pleasing than those crowned with fruition. In the first case we cook the dish to our own appetite ! in the latter, nature cooks it for us. It is impossible to repeat the train of agreeable reveries we called up for our entertainment. We looked upon our fortunes as once more rising; and as the whole parish asserted that the 'Squire was in love with my daughter, she was actually so with him; for they persuaded her into the passion. In this agreeable interval, my wife had the most lucky dreams in the world, which she took care to tell us every morning with great solemnity and exactness. It was one night a coffin and cross bones, the sign of an approaching wedding; at another time she imagined her daughter's pockets filled with farthings, a certain sign of their being shortly stuffed with gold. The girls themselves had their omens. They felt strange kisses on their lips; they saw rings in the candle, purses bounced from the fire, and true love-knots lurked in the bottom of every tea-cup.

Towards the end of the week we received a card from the town ladies; in which, with their compliments, they hoped to see all our family at church the Sunday following. All Saturday morning I could perceive, in consequence of this, my wife and daughters in close conference together, and now and then glancing at me with looks that betrayed a latent plot. To be sincere, I had strong suspicions that some absurd proposal was preparing for appearing with splendour next day.—In the evening they began their operations in a very regular manner, and my wife undertook to conduct the siege. After tea, when I seemed in spirits, she began thus :—" I fancy, Charles, my dear, we shall have a great deal of good company at our church to-morrow." —" Perhaps we may, my dear," returned I, " though you need be under no uneasiness about that, you shall have a sermon whether there be or not."—" That is what I expect," returned she ; " but I think, my dear, we ought to appear there as decently as possible, for who knows what may happen ? "—" Your precautions," replied I, " are highly commendable. A decent behaviour and appearance in church is what charms me. We should be devout and humble, cheerful and serene."—" Yes," cried she, " I know that; but I mean we should go there in as proper a manner as possible; not altogether like the scrubs about us."—" You are quite right, my dear," returned I, " and I was going to make the very same proposal. The proper manner of going is, to go there as early as possible, to have time for meditation before the service begins."—" Phoo, Charles," interrupted she, " all that is very true; but not what I would be at. I mean, we should go there genteelly. You know the church is two miles off, and I protest I don't like to see my daughters trudging up to their pew all blowzed and red with walking, and looking for all the world as if they had been winners at a smock race. Now, my dear, my proposal is this : there are our two plough horses, the colt that has been in our family these nine years, and his companion Blackberry, that has scarcely done an earthly thing for this month past. They are both grown fat and lazy. Why should not they do something as well as we ? And let me tell you, when Moses has trimmed them a little, they will cut a very tolerable figure."

To this proposal I objected, that walking would be twenty times more genteel than such a paltry conveyance, as Blackberry was wall-eyed, and the colt wanted the tail; that they had never been broke to the rein, but had a hundred vicious tricks : and that we had but one saddle and pillion in the whole house. All these objections, however, were overruled; so that I was obliged to comply. The next morning I perceived them not a little busy in collecting such materials as might be necessary for the expedition; but, as I found it would be a business of time, I walked on to the church before, and they promised speedily to follow. I waited near an hour in the reading desk for their arrival; but not finding them come as expected, I was obliged to begin, and went through the service, not without some uneasiness at finding them absent. This was increased when all was finished, and no appearance of the family. I therefore walked back by the horse-way, which was five miles round, though the foot-way was but two, and when got about half way home, perceived the procession marching slowly forwards towards the church; my son, my wife, and the two little ones, exalted on one horse, and my two daughters upon the other. I demanded the cause of their delay; but I soon found by their looks they had met with a thousand misfortunes on the road. The horse had at first refused to move from the door, till Mr. Burchell was kind enough to beat them forward for about two hundred yards with his cudgel. Next, the straps of my wife's pillion broke down, and they were obliged to stop to repair them before they could proceed. After that, one of the horses took into his head to stand still, and neither blows nor entreaties could prevail with him to proceed. He was just recovering from this dismal situation when I found them; but perceiving every thing safe, I own their present mortification did not much displease me, as it would give many opportunities of future triumph, and teach my daughters more humility.

(*The Vicar of Wakefield*.)

III.—A CITY NIGHT-PIECE

The clock just struck two; the expiring taper rises and sinks in the socket; the watchman forgets the hour in slumber; the laborious and the happy are at rest; and nothing wakes but meditation, guilt, revelry, and despair. The drunkard once more fills the destroying bowl; the robber walks his midnight round; and the suicide lifts his guilty arm against his own sacred person.

Let me no longer waste the night over the page of antiquity, or the sallies of contemporary genius, but pursue the solitary walk, where vanity, ever changing, but a few hours past, walked before me; where she kept up the pageants, and now, like a froward child, seems hushed with her own importunities.

What a gloom hangs all round! The dying lamp feebly emits a yellow gleam; no sound is heard but of the chiming clock, or the distant watch-dog. All the bustle of human pride is forgotten; an hour like this may well display the emptiness of human vanity.

There will come a time, when this temporary solitude may be made continual; and the city itself, like its inhabitants, fade away, and leave a desert in its room.

What cities as great as this have once triumphed in existence; had their victories as great, joy as just, and as unbounded; and, with short-sighted presumption, promised themselves immortality! Posterity can hardly trace the situation of some; the sorrowful traveller wanders over the awful ruins of others; and, as he beholds, he learns wisdom, and feels the transience of every sublunary possession.

"Here," he cries, "stood their citadel, now grown over with weeds; there their senate house, but now the haunt of every noxious reptile; temples and theatres stood here, now only an undistinguished heap of ruin. They are fallen; for luxury and avarice first made them feeble. The rewards of the state were conferred on amusing, and not on useful, members of society. Their riches and opulence invited the invaders, who, though at first repulsed, returned again, conquered by perseverance, and at last swept the defendants into undistinguished destruction."

How few appear in those streets which, but some few hours ago, were crowded! And those, who appear, now no longer wear their daily mask, nor attempt to hide their lewdness or their misery.

But who are those who make the streets their couch, and find a short repose from wretchedness at the doors of the opulent? These are strangers, wanderers, and orphans, whose circumstances are too humble to expect redress, and whose distresses are too great even for pity. Their wretchedness excites rather horror than pity. Some are without the covering even of rags, and others emaciated with disease; the world has disclaimed them; society turns its back upon their distress, and has given them up to nakedness and hunger. These poor shivering females have once seen happier days, and been flattered into beauty. They have been prostituted to the gay luxurious villain, and are now turned out to meet the severity of winter. Perhaps now, lying at the doors of their betrayers, they sue to wretches whose hearts are insensible, or debauchees, who may curse, but will not relieve them.

Why, why was I born a man, and yet see the sufferings of

wretches I cannot relieve? Poor houseless creatures! The world will give you reproaches, but will not give you relief. The slightest misfortunes of the great, the most imaginary uneasiness of the rich, are aggravated with all the power of eloquence, and held up to engage our attention and sympathetic sorrow. The poor weep unheeded, persecuted by every sub-ordinate species of tyranny; and every law, which gives others security, becomes an enemy to them.

Why was this heart of mine formed with so much sensibility; or why was not my fortune adapted to its impulse? Tenderness, without a capacity of relieving, only makes the man, who feels it, more wretched than the object, which sues for assistance. Adieu.

(The Citizen of the World.)

EDMUND BURKE (1729-1797)

I.—MARIE ANTOINETTE

IT is now sixteen or seventeen years since I saw the Queen of France, then the dauphiness, at Versailles; and surely never lighted on this orb, which she hardly seemed to touch, a more delightful vision. I saw her just above the horizon, decorating and cheering the elevated sphere she just began to move in,— glittering like the morning-star, full of life, and splendour, and joy. Oh! what a revolution! and what a heart must I have, to contemplate without emotion that elevation and that fall! Little did I dream when she added titles of veneration to those of enthusiastic, distant, respectful love, that she should ever be obliged to carry the sharp antidote against disgrace concealed in that bosom; little did I dream that I should have lived to see such disasters fall upon her in a nation of gallant men, in a nation of men of honour, and of cavaliers. I thought ten thousand swords must have leaped from their scabbards to avenge even a look that threatened her with insult. But the age of chivalry is gone. That of sophisters, economists, and calculators has succeeded; and the glory of Europe is extinguished for ever. Never, never more shall we behold that generous loyalty to rank and sex, that proud submission, that dignified obedience, that subordination of the heart, which kept alive, even in servitude itself, the spirit of an exalted freedom. The unbought grace of life, the cheap defence of nations, the nurse of manly sentiment, and heroic enterprise, is gone! It is gone, that sensibility of principle, that chastity of honour, which felt a stain like a wound, which inspired courage whilst it mitigated ferocity, which ennobled whatever it touched, and under which vice itself lost half its evil, by losing all its grossness.

(*Reflections on the French Revolution.*)

II.—SOCIETY

Society is indeed a contract. Subordinate contracts for objects of mere occasional interest may be dissolved at pleasure—but the state ought not to be considered nothing better than a partnership agreement in a trade of pepper and coffee, calico or tobacco, or some other such low concern, to be taken up for a little temporary interest, and to be dissolved by the fancy of the parties. It is to be looked on with other reverence; because it is not a partnership in things subservient only to the gross animal existence of a temporary and perishable nature. It is a partnership in all science; a partnership in all art; a partnership in every virtue, and in all perfection. As the ends of such a partnership cannot be obtained in many generations, it becomes a partnership not only between those who are living, but between those who are living, those who are dead, and those who are to be born. Each contract of each particular state is but a clause in the great primæval contract of eternal society, linking the lower with the higher natures, connecting the visible and invisible world, according to a fixed compact sanctioned by the inviolable oath which holds all physical and all moral natures, each in their appointed place. This law is not subject to the will of those, who by an obligation above them, and infinitely superior, are bound to submit their will to that law. The municipal corporations of that universal kingdom are not morally at liberty at their pleasure, and on their speculations of a contingent improvement, wholly to separate and tear asunder the bands of their subordinate community, and to dissolve it into an unsocial, uncivil, unconnected chaos of elementary principles. It is the first and supreme necessity only, a necessity that is not chosen, but chooses, a necessity paramount to deliberation, that admits no discussion, and demands no evidence, which alone can justify a resort to anarchy. This necessity is no exception to the rule; because this necessity itself is a part too of that moral and physical disposition of things, to which man must be obedient by consent of force: but if that which is only submission to necessity should be made the object of choice, the law is broken, nature is disobeyed, and the rebellious are outlawed, cast forth, and exiled, from this world of reason, and order, and peace, and virtue, and fruitful penitence, into the antagonist world of madness, discord, vice, confusion, and unavailing sorrow.

(*Reflections on the French Revolution.*)

III.—THE IMPEACHMENT OF WARREN HASTINGS

My lords, what is it that we want here to a great act of national justice? Do we want a cause, my lords? You have the cause of oppressed princes, of undone women of the first rank, of desolated provinces and of wasted kingdoms.

Do you want a criminal, my lords? When was there so much iniquity ever laid to the charge of any one! No, my lords, you must not look to punish any other such delinquent from India. Warren Hastings has not left substance enough in India to nourish such another delinquent.

My lords, is it a prosecutor you want? You have before you the Commons of Great Britain as prosecutors; and I believe, my lords, that the sun, in his beneficent progress round the world, does not behold a more glorious sight than that of men, separated from a remote people by the material bounds and barriers of nature, united by the bond of a social and moral community; all the Commons of England resenting, as their own, the indignities and cruelties that are offered to the people of India.

Do we want a tribunal? My lords, no example of antiquity, nothing in the modern world, nothing in the range of human imagination, can supply us with a tribunal like this. My lords, here we see virtually in the mind's eye that sacred majesty of the crown, under whose authority you sit and whose power you exercise. We see in that invisible authority what we all feel in reality and life, the beneficent powers and protecting justice of his majesty. We have here the heir apparent to the crown, such as the fond wishes of the people of England wish an heir apparent of the crown to be. We have here all the branches of the royal family in a situation between majesty and subjection, between the sovereign and the subject, offering a pledge in that situation for the support of the rights of the crown and the liberties of the people, both which extremities they touch. My lords, we have a great hereditary peerage here; those who have their own honour, the honour of their ancestors, and of their posterity to guard; and who will justify, as they have always justified, that provision in the constitution by which justice is made a hereditary office. My lords, we have here a new nobility, who have risen and exalted themselves by various merits, by great military services, which have extended the fame of this country from the rising to the setting sun; we have those who, by various civil merits and various civil talents, have been exalted to a situation which they well deserve, and in which they will justify the favour of their sovereign and the good opinion of their fellow-subjects, and make them rejoice to see those virtuous characters, that were the other day upon a level with them, now exalted above them in rank, but feeling with them in sympathy what they felt in common with them before. We have persons exalted from the practice of the law, from the place in which they administered high, though subordinate justice, to a seat here, to enlighten with their knowledge, and to strengthen with their votes, those principles which have distinguished the courts in which they have presided.

My lords, you have here also the lights of our religion; you have the bishops of England. My lords, you have that true image of the primitive church in its ancient form, in its ancient ordinances, purified from the superstitions and the vices which a long succession of ages will bring upon the best institutions. You have the representatives of that religion which says, that their God is love, that the very vital spirit of their institution is charity; a religion which so much hates oppression, that, when the God whom we adore appeared in human form, He did not appear in a form of greatness and majesty, but in sympathy with the lowest of the people, and thereby made it a firm and ruling principle, that their welfare was the object of all government, since the person who was the Master of Nature chose to appear himself in a subordinate situation. These are the considerations which influence them, which animate them, against all oppression; knowing that He, who is called first among them, and first among us all, both of the flock that is fed and of those who feed it, made himself " the servant of all."

My lords, these are the securities which we have in all the constituent parts of the body of this House. We know them, we reckon, we rest upon them, and commit safely the interests of India and of humanity into your hands. Therefore it is with confidence that, ordered by the Commons,

I impeach Warren Hastings, Esquire, of high crimes and misdemeanors.

I impeach him in the name of the Commons of Great Britain in Parliament assembled, whose parliamentary trust he has betrayed.

I impeach him in the name of all the Commons of Great Britain, whose national character he has dishonoured.

I impeach him in the name of the people of India, whose laws, rights and liberties he has subverted, whose properties he has destroyed, whose country he has laid waste and desolate.

I impeach him in the name and by virtue of those eternal laws of justice which he has violated.

I impeach him in the name of human nature itself, which he has cruelly outraged, injured and oppressed in both sexes, in every age, rank, situation, and condition of life.

(*Speech on the Impeachment of Warren Hastings.*)

JAMES MACPHERSON (1736–1796)

OSSIAN'S SONG TO THE SUN

I FEEL the sun, O Malvina! leave me to my rest. Perhaps they may come to my dreams; I think I hear a feeble voice! The beam of heaven delights to shine on the grave of Carthon: I feel it warm around.

O thou that rollest above, round as the shield of my fathers! Whence are thy beams, O sun! thy everlasting light? Thou comest forth in thy awful beauty; the stars hide themselves in the sky; the moon, cold and pale, sinks in the western wave; but thou thyself movest alone. Who can be a companion of thy course? The oaks of the mountains fall; the mountains themselves decay with years; the ocean shrinks and grows again; the moon herself is lost in heaven, but thou art for ever the same, rejoicing in the brightness of thy course. When the world is dark with tempests, when thunder rolls, and lightning flies, thou lookest in thy beauty from the clouds, and laughest at the storm. But to Ossian thou lookest in vain, for he beholds thy beams no more; whether thy yellow hair flows on the eastern clouds, or thou tremblest at the gates of the west. But thou art perhaps like me, for a season; thy years will have an end. Thou shalt sleep in thy clouds, careless of the voice of the morning. Exult then, O sun, in the strength of thy youth! Age is dark and unlovely; it is like the glimmering light of the moon when it shines through broken clouds, and the mist is on the hills: the blast of the north is on the plain; the traveller shrinks in the midst of his journey.

(*Fragments of Ancient Poetry . . . from the Erse Language.*)

EDWARD GIBBON (1737–1794)

I.—CONSTANTINE'S INVASION OF ITALY

WHILE Constantine signalized his conduct and valour in the field, the sovereign of Italy appeared insensible of the calamities and danger of a civil war which raged in the heart of his dominions. Pleasure was still the only business of Maxentius. Concealing, or at least attempting to conceal, from the public knowledge the misfortunes of his arms, he indulged himself in vain confidence which deferred the remedies of the appoaching evil, without deferring the evil itself. The rapid progress of Constantine was scarcely sufficient to awaken him from this fatal security; he flattered himself that his well-known liberality, and the majesty of the Roman name, which had already delivered him from two invasions, would dissipate with the same facility the rebellious army of Gaul. The officers of experience and ability who had served under the banners of Maximian were at length compelled to inform his effeminate son of the imminent danger to which he was reduced; and, with a freedom that at once surprised and convinced him, to urge the necessity of preventing his ruin by a vigorous exertion of his remaining power. The resources of Maxentius, both of men and money, were still considerable. The Praetorian guards felt how strongly their own interest and safety were connected with his cause; and a third army was soon collected, more numerous than those which had been lost in the battles of Turin and Verona. It was far from the intention of the emperor to lead his troops in person. A stranger to the exercises of war, he trembled at the apprehension of so dangerous a contest; and, as fear is commonly superstitious, he listened with melancholy attention to the rumours of omens and presages which seemed to menace his life and empire. Shame at length supplied the place of courage, and forced him to take the field. He was unable to sustain the contempt of the Roman people. The circus resounded with their indignant clamours, and they tumultuously besieged the gates of the palace, reproaching the pusillanimity of their indolent sovereign, and celebrating the heroic spirit of Constantine. Before Maxentius left Rome, he consulted the Sibylline books. The guardians of these ancient oracles were as well versed in the arts of this world, as they were ignorant of the secrets of fate; and they returned him a very prudent answer, which might adapt itself to the event, and secure their reputation whatever should be the chance of arms.

The celerity of Constantine's march has been compared to the rapid conquest of Italy by the first of the Caesars; nor is the flattering parallel repugnant to the truth of history, since no more than fifty-eight days elapsed between the surrender of Verona and the final decision of the war. Constantine had always

apprehended that the tyrant would obey the dictates of fear,
and perhaps of prudence; and that, instead of risking his last
hopes in a general engagement, he would shut himself up within
the walls of Rome. His ample magazines secured him against
the danger of famine; and, as the situation of Constantine
admitted not of delay, he might have been reduced to the sad
necessity of destroying with fire and sword the Imperial city,
the noblest reward of his victory, and the deliverance of which
had been the motive, or rather indeed the pretence, of the civil
war. It was with equal surprise and pleasure that, on his arrival
at a place called Saxa Rubra, about nine miles from Rome,
he discovered the army of Maxentius prepared to give him
battle. Their long front filled a very spacious plain, and their
deep array reached to the banks of the Tiber, which covered
their rear, and forbade their retreat. We are informed, and we
may believe, that Constantine disposed his troops with consummate skill, and that he chose for himself the post of honour
and danger. Distinguished by the splendour of his arms, he
charged in person the cavalry of his rival; and his irresistible
attack determined the fortune of the day. The cavalry of
Maxentius was principally composed either of unwieldy cuiras-
siers [1] or of light Moors and Numidians. They yielded to the
vigour of the Gallic horse, which possessed more activity than
the one, more firmness than the other. The defeat of the two
wings left the infantry without any protection on its flanks, and
the undisciplined Italians fled without reluctance from the
standard of a tyrant whom they had always hated, and whom
they no longer feared. The Praetorians, conscious that their
offences were beyond the reach of mercy, were animated by
revenge and despair. Notwithstanding their repeated efforts,
those brave veterans were unable to recover the victory:
they obtained, however, an honourable death; and it was
observed that their bodies covered the same ground which
had been occupied by their ranks. The confusion then became
general, and the dismayed troops of Maxentius, pursued by
an implacable enemy, rushed by thousands into the deep and
rapid stream of the Tiber. The emperor himself attempted
to escape back into the city over the Milvian bridge, but the
crowds which pressed together through that narrow passage
forced him into the river, where he was immediately drowned
by the weight of his armour. His body, which had sunk very
deep into the mud, was found with some difficulty the next
day. The sight of his head, when it was exposed to the eyes

---

[1] Cuirass: the body-armour worn by heavy cavalry.

of the people, convinced them of their deliverance, and admonished them to receive with acclamations of loyalty and gratitude the fortunate Constantine, who thus achieved by his valour and ability the most splendid enterprise of his life.

(The Decline and Fall of the Roman Empire.)

II.—A Retrospect

When I contemplate the common lot of mortality, I must acknowledge that I have drawn a high prize in the lottery of life. The far greater part of the globe is overspread with barbarism or slavery; in the civilised world the most numerous class is condemned to ignorance and poverty; and the double fortune of my birth in a free and enlightened country, in an honourable and wealthy family, is the lucky chance of a unit against millions. The general probability is about three to one that a new-born infant will not live to complete his fiftieth year. I have now passed that age, and may fairly estimate the present value of my existence in the three-fold division of mind, body, and estate.

1. The first and indispensable requisite of happiness is a clear conscience, unsullied by the reproach or remembrance of any unworthy action.

——Hic murus aheneus esto,
Nil conscire sibi, nullâ pallescere culpâ.

I am endowed with a cheerful temper, a moderate sensibility, and a natural disposition to repose rather than to activity : some mischievous appetites and habits have perhaps been corrected by philosophy or time. The love of study, a passion which derives fresh vigour from enjoyment, supplies each day, each hour, with a perpetual source of independent and rational pleasure; and I am not sensible of any decay of the mental faculties. The original soil has been highly improved by cultivation; but it may be questioned whether some flowers of fancy, some grateful errors, have not been eradicated with the weeds of prejudice. 2. Since I have escaped from the long perils of my childhood, the serious advice of a physician has seldom been requisite. "The madness of superfluous health" I have never known, but my tender constitution has been fortified by time, and the inestimable gift of the sound and peaceful slumbers of infancy may be imputed both to the mind and body. 3. I have already described the merits of my society and situation ; but these enjoyments would be tasteless or bitter if their possession were not assured by an annual and adequate supply. According to the scale of Switzerland

I am a rich man; and I am indeed rich, since my income is superior to my expense, and my expense is equal to my wishes. My friend Lord Sheffield has kindly relieved me from the cares to which my taste and temper are most adverse: shall I add that, since the failure of my first wishes, I have never entertained any serious thoughts of a matrimonial connection?

I am disgusted with the affectation of men of letters, who complain that they have renounced a substance for a shadow, and that their fame (which sometimes is no insupportable weight) affords a poor compensation for envy, censure, and persecution. My own experience, at least, has taught me a very different lesson: twenty happy years have been animated by the labour of my *History*, and its success has given me a name, a rank, a character in the world to which I should not otherwise have been entitled. The freedom of my writings has indeed provoked an implacable tribe; but, as I was safe from the stings, I was soon accustomed to the buzzing of the hornets: my nerves are not tremblingly alive, and my literary temper is so happily framed that I am less sensible of pain than of pleasure. The rational pride of an author may be offended, rather than flattered, by vague indiscriminate praise; but he cannot, he should not, be indifferent to the fair testimonies of private and public esteem. Even his moral sympathy may be gratified by the idea that now, in the present hour, he is imparting some degree of amusement or knowledge to his friends in a distant land; that one day his mind will be familiar to the grandchildren of those who are yet unborn. I cannot boast of the friendship or favour of princes; the patronage of English literature has long since been devolved on our booksellers, and the measure of their liberality is the least ambiguous test of our common success. Perhaps the golden mediocrity of my fortune has contributed to fortify my application.

The present is a fleeting moment, the past is no more; and our prospect of futurity is dark and doubtful. This day may *possibly* be my last: but the laws of probability, so true in general, so fallacious in particular, still allow about fifteen years. I shall soon enter into the period which, as the most agreeable of his long life, was selected by the judgment and experience of the sage Fontenelle. His choice is approved by the eloquent historian of nature, who fixes our moral happiness to the mature season, in which our passions are supposed to be calmed, our duties fulfilled, our ambition satisfied, our fame and fortune established on a solid basis. In private conversation, that great and amiable man added the weight of his own experience; and this autumnal felicity might be exemplified in the lives of Voltaire, Hume, and many other men of letters. I am far more inclined to embrace than to dispute this comfortable doctrine. I will not suppose any premature decay of the mind or body; but I must reluctantly observe that two causes, the abbreviation of time, and the failure of hope, will always tinge with a browner shade the evening of life.

(The Autobiography.)

JAMES BOSWELL (1740–1795)

I.—DR. GOLDSMITH

As Dr. Oliver Goldsmith will frequently appear in this narrative, I shall endeavour to make my readers in some degree acquainted with his singular character. He was a native of Ireland, and a contemporary with Mr. Burke, at Trinity College, Dublin, but did not then give much promise of future celebrity. He, however, observed to Mr. Malone, that " though he made no great figure in mathematicks, which was a study in much repute there, he could turn an Ode of Horace into English better than any of them. " He afterwards studied physick at Edinburgh, and upon the Continent : and I have been informed, was enabled to pursue his travels on foot, partly by demanding at Universities to enter the lists as a disputant, by which, according to the custom of many of them, he was entitled to the premium of a crown, when luckily for him his challenge was not accepted ; so that, as I once observed to Dr. Johnson, he *disputed* his passage through Europe. He then came to England, and was employed successively in the capacities of an usher to an academy, a corrector of the press, a reviewer, and a writer for a news-paper. He had sagacity enough to cultivate assiduously the acquaintance of Johnson, and his faculties were gradually enlarged by the contemplation of such a model. To me and many others it appeared that he studiously copied the manner of Johnson, though, indeed, upon a smaller scale.

At this time I think he had published nothing with his name, though it was pretty generally known that *one Dr. Goldsmith* was the authour of " An Enquiry into the present State of polite Learning in Europe," and of " The Citizen of the World," a series of letters supposed to be written from London by a Chinese. No man had the art of displaying with more advantage as a writer, whatever literary acquisitions he made.

*H 675

"*Nihil quod tetigit non ornavit.*" His mind resembled a fertile, but thin soil. There was a quick, but not a strong vegetation, of whatever chanced to be thrown upon it. No deep root could be struck. The oak of the forest did not grow there : but the elegant shrubbery and the fragrant parterre appeared in gay succession. It has been generally circulated and believed that he was a mere fool in conversation; but, in truth, this has been greatly exaggerated. He had, no doubt, a more than common share of that hurry of ideas which we often find in his countrymen, and which sometimes produces a laughable confusion in expressing them. He was very much what the French call *un étourdi*, and from vanity and an eager desire of being conspicuous wherever he was, he frequently talked carelessly without knowledge of the subject, or even without thought. His person was short, his countenance coarse and vulgar, his deportment that of a scholar awkwardly affecting the easy gentleman. Those who were in any way distinguished excited envy in him to so ridiculous an excess, that the instances of it are hardly credible. When accompanying two beautiful young ladies with their mother on a tour in France, he was seriously angry that more attention was paid to them than to him, and once at the exhibition of the *Fantoccini* in London, when those who sat next him observed with what dexterity a puppet was made to toss a pike, he could not bear that it should have such praise, and exclaimed with some warmth, " Pshaw ! I can do it better myself."

He, I am afraid, had no settled system of any sort, so that his conduct must not be strictly scrutinized; but his affections were social and generous, and when he had money he gave it away very liberally. His desire of imaginary consequence predominated over his attention to truth. When he began to rise into notice, he said he had a brother who was Dean of Durham, a fiction so easily detected, that it is wonderful how he should have been so inconsiderate as to hazard it. He boasted to me at this time of the power of his pen in commanding money, which I believe was true in a certain degree, though in the instance he gave he was by no means correct. He told me that he had sold a novel for four hundred pounds. This was his " Vicar of Wakefield." But Johnson informed me, that he had made the bargain for Goldsmith, and the price was sixty pounds. " And, Sir, (said he,) a sufficient price too, when it was sold; for then the fame of Goldsmith had not been elevated, as it afterwards was, by his ' Traveller; ' and the bookseller had such faint hopes of profit by his bargain, that he kept the manuscript by him a long time, and did not publish it till after the 'Traveller' had appeared. Then, to be sure, it was accidentally worth more money."

Mrs. Piozzi and Sir John Hawkins have strangely mis-stated the history of Goldsmith's situation and Johnson's friendly interference, when this novel was sold. I shall give it authentically from Johnson's own exact narration:

"I received one morning a message from poor Goldsmith that he was in great distress, and as it was not in his power to come to me, begging that I would come to him as soon as possible. I sent him a guinea, and promised to come to him directly. I accordingly went as soon as I was drest, and found that his landlady had arrested him for his rent, at which he was in a violent passion. I perceived that he had already changed my guinea, and had got a bottle of Madeira and a glass before him. I put the cork into the bottle, desired he would be calm, and began to talk to him of the means by which he might be extricated. He then told me that he had a novel ready for the press, which he produced to me. I looked into it, and saw its merit; told the landlady I should soon return, and having gone to a bookseller, sold it for sixty pounds. I brought Goldsmith the money, and he discharged his rent, not without rating his landlady in a high tone for having used him so ill."

(*The Life of Dr. Samuel Johnson.*)

II.—Dr. Johnson and Mr. Wilkes

Notwithstanding the high veneration which I entertain for Dr. Johnson, I was sensible that he was sometimes a little actuated by the spirit of contradiction, and by means of that I hoped I should gain my point. I was persuaded that if I had come upon him with a direct proposal, "Sir, will you dine in company with Jack Wilkes?" he would have flown into a passion, and would probably have answered, "Dine with Jack Wilkes, Sir! I'd as soon dine with Jack Ketch."[1] I there-fore, while we were sitting by ourselves at his house in an evening, took occasion to open my plan thus:—"Mr. Dilly, Sir, sends his respectful compliments to you, and would be happy if you would do him the honour to dine with him on Wednesday next along with me, as I must soon go to Scot-land." Johnson. "Sir, I am obliged to Mr. Dilly. I will

[1] This has been circulated as if actually said by Johnson; when the truth is, it was only *supposed* by me.

wait upon him—" BOSWELL. "Provided, Sir, I suppose, that the company which he is to have, is agreeable to you." JOHNSON. "What do you mean, Sir? What do you take me for? Do you think I am so ignorant of the world, as to imagine that I am to prescribe to a gentleman what company he is to have at his table?" BOSWELL. "I beg your pardon, Sir, for wishing to prevent you from meeting people whom you might not like. Perhaps he may have some of what he calls his patriotick friends with him." JOHNSON. "Well, Sir, and what then? What care *I* for his *patriotick friends?* Poh!" BOSWELL. "I should not be surprized to find Jack Wilkes there." JOHNSON. "And if Jack Wilkes *should* be there, what is that to *me*, Sir? My dear friend, let us have no more of this. I am sorry to be angry with you; but really it is treating me strangely to talk to me as if I could not meet any company whatever, occasionally." BOSWELL. "Pray, forgive me, Sir: I meant well. But you shall meet whoever comes, for me." Thus I secured him, and told Dilly that he would find him very well pleased to be one of his guests on the day appointed.

Upon the much expected Wednesday, I called on him about half an hour before dinner, as I often did when we were to dine out together, to see that he was ready in time, and to accompany him. I found him buffeting his books, as upon a former occasion, covered with dust, and making no preparation for going abroad. "How is this, Sir? (said I). Don't you recollect that you are to dine at Mr. Dilly's?" JOHNSON. "Sir, I did not think of going to Dilly's: it went out of my head. I have ordered dinner at home with Mrs. Williams." BOSWELL. "But, my dear Sir, you know you were engaged to Mr. Dilly, and I told him so. He will expect you, and will be much disappointed if you don't come." JOHNSON. "You must talk to Mrs. Williams about this."

Here was a sad dilemma. I feared that what I was so confident I had secured, would yet be frustrated. He had accustomed himself to shew Mrs. Williams such a degree of humane attention, as frequently imposed some restraint upon him; and I knew that if she should be obstinate, he would not stir. I hastened down stairs to the blind lady's room, and told her I was in great uneasiness, for Dr. Johnson had engaged to me to dine this day at Mr. Dilly's, but that he had told me he had forgotten his engagement, and had ordered dinner at home. "Yes, Sir, (said she, pretty peevishly,) Dr. Johnson is to dine at home."—"Madam, (said I,) his respect for you is such, that

I know he will not leave you, unless you absolutely desire it. But as you have so much of his company, I hope you will be good enough to forego it for a day: as Mr. Dilly is a very worthy man, has frequently had agreeable parties at his house for Dr. Johnson, and will be vexed if the doctor neglects him to-day. And then, Madam, be pleased to consider my situation; I carried the message, and I assured Mr. Dilly that Dr. Johnson was to come; and no doubt he has made a dinner, and invited a company, and boasted of the honour he expected to have. I shall be quite disgraced if the Doctor is not there." She gradually softened to my solicitations, which were certainly as earnest as most entreaties to ladies upon any occasion, and was graciously pleased to empower me to tell Dr. Johnson, "That all things considered, she thought he should certainly go." I flew back to him, still in dust, and careless of what should be the event, "indifferent in his choice to go or stay;" but as soon as I had announced to him Mrs. Williams's consent, he roared, "Frank, a clean shirt," and was very soon drest. When I had him fairly seated in a hackney-coach with me, I exulted as much as a fortune-hunter who has got an heiress into a post-chaise with him to set out for Gretna-Green.

When we entered Mr. Dilly's drawing-room, he found himself in the midst of a company he did not know. I kept myself snug and silent, watching how he would conduct himself. I observed him whispering to Mr. Dilly, "Who is that gentleman, sir?"—"Mr. Arthur Lee." — JOHNSON. "Too, too, too," (under his breath,) which was one of his habitual mutterings. Mr. Arthur Lee could not but be very obnoxious to Johnson, for he was not only a *patriot*, but an *American*. He was afterwards minister from the United States at the court of Madrid. "And who is the gentleman in lace?"—"Mr. Wilkes, Sir." This information confounded him still more; he had some difficulty to restrain himself, and taking up a book, sat down upon a window-seat and read, or at least kept his eye upon it intently for some time, till he composed himself. His feelings, I dare say, were awkward enough. But he no doubt recollected his having rated me for supposing that he could be at all disconcerted by any company, and he, therefore, resolutely set himself to behave quite as an easy man of the world, who could adapt himself at once to the disposition and manners of those whom he might chance to meet.

The cheering sound of "Dinner is upon the table," dissolved his reverie, and we *all* sat down without any symptom of ill humour. There were present, beside Mr. Wilkes, and Mr. Arthur Lee, who was an old companion of mine when he studied physick at Edinburgh, Mr. (now Sir John) Miller, Dr. Lettsom, and Mr. Slater, the druggist. Mr. Wilkes placed himself next to Dr. Johnson, and behaved to him with so much attention and politeness, that he gained upon him insensibly. No man eat more heartily than Johnson, or loved better what was nice and delicate. Mr. Wilkes was very assiduous in helping him to some fine veal. "Pray give me leave, Sir;—It is better here—A little of the brown—Some fat, Sir—A little of the stuffing—Some gravy—Let me have the pleasure of giving you some butter—Allow me to recommend a squeeze of this orange;—or the lemon, perhaps, may have more zest."—"Sir, Sir, I am obliged to you, Sir," cried Johnson, bowing, and turning his head to him with a look for some time of "surly virtue,"[1] but, in a short while, of complacency.

Foote being mentioned, Johnson said, "He is not a good mimick." One of the company added, "A merry Andrew, a buffoon." JOHNSON. "But he has wit too, and is not deficient in ideas, or in fertility and variety of imagery, and not empty of reading ; he has knowledge enough to fill up his part. One species of wit he has in an eminent degree, that of escape. You drive him into a corner with both hands; but he's gone, Sir, when you think you have got him—like an animal that jumps over your head. Then he has a great range for wit; he never lets truth stand between him and a jest, and he is sometimes mighty coarse. Garrick is under many restraints from which Foote is free." WILKES. "Garrick's wit is more like Lord Chesterfield's." JOHNSON. "The first time I was in company with Foote was at Fitzherbert's. Having no good opinion of the fellow, I was resolved not to be pleased; and it is very difficult to please a man against his will. I went on eating my dinner pretty sullenly, affecting not to mind him. But the dog was so very comical, that I was obliged to lay down my knife and fork, throw myself back upon my chair, and fairly laugh it out. No, Sir, he was irresistible."[2] He upon one occasion experienced, in an extraordinary degree, the efficacy of his powers of entertaining. Amongst the many and various modes which he tried of getting money, he became a partner with a small-beer brewer, and he was to

---

[1] Johnson's *London, a Poem,* v. 145.
[2] Foote told me, that Johnson said of him, "For loud obstreperous broad-faced mirth I know not his equal."

have a share of profits for procuring customers amongst his numerous acquaintance. Fitzherbert was one who took his small-beer; but it was so bad that the servants resolved not to drink it. They were at some loss how to notify their resolution, being afraid of offending their master, who they knew liked Foote much as a companion. At last they fixed upon a little black boy, who was rather a favourite, to be their deputy, and deliver their remonstrance; and having invested him with the whole authority of the kitchen, he was to inform Mr. Fitzherbert, in all their names, upon a certain day, that they would drink Foote's small-beer no longer. On that day Foote happened to dine at Fitzherbert's, and this boy served at table ; he was so delighted with Foote's stories, and merriment, and grimace, that when he went down stairs, he told them, " This is the finest man I have ever seen. I will not deliver your message. I will drink his small-beer."

Somebody observed that Garrick could not have done this. WILKES. " Garrick would have made the small-beer still smaller. He is now leaving the stage; but he will play *Scrub* all his life." I knew that Johnson would let nobody attack Garrick but himself, as Garrick said to me, and I had heard him praise his liberality; so to bring out his commendation of his celebrated pupil, I said, loudly, " I have heard Garrick is liberal." JOHNSON. " Yes, Sir, I know that Garrick has given away more money than any man in England that I am acquainted with, and that not from ostentatious views. Garrick was very poor when he began life ; so when he came to have money, he probably was very unskilful in giving away, and saved when he should not. But Garrick began to be liberal as soon as he could; and I am of opinion, the reputation of avarice which he has had, has been very lucky for him, and prevented his having many enemies. You despise a man for avarice, but do not hate him. Garrick might have been much better attacked for living with more splendour than is suitable to a player : if they had had the wit to have assaulted him in that quarter they might have galled him more. But they have kept clamouring about his avarice, which has rescued him from much obloquy and envy."

Talking of the great difficulty of obtaining authentick information for biography, Johnson told us, " When I was a young fellow I wanted to write the ' Life of Dryden,' and in order to get materials, I applied to the only two persons then alive who had seen him; these were old Swinney, and old Cibber. Swinney's information was no more than this, ' That at Will's coffee-house Dryden had a particular chair for himself, which was set by the fire in winter, and was then called his winter-chair ; and that it was carried out for him to the balcony in summer, and was then called his summer-chair.' Cibber could tell no more but ' That he remembered him a decent old man, arbiter of critical disputes at Will's.' You are to consider that Cibber was then at a great distance from Dryden, had perhaps one leg only in the room, and durst not draw in the other." BOSWELL. "Yet Cibber was a man of observation?" JOHNSON. "I think not." BOSWELL. "You will allow his 'Apology' to be well done." JOHNSON. "Very well done, to be sure, Sir. That book is a striking proof of the justice of Pope's remark :

> "'Each might his several province well command,
> Would all but stoop to what they understand.'"

BOSWELL. "And his plays are good." JOHNSON. "Yes; but that was his trade ; *l'esprit du corps* ; he had been all his life among players and play-writers. I wondered that he had so little to say in conversation, for he had kept the best company, and learnt all that can be got by the ear. He abused Pindar to me and then shewed me an ode of his own, with an absurd couplet, making a linnet soar on an eagle's wing. I told him that when the ancients made a simile, they always made it like something real."

Mr. Wilkes remarked, that "among all the bold flights of Shakspeare's imagination, the boldest was making Birnam-wood march to Dunsinane ; creating a wood where there never was a shrub ; a wood in Scotland ! ha ! ha ! ha ! " And he also observed, that "the clannish slavery of the Highlands of Scotland was the single exception to Milton's remark of 'The Mountain Nymph, sweet Liberty,' being worshipped in all hilly countries."—" When I was at Inverary (said he,) on a visit to my old friend Archibald, Duke of Argyle, his dependents congratulated me on being such a favourite of his Grace. I said, ' It is then, gentlemen, truly lucky for me ; for if I had displeased the Duke, and he had wished it, there is not a Campbell among you but would have been ready to bring John Wilkes's head to him in a charger. It would have been only

> "'Off with his head ! so much for *Aylesbury*'

I was then member for Aylesbury."

Dr. Johnson and Mr. Wilkes talked of the contested passage in Horace's Art of Poetry, "*Difficile est propriè communia dicere*." Mr. Wilkes, according to my note, gave the interpretation thus :

" It is difficult to speak with propriety of common things; as, if a poet had to speak of Queen Caroline drinking tea, he must endeavour to avoid the vulgarity of cups and saucers." But upon reading my note, he tells me that he meant to say, that " the word *communia* being a Roman law-term, signifies here things *communis juris*, that is to say, what have never yet been treated by any body; and this appears clearly from what followed.

"————Tuque
Rectiùs Iliacum carmen deducis in actus
Quàm si proferres ignota indictaque primus.

" You will easier make a tragedy out of the Iliad than on any subject not handled before." JOHNSON. " He means that it is difficult to appropriate to particular persons qualities which are common to all mankind, as Homer had done."

WILKES. " We have no City-Poet now: that is an office which has gone into disuse. The last was Elkanah Settle. There is something in *names* which one cannot help feeling. Now *Elkanah Settle* sounds so *queer*, who can expect much from that name? We should have no hesitation to give it for John Dryden, in preference to Elkanah Settle, from the names only, without knowing their different merits." JOHNSON. " I suppose, Sir, Settle did as well for Aldermen in his time, as John Home could do now. Where did Beckford, and Trecothick learn English? "

Mr. Arthur Lee mentioned some Scotch who had taken possession of a barren part of America, and wondered why they should choose it. JOHNSON. " Why, Sir, all barrenness is comparative. The *Scotch* would not know it to be barren." BOSWELL. " Come, come, he is flattering the English. You have now been in Scotland, Sir, and say if you did not see meat and drink enough there." JOHNSON. " Why yes, Sir, meat and drink enough to give the inhabitants sufficient strength to run away from home." All these quick and lively sallies were said sportively, quite in jest, and with a smile, which showed that he meant only wit. Upon this topick he and Mr. Wilkes could perfectly assimilate; here was a bond of union between them, and I was conscious that as both of them had visited Caledonia, both were fully satisfied of the strange narrow ignorance of those who imagine that it is a land of famine. But they amused themselves with persevering in the old jokes. When I claimed a superiority for Scotland over England in one respect, that no man can be arrested there for a debt merely because another swears it against him; but there must first be the judgement of a court of law ascertaining its justice; and that a seizure of the person, before judgement is obtained, can take place only, if his creditor should swear that he is about to fly from the country, or, as it is technically expressed, is *in meditatione fugæ*: WILKES. "That, I should think, may be safely sworn of all the Scotch nation." JOHNSON. (To Mr. Wilkes) "You must know, Sir, I lately took my friend Boswell, and shewed him genuine civilized life in an English provincial town. I turned him loose at Lichfield, my native city, that he might see for once real civility: for you know he lives among savages in Scotland, and among rakes in London." WILKES. "Except when he is with grave, sober, decent people, like you and me." JOHNSON. (smiling) "And we ashamed of him."

They were quite frank and easy. Johnson told the story of his asking Mrs. Macaulay to allow her footman to sit down with them, to prove the ridiculousness of the arguments for the equality of mankind; and he said to me afterwards, with a nod of satisfaction, "You saw Mr. Wilkes acquiesced." Wilkes talked with all imaginable freedom of the ludicrous title given to the Attorney-General, *Diabolus Regis*; adding, "I have reason to know something about that officer; for I was prosecuted for a libel." Johnson, who many people would have supposed must have been furiously angry at hearing this talked of so lightly, said not a word. He was now, *indeed*, "a good-humoured fellow."

After dinner we had an accession of Mrs. Knowles, the Quaker lady, well known for her various talents, and of Mr. Alderman Lee. Amidst some patriotick groans, somebody (I think the Alderman) said, "Poor old England is lost." JOHNSON. "Sir, it is not so much to be lamented that old England is lost, as that the Scotch have found it." WILKES. "Had Lord Bute governed Scotland only, I should not have taken the trouble to write his eulogy, and dedicate 'MORTIMER' to him."

Mr. Wilkes held a candle to shew a fine print of a beautiful female figure which hung in the room, and pointed out the elegant contour of the bosom with the finger of an arch connoisseur. He afterwards in a conversation with me waggishly insisted, that all the time Johnson shewed visible signs of a fervent admiration of the corresponding charms of the fair Quaker.

This record, though by no means so perfect as I could wish, will serve to give a notion of a very curious interview, which was not only pleasing at the time, but had the agreeable and benignant effect of reconciling any animosity and sweetening any acidity, which, in the various bustle of political contest, had been produced in the minds of two men, who though widely different, had so many things in common—classical learning, modern literature, wit and humour, and ready repartee —that it would have been much to be regretted if they had been for ever at a distance from each other.

Mr. Burke gave me much credit for this successful *negotiation ;* and pleasantly said, " that there was nothing equal to it in the whole history of the *Corps Diplomatique.*"

I attended Dr. Johnson home, and had the satisfaction to hear him tell Mrs. Williams how much he had been pleased with Mr. Wilkes's company, and what an agreeable day he had passed.

(*The Life of Dr. Samuel Johnson.*)

SIR WALTER SCOTT (1771–1832)

I.—JEANIE DEANS AND QUEEN CAROLINE

" WE will not prosecute a topic on which we may probably differ," said the Queen. " One word, however, I may say in private—You know our good Lady Suffolk is a little deaf—the Duke of Argyle, when disposed to renew his acquaintance with his master and mistress, will hardly find many topics on which we should disagree."

" Let me hope," said the Duke, bowing profoundly to so flattering an intimation, " that I shall not be so unfortunate as to have found one on the present occasion."

" I must first impose on your Grace the duty of confession," said the Queen, " before I grant you absolution. What is your particular interest in this young woman? She does not seem " (and she scanned Jeanie, as she said this, with the eye of a connoisseur) " much qualified to alarm my friend the Duchess's jealousy."

" I think your Majesty," replied the Duke, smiling in his turn, " will allow my taste may be a pledge for me on that score."

" Then, though she has not much the air *d'une grande dame,* I suppose she is some thirtieth cousin in the terrible chapter of Scottish genealogy? "

" No, madam," said the Duke; " but I wish some of my nearer relations had half her worth, honesty, and affection."

" Her name must be Campbell, at least? " said Queen Caroline.

" No, madam; her name in not quite so distinguished, if I may be permitted to say so," answered the Duke.

" Ah ! but she comes from Inverary or Argyleshire ? " said the sovereign.

" She has never been farther north in her life than Edinburgh, madam."

" Then my conjectures are all ended," said the Queen, " and your Grace must yourself take the trouble to explain the affair of your protégée."

With this precision and easy brevity which is only acquired by habitually conversing in the higher ranks of society, and which is the diametrical opposite of that protracted style of disquisition,

> Which squires call potter, and which men call prose,

the Duke explained the singular law under which Effie Deans had received sentence of death, and detailed the affectionate exertions which Jeanie had made in behalf of her sister, for whose sake she was willing to sacrifice all but truth and conscience.

Queen Caroline listened with attention ; she was rather fond, it must be remembered, of an argument, and soon found matter in what the Duke told her for raising difficulties to his request.

" It appears to me, my Lord," she replied, " that this is a severe law. But still it is adopted upon good grounds, I am bound to suppose, as the law of the country, and the girl has been convicted under it. The very presumptions which the law construes into a positive proof of guilt exist in her case ; and all that your Grace has said concerning the possibility of her innocence may be a very good argument for annulling the Act of Parliament, but cannot, while it stands good, be admitted in favour of any individual convicted upon the statute."

The Duke saw and avoided the snare ; for he was conscious, that, by replying to the argument, he must have been inevitably led to a discussion, in the course of which the Queen was likely to be hardened in her own opinion, until she became obliged, out of mere respect to consistency, to let the criminal suffer. " If your Majesty," he said, " would condescend to hear my poor countrywoman herself, perhaps she may find an advocate in your own heart, more able than I am, to combat the doubts suggested by your understanding."

The Queen seemed to acquiesce, and the Duke made a signal for Jeanie to advance from the spot where she had hitherto remained watching countenances, which were too long accustomed to suppress all apparent signs of emotion, to convey to her any interesting intelligence. Her Majesty could not help smiling at the awe-struck manner in which the quiet demure figure of the little Scotchwoman advanced towards her, and yet more at the first sound of her broad northern accent. But Jeanie had a voice low and sweetly toned, an admirable thing in woman, and eke besought " her Leddyship to have pity on a poor misguided young creature," in tones so affecting, that, like the notes of some of her native songs, provincial vulgarity was lost in pathos.

"Stand up, young woman," said the Queen, but in a kind tone, "and tell me what sort of a barbarous people your countryfolk are, where child-murder is become so common as to require the restraint of laws like yours ? "

" If your Leddyship pleases," answered Jeanie, " there are mony places beside Scotland where mothers are unkind to their ain flesh and blood."

It must be observed, that the disputes between George the Second, and Frederick, Prince of Wales, were then at the highest, and that the good-natured part of the public laid the blame on the Queen. She coloured highly, and darted a glance of a most penetrating character first at Jeanie, and then at the Duke. Both sustained it unmoved ; Jeanie from total unconsciousness of the offence she had given, and the Duke from his habitual composure. But in his heart he thought, My unlucky protégée has, with this luckless answer, shot dead, by a kind of chance medley, her only hope of success.

Lady Suffolk, good-humouredly and skillfully, interposed in this awkward crisis. " You should tell this lady," she said to Jeanie, " the particular causes which render this crime common in your country."

" Some thinks it's the Kirk-Session—that is—it's the—it's the cutty-stool, if your Leddyship pleases," said Jeanie, looking down, and courtesying.

" And what ? " said Lady Suffolk, to whom the phrase was new, and who besides was rather deaf.

" That's the stool of repentance, madam, if it please your Leddyship," answered Jeanie, " for light life and conversation, and for breaking the seventh command." Here she raised her eyes to the Duke, saw his hand at his chin, and totally unconscious of what she had said out of joint, gave double effect to the innuendo, by stopping short and looking embarrassed.

As for Lady Suffolk, she retired like a covering party, which, having interposed betwixt their retreating friends and the enemy, have suddenly drawn on themselves a fire unexpectedly severe.

The deuce take the lass, thought the Duke of Argyle to himself : there goes another shot—and she has hit with both barrels right and left !

Indeed the Duke had himself his share of the confusion, for, having acted as master of ceremonies to this innocent offender, he felt much in the circumstances of a country squire, who, having introduced his spaniel into a well-appointed drawing-room, is doomed to witness the disorder and damage which arises to china and to dress-gowns, in consequence of its untimely frolics. Jeanie's last chance hit, however, obliterated the ill impression which had arisen from the first ; for her Majesty had not so lost the feelings of a wife in those of a Queen, but that she could enjoy a jest at the expence of " her good Suffolk." She turned towards the Duke of Argyle with a smile, which marked that she enjoyed the triumph, and observed, " the Scotch are a rigidly moral people." Then again applying herself to Jeanie, she asked, how she travelled up from Scotland.

" Upon my foot mostly, madam," was the reply.

" What, all that immense way upon foot ?—How far can you walk in a day ? "

" Five-and-twenty miles and a bittock."

" And a what ? " said the Queen, looking towards the Duke of Argyle.

" And about five miles more," replied the Duke.

" I thought I was a good walker," said the Queen, " but this shames me sadly."

" May your Leddyship never hae sae weary a heart, that ye canna be sensible of the weariness of the limbs ! " said Jeanie.

That came better off, thought the Duke ; it's the first thing she has said to the purpose.

" And I didna just a'thegither walk the haill way neither, for I had whiles the cast of a cart ; and I had the cast of a horse from Ferrybridge—and divers other easements," said Jeanie, cutting short her story, for she observed the Duke made the sign he had fixed upon.

" With all these accommodations," answered the Queen, " you must have had a very fatiguing journey, and, I fear, to little purpose ; since, if the King were to pardon your sister, in all probability it would do her little good, for I suppose your people of Edinburgh would hang her out of spite."

She will sink herself now outright, thought the Duke.

But he was wrong. The shoals on which Jeanie had touched in this delicate conversation lay underground, and were unknown to her; this rock was above water, and she avoided it.

"She was confident," she said, "that baith town and country wad rejoice to see his Majesty taking compassion on a poor unfriended creature."

"His Majesty has not found it so in a late instance," said the Queen; "but, I suppose, my Lord Duke would advise him to be guided by the votes of the rabble themselves, who should be hanged and who should be spared?"

"No, madam," said the Duke; "but I would advise his Majesty to be guided by his own feelings, and those of his royal consort; and then, I am sure, punishment will only attach itself to guilt, and even then with cautious reluctanc."

"Well, my lord," said her Majesty, "all these fine speeches do not convince me of the propriety of so soon showing any mark of favour to your—I suppose I must not say rebellious? —but, at least, your very disaffected and intractable metropolis. Why, the whole nation is in a league to screen the savage and abominable murderers of that unhappy man; otherwise, how is it possible but that, of so many perpetrators, and engaged in so public an action for such a length of time, one at least must have been recognised? Even this wench, for aught I can tell, may be a depository of the secret.—Hark you, young woman, had you any friends engaged in the Porteous mob?"

"No, madam," answered Jeanie, happy that the question was so framed that she could, with a good conscience, answer it in the negative.

"But I suppose," continued the Queen, "if you were possessed of such a secret, you would hold it matter of conscience to keep it to yourself?"

"I would pray to be directed and guided what was the line of duty, madam," answered Jeanie.

"Yes, and take that which suited your own inclinations," replied her Majesty.

"If it like you, madam," said Jeanie, "I would hae gaen to the end of the earth to save the life of John Porteous, or any other unhappy man in his condition; but I might lawfully doubt how far I am called upon to be the avenger of his blood, though it may become the civil magistrate to do so. He is dead and gane to his place, and they that have slain him must answer for their ain act. But my sister, my puir sister Effie, still lives, though her days and hours are numbered!—She still lives, and a word of the King's mouth might restore her to a broken-hearted auld man, that never, in his daily and nightly exercise, forgot to pray that his Majesty might be blessed with a long and a prosperous reign, and that his throne, and the throne of his posterity, might be established in right-eousness. Oh, madam, if ever ye kend what it was to sorrow for and with a sinning and a suffering creature, whose mind is sae tossed that she can be neither ca'd fit to live or die, have some compassion on our misery!—Save an honest house from dishonour, and an unhappy girl, not eighteen years of age, from an early and dreadful death! Alas! it is not when we sleep soft and wake merrily ourselves, that we think on other people's sufferings. Our hearts are waxed light within us then, and we are for righting our ain wrangs and fighting our ain battles. But when the hour of trouble comes to the mind or to the body—and seldom may it visit your Leddyship —and when the hour of death comes, that comes to high and low—lang and late may it be yours—Oh, my Leddy, then it isna what we hae dune for oursells, but what we hae dune for others, that we think on maist pleasantly. And the thoughts that ye hae intervened to spare the puir thing's life will be sweeter in that hour, come when it may, than if a word of your mouth could hang the haill Porteous mob at the tail of ae tow."

Tear followed tear down Jeanie's cheeks, as, her features glowing and quivering with emotion, she pleaded her sister's cause with a pathos which was at once simple and solemn.

"This is eloquence," said her Majesty to the Duke of Argyle. "Young woman," she continued, addressing herself to Jeanie, "*I* cannot grant a pardon to your sister—but you shall not want my warm intercession with his Majesty. Take this housewife case," she continued, putting a small embroidered needle-case into Jeanie's hands; "do not open it now, but at your leisure you will find something in it which will remind you that you have had an interview with Queen Caroline."

Jeanie having her suspicions thus confirmed, dropped on her knees, and would have expanded herself in gratitude; but the Duke, who was upon thorns lest she should say more or less than just enough, touched her chin once more.

"Our business is, I think, ended for the present, my Lord Duke," said the Queen, "and, I trust, to your satisfaction. Hereafter I hope to see your Grace more frequently, both at Richmond and at St. James's.—Come, Lady Suffolk, we must wish his Grace good morning."

They exchanged their parting reverences, and the Duke, so

soon as the ladies had turned their backs, assisted Jeanie to rise from the ground, and conducted her back through the avenue, which she trode with the feeling of one who walks in her sleep.

(The Heart of Mid-Lothian.)

II.—A Scotch Gardener

As I sauntered on, I found the gardener hard at his evening employment, and saluted him, as I paused to look at his work. " Good even, my friend."

" Gude e'en, gude e'en t'ye," answered the man, without looking up, and in a tone which at once indicated his Northern extraction.

" Fine weather for your work, my friend."

" It's no that muckle to be compleened o'," answered the man with that limited degree of praise which gardeners and farmers usually bestow on the very best weather. Then raising his head, as if to see who spoke to him, he touched his Scotch bonnet with an air of respect, as he observed, " Eh, Gude safe us ! it's a sight for sair een to see a gold-laced jeistiecor in the Ha' garden sae late at e'en."

" A gold-laced what, my good friend ?"

" Ou, a jeistiecor,[1]—that's a jacket like your ain, there. They hae other things to do wi' them up yonder,—unbuttoning them to make room for the beef and the bag-puddings, and the claret-wine, nae doubt ; that's the ordinary for evening lecture on this side the Border."

" There's no such plenty of good cheer in your country, my good friend," I replied, " as to tempt you to sit so late at it."

" Hout, sir, ye ken little about Scotland ; it's no for want of gude vivers,—the best of fish, flesh, and fowl hae we, by sybos, ingans, turneeps, and other garden fruit. But we hae mense and discretion, and are moderate of our mouths ; but here, frae the kitchen to the ha', it's fill and fetch mair, frae the tae end of the four-and-twenty till the tother. Even their fast days,—they ca' it fasting when they hae the best o' sea-fish frae Hartlepool and Sunderland by land carriage, forbye trouts, grilses, salmon, and a' the lave o't, and so they make their very fasting a kind of luxury and abomination ; and then the awfu' masses and matins of the puir deceived souls,—but I shouldna speak about them, for your honour will be a Roman, I'se warrant, like the lave."

" Not I, my friend ; I was bred an English Presbyterian, or Dissenter."

[1] Perhaps from the French *Justaucorps*.

"The right hand of fellowship to your honour then," quoth the gardener, with as much alacrity as his hard features were capable of expressing; and, as if to show that his good-will did not rest on words, he plucked forth a huge horn snuff-box, or mull, as he called it, and proffered me a pinch with a most fraternal grin.

Having accepted his courtesy, I asked him if he had been long a domestic at Osbaldistone Hall.

"I have been fighting with wild beasts at Ephesus," said he, looking towards the building, "for the best part of these four-and-twenty years, as sure as my name's Andrew Fairservice."

"But, my excellent friend Andrew Fairservice, if your religion and your temperance are so much offended by Roman rituals and Southern hospitality, it seems to me that you must have been putting yourself to an unnecessary penance all this while, and that you might have found a service where they eat less, and are more orthodox in their worship. I dare say it cannot be want of skill which prevented your being placed more to your satisfaction."

"It disna become me to speak to the point of my quali-fications," said Andrew, looking round him with great com-placency; "but nae doubt I should understand my trade of horticulture, seeing I was bred in the parish of Dreepdaily, where they raise lang-kale under glass, and force the early nettles for their spring kale. And to speak truth, I hae been flitting every term these four-and-twenty years; but when the time comes, there's aye something to saw that I would like to see sawn, or something to maw that I would like to see mawn, or something to ripe that I would like to see ripen,—and sae I e'en daiker on wi' the family frae year's end to year's end. And I wad say for certain that I am gaun to quit at Cannlemas, only I was just as positive on it twenty years syne, and I find mysell still turning up the mouls here, for a' that. Forbye that, to tell your honour the evendown truth there's nae better place ever offered to Andrew. But if your honour wad wush me to ony place where I wad hear pure doctrine, and hae a free cow's grass, and a cot, and a yard, and mair than ten punds of annual fee, and where there's nae leddy about the town to count the apples, I'se hold mysell muckle indebted t' ye."

"Bravo, Andrew; I perceive you'll lose no preferment for want of asking patronage."

"I canna see what for I should," replied Andrew; "it's no a generation to wait till ane's worth's discovered, I trow."

"But you are no friend, I observe, to the ladies."

"Na, by my troth, I keep up the first gardener's quarrel to them. They're fasheous bargains,—aye crying for apricocks, pears, plums, and apples, summer and winter, without distinction o' seasons; but we hae nae slices o' the spare rib here, be praised for't!—except auld Martha, and she's weel eneugh pleased wi' the freedom o' the berry-bushes to her sister's weans, when they come to drink tea in a holiday in the housekeeper's room, and wi' a wheen codlings now and then for her ain private supper."

"You forget your young mistress."

"What mistress do I forget?—whae's that?"

"Your young mistress, Miss Vernon."

"What! the lassie Vernon?—She's nae mistress o' mine, man. I wish she was her own mistress; and I wish she mayna be some other body's mistress or it's lang. She's a wild slip that."

"Indeed!" said I, more interested than I cared to own to myself, or to show to the fellow,—"why, Andrew, you know all the secrets of this family."

"If I ken them, I can keep them," said Andrew; "they winna work in my wame like barm in a barrel, I'se warrant ye. Miss Die is— But it's neither beef nor brose o' mine."

And he began to dig with a great semblance of assiduity.

"What is Miss Vernon, Andrew? I am a friend of the family, and should like to know."

"Other than a gude ane, I'm fearing," said Andrew, closing one eye hard, and shaking his head with a grave and mysterious look,—"something glee'd; your honour understands me?"

"I cannot say I do," said I, "Andrew, but I should like to hear you explain yourself;" and therewithal I slipped a crown-piece into Andrew's horn-hard hand. The touch of the silver made him grin a ghastly smile, as he nodded slowly, and thrust it into his breeches pocket; and then, like a man who well understood that there was value to be returned, stood up, and rested his arms on his spade, with his features composed into the most important gravity, as for some serious communication.

"Ye maun ken, then, young gentleman, since it imports you to know, that Miss Vernon is—— "

Here breaking off, he sucked in both his cheeks till his lantern jaws and long chin assumed the appearance of a pair of nut-crackers, winked hard once more, frowned, shook his head, and seemed to think his physiognomy had completed the information which his tongue had not fully told.

"Good God!" said I, "so young, so beautiful, so early lost."

"Troth, ye may say sae,—she's in a manner lost body and saul; forby being a papist, I'se uphaud her for—" and his Northern caution prevailed, and he was again silent.

"For what, sir?" said I, sternly. "I insist on knowing the plain meaning of all this."

"Ou, just for the bitterest Jacobite in the haill shire."

"Pshaw! a Jacobite?—is that all?"

Andrew looked at me with some astonishment, at hearing his information treated so lightly; and then muttering, "Aweel, it's the warst thing I ken aboot the lassie, howsoe're," he resumed his spade, like the King of the Vandals, in Marmontel's late novel.

(*Rob Roy*.)

SAMUEL TAYLOR COLERIDGE (1772–1834)

I.—The Lyrical Ballads

DURING the first year that Mr. Wordsworth and I were neighbours, our conversations turned frequently on the two cardinal points of poetry, the power of exciting the sympathy of the reader by a faithful adherence to the truth of nature, and the power of giving the interest of novelty by the modifying colours of imagination. The sudden charm which accidents of light and shade, which moonlight or sunset, diffused over a known and familiar landscape, appeared to represent the practicability of combining both. These are the poetry of nature. The thought suggested itself (to which of us I do not recollect) that a series of poems might be composed of two sorts. In the one, the incidents and agents were to be in part at least, supernatural; and the excellence aimed at was to consist in the interesting of the affections by the dramatic truth of such emotions, as would naturally accompany such situations, supposing them real. And real in this sense they have been to every human being who, from whatever source of delusion, has at any time believed himself under supernatural agency. For the second class, subjects were to be chosen from ordinary life; the characters and incidents were to be such as will be found in every village and its vicinity where there is a meditative mind to seek after them, or to notice them when they present themselves.

In this idea originated the plan of the "Lyrical Ballads"; in which it was agreed that my endeavours should be directed to persons and characters supernatural, or at least romantic; yet so as to transfer from our inward nature a human interest and a semblance of truth sufficient to procure for these shadows of imagination that willing suspension of disbelief for the moment, which constitutes poetic faith. Mr. Wordsworth, on the other hand, was to propose to himself as his object, to give the charm of novelty to things of every day, and to excite a feeling analogous to the supernatural, by awakening the mind's attention from the lethargy of custom, and directing it to the loveliness and the wonders of the world before us; an inexhaustible treasure, but for which, in consequence of the film of familiarity and selfish solicitude, we have eyes, yet see not, ears that hear not, and hearts that neither feel nor understand.

With this view I wrote the "Ancient Mariner," and was preparing among other poems, the "Dark Ladie," and the "Christabel," in which I should have more nearly realised my ideal than I had done in my first attempt. But Mr. Wordsworth's industry had proved so much more successful, and the number of his poems so much greater, that my compositions, instead of forming a balance, appeared rather an interpolation of heterogeneous matter. Mr. Wordsworth added two or three poems written in his own character, in the impassioned, lofty, and sustained diction which is characteristic of his genius. In this form the "Lyrical Ballads" were published; and were presented by him as an experiment, whether subjects, which from their nature rejected the usual ornaments and extra-colloquial style of poems in general, might not be so managed in the language of ordinary life as to produce the pleasurable interest which it is the peculiar business of poetry to impart.

(Biographia Literaria.)

II.—HAMLET

The seeming inconsistencies in the conduct and character of Hamlet have long exercised the conjectural ingenuity of critics; and, as we are always loth to suppose that the cause of defective apprehension is in ourselves, the mystery has been too commonly explained by the very easy process of setting it down as in fact inexplicable, and by resolving the phenomenon into a misgrowth or *lusus* of the capricious and irregular genius of Shakespeare. The shallow and stupid arrogance of these vulgar and indolent decisions I would fain do my best to expose. I believe the character of Hamlet may be traced to Shakespeare's deep and accurate science in mental philosophy. Indeed, that this character must have some connection with the common fundamental laws of our nature may be assumed from the fact that Hamlet has been the darling of every country in which the literature of England has been fostered. In order to understand him, it is essential that we should reflect on the constitution of our own minds. Man is distinguished from the brute animals in proportion as thought prevails over sense: but in the healthy processes of the mind, a balance is constantly maintained between the impressions from outward objects and the inward operations of the intellect;—for if there be an over-balance in the contemplative faculty, man thereby becomes the centre of mere meditation, and loses his natural power of action. Now one of Shakespeare's modes of creating characters is, to conceive any one intellectual or moral faculty in morbid excess, and then to place himself, Shakespeare, thus mutilated or diseased, under given circumstances. In Hamlet he seems to have wished to exemplify the moral necessity of a due balance between our attention to the objects of our senses and our meditation on the workings of our minds—an equilibrium between the real and the imaginary worlds. In Hamlet this balance is disturbed: his thoughts, and the images of his fancy, are far more vivid than his actual perceptions, and his very perceptions, instantly passing through the medium of his contemplations, acquire, as they pass, a form and a colour not naturally their own. Hence we see a great, an almost enormous, intellectual activity, and a proportionate aversion to real action consequent upon it, with all its symptoms and accompanying qualities. This character Shakespeare places in circumstances under which it is obliged to act on the spur of the moment :— Hamlet is brave and careless of death, but he vacillates from sensibility, and procrastinates from thought, and loses the power of action in the energy of resolve. Thus it is that this tragedy presents a direct contrast to that of Macbeth; the one proceeds with the utmost slowness, the other with a crowded and breathless rapidity.

(Lectures on Shakespeare.)

JANE AUSTEN (1775–1817)

A FAMILY QUARREL

IT is a truth universally acknowledged, that a single man in possession of a good fortune must be in want of a wife.

However little known the feelings or views of such a man may be on his first entering a neighbourhood, this truth is so well fixed in the minds of the surrounding families, that he is considered as the rightful property of some one or other of their daughters.

"My dear Mr. Bennet," said his lady to him one day, "have you heard that Netherfield Park is let at last?"

Mr. Bennet replied that he had not.

"But it is," returned she; "for Mrs. Long has just been here, and she told me all about it."

Mr. Bennet made no answer.

"Do not you want to know who has taken it?" cried his wife impatiently.

"*You* want to tell me, and I have no objection to hearing it."

This was invitation enough.

"Why, my dear, you must know, Mrs. Long says that Netherfield is taken by a young man of large fortune from the north of England; that he came down on Monday in a chaise and four to see the place, and was so much delighted with it, that he agreed with Mr. Morris immediately; that he is to take possession before Michaelmas, and some of his servants are to be in the house by the end of next week."

"What is his name?"

"Bingley."

"Is he married or single?"

"Oh! single, my dear, to be sure! A single man of large fortune; four or five thousand a-year. What a fine thing for our girls!"

"How so? how can it affect them?"

"My dear Mr. Bennet," replied his wife, "how can you be so tiresome! you must know that I am thinking of his marrying one of them."

"Is that his design in settling here?"

"Design! nonsense, how can you talk so! But it is very likely that he *may* fall in love with one of them, and therefore you must visit him as soon as he comes."

"I see no occasion for that. You and the girls may go, or you may send them by themselves, which perhaps will be still better, for as you are as handsome as any of them, Mr. Bingley might like you the best of the party."

"My dear, you flatter me. I certainly *have* had my share of beauty, but I do not pretend to be anything extraordinary now. When a woman has five grown-up daughters, she ought to give over thinking of her own beauty."

"In such cases, a woman has not often much beauty to think of."

"But, my dear, you must indeed go and see Mr. Bingley when he comes into the neighbourhood."

" It is more than I engage for, I assure you."

" But consider your daughters. Only think what an establishment it would be for one of them. Sir William and Lady Lucas are determined to go, merely on that account, for in general, you know, they visit no new-comers. Indeed, you must go, for it will be impossible for *us* to visit him if you do not."

" You are over-scrupulous, surely. I dare say Mr. Bingley will be very glad to see you ; and I will send a few lines by you to assure him of my hearty consent to his marrying whichever he chuses of the girls : though I must throw in a good word for my little Lizzy."

" I desire you will do no such thing. Lizzy is not a bit better than the others ; and I am sure she is not half so handsome as Jane, nor half so good-humoured as Lydia. But you are always giving *her* the preference."

" They have none of them much to recommend them," replied he ; " they are all silly and ignorant, like other girls ; but Lizzy has something more of quickness than her sisters."

" Mr. Bennet, how can you abuse your own children in such a way ! You take delight in vexing me. You have no compassion on my poor nerves."

" You mistake me, my dear. I have a high respect for your nerves. They are my old friends. I have heard you mention them with consideration these twenty years at least."

" Ah ! you do not know what I suffer."

" But I hope you will get over it, and live to see many young men of four thousand a-year come into the neighbourhood."

" It will be no use to us, if twenty such should come, since you will not visit them."

" Depend upon it, my dear, that when there are twenty, I will visit them all."

Mr. Bennet was so odd a mixture of quick parts, sarcastic humour, reserve, and caprice, that the experience of three-and-twenty years had been insufficient to make his wife understand his character. *Her* mind was less difficult to develope. She was a woman of mean understanding, little information, and uncertain temper. When she was discontented, she fancied herself nervous. The business of her life was to get her daughters married ; its solace was visiting and news.

Mr. Bennet was among the earliest of those who waited on Mr. Bingley. He had always intended to visit him, though to the last always assuring his wife that he should not go ; and till the evening after the visit was paid she had no knowledge of it. It was then disclosed in the following manner :—Observing his second daughter employed in trimming a hat, he suddenly addressed her with—

"I hope Mr. Bingley will like it, Lizzy."

"We are not in a way to know *what* Mr. Bingley likes," said her mother resentfully, "since we are not to visit."

"But you forget, mamma," said Elizabeth, "that we shall meet him at the assemblies, and that Mrs. Long has promised to introduce him."

"I do not believe Mrs. Long will do any such thing. She has two nieces of her own. She is a selfish, hypocritical woman, and I have no opinion of her."

"No more have I," said Mr. Bennet; "and I am glad to find that you do not depend on her serving you."

Mrs. Bennet deigned not to make any reply, but, unable to contain herself, began scolding one of her daughters.

"Don't keep coughing so, Kitty, for Heaven's sake ! Have a little compassion on my nerves. You tear them to pieces."

"Kitty has no discretion in her coughs," said her father; "she times them ill."

"I do not cough for my own amusement," replied Kitty fretfully. "When is your next ball to be, Lizzy ? "

"To-morrow fortnight."

"Aye, so it is," cried her mother, "and Mrs. Long does not come back till the day before; so it will be impossible for her to introduce him, for she will not know him herself."

"Then, my dear, you may have the advantage of your friend, and introduce Mr. Bingley to *her*."

"Impossible, Mr. Bennet, impossible, when I am not acquainted with him myself; how can you be so teazing ? "

"I honour your circumspection. A fortnight's acquaintance is certainly very little. One cannot know what a man really is by the end of a fortnight. But if *we* do not venture somebody else will; and after all, Mrs. Long and her nieces must stand their chance; and, therefore, as she will think it an act of kindness, if you decline the office, I will take it on myself."

The girls stared at their father. Mrs. Bennet said only, "Nonsense, nonsense ! "

"What can be the meaning of that emphatic exclamation ? " cried he. "Do you consider the forms of introduction, and the stress that is laid on them, as nonsense ? I cannot quite agree with you *there*. What say you, Mary ? for you are a young lady of deep reflection, I know, and read great books and make extracts."

Mary wished to say something very sensible, but knew not how.

"While Mary is adjusting her ideas," he continued, "let us return to Mr. Bingley."

"I am sick of Mr. Bingley," cried his wife.

"I am sorry to hear *that*; but why did not you tell me so before? If I had known as much this morning I certainly would not have called on him. It is very unlucky; but as I have actually paid the visit, we cannot escape the acquaintance now."

The astonishment of the ladies was just what he wished; that of Mrs. Bennet perhaps surpassing the rest; though, when the first tumult of joy was over, she began to declare that it was what she had expected all the while.

"How good it was in you, my dear Mr. Bennet! But I knew I should persuade you at last. I was sure you loved your girls too well to neglect such an acquaintance. Well, how pleased I am! and it is such a good joke, too, that you should have gone this morning and never said a word about it till now."

"Now, Kitty, you may cough as much as you chuse," said Mr. Bennet; and, as he spoke, he left the room, fatigued with the raptures of his wife.

"What an excellent father you have, girls!" said she, when the door was shut. "I do not know how you will ever make him amends for his kindness; or me either, for that matter. At our time of life it is not so pleasant, I can tell you, to be making new acquaintance every day; but for your sakes, we would do anything. Lydia, my love, though you *are* the youngest, I dare say Mr. Bingley will dance with you at the next ball."

"Oh!" said Lydia stoutly, "I am not afraid; for though I *am* the youngest, I'm the tallest."

The rest of the evening was spent in conjecturing how soon he would return Mr. Bennet's visit, and determining when they should ask him to dinner.

(*Pride and Prejudice.*)

WALTER SAVAGE LANDOR (1775–1864)

A Vision of Love, Sleep, and Death

Two beautiful youths appeared beside me; each was winged; but the wings were hanging down and seemed ill-adapted to flight. One of them, whose voice was the softest I ever heard, looking at me frequently, said to the other—

"He is under my guardianship for the present, do not

awaken him with that feather." Methought, hearing the whisper, I saw something like the feather on an arrow; and then the arrow itself; the whole of it, even to the point; although he carried it in such a manner that it was difficult at first to discover more than a palm's length of it : the rest of the shaft, and the whole of the barb, was behind his ankles.

"This feather never awakens any one," replied he rather petulantly; "but it brings more confident security, and more of cherished dreams, than you without me are capable of imparting."

"Be it so!" answered the gentler; "none is less inclined to quarrel or dispute than I am. Many whom you have wounded grievously call upon me for succour. But so little am I disposed to thwart you, it is seldom I venture to do more for them than to whisper a few words of comfort in passing. How many reproaches on these occasions have been cast upon me for indifference and infidelity! Nearly as many, and nearly in the same terms, as upon you!"

"Odd enough that we, O Sleep! should be thought so alike!" said Love, contemptuously. "Yonder is he who bears a nearer resemblance to you : the dullest have observed it." I fancied I turned my eyes to where he was pointing, and saw at a distance the figure he designated. Meanwhile the contention went on uninterruptedly. Sleep was slow in asserting his power or his benefits. Love recapitulated them; but only that he might assert his own above them. Suddenly he called on me to decide, and to choose my patron. Under the influence, first of the one, then of the other, I sprang from repose to rapture, I alighted from rapture on repose . . . and knew not which was sweetest. Love was very angry with me, and declared he would cross me throughout the whole of my existence. Whatever I might on other occasions have thought of his veracity, I now felt too surely the conviction that he would keep his word. At last, before the close of the altercation, the third genius had advanced, and stood near us. I cannot tell how I knew him, but I knew him to be the genius of Death. Breathless as I was at beholding him, I soon became familiar with his features. First they seemed only calm; presently they grew contemplative; and lastly beautiful : those of the graces themselves are less regular, less harmonious, less composed. Love glanced at him unsteadily, with a countenance in which there was somewhat of anxiety, somewhat of disdain; and cried, "Go away! go away! nothing that thou touchest, lives!" "Say rather, child!" replied the advancing form, and advancing grew loftier

and statelier, " Say rather that nothing of beautiful or of glorious
lives its own true life until my wing hath passed over it."

Love pouted, and rumpled and bent down with his forefinger
the stiff short feathers on his arrow head; but replied not.
Although he frowned worse than ever, and at me, I dreaded him
less and less, and scarcely looked toward him. The milder and
calmer genius, the third, in proportion as I took courage to
contemplate him, regarded me with more and more complacency.
He held neither flower nor arrow, as the others did; but, throwing back the cluster of dark curls that overshadowed his countenance, he presented to me his hand, openly and benignly. I
shrank on looking at him so near, and yet I sighed to love him.
He smiled, not without an expression of pity, at perceiving my
diffidence, my timidity: for I remembered how soft was the
hand of Sleep, how warm and entrancing was Love's. By
degrees, I became ashamed of my ingratitude; and turning my
face away I held out my arms, and felt my neck within his.
Composure strewed and allayed all the throbbings of my bosom;
the coolness of freshest morning breathed around; the heavens
seemed to open above me; while the beautiful cheek of my
deliverer rested on my head. I would now have looked for those
others; but knowing my intention by my gesture, he said
consolatorily—

" Sleep is on his way to the earth where many are calling
him; but it is not to these he hastens; for every call only makes
him fly farther off. Sedately and gravely as he looks, he is
nearly as capricious and volatile as the more arrogant and
ferocious one."

" And Love ! " said I, " whither is he departed ? If not too
late, I would propitiate and appease him."

" He who cannot follow me, he who cannot overtake and pass
me," said the genius, " is unworthy of the name, the most
glorious in earth or heaven. Look up ! Love is yonder, and
ready to receive thee."

I looked: the earth was under me: I saw only the clear blue
sky, and something brighter above it.

(The Pentameron.)

CHARLES LAMB (1775–1834)

I.—MACKERY END IN HERTFORDSHIRE

BRIDGET ELIA has been my housekeeper for many a long
year. I have obligations to Bridget, extending beyond the
period of memory. We house together, old bachelor and

Anthology of Prose 245

maid, in a sort of double singleness; with such tolerable comfort, upon the whole, that I, for one, find in myself no sort of disposition to go out upon the mountains, with the rash king's offspring, to bewail my celibacy. We agree pretty well in our tastes and habits—yet so, as "with a difference." We are generally in harmony, with occasional bickerings—as it should be among near relations. Our sympathies are rather understood, than expressed; and once, upon my dissembling a tone in my voice more kind than ordinary, my cousin burst into tears, and complained that I was altered. We are both great readers in different directions. While I am hanging over (for the thousandth time) some passage in old Burton, or one of his strange contemporaries, she is abstracted in some modern tale, or adventure, whereof our common reading-table is daily fed with assiduously fresh supplies. Narrative teases me. I have little concern in the progress of events. She must have a story—well, ill, or indifferently told—so there be life stirring in it, and plenty of good or evil accidents. The fluctuations of fortune in fiction—and almost in real life—have ceased to interest, or operate but dully upon me. Out-of-the-way humours and opinions—heads with some diverting twist in them—the oddities of authorship please me most. My cousin has a native disrelish of anything that sounds odd or bizarre. Nothing goes down with her, that is quaint, irregular, or out of the road of common sympathy. She "holds Nature more clever." I can pardon her blindness to the beautiful obliquities of the Religio Medici; but she must apologise to me for certain disrespectful insinuations, which she has been pleased to throw out latterly, touching the intellectuals of a dear favourite of mine, of the last century but one—the thrice noble, chaste, and virtuous,—but again somewhat fantastical, and original-brained, generous Margaret Newcastle.

It has been the lot of my cousin, oftener perhaps than I could have wished, to have had for her associates and mine, free-thinkers—leaders, and disciples, of novel philosophies and systems; but she neither wrangles with, nor accepts, their opinions. That which was good and venerable to her, when a child, retains its authority over her mind still. She never juggles or plays tricks with her understanding.

We are both of us inclined to be a little too positive; and I have observed the result of our disputes to be almost uniformly this—that in matters of fact, dates, and circumstances, it turns out that I was in the right, and my cousin in the wrong. But where we have differed upon moral points; upon something proper to be done, or let alone; whatever heat of opposition, or steadiness of conviction, I set out with, I am sure always, in the long-run, to be brought over to her way of thinking.

I must touch upon the foibles of my kinswoman with a gentle hand, for Bridget does not like to be told of her faults. She hath an awkward trick (to say no worse of it) of reading in company; at which times she will answer *yes* or *no* to a question, without fully understanding its purport—which is provoking, and derogatory in the highest degree to the dignity of the putter of the said question. Her presence of mind is equal to the most pressing trials of life, but will sometimes desert her upon trifling occasions. When the purpose requires it, and is a thing of moment, she can speak to it greatly; but in matters which are not stuff of the conscience, she hath been known sometimes to let slip a word less seasonably.

Her education in youth was not much attended to; and she happily missed all that train of female garniture, which passeth by the name of accomplishments. She was tumbled early, by accident or design, into a spacious closet of good old English reading, without much selection or prohibition, and browsed at will upon that fair and wholesome pasturage. Had I twenty girls, they should be brought up exactly in this fashion. I know not whether their chance in wedlock might not be diminished by it; but I can answer for it, that it makes (if the worst come to the worst) most incomparable old maids.

In a season of distress, she is the truest comforter; but in the teasing accidents, and minor perplexities, which do not call out the *will* to meet them, she sometimes maketh matters worse by an excess of participation. If she does not always divide your trouble, upon the pleasanter occasions of life she is sure always to treble your satisfaction. She is excellent to be at a play with, or upon a visit; but best, when she goes a journey with you.

We made an excursion together a few summers since into Hertfordshire, to beat up the quarters of some of our less-known relations in that fine corn country.

The oldest thing I remember is Mackery End—or Mackarel End, as it is spelt, perhaps more properly, in some old maps of Hertfordshire—a farm-house, delightfully situated within a gentle walk from Wheathampstead. I can just remember having been there, on a visit to a great-aunt, when I was a child, under the care of Bridget; who, as I have said, is older than myself by some ten years. I wish that I could throw into a heap the remainder of our joint existences, that we

might share them in equal division. But that is impossible.
The house was at that time in the occupation of a substantial
yeoman, who had married my grandmother's sister. His name
was Gladman. My grandmother was a Bruton, married to a
Field. The Gladmans and the Brutons are still flourishing in
that part of the county, but the Fields are almost extinct.
More than forty years had elapsed since the visit I speak of;
and, for the greater portion of that period, we had lost sight
of the other two branches also. Who or what sort of persons
inherited Mackery End—kindred or strange folk—we were
afraid almost to conjecture, but determined some day to explore.

By somewhat a circuitous route, taking the noble park at
Luton in our way from Saint Albans, we arrived at the spot of
our anxious curiosity about noon. The sight of the old farm-
house, though every trace of it was effaced from my recollection,
affected me with a pleasure which I had not experienced for
many a year. For though _I_ had forgotten it, _we_ had never
forgotten being there together, and we had been talking about
Mackery End all our lives, till memory on my part became
mocked with a phantom of itself, and I thought I knew the
aspect of a place, which, when present, O how unlike it was to
that, which I had conjured up so many times instead of it!

Still the air breathed balmily about it; the season was in the
" heart of June," and I could say with the poet—

> But thou, that didst appear so fair
> To fond imagination,
> Dost rival in the light of day
> Her delicate creation!

Bridget's was more a waking bliss than mine, for she easily
remembered her old acquaintance again—some altered features,
of course, a little grudged at. At first, indeed, she was ready
to disbelieve for joy; but the scene soon re-confirmed itself in
her affections—and she traversed every outpost of the old
mansion, to the wood-house, the orchard, the place where the
pigeon-house had stood (house and birds were alike flown)—
with a breathless impatience of recognition, which was more
pardonable perhaps than decorous at the age of fifty odd. But
Bridget in some things is behind her years.

The only thing left was to get into the house—and that was
a difficulty which to me singly would have been insurmount-
able; for I am terribly shy in making myself known to strangers
and out-of-date kinsfolk. Love, stronger than scruple, winged
my cousin in without me; but she soon returned with a creature
that might have sat to a sculptor for the image of Welcome.

It was the youngest of the Gladmans; who, by marriage with a Bruton, had become mistress of the old mansion. A comely brood are the Brutons. Six of them, females, were noted as the handsomest young women in the county. But this adopted Bruton, in my mind, was better than they all—more comely. She was born too late to have remembered me. She just recollected in early life to have had her cousin Bridget once pointed out to her, climbing a stile. But the name of kindred, and of cousinship, was enough. Those slender ties, that prove slight as gossamer in the rending atmosphere of a metropolis, bind faster, as we found it, in hearty, homely, loving Hertfordshire. In five minutes we were as thoroughly acquainted as if we had been born and bred up together; were familiar, even to the calling each other by our Christian names. So Christians should call one another. To have seen Bridget, and her—it was like the meeting of the two scriptural cousins! There was a grace and dignity, an amplitude of form and stature, answering to her mind, in this farmer's wife, which would have shined in a palace—or so we thought it. We were made welcome by husband and wife equally—we, and our friend that was with us—I had almost forgotten him—but B. F. will not so soon forget that meeting, if peradventure he shall read this on the far distant shores where the kangaroo haunts. The fatted calf was made ready, or rather was already so, as if in anticipation of our coming; and, after an appropriate glass of native wine, never let me forget with what honest pride this hospitable cousin made us proceed to Wheathampstead, to introduce us (as some new found rarity) to her mother and sister Gladmans, who did indeed know something more of us, at a time when she almost knew nothing.—With what corresponding kindness we were received by them also—how Bridget's memory, exalted by the occasion, warmed into a thousand half-obliterated recollections of things and persons, to my utter astonishment, and her own—and to the astoundment of B. F., who sat by, almost the only thing that was not a cousin there—old effaced images of more than half-forgotten names and circumstances still crowding back upon her, as words written in lemon come out upon exposure to a friendly warmth,—when I forget all this, then may my country cousins forget me; and Bridget no more remember, that in the days of weakling infancy I was her tender charge—as I have been her care in foolish manhood since—in those pretty pastoral walks, long ago, about Mackery End, in Hertfordshire.

(*Essays of Elia.*)

II.—A Quakers' Meeting

Reader, wouldst thou know what true peace and quiet mean; wouldst thou find a refuge from the noises and clamours of the multitude; wouldst thou enjoy at once solitude and society; wouldst thou possess the depth of thine own spirit in stillness, without being shut out from the consolatory faces of thy species; wouldst thou be alone and yet accompanied; solitary, yet not desolate; singular, yet not without some to keep thee in countenance; a unit in aggregate; a simple in composite :—come with me into a Quakers' Meeting.

Dost thou love silence deep as that " before the winds were made "? go not out into the wilderness, descend not into the profundities of the earth; shut not up thy casements; nor pour wax into the little cells of thy ears, with little-faith'd self-mistrusting Ulysses.—Retire with me into a Quakers' Meeting.

For a man to refrain even from good words, and to hold his peace, it is commendable; but for a multitude it is great mastery.

What is the stillness of the desert compared with this place? what the uncommunicating muteness of fishes?—here the goddess reigns and revels.—" Boreas, and Cesias, and Argestes loud," do not with their interconfounding uproars more augment the brawl—nor the waves of the blown Baltic with their clubbed sounds—than their opposite (Silence her sacred self) is multiplied and rendered more intense by numbers, and by sympathy. She too hath her deeps, that call unto deeps. Negation itself hath a positive more and less : and closed eyes would seem to obscure the great obscurity of midnight.

There are wounds which an imperfect solitude cannot heal. By imperfect I mean that which a man enjoyeth by himself. The perfect is that which he can sometimes attain in crowds, but nowhere so absolutely as in a Quakers' Meeting.—Those first hermits did certainly understand this principle, when they retired into Egyptian solitudes, not singly, but in shoals, to enjoy one another's want of conversation. The Carthusian is bound to his brethren by this agreeing spirit of incommunicativeness. In secular occasions, what so pleasant as to be reading a book through a long winter evening, with a friend sitting by—say, a wife—he, or she, too (if that be probable), reading another without interruption, or oral communication? —can there be no sympathy without the gabble of words?— away with this inhuman, shy, single, shade-and-cavern-haunting solitariness. Give me, Master Zimmerman, a sympathetic solitude.

To pace alone in the cloisters or side aisles of some cathedral, time-stricken;

> Or under hanging mountains,
> Or by the fall of fountains ;

is but a vulgar luxury compared with that which those enjoy who come together for the purposes of more complete, abstracted solitude. This is the loneliness " to be felt."—The Abbey Church of Westminster hath nothing so solemn, so spirit soothing, as the naked walls and benches of a Quakers' Meeting. Here are no tombs, no inscriptions.

> ——Sands, ignoble things,
> Dropt from the ruined sides of kings—

but here is something which throws Antiquity herself into the foreground—SILENCE—eldest of things—language of old Night —primitive discourser—to which the insolent decays of mouldering grandeur have but arrived by a violent, and, as we may say, unnatural progression.

> How reverend is the view of these hushed heads,
> Looking tranquillity !

Nothing-plotting, nought-caballing, unmischievous synod ! convocation without intrigue ! parliament without debate ! what a lesson dost thou read to council, and to consistory !— if my pen treat of you lightly—as haply it will wander—yet my spirit hath gravely felt the wisdom of your custom, when, sitting among you in deepest peace, which some out-welling tears would rather confirm than disturb, I have reverted to the times of your beginnings, and the sowings of the seed by Fox and Dewesbury.—I have witnessed that which brought before my eyes your heroic tranquillity, inflexible to the rude jests and serious violences of the insolent soldiery, republican or royalist, sent to molest you—for ye sate betwixt the fires of two persecutions, the outcast and offscouring of church and presbytery.—I have seen the reeling sea-ruffian, who had wandered into your receptacle with the avowed intention of disturbing your quiet, from the very spirit of the place receive in a moment a new heart, and presently sit among ye as a lamb amidst lambs. And I remember Penn before his accusers, and Fox in the bail dock, where he was lifted up in spirit, as he tells us, and " the Judge and the Jury became as dead men under his feet."

Reader, if you are not acquainted with it, I would recommend to you, above all church-narratives, to read Sewel's *History of the Quakers*. It is in folio, and is the abstract of the journals of Fox and the primitive Friends. It is far more edifying and affecting than anything you will read of Wesley and his colleagues. Here is nothing to stagger you, nothing to make you mistrust, no suspicion of alloy, no drop or dreg of the worldly or ambitious spirit. You will here read the true story of that much-injured, ridiculed man (who perhaps hath been a byword in your mouth)—James Naylor: what dreadful sufferings, with what patience, he endured, even to the boring through of his tongue with red-hot irons, without a murmur; and with what strength of mind, when the delusion he had fallen into, which they stigmatized for blasphemy, had given way to clearer thoughts, he could renounce his error, in a strain of the beautifullest humility, yet keep his first grounds, and be a Quaker still !—so different from the practice of your common converts from enthusiasm, who, when they apostatize *apostatize all*, and think they can never get far enough from the society of their former errors, even to the renunciation of some saving truths, with which they had been mingled, not implicated.

Get the writings of John Woolman [1] by heart; and love the early Quakers.

How far the followers of these good men in our days have kept to the primitive spirit, or in what proportion they have substituted formality for it, the Judge of Spirits can alone determine. I have seen faces in their assemblies upon which the dove sate visibly brooding. Others, again, I have watched, when my thoughts should have been better engaged, in which I could possibly detect nothing but a blank inanity. But quiet was in all, and the disposition to unanimity, and the absence of the fierce controversial workings.—If the spiritual pretensions of the Quakers have abated, at least they make few pretences. Hypocrites they certainly are not in their preaching. It is seldom, indeed, that you shall see one get up amongst them to hold forth. Only now and then a trembling, female, generally *ancient*, voice is heard—you cannot guess from what part of the meeting it proceeds—with a low, buzzing, musical sound, laying out a few words which " she thought might suit the condition of some present," with a quaking diffidence, which leaves no possibility of supposing that anything of female vanity was mixed up, where the tones were so full of tenderness, and a restraining modesty.—The men, for what I have observed, speak seldomer.

[1] 1720–72. One of the best known of the American Quakers.

Once only, and it was some years ago, I witnessed a sample of the old Foxian orgasm. It was a man of giant stature, who, as Wordsworth phrases it, might have danced " from head to foot equipt in iron mail." His frame was of iron too. But *he* was malleable. I saw him shake all over with the spirit—I dare not say of delusion. The strivings of the outer man were unutterable—he seemed not to speak, but to be spoken from. I saw the strong man bowed down, and his knees to fail—his joints all seemed loosening—it was a figure to set off against Paul preaching—the words he uttered were few, and sound— he was evidently resisting his will—keeping down his own word-wisdom with more mighty effort than the world's orators strain for theirs. " He had been a WIT in his youth," he told us, with expressions of a sober remorse. And it was not till long after the impression had begun to wear away that I was enabled, with something like a smile, to recall the striking incongruity of the confession—understanding the term in its worldly accepta-tion—with the frame and physiognomy of the person before me. His brow would have scared away the Levites—the Jocos Risus-que—faster than the Loves fled the face of Dis at Enna.— By *wit*, even in his youth, I will be sworn he understood some-thing far within the limits of an allowable liberty.

More frequently the Meeting is broken up without a word having been spoken. But the mind has been fed. You go away with a sermon not made with hands. You have been in milder caverns of Trophonius; or as in some den, where that fiercest and savagest of all wild creatures, the TONGUE, that unruly member, has strangely lain tied up and captive. You have bathed with stillness.—Oh, when the spirit is sore fretted, even tired to sickness of the janglings and nonsense-noises of the world, what a balm and a solace it is to go and seat yourself for a quiet half-hour upon some undisputed corner of a bench, among the gentle Quakers !

Their garb and stillness conjoined present a uniformity, tran-quil and herd-like—as in the pasture—" forty feeding like one."

The very garments of a Quaker seem incapable of receiving a soil ; and cleanliness in them to be something more than the absence of its contrary. Every Quakeress is a lily ; and when they come up in bands to their Whitsun conferences, whitening the easterly streets of the metropolis, from all part of the United Kingdom, they show like troops of the Shining Ones.

                                              (*Essays of Elia.*)

III.—Dream Children : A Reverie

Children love to listen to stories about their elders, when *they* were children; to stretch their imagination to the conception of a traditional great-uncle, or granddame, whom they never saw. It was in this spirit that my little ones crept about me the other evening to hear about their great-grandmother Field, who lived in a great house in Norfolk (a hundred times bigger than that in which they and papa lived) which had been the scene—so at least it was generally believed in that part of the country—of the tragic incidents which they had lately become familiar with from the ballad of the " Children in the Wood." Certain it is that the whole story of the children and their cruel uncle was to be seen fairly carved out in wood upon the chimney-piece of the great hall, the whole story down to the Robin Redbreasts; till a foolish rich person pulled it down to set up a marble one of modern invention in its stead, with no story upon it. Here Alice put out one of her dear mother's looks, too tender to be called upbraiding. Then I went on to say, how religious and how good their great-grandmother Field was, how beloved and respected by everybody, though she was not indeed the mistress of this great house, but had only the charge of it (and yet in some respects she might be said to be the mistress of it too) committed to her by the owner, who preferred living in a newer and more fashionable mansion which he had purchased somewhere in the adjoining county; but still she lived in it in a manner as if it had been her own, and kept up the dignity of the great house, in a sort while she lived which afterwards came to decay, and was nearly pulled down, and all its old ornaments stripped and carried away to the owner's other house, where they were set up, and looked as awkward as if some one were to carry away the old tombs they had seen lately at the Abbey, and stick them up in Lady C.'s tawdry gilt drawing-room. Here John smiled, as much as to say, " that would be foolish indeed." And then I told how, when she came to die, her funeral was attended by a concourse of all the poor, and some of the gentry too, of the neighbourhood for many miles round, to show their respect for her memory, because she had been such a good and religious woman; so good indeed that she knew all the Psaltery by heart, ay, and a great part of the Testament besides. Here little Alice spread her hands. Then I told what a tall, upright, graceful person their great-grandmother Field once was; and how in her youth she was esteemed the best dancer—here Alice's little right foot played an involuntary movement, till, upon my looking grave, it desisted—the best dancer, I was saying, in the county, till a cruel disease called a cancer, came, and bowed her down with pain; but it could never bend her good spirits, or make them stoop, but they were still upright, because she was so good and religious. Then I told how she was used to sleep by herself in a lone chamber of the great lone house; and how she believed that an apparition of two infants was to be seen at midnight gliding up and down the great staircase near where she slept, but she said " those innocents would do her no harm "; and how frightened I used to be, though in those days I had my maid to sleep with me, because I was never half so good or religious as she—and yet I never saw the infants. Here John expanded all his eyebrows and tried to look courageous. Then I told how good she was to all her grandchildren, having us to the great house in the holydays, where I in particular used to spend many hours by myself, in gazing upon the old busts of the twelve Cæsars, that had been Emperors of Rome, till the old marble heads would seem to live again, or I to be turned into marble with them; how I never could be tired with roaming about that huge mansion, with its vast empty rooms, with their worn-out hangings, fluttering tapestry, and carved oaken panels, with the gilding almost rubbed out—sometimes in the spacious old-fashioned gardens, which I had almost to myself, unless when now and then a solitary gardening man would cross me—and how the nectarines and peaches hung upon the walls, without my ever offering to pluck them, because they were forbidden fruit, unless now and then,—and because I had more pleasure in strolling about among the old melancholy-looking yew-trees, or the firs, and picking up the red berries, and the fir-apples, which were good for nothing but to look at—or in lying about upon the fresh grass with all the fine garden smells around me—or basking in the orangery, till I could almost fancy myself ripening too along with the oranges and the limes in that grateful warmth—or in watching the dace that darted to and fro in the fish-pond, at the bottom of the garden, with here and there a great sulky pike hanging midway down the water in silent state, as if it mocked at their impertinent friskings,—I had more pleasure in these busy-idle diversions than in all the sweet flavours of peaches, nectarines, oranges, and such-like common baits of children. Here John slyly deposited back upon the plate a bunch of grapes, which, not unobserved by Alice, he had meditated dividing with her, and both seemed willing to relinquish them for the present as irrelevant. Then, in somewhat a more heightened tone, I told how, though their great-grandmother Field loved all her grandchildren, yet in an especial manner she might be said to love their uncle, John L——, because he was so handsome and spirited a youth, and a king to the rest of us; and, instead of moping about in solitary corners, like some of us, he would mount the most mettlesome horse he could get, when but an imp no bigger than themselves, and make it carry him half over the county in a morning, and join the hunters when there were any out—and yet he loved the old great house and gardens too, but had too much spirit to be always pent up within their boundaries—and how their uncle grew up to man's estate as brave as he was handsome, to the admiration of everybody, but of their great-grandmother Field most especially; and how he used to carry me upon his back when I was a lame-footed boy—for he was a good bit older than me—many a mile when I could not walk for pain;— and how in after life he became lame-footed too, and I did not always (I fear) make allowances enough for him when he was impatient and in pain, nor remember sufficiently how considerate he had been to me when I was lame-footed; and how when he died, though he had not been dead an hour, it seemed as if he had died a great while ago, such a distance there is betwixt life and death; and how I bore his death as I thought pretty well at first, but afterwards it haunted and haunted me; and though I did not cry or take it to heart as some do, and as I think he would have done if I had died, yet I missed him all day long, and knew not till then how much I had loved him. I missed his kindness, and I missed his crossness, and wished him to be alive again, to be quarrelling with him (for we quarrelled sometimes), rather than not to have him again, and was as uneasy without him, as he, their poor uncle, must have been when the doctor took off his limb.—Here the children fell a-crying, and asked if their little mourning which they had on was not for uncle John, and they looked up, and prayed me not to go on about their uncle, but to tell them some stories about their pretty dead mother. Then I told how for seven long years, in hope sometimes, sometimes in despair, yet persisting ever, I courted the fair Alice W——n; and as much as children could understand, I explained to them what coyness, and difficulty, and denial, meant in maidens—when suddenly turning to Alice, the soul of the first Alice looked out at her eyes with such a reality of re-presentment, that I became in doubt which of them stood there before me, or whose that bright hair was; and while I stood gazing, both the children gradually grew fainter to my view, receding, and still receding, till nothing at last but two mournful features were seen in the uttermost distance, which, without speech, strangely impressed upon me the effects of speech : " We are not of Alice, nor of thee, nor are we children at all. The children of Alice call Bertrum father. We are nothing; less than nothing, and dreams. We are only what might have been, and must wait upon the tedious shores of Lethe millions of ages before we have existence, and a name "—and immediately awaking, I found myself quietly seated in my bachelor armchair, where I had fallen asleep, with the faithful Bridget unchanged by my side— but John L. (or James Elia) was gone for ever.

(*Essays of Elia.*)

WILLIAM HAZLITT (1778–1830)

I.—On a Landscape of Nicolas Poussin

POUSSIN was, of all painters, the most poetical. He was the painter of ideas. No one ever told a story half so well, nor so well knew what was capable of being told by the pencil. He seized on, and struck off with grace and precision, just that point of view which would be likely to catch the reader's fancy. There is a significance, a consciousness in whatever he does (sometimes a vice, but oftener a virtue) beyond any other painter. His Giants sitting on the tops of craggy mountains, as huge themselves, and playing idly on their Pan's-pipes, seem to have been seated there these three thousand years, and to know the beginning and the end of their own story. An infant Bacchus or Jupiter is big with his future destiny. Even inanimate and dumb things speak a language of their own. His snakes, the messengers of fate, are inspired with human intellect. His trees grow and expand their leaves in the air, glad of the rain, proud of the sun, awake to the winds of heaven. In his Plague of Athens, the very buildings seem stiff with horror. His picture of the Deluge is, perhaps, the finest historical landscape in the world. You see a waste of waters, wide, interminable; the sun is labouring, wan and weary, up the sky; the clouds, dull and leaden, lie like a load upon the eye, and heaven and earth seem commingling into one confused mass ! His human figures are sometimes " o'er-informed " with this kind of feeling. Their actions have too much gesticulation, and the set expression of the features borders too much on the mechanical and caricatured style. In this respect they form a contrast to Raphael's, whose figures never appear to be sitting for their pictures, or to be conscious of a spectator, or to have come from the painter's hand. In Nicolas Poussin, on the contrary, everything seems to have a distinct understanding with the artist; "the very stones prate of their whereabout"; each object has its part and place assigned, and is in a sort of compact with the rest of the picture. It is this conscious keeping, and, as it were, *internal* design, that gives their peculiar character to the works of this artist. There was a picture of Aurora in the British Gallery a year or two ago. It was a suffusion of golden light. The Goddess wore her saffron-coloured robes, and appeared just risen from the gloomy bed of old Tithonus. Her very steeds, milk-white, were tinged with the yellow dawn. It was a personification of the morning. Poussin succeeded better in classic than in sacred subjects. The latter are comparatively heavy, forced, full of violent contrasts of colour, of red, blue, and black, and without the true prophetic inspiration of the characters. But in his pagan allegories and fables he was quite at home. The native gravity and native levity of the Frenchman were combined with Italian scenery and an antique gusto, and gave even to his colouring an air of learned indifference. He wants, in one respect, grace, form, expression; but he has everywhere sense and meaning, perfect costume and propriety. His personages always belong to the class and time represented, and are strictly versed in the business in hand. His grotesque compositions in particular, his Nymphs and Fauns, are superior (at least, as far as style is concerned) even to those of Rubens. They are taken more immediately out of fabulous history. Rubens' Satyrs and Bacchantes have a more jovial and voluptuous aspect, are more drunk with pleasure, more full of animal spirits and riotous impulses; they laugh and bound along—

Leaping like wanton kids in pleasant spring:

but those of Poussin have more of the intellectual part of the character, and seem vicious on reflection, and of set purpose. Rubens' are noble specimens of a class; Poussin's are allegorical abstractions of the same class, with bodies less pampered, but with minds more secretly depraved. The Bacchanalian groups of the Flemish painter were, however, his masterpieces in composition. Witness those prodigies of colour, character, and expression at Blenheim. In the more chaste and refined delineation of classic fable, Poussin was without a rival. Rubens, who was a match for him in the wild and picturesque, could not pretend to vie with the elegance and purity of thought in his picture of Apollo giving a poet a cup of water to drink, nor with the gracefulness of design in the figure of a nymph squeezing the juice of a bunch of grapes from her fingers (a rosy wine-press) which falls into the mouth of a chubby infant below. But, above all, who shall celebrate, in terms of fit praise, his picture of the shepherds in the Vale of Tempe going out in a fine morning of the spring, and coming to a tomb with this inscription: ET EGO IN ARCADIA VIXI! The eager curiosity of some, the expression of others who start back with fear and surprise, the clear breeze playing with the branches of the shadowing trees, "the valleys low, where the mild zephyrs use," the distant, uninterrupted, sunny prospect speak (and for ever will speak on) of ages past to ages yet to come! [1]

Pictures are a set of chosen images, a stream of pleasant thoughts passing through the mind. It is a luxury to have the walls of our rooms hung round with them, and no less so to have such a gallery in the mind, to con over the relics of ancient art bound up "within the book and volume of the brain, unmixed (if it were possible) with baser matter!" A life passed among pictures, in the study and the love of art, is a happy noiseless dream: or rather, it is to dream and to be awake at the same time; for it has all "the sober certainty of waking bliss," with the romantic voluptuousness of a visionary and abstracted being. They are the bright consummate essences of things, and "he who knows of these delights to taste and interpose them oft, is not unwise!"—The Orion, which I have here taken occasion to descant upon, is one of a collection of excellent pictures, as this collection is itself one of a series from the old masters, which have for some years back embrowned the walls of the British Gallery, and enriched the public eye. What hues (those of nature mellowed by time) breathe around as we enter! What forms are there, woven into the memory! What looks, which only the answering looks of the spectator can express! What intellectual stores have been yearly poured forth from the shrine of ancient art! The works are various, but the names the same—heaps of Rembrandts frowning from the darkened walls, Rubens' glad gorgeous groups, Titians more rich and rare, Claudes always exquisite, sometimes beyond

---

[1] Poussin has repeated this subject more than once, and appears to have revelled in its witcheries. I have before alluded to it, and may again. It is hard that we should not be allowed to dwell as often as we please on what delights us, when things that are disagreeable recur so often against our will.

compare, Guido's endless cloying sweetness, the learning of Poussin and the Caracci, and Raphael's princely magnificence crowning all. We read certain letters and syllables in the Catalogue, and at the well-known magic sound a miracle of skill and beauty starts to view. One might think that one year's prodigal display of such perfection would exhaust the labours of one man's life; but the next year, and the next to that, we find another harvest reaped and gathered in to the great garner of art, by the same immortal hands—

> Old GENIUS the porter of them was ;
> He letteth in, he letteth out to wend.—

Their works seem endless as their reputation—to be many as they are complete—to multiply with the desire of the mind to see more and more of them ; as if there were a living power in the breath of Fame, and in the very names of the great heirs of glory " there were propagation too " ! It is something to have a collection of this sort to count upon once a year ; to have one last, lingering look yet to come. Pictures are scattered like stray gifts through the world ; and while they remain, earth has yet a little gilding left, not quite rubbed off, dishonoured, and defaced. There are plenty of standard works still to be found in this country, in the collections at Blenheim, at Burleigh, and in those belonging to Mr. Angerstein, Lord Grosvenor, the Marquis of Stafford, and others, to keep up this treat to the lovers of art for many years ; and it is the more desirable to reserve a privileged sanctuary of this sort, where the eye may dote, and the heart take its fill of such pictures as Poussin's Orion, since the Louvre is stripped of its triumphant spoils, and since he who collected it, and wore it as a rich jewel in his Iron Crown, the hunter of greatness and of glory, is himself a shade.

(*Table Talk.*)

II.—ELIA

Mr. Lamb has succeeded, not by conforming to the *Spirit of the Age,* but in opposition to it. He does not march boldly along with the crowd, but steals off the pavement to pick his way in the contrary direction. He prefers *bye-ways* to *highways*. When the full tide of human life pours along to some festive show, to some pageant of a day, Elia would stand on one side to look over an old book-stall, or stroll down some deserted pathway in search of a pensive description over a tottering doorway, or some quaint device in architecture, illustrative of embryo art and ancient manners. Mr. Lamb has the very soul of an antiquarian, as this implies a reflecting humanity; the film of the past hovers forever before him. He is shy, sensitive, the reverse of every thing coarse, vulgar, obtrusive, and *common-place*. He would fain " shuffle off this mortal coil "; and his spirit clothes itself in the garb of elder time, homelier, but more durable. He is borne along with no pompous paradoxes, shines in no glittering tinsel of a fashionable phraseology, is neither fop nor sophist. He has none of the turbulence or froth of new-fangled opinions. His style runs pure and clear, though it may often take an underground course, or be conveyed through old-fashioned conduit-pipes. Mr. Lamb does not court popularity, nor strut in gaudy plumes, but shrinks from every kind of ostentatious and obvious pretension into the retirement of his own mind.

> " The self-applauding bird, the peacock see :—
> Mark what a sumptuous pharisee is he !
> Meridian sun-beams tempt him to unfold
> His radiant glories, azure, green, and gold ;
> He treads as if, some solemn music near,
> His measured step were governed by his ear :
> And seems to say—' Ye meaner fowl, give place,
> I am all splendour, dignity, and grace ! '
> Not so the pheasant on his charms presumes,
> Though he too has a glory in his plumes.
> He, Christian-like, retreats with modest mien
> To the close copse or far sequestered green,
> And shines without desiring to be seen."

These lines well describe the modest and delicate beauties of Mr. Lamb's writings, contrasted with the lofty and vainglorious pretensions of some of his contemporaries. This gentleman is not one of those who pay all their homage to the prevailing idol : he thinks that

> " New-born gauds are made and moulded of things past,"

nor does he

> " Give to dust that is a little gilt
> More laud than gilt o'er-dusted."

His convictions " do not in broad rumour lie," nor are they " set off to the world in the glistering foil " of fashion, but " live and breathe aloft in those pure eyes, and perfect judgment of all-seeing *time*."

Mr. Lamb rather affects and is tenacious of the obscure and remote, of that which rests on its own intrinsic and silent merit ; which scorns all alliance or even the suspicion of owing any thing to noisy clamour, to the glare of circumstances. There is a fine tone of *chiaroscuro*, a moral perspective in his writings.

He delights to dwell on that which is fresh to the eye of memory; he yearns after and covets what soothes the frailty of human nature. That touches him most nearly which is withdrawn to a certain distance, which verges on the borders of oblivion: that piques and provokes his fancy most, which is hid from a superficial glance. That which, though gone by, is still remembered, is in his view more genuine, and has given more "vital signs that it will live," than a thing of yesterday, that may be forgotten to-morrow. Death has in this sense the spirit of life in it; and the shadowy has to our author something substantial in it. Ideas savour most of reality in his mind; or rather his imagination loiters on the edge of each, and a page of his writings recalls to our fancy the *stranger* on the grate, fluttering in its dusky tenuity, with its idle superstition and hospitable welcome!

Mr. Lamb has a distaste to new faces, to new books, to new buildings, to new customs. He is shy of all imposing appearances, of all assumptions of self-importance, of all adventitious ornaments, of all mechanical advantages, even to a nervous excess. It is not merely that he does not rely upon, or ordinarily avail himself of them; he holds them in abhorrence; he utterly abjures and discards them and places a great gulph between him and them. He disdains all the vulgar artifices of authorship, all the cant of criticism and helps to notoriety. He has no grand swelling theories to attract the visionary and the enthusiast, no passing topics to allure the thoughtless and the vain. He evades the present; he mocks the future. His affections revert to, and settle on the past; but then even this must have something personal and local in it to interest him deeply and thoroughly. He pitches his tent in the suburbs of existing manners, brings down the account of character to the few straggling remains of the last generation, seldom ventures beyond the bills of mortality, and occupies that nice point between egotism and disinterested humanity. No one makes the tour of our southern metropolis, or describes the manners of the last age, so well as Mr. Lamb: with so fine and yet so formal an air: with such vivid obscurity: with such arch piquancy, such picturesque quaintness, such smiling pathos.

How admirably he has sketched the former inmates of the South-Sea House; what "fine fretwork he makes of their double and single entries!" With what firm, yet subtle pencil he has embodied *Mrs. Battle's Opinions on Whist!* How notably he embalms a battered *beau;* how delightfully an amour, that was cold forty years ago, revives in his pages!

With what well-disguised humour he introduces us to his relations, and how freely he serves up his friends ! Certainly, some of his portraits are *fixtures*, and will do to hang up as lasting and lively emblems of human infirmity. Then there is no one who has so sure an ear for " the chimes at midnight," not even excepting Mr. Justice Shallow; nor could Master Silence himself take his " cheese and pippins " with a more significant and satisfactory air. With what a gusto Mr. Lamb describes the Inns and Courts of law, the Temple and Gray's-Inn, as if he had been a student there for the last two hundred years, and had been as well acquainted with the person of Sir Francis Bacon as he is with his portrait or writings ! It is hard to say whether St. John's Gate is connected with more intense and authentic associations in his mind, as a part of old London Wall, or as the frontispiece (time out of mind) of the *Gentleman's Magazine*. He haunts Watling-street like a gentle spirit; the avenues to the play-houses are thick with panting recollections; and Christ's-Hospital still breathes the balmy breath of infancy in his description of it ! Whittington and his Cat are a fine hallucination for Mr. Lamb's historic Muse, and we believe he never heartily forgave a certain writer who took the subject of Guy Faux out of his hands. The streets of London are his fairy-land, teeming with wonder, with life and interest to his retrospective glance, as it did to the eager eye of childhood; he has contrived to weave its tritest traditions into a bright and endless romance !

(The Spirit of the Age.)

JAMES HENRY LEIGH HUNT (1784–1859)
MY BOOKS

SITTING last winter among my books, and walled round with all the comfort and protection which they and my fireside could afford me—to wit, a table of high-piled books at my back, my writing-desk on one side of me, some shelves on the other, and the feeling of the warm fire at my feet—I began to consider how I loved the authors of those books : how I loved them too, not only for the imaginative pleasures they afforded me, but for their making me love the very books themselves, and delight to be in contact with them. I looked sideways at my *Spenser*, my *Theocritus*, and my *Arabian Nights ;* then above them at my Italian poets; then behind me at my *Dryden* and *Pope*, my romances, and my Boccaccio; then on my left side at my *Chaucer* who lay on a writing-desk; and thought how natural it was in

C. L. to give a kiss to an old folio, as I once saw him do to *Chapman's Homer*. At the same time I wondered how he could sit in that front room of his with nothing but a few unfeeling tables and chairs, or at best a few engravings in trim frames, instead of putting a couple of arm-chairs into the back-room with the books in it, where there is but one window. Would I were there, with both the chairs properly filled, and one or two more besides ! " We had talk, sir "—the only talk capable of making one forget the books.

I entrench myself in my books equally against sorrow and the weather. If the wind comes through a passage, I look about to see how I can fence it off by a better disposition of my movables ; if a melancholy thought is importunate, I give another glance at my *Spenser*. When I speak of being in contact with my books I mean it literally. I like to lean my head against them. Living in a southern climate, though in a part sufficiently northern to feel the winter, I was obliged during that season to take some of the books out of the study, and hang them up near the fire-place in the sitting-room, which is the only room that has such a convenience. I therefore walled myself in, as well as I could, in the manner above-mentioned. I took a walk every day, to the astonishment of the Genoese, who used to huddle against a bit of sunny wall like flies on a chimney-piece ; but I did this only that I might so much the more enjoy my *English* evening. The fire was a wood fire instead of a coal ; but I imagined myself in the country. I remembered at the very worst, that one end of my native land was not nearer the other than England is to Italy.

While writing this article I am in my study again. Like the rooms in all the houses in this country which are not hovels, it is handsome and ornamented. On one side it looks towards a garden and the mountains ; on another, to the mountains and the sea. What signifies all this ? I turn my back upon the sea ; I shut up even one of the side windows looking upon the mountains, and retain no prospect but that of the trees. On the right and left of me are book-shelves ; a bookcase is affectionately open in front of me ; and thus kindly enclosed with my books and the green leaves, I write. If all this is too luxurious and effeminate, of all luxuries it is the one that leaves you the most strength. And this is to be said for scholarship in general. It unfits a man for activity ; for his bodily part in the world ; but it often doubles both the power and the sense of his mental duties ; and with much indignation against his body, and more against those who tyrannise over the intellectual claims of

mankind, the man of letters, like the magician of old, is prepared
" to play the devil " with the great men of this world, in a style
that astonishes both the sword and the toga.

I do not like this fine large study. I like elegance. I like
room to breathe in, and even walk about, when I want to
breathe and walk about. I like a great library next my study;
but for the study itself give me a small snug place, almost
entirely walled with books. There should be only one window
in it, looking upon trees. Some prefer a place with few or no
books at all—nothing but a chair, or a table, like Epictetus;
but I should say that these were philosophers, not lovers of
books; if I did not recollect that Montaigne was both. He had
a study in a round tower, walled as aforesaid. It is true, one
forgets one's books while writing—at least they say so. For
my part, I think I have them in a sort of sidelong mind's eye;
like a second thought, which is more—like a waterfall, or a
whispering wind.

(*Essays*.)

THOMAS DE QUINCEY (1785–1859)

I.—DREAMS

I THOUGHT that it was a Sunday morning in May; that it was
Easter Sunday, and as yet very early in the morning. I was
standing, as it seemed to me, at the door of my own cottage.
Right before me lay the very scene which could really be commanded from that situation, but exalted, as was usual, and
solemnised by the power of dreams. There were the same
mountains, and the same lovely valley at their feet; but the
mountains were raised to more than Alpine height, and there
was interspace far larger between them of savannahs and forest
lawns; the hedges were rich with white roses; and no living
creature was to be seen, excepting that in the green churchyard
there were cattle tranquilly reposing upon the verdant graves,
and particularly round about the grave of a child whom I had
once tenderly loved, just as I had really beheld them, a little
before sunrise, in the same summer when that child died. I
gazed upon the well-known scene, and I said to myself, " It yet
wants much of sunrise; and it is Easter Sunday; and that is
the day on which they celebrate the first-fruits of Resurrection.
I will walk abroad; old griefs shall be forgotten to-day : for
the air is cool and still, and the hills are high, and stretch away
to heaven; and the churchyard is as verdant as the forest lawns,
and the forest lawns are as quiet as the churchyard; and with

the dew I can wash the fever from my forehead; and then I shall be unhappy no longer." I turned, as if to open my garden gate, and immediately I saw upon the left a scene far different; but which yet the power of dreams had reconciled into harmony. The scene was an oriental one; and there also it was Easter Sunday, and very early in the morning. And at a vast distance were visible, as a stain upon the horizon, the domes and cupolas of a great city—an image or faint abstraction, caught perhaps in childhood from some picture of Jerusalem. And not a bow-shot from me, upon a stone, shaded by Judean palms, there sat a woman; and I looked, and it was—Ann! She fixed her eyes upon me earnestly; and I said to her at length, "So, then, I have found you at last." I waited; but she answered me not a word. Her face was the same as when I saw it last; the same, and yet, again, how different! Seventeen years ago, when the lamp-light of mighty London fell upon her face, as for the last time I kissed her lips (lips, Ann, that to me were not polluted!), her eyes were streaming with tears. The tears were now no longer seen. Sometimes she seemed altered; yet again sometimes *not* altered; and hardly older. Her looks were tranquil, but with unusual solemnity of expression, and I now gazed upon her with some awe. Suddenly her countenance grew dim; and, turning to the mountains, I perceived vapours rolling between us: in a moment all had vanished; thick darkness came on; and in the twinkling of an eye I was far away from mountains, and by lamp-light in London, walking again with Ann—just as we had walked, when both children, eighteen years before, along the endless terraces of Oxford Street.

Then suddenly would come a dream of far different character —a tumultuous dream—commencing with a music such as now I often heard in sleep—music of preparation and of awakening suspense. The undulations of fast-gathering tumults were like the opening of the Coronation Anthem; and, like *that*, gave the feeling of a multitudinous movement, of infinite cavalcades filing off, and the tread of innumerable armies. The morning was come of a mighty day—a day of crisis and of ultimate hope for human nature, then suffering mysterious eclipse, and labouring in some dread extremity. Somewhere, but I knew not where—somehow, but I knew not how—by some beings, but I knew not by whom—a battle, a strife, an agony, was travelling through all its stages—was evolving itself, like the catastrophe of some mighty drama, with which my sympathy was the more insupportable, from deepening confusion as to its local scene, its cause, its nature, and its undecipherable issue. I (as is usual in dreams where, of necessity, we make ourselves central to every movement) had the power, and yet had not the power, to decide it. I had the power, if I could raise myself to will it; and yet again had not the power, for the weight of twenty Atlantics was upon me, or the oppression of inexpiable guilt. "Deeper than ever plummet sounded," I lay inactive. Then, like a chorus, the passion deepened. Some greater interest was at stake, some mightier cause, than ever yet the sword had pleaded, or trumpet had proclaimed. Then came sudden alarms; hurryings to and fro; trepidations of innumerable fugitives, I knew not whether from the good cause or the bad; darkness and lights; tempest and human faces: and at last, with the sense that all was lost, female forms, and the features that were worth all the world to me; and but a moment allowed—and clasped hands, with heart-breaking partings, and then—everlasting farewells! and, with a sigh such as the caves of hell sighed when the incestuous mother uttered the abhorred name of Death, the sound was reverberated—everlasting farewells! and again, and yet again reverberated—everlasting farewells!

And I awoke in struggles, and cried aloud, "I will sleep no more!"

(Confessions of an English Opium Eater.

II.—DOROTHY WORDSWORTH

A happier life, by far, was hers in youth, coming as near as difference of scenery and difference of relations would permit to that which was promised to Ruth—the Ruth of her brother's creation [1]—by the youth who came from Georgia's shore; for, though not upon American savannah, or Canadian lakes—

> "With all their fairy crowds
> Of islands that together lie
> As quietly as spots of sky
> Amongst the evening clouds,"

yet, amongst the loveliest scenes of sylvan England, and (at intervals) of sylvan Germany—amongst lakes, too, far better

---

[1] "*The Ruth of her brother's creation*":—So I express it; because so much in the development of the story and situations necessarily belongs to the poet. Else, for the mere outline of the story, it was founded upon fact. Wordsworth himself told me, in general terms, that the case which suggested the poem was that of an American lady, whose husband forsook her at the very place of embarkation from England, under circumstances and under expectations, upon her part, very much the same as those of Ruth. I am afraid, however, that the husband was an attorney; which is intolerable; *nisi prius* cannot be harmonized with the dream-like fairyland of Georgia.

fitted to give the *sense* of their own character than the vast
inland *seas* of America, and amongst mountains more romantic
than many of the chief ranges in that country—her time fleeted
away like some golden age, or like the life of primeval man ; and
she, like Ruth, was for years allowed

> " To run, though *not* a bride,
> A sylvan huntress, by the side "

of him to whom she, like Ruth, had dedicated her days, and to
whose children, afterwards, she dedicated a love like that of
mothers. Dear Miss Wordsworth ! How noble a creature did
she seem when I first knew her !—and when, on the very first
night which I passed in her brother's company, he read to me,
in illustration of something he was saying, a passage from Fair-
fax's " Tasso," ending pretty nearly with these words—

> " Amidst the broad fields and the endless wood,
> The lofty lady kept her maidenhood,"

I thought that, possibly, he had his sister in his thoughts. Yet
" lofty " was hardly the right word. Miss Wordsworth was too
ardent and fiery a creature to maintain the reserve essential to
dignity; and dignity was the last thing one thought of in the
presence of one so natural, so fervent in her feelings, and so
embarrassed in their utterance—sometimes, also, in the attempt
to check them. It must not, however, be supposed that there
was any silliness or weakness of enthusiasm about her. She was
under the continual restraint of severe good sense, though
liberated from that false shame which, in so many persons,
accompanies all expressions of natural emotion; and she had
too long enjoyed the ennobling conversation of her brother, and
his admirable comments on the poets, which they read in common, to fail in any essential point of logic or propriety of thought.
Accordingly, her letters, though the most careless and un-
elaborate—nay, the most hurried that can be imagined—are
models of good sense and just feeling. In short, beyond any
person I have known in this world, Miss Wordsworth was the
creature of impulse; but, as a woman most thoroughly virtuous
and well-principled, as one who could not fail to be kept right
by her own excellent heart, and as an intellectual creature from
her cradle, with much of her illustrious brother's peculiarity of
mind—finally, as one who had been, in effect, educated and
trained by that very brother—she won the sympathy and the
respectful regard of every man worthy to approach her. Properly, and in a spirit of prophecy, was she named *Dorothy ;*

in its Greek meaning,[1] *gift of God*, well did this name prefigure the relation in which she stood to Wordsworth, the mission with which she was charged—to wait upon him as the tenderest and most faithful of domestics; to love him as a sister; to sympathise with him as a confidante; to counsel him; to cheer him and sustain him by the natural expression of her feelings—so quick, so ardent, so unaffected—upon the probable effect of whatever thoughts or images he might conceive; finally, and above all other ministrations, to ingraft, by her sexual sense of beauty, upon his masculine austerity that delicacy and those graces which else (according to the grateful acknowledgments of his own maturest retrospect) it never could have had—

> "The blessing of my later years
> Was with me when I was a boy:
> She gave me hopes, she gave me fears
> A heart the fountain of sweet tears,
> . . . .
> And love, and thought and joy."

And elsewhere he describes her, in a philosophic poem, still in MS., as one who planted flowers and blossoms with her feminine hand upon what might else have been an arid rock—massy, indeed, and grand, but repulsive from the severity of its features. I may sum up in one brief abstract the amount of Miss Wordsworth's character, as a companion, by saying, that she was the very wildest (in the sense of the most natural) person I have ever known; and also the truest, most inevitable, and at the same time the quickest and readiest in her sympathy with either joy or sorrow, with laughter or with tears, with the realities of life or the larger realities of the poets!

(*Reminiscences of the English Lake Poets.*)

THOMAS CARLYLE (1795–1881)
I.—ODIN

WE will fancy him to be the Type Norseman; the finest Teuton whom that race had yet produced. The rude Norse heart burst-up into *boundless* admiration round him; into adoration. He is as a root of so many great things; the fruit of him is found growing, from deep thousands of years, over the whole field of Teutonic Life. Our own Wednesday, as I said, is it not still

---

[1] Of course, therefore, it is essentially the same name as *Theodora*, the same elements being only differently arranged. Yet how opposite is the impression upon the mind! and chiefly, I suppose, from the too prominent emblazonment of this name in the person of Justinian's scandalous wife; though for my own part, I am far from believing all the infamous stories which we read about her.

Odin's Day? Wednesday, Wansborough, Wanstead, Wandsworth: Odin grew into England too, these are still leaves from that root! He was the Chief God to all the Teutonic Peoples; their Pattern Norseman;—in such way did *they* admire their Pattern Norseman; that was the fortune he had in the world.

Thus if the man Odin himself have vanished utterly, there is this huge Shadow of him which still projects itself over the whole History of his People. For this Odin once admitted to be God, we can understand well that the whole Scandinavian Scheme of Nature, or dim No-scheme, whatever it might before have been, would now begin to develop itself altogether differently, and grow thenceforth in a new manner. What this Odin saw into, and taught with his runes and his rhymes, the whole Teutonic People laid to heart and carried forward. His way of thought became their way of thought:—such, under new conditions, is the history of every great thinker still. In gigantic confused lineaments, like some enormous camera-obscura shadow thrown upwards from the dead deeps of the Past, and covering the whole Northern Heaven, is not that Scandinavian Mythology in some sort the Portraiture of this man Odin? The gigantic image of *his* natural face, legible or not legible there, expanded and confused in that manner! Ah, Thought, I say, is always Thought. No great man lives in vain. The History of the world is but the Biography of great men.

To me there is something very touching in this primeval figure of Heroism; in such artless, helpless, but hearty entire reception of a Hero by his fellow-men. Never so helpless in shape, it is the noblest of feelings, and a feeling in some shape or other perennial as man himself. If I could show in any measure, what I feel deeply for a long time now, That it is the vital element of manhood, the soul of man's history here in our world,—it would be the chief use of this discoursing at present. We do not now call our great men Gods, nor admire *without* limit; ah no, *with* limit enough! But if we have no great men, or do not admire at all,—that were a still worse case.

This poor Scandinavian Hero-worship, that whole Norse way of looking at the Universe, and adjusting oneself there, has an indestructible merit for us. A rude childlike way of recognising the divineness of Nature, the divineness of Man; most rude, yet heartfelt, robust, giantlike; betokening what a giant of a man this child would yet grow to!—It was a truth, and is none. Is it not as the half-dumb stifled voice of the long-buried generations of our own Fathers, calling out of the depths of ages to us, in whose veins their blood still runs: " This then, this is what *we* made of the world : this is all the image and notion we could form to ourselves of this great mystery of a Life and Universe. Despise it not. You are raised high above it, to large free scope of vision; but you too are not yet at the top. No, your notion too, so much enlarged, is but a partial, imperfect one; that matter is a thing no man will ever, in time or out of time, comprehend; after thousands of years of ever-new expansion, man will find himself but struggling to comprehend again a part of it : the thing is larger than man, not to be comprehended by him; an Infinite thing ! "

The essence of the Scandinavian, as indeed of all Pagan Mythologies, we found to be recognition of the divineness of Nature; sincere communion of man with the mysterious invisible Powers visibly seen at work in the world round him. This, I should say, is more sincerely done in the Scandinavian than in any Mythology I know. Sincerity is the great characteristic of it. Superior sincerity (far superior) consoles us for the total want of old Grecian grace. Sincerity, I think, is better than grace. I feel that these old Northmen were looking into Nature with open eye and soul : most earnest, honest; childlike, and yet manlike; with a great-hearted simplicity and depth and freshness, in a true, loving, admiring, unfearing way. A right valiant, true old race of men. Such recognition of Nature one finds to be the chief element of Paganism : recognition of Man, and his Moral Duty, though this too is not wanting, comes to be the chief element only in purer forms of religion. Here, indeed, is a great distinction and epoch in Human Beliefs; a great landmark in the religious development of Mankind. Man first puts himself in relation with Nature and her Powers, wonders and worships over those; not till a later epoch does he discern that all Power is Moral, that the grand point is the distinction for him of Good and Evil, of *Thou shalt* and *Thou shalt not.*

With regard to all these fabulous delineations in the *Edda*, I will remark, moreover, as indeed was already hinted, that most probably they must have been of much newer date; most probably, even from the first, were comparatively idle for the old Norsemen, and as it were a kind of Poetic sport. Allegory and Poetic Delineation, as I said above, cannot be religious Faith; the Faith itself must first be there, then Allegory enough will gather round it, as the fit body round its soul. The Norse Faith, I can well suppose, like other Faiths, was most active while it lay mainly in the silent state, and had not yet much to say about itself, still less to sing.

Among those shadowy *Edda* matters, amid all that fantastic congeries of assertions, and traditions, in their musical Mythologies, the main practical belief a man could have was probably not much more than this : of the *Valkyrs* and the *Hall of Odin ;* of an inflexible *Destiny ;* and that the one thing needful for a man was *to be brave.* The *Valkyrs* are Choosers of the Slain ; a Destiny inexorable, which it is useless trying to bend or soften, has appointed who is to be slain ; this was a fundamental point for the Norse believer ;—as indeed it is for all earnest men everywhere, for a Mahomet, a Luther, for a Napoleon too. It lies at the basis this for every such man ; it is the woof out of which his whole system of thought is woven. The *Valkyrs ;* and then that these *Choosers* lead the brave to a heavenly *Hall of Odin ;* only the base and slavish being thrust elsewhither, into the realms of Hela the Death-goddess : I take this to have been the soul of the whole Norse Belief. They understood in their heart that it was indispensable to be brave ; that Odin would have no favour for them, but despise and thrust them out, if they were not brave. Consider too whether there is not something in this ! It is an everlasting duty, valid in our day as in that, the duty of being brave. *Valour* is still *value.* The first duty for a man is still that of subduing *Fear.* We must get rid of Fear ; we cannot act at all till then. A man's acts are slavish, not true but specious ; his very thoughts are false, he thinks too as a slave and coward, till he have got Fear under his feet. Odin's creed, if we disentangle the real kernel of it, is true to this hour. A man shall and must be valiant ; he must march forward, and quit himself like a man, —trusting imperturbably in the appointment and *choice* of the upper Powers ; and, on the whole, not fear at all. Now and always, the completeness of his victory over Fear will determine how much of a man he is.

It is doubtless very savage that kind of valour of the old Northmen. Snorro tells us they thought it a shame and misery not to die in battle ; and if natural death seemed to be coming on, they would cut wounds in their flesh, that Odin might receive them as warriors slain. Old kings, about to die, had their body laid into a ship ; the ship sent forth, with sails set and slow fire burning it ; that, once out at sea, it might blaze-up in flame, and in such manner bury worthily the old hero, at once in the sky and in the ocean ! Wild bloody valour ; yet valour of its kind ; better, I say, than none. In the old Sea-kings too, what an indomitable rugged energy ! Silent, with closed lips, as I fancy them, unconscious that they were specially brave ; defying

the wild ocean with its monsters, and all men and things;—
progenitors of our own Blakes and Nelsons ! No Homer sang
these Norse Sea-kings; but Agamemnon's was a small audacity,
and of small fruit in the world, to some of them;—to Hrolf's of
Normandy, for instance ! Hrolf, or Rollo Duke of Normandy,
the wild Sea-king, has a share in governing England at this hour.

Nor was it altogether nothing, even that wild sea-roving and
battling, through so many generations. It needed to be ascer-
tained which was the *strongest* kind of men; who were to be
ruler over whom. Among the Northland Sovereigns, too, I
find some who got the title *Wood-cutter ;* Forest-felling Kings.
Much lies in that. I suppose at bottom many of them were
forest-fellers as well as fighters, though the Skalds talk mainly
of the latter,—misleading certain critics not a little; for no
nation of men could ever live by fighting alone; there could
not produce enough come out of that ! I suppose the right good
fighter was oftenest also the right good forest-feller,—the right
good improver, discerner, doer and worker in every kind; for
true valour, different enough from ferocity, is the basis of all.
A more legitimate kind of valour that; showing itself against
the untamed Forests and dark brute Powers of Nature, to
conquer Nature for us. In the same direction have not we
their descendants since carried it far? May such valour last
forever with us !

That the man Odin, speaking with a Hero's voice and heart,
as with an impressiveness out of Heaven, told his People the
infinite importance of Valour, how man thereby became a god;
and that his People, feeling a response to it in their own hearts,
believed this message of his, and thought it a message out of
Heaven, and him a Divinity for telling it them : this seems to
me the primary seed-grain of the Norse Religion, from which
all manner of mythologies, symbolic practices, speculations,
allegories, songs and sagas would naturally grow. Grow,—
how strangely ! I called it a small light shining and shaping
in the huge vortex of Norse darkness. Yet the darkness itself
was *alive ;* consider that. It was the eager inarticulate un-
instructed Mind of the whole Norse People, longing only to
become articulate, to go on articulating ever farther ! The
living doctrine grows, grows;—like a Banyan-tree; the first
seed is the essential thing : any branch strikes itself down into
the earth, becomes a new root; and so, in endless complexity,
we have a whole wood, a whole jungle, one seed the parent of
it all. Was not the whole Norse Religion, accordingly, in some
sense, what we called " the enormous shadow of this man's

likeness ? " Critics trace some affinity in some Norse mythuses, of the Creation and suchlike, with those of the Hindoos. The Cow Adumbla, " licking the rime from the rocks," has a kind of Hindoo look. A Hindoo Cow, transported into frosty countries. Probably enough; indeed we may say undoubtedly, these things will have a kindred with the remotest lands, with the earliest times. Thought does not die, but only is changed. The first man that began to think in this Planet of ours, he was the beginner of all. And then the second man, and the third man;—nay, every true Thinker to this hour is a kind of Odin, teaches men *his* way of thought, spreads a shadow of his own likeness over sections of the History of the World.

(Heroes and Hero-Worship.)

II.—The Everlasting Yea

" Beautiful it was to sit there, as in my skyey Tent, musing and meditating; on the high table-land, in front of the Mountains; over me, as roof, the azure Dome, and around me, for walls, four azure-flowing curtains,—namely, of the Four azure winds, on whose bottom-fringes also I have seen gilding. And then to fancy the fair Castles that stood sheltered in these Mountain hollows; with their green flower-lawns, and white dames and damosels, lovely enough : or better still, the straw-roofed Cottages wherein stood many a Mother baking bread, with her children round her :—all hidden and protectingly folded-up in the valley-folds; yet there and alive, as sure as if I beheld them. Or to see, as well as fancy, the nine Towns and Villages, that lay round my mountain-seat, which, in still weather, were wont to speak to me (by their steeple-bells) with metal tongue; and, in almost all weather, proclaimed their vitality by repeated Smoke-clouds; whereon, as on a culinary horologe, I might read the hour of the day. For it was the smoke of cookery, as kind housewives at morning, midday, eventide, were boiling their husbands' kettles; and ever a blue pillar rose up into the air, successively or simultaneously, from each of the nine, saying, as plainly as smoke could say : Such and such a meal is getting ready here. Not uninteresting ! For you have the whole Borough, with all its love-makings and scandal-mongeries, contentions and contentments, as in miniature, and could cover it all with your hat.—If, in my wide Way-farings, I had learned to look into the business of the World in its details, here perhaps was the place for combining it into general propositions, and deducing inferences therefrom.

" Often also could I see the black Tempest marching in anger through the Distance : round some Schreckhorn, as yet grim-blue, would the eddying vapour gather, and there tumultuously eddy, and flow down like a mad witch's hair; till, after a space, it vanished, and, in the clear sunbeam, your Schreckhorn stood smiling grim-white, for the vapour had held snow. How thou fermentest and elaboratest, in thy great fermenting-vat and laboratory of an Atmosphere, of a World, O Nature !—Or what is Nature ? Ha ! why do I not name thee GOD ? Art thou not the ' Living Garment of GOD ? ' O Heavens, is it, in very deed, HE then that ever speaks through thee; that lives and loves in thee, that lives and loves in me ?

" Fore-shadows, call them rather fore-splendours, of that Truth, and Beginning of Truths, fell mysteriously over my soul. Sweeter than Dayspring to the Shipwrecked in Nova Zembla; ah ! like the mother's voice to her little child that strays bewildered, weeping, in unknown tumults; like soft streamings of celestial music to my too-exasperated heart, came that Evangel. The Universe is not dead and demoniacal, a charnel-house with spectres; but godlike, and my Father's !

" With other eyes, too, could I now look upon my fellow man ; with an infinite Love, an infinite Pity. Poor, wandering, wayward man ! Art thou not tried, and beaten with stripes, even as I am ? Ever, whether thou bear the royal mantle or the beggar's gabardine, art thou not so weary, so heavy-laden; and thy Bed of Rest is but a Grave. O my Brother, my Brother, why cannot I shelter thee in my bosom, and wipe away all tears from thy eyes !—Truly, the din of many-voiced Life, which, in this solitude, with the mind's organ, I could hear, was no longer a maddening discord, but a melting one; like inarticulate cries, and sobbings of a dumb creature which in the ear of Heaven are prayers. The poor Earth, with her poor joys, was now my needy Mother, not my cruel Stepdame; Man, with his so mad Wants and so mean Endeavours, had become the dearer to me; and even for his sufferings and his sins, I now first named him Brother. Thus was I standing in the porch of that ' Sanctuary of Sorrow ; ' by strange, steep ways, had I too been guided thither; and ere long its sacred gates would open, and the ' Divine Depth of Sorrow ' lie disclosed to me."

(Sartor Resartus.)

III.—HAPPINESS

All work, even cotton-spinning, is noble ; work is alone noble : be that here said and asserted once more. And in like manner, too, all dignity is painful; a life of ease is not for any man, nor for any god. The life of all gods figures itself to us as a Sublime Sadness,—earnestness of Infinite Battle against Infinite Labour. Our highest religion is named the " Worship of Sorrow." For the son of man there is no noble crown, well worn, or even ill worn, but is a crown of thorns !—These things, in spoken words, or still better, in felt instincts alive in every heart, were once well known.

Does not the whole wretchedness, the whole *Atheism* as I call it, of man's ways, in these generations, shadow itself for us in that unspeakable Life-philosophy of his : The pretension to be what he calls " happy ? " Every pitifullest whipster that walks within a skin has his head filled with the notion that he is, shall be, or by all human and divine laws ought to be, " happy." His wishes, the pitifullest whipster's, are to be fulfilled for him ; his days, the pitifullest whipster's, are to flow on in ever-gentle current of enjoyment, impossible even for the gods. The prophets preach to us, Thou shalt be happy ; thou shalt love pleasant things, and find them. The people clamour, Why have we not found pleasant things ?

We construct our theory of Human Duties, not on any Greatest-Nobleness Principle, never so mistaken ; no, but on a Greatest-Happiness Principle. " The word *Soul* with us, as in some Slavonic dialects, seems to be synonymous with *Stomach*." We plead and speak, in our Parliaments and elsewhere, not as from the Soul, but from the Stomach ;—wherefore, indeed, our pleadings are so slow to profit. We plead not for God's Justice ; we are not ashamed to stand clamouring and pleading for our own " interests," our own rents and trade-profits ; we say, They are the " interests " of so many ; there is such an intense desire in us for them ! We demand Free-Trade, with much just vociferation and benevolence. That the poorer classes, who are terribly ill-off at present, may have cheaper New-Orleans bacon. Men ask on Free-trade platforms, How can the indomitable spirit of Englishmen be kept up without plenty of bacon ? We shall become a ruined Nation !—Surely, my friends, plenty of bacon is good and indispensable : but, I doubt, you will never get even bacon by aiming only at that. You are men, not animals of prey, well-used or ill-used ! Your Greatest-Happiness Principle seems to me fast becoming a rather unhappy one.—What if we should cease babbling about " happiness," and leave *it* resting on its own basis, as it used to do !

A gifted Byron rises in his wrath ; and feeling too surely that he for his part is not " happy," declares the same in very violent language, as a piece of news that may be interesting. It evidently has surprised him much. One dislikes to see a man and poet reduced to proclaim on the streets such tidings : but on the whole, as matters go, that is not the most dislikable. Byron speaks the *truth* in this matter. Byron's large audience indicates how true it is felt to be.

"Happy," my brother? First of all, what difference is it whether thou art happy or not! To-day becomes Yesterday so fast, all To-morrows become Yesterdays; and then there is no question whatever of the "happiness," but quite another question. Nay, thou hast such a sacred pity left at least for thyself, thy very pains, once gone over into Yesterday, become joys to thee. Besides, thou knowest not what heavenly blessedness and indispensable sanative virtue was in them; thou shalt only know it after many days, when thou art wiser!—A benevolent old Surgeon sat once in our company, with a Patient fallen sick by gourmandising, whom he had just, too briefly in the Patient's judgment, been examining. The foolish Patient still at intervals continued to break in on our discourse, which rather promised to take a philosophic turn : "But I have lost my appetite," said he, objurgatively, with a tone of irritated pathos; "I have no appetite; I can't eat!"—"My dear fellow," answered the Doctor in mildest tone, "it isn't of the slightest consequence;"—and continued his philosophical discoursings with us!

Or does the reader not know the history of that Scottish iron Misanthrope? The inmates of some town-mansion, in those Northern parts, were thrown into the fearfullest alarm by indubitable symptoms of a ghost inhabiting the next house, or perhaps even the partition-wall! Ever at a certain hour, with preternatural gnarring, growling and screeching, which attended as running bass, there began, in a horrid, semi-articulate, unearthly voice, this song : "Once I was hap-hap-happy, but now I'm *mees*-erable! Clack-clack-clack, gnarr-r-r, whuz-z : Once I was hap-hap-happy, but now I'm *mees*-erable!"—Rest, rest, perturbed spirit;—or indeed, as the good old Doctor said : My dear fellow, it isn't of the slightest consequence! But no; the perturbed spirit could not rest; and to the neighbours, fretted, affrighted, or at least insufferably bored by him, it *was* of such consequence that they had to go and examine in his haunted chamber. In his haunted chamber, they find that the perturbed spirit is an unfortunate—Imitator of Byron? No, is an unfortunate rusty Meat-jack, gnarring and creaking with rust and work; and this, in Scottish dialect, is *its* Byronian musical Life-philosophy, sung according to ability!

(Past and Present.)

THOMAS BABINGTON MACAULAY (1800–1859)
I.—ADDISON, VOLTAIRE, AND SWIFT

In wit, properly so called, Addison was not inferior to Cowley or Butler. No single ode of Cowley contains so many happy analogies as are crowded into the lines to Sir Godfrey Kneller; and we would undertake to collect from the *Spectators* as great a number of ingenious illustrations as can be found in *Hudibras*. The still higher faculty of invention Addison possessed in still larger measure. The numerous fictions, generally original, often wild and grotesque, but always singularly graceful and happy, which are found in his essays, fully entitle him to the rank of a great poet, a rank to which his metrical compositions give him no claim. As an observer of life, of manners, of all the shades of human character, he stands in the first class. And what he observed he had the art of communicating in two widely different ways. He could describe virtues, vices, habits, whims, as well as Clarendon. But he could do something better. He could call human beings into existence, and make them exhibit themselves. If we wish to find anything more vivid than Addison's best portraits, we must go either to Shakespeare or to Cervantes.

But what shall we say of Addison's humour, of his sense of the ludicrous, of his power of awakening that sense in others, and of drawing mirth from incidents which occur every day, and from little peculiarities of temper and manner, such as may be found in every man? We feel the charm: we give ourselves up to it: but we strive in vain to analyse it.

Perhaps the best way of describing Addison's peculiar pleasantry is to compare it with the pleasantry of some other great satirists. The three most eminent masters of the art of ridicule, during the eighteenth century, were, we conceive, Addison, Swift, and Voltaire. Which of the three had the greatest power of moving laughter may be questioned. But each of them, within his own domain, was supreme.

Voltaire is the prince of buffoons. His merriment is without disguise or restraint. He gambols; he grins; he shakes his sides; he points the finger; he turns up the nose; he shoots out the tongue. The manner of Swift is the very opposite to this. He moves laughter, but never joins in it. He appears in his works such as he appeared in society. All the company are convulsed with merriment, while the Dean, the author of all the mirth, preserves an invincible gravity, and even sourness of aspect, and gives utterance to the most eccentric and ludicrous fancies, with the air of a man reading the commination service.

The manner of Addison is as remote from that of Swift as from that of Voltaire. He neither laughs out like the French wit, nor, like the Irish wit, throws a double portion of severity into his countenance while laughing inwardly; but preserves a look peculiarly his own, a look of demure serenity, disturbed only by an arch sparkle of the eye, an almost imperceptible elevation of the brow, an almost imperceptible curl of the lip. His tone is never that either of a Jack Pudding or of a Cynic. It is that of a gentleman, in whom the quickest sense of the ridiculous is constantly tempered by good nature and good breeding.

We own that the humour of Addison is, in our opinion, of a more delicious flavour than the humour of either Swift or Voltaire. Thus much, at least, is certain, that both Swift and Voltaire have been successfully mimicked, and that no man has yet been able to mimic Addison. The letter of the Abbé Coyer to Pansophe is Voltaire all over, and imposed, during a long time, on the Academicians of Paris. There are passages in Arbuthnot's satirical works which we, at least, cannot distinguish from Swift's best writing. But of the many eminent men who have made Addison their model, though several have copied his mere diction with happy effect, none has been able to catch the tone of his pleasantry. In the *World*, in the *Connoisseur*, in the *Mirror*, in the *Lounger*, there are numerous papers written in obvious imitation of his *Tatlers* and *Spectators*. Most of those papers have some merit; many are very lively and amusing; but there is not a single one which could be passed off as Addison's on a critic of the smallest perspicacity.

But that which chiefly distinguishes Addison from Swift, from Voltaire, from almost all the other great masters of ridicule, is the grace, the nobleness, the moral purity, which we find even in his merriment. Severity, gradually hardening and darkening into misanthropy, characterizes the works of Swift. The nature of Voltaire, was indeed, not inhuman; but he venerated nothing. Neither in the masterpieces of art nor in the purest examples of virtue, neither in the Great First Cause nor in the awful enigma of the grave, could he see anything but subjects for drollery. The more solemn and august the theme, the more monkey-like was his grimacing and chattering. The mirth of Swift is the mirth of Mephistopheles; the mirth of Voltaire is the mirth of Puck. If, as Soame Jenyns oddly imagined, a portion of the happiness of Seraphim and just men made perfect be derived from an exquisite perception of the ludicrous, their mirth must surely be none other than the mirth of Addison; a mirth consistent with tender compassion for all that is frail, and with profound reverence for all that is sublime. Nothing great, nothing amiable, no moral duty, no doctrine of natural or revealed religion, has ever been associated by Addison with any degrading idea. His humanity is without a parallel in literary history. The highest proof of virtue is to possess boundless power without abusing it. No kind of power is more formidable than the power of making men ridiculous; and that power Addison possessed in boundless measure. How grossly that power was abused by Swift and by Voltaire is well known. But of Addison it may be confidently affirmed that he has blackened no man's character, nay, that it would be difficult, if not impossible, to find in all the volumes which he has left us a single taunt which can be called ungenerous or unkind. Yet he had detractors, whose malignity might have seemed to justify as terrible a revenge as that which men, not superior to him in genius, wreaked on Bettesworth and on Franc de Pompignan. He was a politician; he was the best writer of his party; he lived in times of fierce excitement, in times when persons of high character and station stooped to scurrility such as is now practised only by the basest of mankind. Yet no provocation and no example could induce him to return railing for railing.

(*Essay on Addison.*)

II.—THE WRITINGS OF HORACE WALPOLE

It is impossible to deny that Walpole's writings have real merit, and merit of a very rare, though not of a very high kind. Sir Joshua Reynolds used to say that, though nobody would for a moment compare Claude to Raphael, there would be another Raphael before there was another Claude. And we own that we expect to see fresh Humes and fresh Burkes before we again fall in with that peculiar combination of moral and intellectual qualities to which the writings of Walpole owe their extraordinary popularity.

It is easy to describe him by negatives. He had not a creative imagination. He had not a pure taste. He was not a great reasoner. There is indeed scarcely any writer in whose works it would be possible to find so many contradictory judgments, so many sentences of extravagant nonsense. Nor was it only in his familiar correspondence that he wrote in this flighty and inconsistent manner, but in long and elaborate books, in books repeatedly transcribed and intended for the public eye. We will give an instance or two; for, without instances, readers not very familiar with his works will scarcely understand our meaning. In the *Anecdotes of Painting*, he states, very truly, that the art declined after the commencement of the civil wars. He proceeds to inquire why this happened. The explanation, we should have thought, would have been easily found. He might have mentioned the loss of the most munificent and judicious patron that the fine arts ever had in England, the troubled state of the country, the distressed condition of many of the aristocracy, perhaps also the austerity of the victorious party. These circumstances, we conceive, fully account for the phænomenon. But this solution was not odd enough to satisfy Walpole. He discovers another cause for the decline of the art, the want of models. Nothing worth painting, it seems, was left to paint. "How picturesque," he exclaims, "was the figure of an Anabaptist!"—as if puritanism had put out the sun and withered the trees; as if the civil wars had blotted out the expression of character and passion from the human lip and brow; as if many of the men whom Vandyke painted had not been living in the time of the Commonwealth, with faces little the worse for wear; as if many of the beauties afterwards portrayed by Lely were not in their prime before the Restoration; as if the garb or the features of Cromwell and Milton were less picturesque than those of the round-faced peers, as like each other as eggs to eggs, who look out from the middle of the periwigs of Kneller. In the *Memoirs*, again, Walpole sneers at the Prince of Wales, afterwards George the Third, for presenting a collection of books to one of the American colleges during the Seven Years' War, and says that, instead of books, his Royal Highness ought to have sent arms and ammunition, as if a war ought to suspend all study and all education, or as if it were the business of the Prince of Wales to supply the colonies with military stores out of his own pocket. We have perhaps dwelt too long on these passages; but we have done so because they are specimens of Walpole's manner. Everybody who reads his works with attention will find that they swarm with loose and foolish observations like those which we have cited; observations which might pass in conversation or in a hasty letter, but which are unpardonable in books deliberately written and repeatedly corrected.

He appears to have thought that he saw very far into men; but we are under the necessity of altogether dissenting from his opinion. We do not conceive that he had any power of discerning the finer shades of character. He practised an art, however, which, though easy and even vulgar, obtains for those who practise it the reputation of discernment with ninety-nine people out of a hundred. He sneered at everybody, put on every action the worst construction which it would bear, " spelt every man backward," to borrow the Lady Hero's phrase,

> " Turned every man the wrong side out,
> And never gave to truth and virtue that
> Which simpleness and merit purchaseth."

In this way any man may, with little sagacity and little trouble, be considered by those whose good opinion is not worth having as a great judge of character.

It is said that the hasty and rapacious Kneller used to send away the ladies who sate to him as soon as he had sketched their faces, and to paint the figure and hands from his housemaid. It was in much the same way that Walpole portrayed the minds of others. He copied from the life only those glaring and obvious peculiarities which could not escape the most super-ficial observation. The rest of the canvas he filled up, in a careless dashing way, with knave and fool, mixed in such proportions as pleased Heaven. What a difference between these daubs and the masterly portraits of Clarendon !

There are contradictions without end in the sketches of char-acter which abound in Walpole's works. But if we were to form our opinion of his eminent contemporaries from a general survey of what he has written concerning them, we should say that Pitt was a strutting, ranting, mouthing actor, Charles Townshend an impudent and voluble jack-pudding, Murray a demure, cold-blooded, cowardly hypocrite, Hardwicke an insolent upstart, with the understanding of a pettifogger and the heart of a hangman, Temple an impertinent poltroon, Egmont a solemn coxcomb, Lyttelton a poor creature whose only wish was to go to heaven in a coronet, Onslow a pompous proser, Washington a braggart, Lord Camden sullen, Lord Townshend malevolent, Secker an atheist who had shammed Christian for a mitre, Whitefield an impostor who swindled his converts out of their watches. The Walpoles fare little better than their neighbours. Old Horace is constantly represented as a coarse, brutal, niggardly buffoon, and his son as worthy of such a father. In short, if we are to trust this discerning judge of human nature, England in his time contained little sense and no virtue, except what was distributed between himself, Lord Waldgrave, and Marshal Conway.

Of such a writer it is scarcely necessary to say, that his works are destitute of every charm which is derived from elevation or from tenderness of sentiment. When he chose to be humane and magnanimous,—for he sometimes, by way of variety, tried this affectation,—he overdid his part most ludicrously. None of his many disguises sat so awkwardly upon him. For example, he tells us that he did not choose to be intimate with Mr. Pitt. And why? Because Mr. Pitt had been among the persecutors of his father? Or because, as he repeatedly assures us, Mr. Pitt was a disagreeable man in private life? Not at all; but because Mr. Pitt was too fond of war, and was great with too little reluctance. Strange that a habitual scoffer like Walpole should imagine that this cant should impose on the dullest reader! If Molière had put such a speech into the mouth of Tartuffe, we should have said that the fiction was unskilful, and that Orgon could not have been such a fool as to be taken in by it. Of the twenty-six years during which Walpole sat in Parliament, thirteen were years of war. Yet he did not, during all those thirteen years, utter a single word or give a single vote tending to peace. His most intimate friend, the only friend, indeed, to whom he appears to have been sincerely attached, Conway, was a soldier, was fond of his profession, and was perpetually entreating Mr. Pitt to give him employment. In this Walpole saw nothing but what was admirable. Conway was a hero for soliciting the command of expeditions which Mr. Pitt was a monster for sending out.

What then is the charm, the irresistible charm, of Walpole's writings? It consists, we think, in the art of amusing without exciting. He never convinces the reason, or fills the imagination, or touches the heart; but he keeps the mind of the reader constantly attentive, and constantly entertained. He had a strange ingenuity peculiarly his own, an ingenuity which appeared in all that he did, in his building, in his gardening, in his upholstery, in the matter and in the manner of his writings. If we were to adopt the classification, not a very accurate classification, which Akenside has given of the pleasures of the imagination, we should say that with the Sublime and the Beautiful Walpole had nothing to do, but that the third province, the Odd, was his peculiar domain. The motto which he prefixed to his Catalogue of Royal and Noble Authors might have been inscribed with perfect propriety over the door of every room in his house, and on the titlepage of every one of his books: "Dove diavolo, Messer Ludovico, avete pigliate tante coglionerie?" In his villa, every apartment is a museum; every piece of furniture is a curiosity; there is something strange in the form of the shovel; there is a long story belonging to the bell-rope. We wander among a profusion of rarities, of trifling intrinsic value, but so quaint in fashion, or connected with such remarkable names and events, that they may well detain our attention for a moment. A moment is enough. Some new relic, some new unique, some new carved work, some new enamel, is forthcoming in an instant. One cabinet of trinkets is no sooner closed than another is opened. It is the same with Walpole's writings. It is not in their utility, it is not in their beauty, that their attraction lies. They are to the works of great historians and poets, what Strawberry Hill is to the Museum of Sir Hans Sloane or to the Gallery of Florence. Walpole is constantly showing us things, not of very great value indeed, yet things which we are pleased to see, and which we can see nowhere else. They are baubles; but they are made curiosities either by his grotesque workmanship or by some association belonging to them. His style is one of those peculiar styles by which every body is attracted, and which nobody can safely venture to imitate. He is a mannerist whose manner has become perfectly easy to him. His affectation is so habitual and so universal that it can hardly be called affectation. The affectation is the essence of the man. It pervades all his thoughts and all his expressions. If it were taken away, nothing would be left. He coins new words, distorts the senses of old words, and twists sentences into forms which make grammarians stare. But all this he does, not only with an air of ease, but as if he could not help doing it. His wit was, in its essential properties, of the same kind with that of Cowley and Donne. Like theirs, it consisted in an exquisite perception of points of analogy and points of contrast too subtle for common observation. Like them, Walpole perpetually startles us by the ease with which he yokes together ideas between which there would seem, at first sight, to be no connection. But he did not, like them, affect the gravity of a lecture, and draw his illustrations from the laboratory and from the schools. His tone was light and fleering; his topics were the topics of the club and the ball-room; and therefore his strange combinations and far-fetched illusions, though very closely resembling those which tire us to death in the poems of the time of Charles the First, are read with pleasure constantly new.

No man who has written so much is so seldom tiresome. In his books there are scarcely any of those passages which, in our school-days, we used to call *skip*. Yet he often wrote on subjects which are generally considered as dull, on subjects which men of great talents have in vain endeavoured to render popular. When we compare the *Historic Doubts about Richard the Third* with Whitaker's and Chalmers's books on a far more interesting question, the character of Mary Queen of Scots; when we compare the *Anecdotes of Painting* with Nichols's Anecdotes, or even with Mr. D'Israeli's *Quarrels of Authors* and *Calamities of Authors*, we at once see Walpole's superiority, not in industry, not in learning, not in accuracy, not in logical power, but in the art of writing what people will like to read. He rejects all but the attractive parts of his subject. He keeps only what is in itself amusing, or what can be made so by the artifice of his diction. The coarser morsels of antiquarian learning he abandons to others, and sets out an entertainment worthy of a Roman epicure, an entertainment consisting of nothing but delicacies, the brains of singing-birds, the roe of mullets, the sunny halves of peaches. This, we think, is the great merit of his romance. There is little skill in the delineation of the characters. Manfred is as commonplace a tyrant, Jerome as commonplace a confessor, Theodore as commonplace a young gentleman, Isabella and Matilda as commonplace a pair of young ladies, as are to be found in any of the thousand Italian castles in which *condottieri* have revelled or in which imprisoned duchesses have pined. We cannot say that we much admire the big man whose sword is dug up in one quarter of the globe, whose helmet drops from the clouds in another, and who, after clattering and rustling for some days, ends by kicking the house down. But the story, whatever its value may be, never flags for a single moment. There are no digressions, or unseasonable descriptions, or long speeches. Every sentence carries the action forward. The excitement is constantly renewed. Absurd as is the machinery, insipid as are the human actors, no reader probably ever thought the book dull.

Walpole's *Letters* are generally considered as his best performances, and, we think, with reason. His faults are far less offensive to us in his correspondence than in his books. His wild, absurd, and ever-changing opinions about men and things are easily pardoned in familiar letters. His bitter, scoffing, depreciating disposition does not show itself in so unmitigated a manner as in his *Memoirs*. A writer of letters must in general be civil and friendly to his correspondent at least, if to no other person.

He loved letter-writing, and had evidently studied it as an art. It was, in truth, the very kind of writing for such a man, for a man very ambitious to rank among wits, yet nervously afraid that, while obtaining the reputation of a wit, he might lose caste as a gentleman. There was nothing vulgar in writing a letter. Not even Ensign Northerton, not even the Captain described in Hamilton's *Bawn*,—and Walpole, though the author of many quartos, had some feelings in common with those gallant officers,—would have denied that a gentleman might sometimes correspond with a friend. Whether Walpole bestowed much labour on the composition of his letters, it is impossible to judge from internal evidence. There are passages which seem perfectly unstudied. But the appearance of ease may be the effect of labour. There are passages which have a very artificial air. But they may have been produced without effort by a mind of which the natural ingenuity had been improved into morbid quickness by constant exercise. We are never sure that we see him as he was. We are never sure that what appears to be nature is not disguised art. We are never sure that what appears to be art is not merely habit which has become second nature.

(Essay on Walpole.)

WILLIAM EWART GLADSTONE (1809–1898)
The Greek Doctrine of a Future State

The doctrine of the future state, if viewed as a working portion of religion, lost force and did not gain it with the lapse of time under the Egyptian system, which had been so famous for its early inculcation.

Undoubtedly this seems to have been the case also with the Greeks. The genius of that extraordinary people does not appear at any time to have qualified or inclined them to adopt with anything like earnestness or force that belief, which is so marked in the religions of Egypt and of Persia at an early date. Homer is here our principal authority : and what we gather from the " Odyssey " is that the underworld of the Poet is evidently an exotic and imported conception, made up of elements which were chiefly supplied from the religions of Egypt and Assyria. We may also observe that the place he finds for it lies in the outer zone of his geography, beyond the great encircling River Okeanos. In the " Iliad," the great national and patriotic poem of Homer, the doctrine of the future life appears only in the case of Patroklos, and there only as a vague, remote, and shadowy image. The Egyptian name for the kingdom of the dead was Amenti, which seems to reappear in the Greek Rhadamanthos. There is a singular circumstance associated with one of the discoveries of Schliemann at Mycenæ. In a tomb fifteen feet six inches in length, and only five feet six inches in breadth, the bodies of full-grown men are laid, not along but across the space, being thus squeezed in the strangest manner. But they were in this way made to lie east and west, and towards the west : and such we learn was the position in which the Egyptians laid their dead. Minos is also introduced to us as a personage in the underworld of the " Odyssey," and he is engaged in administering justice. So far we follow the Egyptian idea. But the Greek spirit took the heart and life out of the realm of Osiris. Minos sits, so to speak, not as a criminal but as a civil judge : he does not punish the guilty for their misdeeds on earth, but simply meets the wants of a community for an arbitrator of determining authority in their affairs. No one, whom we can certainly call a compatriot of Homer's appears in the underworld as under penal suffering : not, for instance, Aigisthos, or Klutaimnestra, who might have been fit subjects for it. In the ethical code of Homer, there is no clear recognition of penalty for sin; except it be for perjury upon the breach of great public facts; and this penalty is made applicable to gods and men alike. The only case, in which he associates the existence after death with happiness, is that of Menelaos. Menelaos is among the purest characters of the Poems : but the reason given for his fortunate lot is that he was the husband of Helen, and son-in-law of Zeus. It is, however, plain that there must have been a general belief in a future state among his contemporaries, or we should not find it as we now find it, embodied and developed in a poem essentially popular.

It was, then, an article of the national belief in the heroic age. What became of it in the classical period ? It faded out of notice. There grew up instead of it that remarkable idea of the self-sufficiency of life which became a basis for Greek existence. Apart from particular exceptions, and from the mysteries, which remained always only mysteries for the people, things temporal and things seen affixed all round a limit to human interests. The underworld could not have been treated as it is treated by Aristophanes, in any country except one where for the mind of the people at large it had ceased to have a really religious existence. The disputed existence which it obtained in some of the philosophical schools is itself a witness to the fact that for man as such, in the wear and tear of centuries the idea had not, upon the whole, gained ground, but lost it among the most intellectual people ever known.

(*Essay on the Ancient Beliefs in a Future State.*)

ELIZABETH CLEGHORN GASKELL (1810–1865)
OLD LETTERS

ONE night, I remember this candle economy particularly annoyed me. I had been very much tired of my compulsory " blind man's holidays," especially as Miss Matty had fallen asleep, and I did not like to stir the fire and run the risk of awakening her, so I could not even sit on the rug, and scorch myself with sewing by firelight, according to my usual custom. I fancied Miss Matty must be dreaming of her early life; for she spoke one or two words in her uneasy sleep, bearing reference to persons who were dead long before. When Martha brought in the lighted candle and tea, Miss Matty started into wakefulness, with a strange, bewildered look around, as if we were not the people she expected to see about her. There was a little sad expression that shadowed her face as she recognised me; but immediately afterwards she tried to give me her usual smile. All through tea-time her talk ran upon the days of her childhood and youth. Perhaps this reminded her of the desirableness of looking over all the old family letters, and destroying such as ought not to be allowed to fall into the hands of strangers; for she had often spoken of the necessity of this task, but had always shrunk from it, with a timid dread of something painful. To-night, however, she rose up after tea and went for them—in the dark; for she piqued herself on the precise neatness of all her chamber arrangements, and used to look uneasily at me when I lighted a bed-candle to go to another room for anything. When she returned there was a faint, pleasant smell of Tonquin beans in the room. I had always noticed this scent about any of the things which had belonged to her mother; and many of the letters were addressed to her—yellow bundles of love-letters, sixty or seventy years old.

Miss Matty undid the packet with a sigh; but she stifled it directly, as if it were hardly right to regret the flight of time, or of life either. We agreed to look them over separately, each taking a different letter out of the same bundle and describing its contents to the other before destroying it. I never knew what sad work the reading of old letters was before that evening, though I could hardly tell why. The letters were as happy as letters could be—at least those early letters were. There was in them a vivid and intense sense of the present time, which seemed so strong and full, as if it could never pass away, and as if the warm, living hearts that so expressed themselves could never die, and be as nothing to the sunny earth. I should have felt less melancholy, I believe, if the letters had been more so. I saw the tears stealing down the well-worn furrows of Miss Matty's cheeks, and her spectacles often wanted wiping. I trusted at last that she would light the other candle, for my own eyes were rather dim, and I wanted more light to see the pale, faded ink; but no, even through her tears, she saw and remembered her little economical ways.

The earliest set of letters were two bundles tied together, and ticketed (in Miss Jenkyns's handwriting), " Letters interchanged between my ever-honoured father and my dearly-beloved mother prior to their marriage, in July, 1774." I should guess that the rector of Cranford was about twenty-seven years of age when he wrote those letters; and Miss Matty told me that her mother was just eighteen at the time of her wedding. With my idea of the rector, derived from a picture in the dining-parlour, stiff and stately, in a huge full-bottomed wig, with gown, cassock, and bands, and his hand upon a copy of the only sermon he ever published—it was strange to read these letters. They were full of eager, passionate ardour; short, homely sentences, right fresh from the heart (very different from the grand Latinised, Johnsonian style of the printed sermon, preached before some judge at assize time). His letters were a curious contrast to those of his girl-bride. She was evidently rather annoyed at his demands upon her for expressions of love, and could not quite understand what he meant by repeating the same thing over in so many different ways; but what she was quite clear about was a longing for a white " Paduasoy "—whatever that might be; and six or seven letters were principally occupied in asking her lover to use his influence with her parents (who evidently kept her in good order) to obtain this or that article of dress, more especially the white " Paduasoy." He cared nothing how she was dressed; she was always lovely enough for him, as he took pains to assure her, when she begged him to express in his answers a predilection for particular pieces of finery, in order that she might show what he said to her parents. But at length he seemed to find out that she would not be married till she had a " trousseau " to her mind; and then he sent her a letter, which had evidently accompanied a whole box full of finery, and in which he requested that she might be dressed in everything her heart desired. This was the first letter, ticketed in a frail, delicate hand, " From my dearest John." Shortly afterwards they were married —I suppose, from the intermission in their correspondence.

"We must burn them, I think," said Miss Matty, looking doubtfully at me. " No one will care for them when I am gone." And one by one she dropped them into the middle of the fire, watching each blaze up, die out, and rise away, in faint, white, ghostly semblance, up the chimney, before she gave another to the same fate. The room was light enough now; but I, like her, was fascinated into watching the destruction of those letters, into which the honest warmth of a manly heart had been poured forth.

The next letter, likewise docketed by Miss Jenkyns, was endorsed, " Letter of pious congratulation and exhortation from my venerable grandfather to my beloved mother, on occasion of my own birth. Also some practical remarks on the desirability of keeping warm the extremities of infants, from my excellent grandmother."

The first part was, indeed, a severe and forcible picture of the responsibilities of mothers, and a warning against the evils that were in the world, and lying in ghastly wait for the little baby of two days old. His wife did not write, said the old gentleman, because he had forbidden it, she being indisposed with a sprained ankle, which (he said) quite incapacitated her from holding a pen. However, at the foot of the page was a small " т.о.," and on turning it over, sure enough, there was a letter to " my dear, dearest Molly," begging her, when she left her room, whatever she did, to go *up* stairs before going *down* ; and telling her to wrap her baby's feet up in flannel, and keep it warm by the fire, although it was summer, for babies were so tender.

It was pretty to see from the letters, which were evidently exchanged with some frequency between the young mother and the grandmother, how the girlish vanity was being weeded out of her heart by love for her baby. The white " Paduasoy " figured again in the letters, with almost as much vigour as before. In one, it was being made into a christening cloak for the baby. It decked it when it went with its parents to spend a day or two at Arley Hall. It added to its charms, when it was " the prettiest little baby that ever was seen. Dear mother, I wish you could see her ! Without any parshality, I do think she will grow up a regular bewty ! " I thought of Miss Jenkyns, gray, withered, and wrinkled, and I wondered if her mother had known her in the courts of heaven : and then I knew that she had, and that they stood there in angelic guise.

There was a great gap before any of the rector's letters appeared. And then his wife had changed her mode of endorsement. It was no longer from " My dearest John "; it was from " My honoured Husband." The letters were written on occasion of the publication of the same sermon which was represented in the picture. The preaching before " My Lord Judge," and the " publishing by request," was evidently the culminating point—the event of his life. It had been necessary for him to go up to London to superintend it through the press. Many friends had to be called upon, and consulted, before he could decide on any printer fit for so onerous a task ; and at length it was arranged that J. and J. Rivingtons were to have the honourable responsibility. The worthy rector seemed to be strung up by the occasion to a high literary pitch, for he could hardly write a letter to his wife without cropping out into Latin. I remember the end of one of his letters ran thus : " I shall ever hold the virtuous qualities of my Molly in remembrance, *dum memor ipse mei, dum spiritus regit artus* " ; which, considering that the English of his correspondent was sometimes at fault in grammar, and often in spelling, might be taken as a proof of how much he " idealised his Molly "; and, as Miss Jenkyns used to say, " People talk a great deal about idealising nowadays, whatever that may mean." But this was nothing to a fit of writing classical poetry which soon seized him, in which his Molly figured away as " Maria." The letter containing the *carmen* was endorsed by her, " Hebrew verses sent me by my honoured husband. I thowt to have had a letter about killing the pig, but must wait. Mem., to send the poetry to Sir Peter Arley, as my husband desires." And in a *post-scriptum* note in his handwriting it was stated that the ode had appeared in *The Gentleman's Magazine*, December, 1782.

Her letters back to her husband (treasured as fondly by him as if they had been *M. T. Ciceronis Epistolæ*) were more satisfactory to an absent husband and father than his could ever have been to her. She told him how Deborah sewed her seam very neatly every day, and read to her in the books he had set her; how she was a very " forrard," good child, but *would* ask questions her mother could not answer, but how she did not let herself down by saying she did not know, but took to stirring the fire, or sending the " forrard " child on an errand. Matty was now the mother's darling, and promised (like her sister at her age) to be a great beauty. I was reading this aloud to Miss Matty, who smiled and sighed a little at the hope, so fondly expressed, that " little Matty might not be vain, even if she were a bewty."

" I had very pretty hair, my dear," said Miss Matilda; " and not a bad mouth." And I saw her, soon afterwards, adjust her cap and draw herself up.

But to return to Mrs. Jenkyns's letters. She told her husband about the poor in the parish; what homely, domestic medicines she had administered; what kitchen physic she had sent. She had evidently held his displeasure as a rod in pickle over the heads of all the ne'er-do-wells. She asked for his directions about the cows and pigs; and did not always obtain them, as I have shown before.

The kind old grandmother was dead when a little boy was born, soon after the publication of the sermon; but there was another letter of exhortation from the grandfather, more stringent and admonitory than ever, now that there was a boy to be guarded from the snares of the world. He described all the various sins into which men might fall, until I wondered how any man ever came to a natural death. The gallows seemed as if it must have been the termination of the lives of most of the grandfather's friends and acquaintance; and I was not surprised at the way in which he spoke of this life being "a vale of tears."

(Cranford.)

DR. JOHN BROWN (1810–1882)
WALTER SCOTT AND MARJORIE

THE third we all know. What has he not done for every one of us? Who else ever, except Shakspere, so diverted mankind, entertained and entertains a world so liberally, so wholesomely? We are fain to say, not even Shakspere, for his is something deeper than diversion, something higher than pleasure, and yet who would care to split this hair?

Had any one watched him closely before and after the parting, what a change he would see! The bright, broad laugh, the shrewd, jovial word, the man of the Parliament House and of the world; and next step, moody, the light of his eye withdrawn, as if seeing things that were invisible; his shut mouth, like a child's, so impressionable, so innocent, so sad; he was now all within, as before he was all without; hence his brooding look. As the snow blattered in his face, he muttered, "How it raves and drifts! On-ding o' snaw—aye, that's the word—on-ding——" He was now at his own door, "Castle Street, No. 39." He opened the door, and went straight to his den; that wondrous workshop, where, in one year, 1823, when he was fifty-two, he wrote *Peveril of the Peak*, *Quentin Durward*, and *St. Ronan's Well*, besides much else. We once took the foremost of our novelists, the greatest, we would say, since Scott, into this room, and could not but mark the solemnizing effect of sitting where the great magician sat so often and so long, and looking out upon that little shabby bit of sky and that back green, where faithful Camp lies.

He sat down in his large, green morocco elbow-chair, drew himself close to his table, and glowered and gloomed at his writing apparatus, "a very handsome old box, richly carved, lined with crimson velvet, and containing ink-bottles, taper-stand, etc., in silver, the whole in such order, that it might have come from the silversmith's window half an hour before." He took out his paper, then starting up angrily, said, "Go spin, you jade, go spin." No, d—— it, it won't do,—

> "My spinnin' wheel is auld and stiff,
>   The rock o't wunna stand, sir,
> To keep the temper-pin in tiff
>   Employs ower aft my hand, sir."

I am off the fang. I can make nothing of *Waverley* to-day;
I'll awa' to Marjorie. Come wi' me, Maida, you thief." The
great creature rose slowly, and the pair were off, Scott taking
a *maud* (a plaid) with him. "White as a forsted plum-cake,
by Jingo!" said he, when he got to the street. Maida gambolled
and whisked among the snow, and her master strode across to
Young Street, and through it to 1 North Charlotte Street, to
the house of his dear friend, Mrs. William Keith of Corstorphine
Hill, niece of Mrs. Keith of Ravelston, of whom he said at her
death, eight years after, "Much tradition, and that of the best,
has died with this excellent old lady, one of the few persons
whose spirits and *cleanliness* and freshness of mind and body
made old age lovely and desirable."

Sir Walter was in that house almost every day, and had a
key, so in he and the hound went, shaking themselves in the
lobby. "Marjorie! Marjorie!" shouted his friend, "where are
ye, my bonnie wee croodlin doo?" In a moment a bright, eager
child of seven was in his arms, and he was kissing her all over.
Out came Mrs. Keith. "Come yer ways in, Wattie." "No,
not now. I am going to take Marjorie wi' me, and you may
come to your tea in Duncan Roy's sedan, and bring the bairn
home in your lap." "Tak' Marjorie, and it *onding o' snaw!*"
said Mrs. Keith. He said to himself, "On-ding—that's odd—
that is the very word." "Hoot, awa! look here," and he
displayed the corner of his plaid, made to hold lambs—(the
true shepherd's plaid, consisting of two breadths sewed together,
and uncut at one end, making a poke or *cul de sac*). "Tak'
yer lamb," said she, laughing at the contrivance, and so the Pet
was first well happit up, and then put, laughing silently, into the
plaid neuk, and the shepherd strode off, with his lamb,—Maida
gambolling through the snow, and running races in her mirth.

Didn't he face "the angry airt," and make her bield his
bosom, and into his own room with her, and lock the door, and
out with the warm, rosy, little wifie, who took it all with great
composure! There the two remained for three or more hours,
making the house ring with their laughter; you can fancy the
big man's and Maidie's laugh. Having made the fire cheery,
he set her down in his ample chair, and standing sheepishly
before her, began to say his lesson, which happened to be—
"Ziccotty, diccotty, dock, the mouse ran up the clock, the

clock struck wan, down the mouse ran, ziccotty, diccotty, dock."
This done repeatedly till she was pleased, she gave him his new
lesson, gravely and slowly, timing it upon her small fingers,—he
saying it after her,—

> " Wonery, twoery, tickery, seven ;
> Alibi, crackaby, ten and eleven ;
> Pin, pan, musky, dan ;
> Tweedle-um, twoddle-um,
> Twenty-wan ; eerie, orie, ourie,
> You, are, out."

He pretended to great difficulty, and she rebuked him with
most comical gravity, treating him as a child. He used to say
that when he came to Alibi Crackaby he broke down, and Pin-
Pan, Musky-Dan, Tweedle-um, Twoddle-um made him roar with
laughter. He said *Musky-Dan* especially was beyond endurance, bringing up an Irishman and his hat fresh from the Spice
Islands and odoriferous Ind ; she getting quite bitter in her
displeasure at his ill-behaviour and stupidness.

Then he would read ballads to her in his own glorious way,
the two getting wild with excitement over *Gil Morrice* or the
Baron of Smailholm ; and he would take her on his knee, and
make her repeat Constance's speeches in *King John*, till he swayed
to and fro, sobbing his fill. Fancy the gifted little creature, like
one possessed, repeating—

> " For I am sick, and capable of fears,
> Oppressed with wrong, and therefore, full of fears ;
> A widow, husbandless, subject to fears,
> A woman, naturally born to fears."

> " If thou that bidst me be content, were grim,
> Ugly and slanderous to thy mother's womb,
> Lame, foolish, crooked, swart, prodigious——"

Or, drawing herself up " to the height of her great argum

> " I will instruct my sorrows to be proud,
> For grief is proud, and makes his owner stout.
> Here I and sorrow sit."

Scott used to say that he was amazed at her power over him,
saying to Mrs. Keith, " She's the most extraordinary creature
I ever met with, and her repeating of Shakspere overpowers
me as nothing else does."

(Pet Marjorie.)

JOHN BRIGHT (1811–1888)

HOUSE OF COMMONS, DECEMBER 22, 1854

WHEN I look at gentlemen on that Bench, and consider all
their policy has brought about within the last twelve months,

I scarcely dare trust myself to speak of them, either in or out of their presence. We all know what we have lost in this House. Here, sitting near me, very often sat the member for Frome. I met him, a short time before he went out, at Mr. Westerton's, the bookseller, near Hyde Park Corner. I asked him whether he was going out. He answered he was afraid he was; not afraid in the sense of personal fear—he knew not that; but he said, with a look and a tone I shall never forget, "It is no light matter for a man who has a wife and five little children." The stormy Euxine is his grave; his wife is a widow, his children fatherless. On the other side of the House sat a member, with whom I was not acquainted, who has lost his life, and another of whom I knew something. Who is there that does not recollect his frank, amiable and manly countenance? I doubt whether there were any men on either side of the House who were more capable of fixing the good-will and affection of those with whom they were associated. Well, but the place that knew them shall know them no more for ever.

I was in the House of Lords when the vote of thanks was moved. In the gallery were many ladies, three-fourths of whom were dressed in the deepest mourning. Is this nothing? And in every village, cottages are to be found into which sorrow has entered, and, as I believe, through the policy of the Ministry, which might have been avoided. No one supposes that the Government wished to spread the pall of sorrow over the land; but this we had a right to expect, that they would at least show a becoming gravity in discussing a subject, the appalling consequences of which may come home to individuals and to the nation. I recollect when Sir Robert Peel addressed the House on a dispute which threatened hostilities with the United States—I recollect the gravity of his countenance, the solemnity of his tone, his whole demeanour showing that he felt in his soul the responsibility that rested on him. I have seen this, and I have seen the present Ministry. There was the buffoonery at the Reform Club. Was that becoming a matter of this grave nature? Has there been a solemnity of manner in the speeches heard in connection with this war, and have Ministers shown themselves statesmen and Christian men when speaking on a subject of this nature?

It is very easy for the noble Lord, the member for Tiverton, to rise and say that I am against war under all circumstances; and that if an enemy were to land on our shores, I should make a calculation as to whether it would be cheaper to take him in or keep him out, and that my opinion on this subject is not to be considered either by Parliament or the country. I am not afraid of discussing the war with the noble Lord on his own principles. I understand the Blue Books as well as he; and, leaving out all fantastic and visionary notions about what will become of us if something is not done to destroy or to cripple Russia, I say—and I say it with as much confidence as I ever said anything in my life—that the war cannot be justified out of these documents; and that impartial history will teach this to posterity if we do not comprehend it now.

I am not, nor did I ever pretend to be, a statesman; and that character is so tainted and so equivocal in our day that I am not sure that a pure and honourable ambition would aspire to it. I have not enjoyed for thirty years, like these noble Lords, the honours and emoluments of office. I have not set my sails to every passing breeze. I am a plain and simple citizen, sent here by one of the foremost constituencies of the Empire, representing feebly, perhaps, but honestly, I dare aver, the opinions of very many, and the true interests of all those who have sent me here. Let it not be said that I am alone in my condemnation of this war, and of this incapable and guilty Administration. And even if I were alone, if mine were a solitary voice, raised amid the din of arms and the clamours of a venal press, I should have the consolation I have to-night—and which I trust will be mine to the last moment of my existence—the priceless consolation that no word of mine has tended to the squandering of my country's treasure or the spilling of one single drop of my country's blood.

(Speech on the Crimean War.)

WILLIAM MAKEPEACE THACKERAY (1811–1863)

THE FAMOUS MR. JOSEPH ADDISON

THE gentlemen ushers had a table at Kensington, and the guard a very splendid dinner daily at St. James's, at either of which ordinaries Esmond was free to dine. Dick Steele liked the guard-table better than his own at the gentlemen ushers', where there was less wine and more ceremony; and Esmond had many a jolly afternoon in company of his friend, and a hundred times at least saw Dick into his chair. If there is verity in wine, according to the old adage, what an amiable-natured character Dick's must have been! In proportion as he took in wine he overflowed with kindness. His talk was not witty so much as charming. He never said a word that could anger anybody, and only became the more benevolent the more tipsy he grew. Many of the wags derided the poor fellow in his cups, and chose him as a butt for their satire; but there was a kindness about him, and a sweet playful fancy, that seemed to Esmond far more charming than the pointed talk of the brightest wits, with their elaborate repartees and affected severities. I think Steele shone rather than sparkled. Those famous *beaux-esprits* of the coffee-houses (Mr. William Congreve, for instance, when his gout and his grandeur permitted him to come among us) would make many brilliant hits—half a dozen in a night sometimes—but, like sharp-shooters, when they had fired their shot, they were obliged to retire under cover, till their pieces were loaded again, and wait till they got another chance at their enemy; whereas Dick never thought that his bottle-companion was a butt to aim at—only a friend to shake by the hand. The poor fellow had half the town in his confidence; everybody knew everything about his loves and his debts, his creditors or his mistress's obduracy. When Esmond first came on to the town honest Dick was all flames and raptures for a young lady, a West India fortune, whom he married. In a couple of years the lady was dead, the fortune was all but spent, and the honest widower was as eager in pursuit of a new paragon of beauty as if he had never courted and married and buried the last one.

Quitting the guard-table on one sunny afternoon, when by chance Dick had a sober fit upon him, he and his friend were making their way down Germain Street, and Dick all of a sudden left his companion's arm, and ran after a gentleman, who was poring over a folio volume at the bookshop near to St. James's Church. He was a fair, tall man, in a snuff-coloured suit, with a plain sword, very sober and almost shabby in appearance—at least, when compared to Captain Steele, who loved to adorn his jolly round person with the finest of clothes, and shone in scarlet and gold lace. The Captain rushed up, then, to the student of the book-stall, took him in his arms, hugged him, and would have kissed him—for Dick was always hugging and bussing his friends, —but the other stepped back with a flush on his pale face, seeming to decline this publick manifestation of Steele's regard.

" My dearest Joe, where hast thou hidden thyself this age? " cries the Captain, still holding both his friend's hands; " I have been languishing for thee this fortnight."

" A fortnight is not an age, Dick," says the other, very good-humouredly. (He had light blue eyes, extraordinary bright, and a face perfectly regular and handsome like a tinted statue.) " And I have been hiding myself—where do you think? "

"What! not across the water, my dear Joe?" says Steele with a look of great alarm: "thou knowest I have always——"

"No," says his friend, interrupting him with a smile: "we are not come to such straits as that, Dick. I have been hiding, sir, at a place where people never think of finding you—at my own lodgings, whither I am going to smoke a pipe now and drink a glass of sack; will your honour come?"

"Harry Esmond, come hither," cries out Dick. "Thou hast heard me talk over and over again at my dearest Joe, my guardian-angel."

"Indeed," says Mr. Esmond, with a bow, "it is not from you only that I have learnt to admire Mr. Addison. We loved good poetry at Cambridge as well as at Oxford; and I have some of yours by heart though I have put on a red coat. . . . 'O qui canoro blandius Orpheo vocale ducis carmen;' shall I go on sir?" says Mr. Esmond, who, indeed, had read and loved the charming Latin poems of Mr. Addison, as every scholar of that time knew and admired them.

"This is Captain Esmond, who was at Blenheim," says Steele.

"Lieutenant Esmond," says the other, with a low bow; "at Mr. Addison's service."

"I have heard of you," says Mr. Addison, with a smile; as, indeed, everybody about town had heard that unlucky story about Esmond's dowager aunt and the Duchess.

"We were going to the George, to take a bottle before the play," says Steele; "wilt thou be one, Joe?"

Mr. Addison said his own lodgings were hard by, where he was still rich enough to give a good bottle of wine to his friends; and invited the two gentlemen to his apartment in the Haymarket, whither we accordingly went.

"I shall get credit with my landlady," says he, with a smile, "when she sees two such fine gentlemen as you come up my stair." And he politely made his visitors welcome to his apartment, which was indeed but a shabby one, though no grandee of the land could receive his guests with a more perfect and courtly grace than this gentleman. A frugal dinner, consisting of a slice of meat and a penny loaf, was awaiting the owner of the lodgings. "My wine is better than my meat," says Mr. Addison; "my Lord Halifax sent me the Burgundy." And he set a bottle and glasses before his friends, and ate his simple dinner in a very few minutes; after which the three fell to, and began to drink. "You see," says Mr. Addison, pointing to his writing-table, whereon was a map of the action at Hochstedt and several other gazettes and pamphlets relating to the battle, "that I, too, am busy about your affairs, captain. I am engaged as a poetical gazetteer, to say truth, and am writing a poem on the campaign."

So Esmond, at the request of his host, told him what he knew about the famous battle, drew the river on the table *aliquo mero*, and with the aid of some bits of tobacco-pipe, showed the advance of the left wing, where he had been engaged.

A sheet or two of the verses lay already on the table beside our bottles and glasses, and Dick having plentifully refreshed himself from the latter, took up the pages of manuscript, writ out with scarce a blot or correction, in the author's slim, neat handwriting, and began to read therefrom with great emphasis and volubility. At pauses of the verse the enthusiastick reader stopped and fired off a great salvo of applause.

Esmond smiled at the enthusiasm of Addison's friend. " You are like the German Burghers," says he, " and the Princes on the Mozelle; when our army came to a halt, they always sent a deputation to compliment the chief, and fired a salute with all their artillery from their walls."

" And drunk the great chief's health afterward, did not they ? " says Captain Steele, gaily filling up a bumper;—he never was tardy at that sort of acknowledgment of a friend's merit.

" And the Duke, since you will have me act his Grace's part," says Mr. Addison, with a smile and something of a blush, " pledged his friends in return. Most Serene Elector of Covent Garden, I drink to your Highness's health," and he filled himself a glass. Joseph required scarce more pressing than Dick to that sort of amusement; but the wine never seemed at all to fluster Mr. Addison's brains; it only unloosed his tongue, whereas Captain Steele's head and speech were quite overcome by a single bottle.

No matter what the verses were, and, to say truth, Mr. Esmond found some of them more than indifferent, Dick's enthusiasm for his chief never faltered, and in every line from Addison's pen, Steele found a master-stroke. By the time Dick had come to that part of the poem, wherein the bard describes, as blandly as though he were recording a dance at the opera, or a harmless bout of bucolick cudgelling at a village fair, that bloody and ruthless part of our campaign, with the remembrance whereof every soldier who bore a part in it must sicken with shame—when we were ordered to ravage and lay waste the Elector's country; and with fire and murder, slaughter and crime, a great part of his dominions was overrun;—when Dick came to the lines :

" In vengeance roused the soldier fills his hand
 With sword and fire, and ravages the land.

In crackling flames a thousand harvests burn,
A thousand villages to ashes turn.
To the thick woods the woolly flocks retreat,
And mixed with bellowing herds confusedly bleat.
Their trembling lords the common shade partake,
And cries of infants sound in every brake.
The listening soldier fixed in sorrow stands,
Loth to obey his leader's just commands.
The leader grieves, by generous pity swayed,
To see his just commands so well obeyed : "

by this time wine and friendship had brought poor Dick to a
perfectly maudlin state, and he hiccupped out the last line with
a tenderness that set one of his auditors a-laughing.

"I admire the licence of you poets," says Esmond to Mr.
Addison. (Dick, after reading of the verses, was fain to go
off, insisting on kissing his two dear friends before his departure,
and reeling away with his perriwig over his eyes.) "I admire
your art : the murder of the campaign is done to military musick
like a battle at the opera, and the virgins shriek in harmony,
as our victorious grenadiers march into their villages. Do you
know what a scene it was?" (By this time, perhaps, the wine
had warmed Mr. Esmond's head too)—" what a triumph you
are celebrating? what scenes of shame and horror were
enacted, over which the commander's genius presided, as calm
as though he didn't belong to our sphere? You talk of the
' listening soldier fixed in sorrow,' the ' leader's grief swayed by
generous pity;' to my belief the leader cared no more for
bleating flocks than he did for infants' cries, and many of our
ruffians butchered one or the other with equal alacrity. I was
ashamed of my trade when I saw those horrors perpetrated,
which came under every man's eyes. You hew out of your
polished verses a stately image of smiling victory; I tell you
'tis an uncouth, distorted, savage idol; hideous, bloody, and
barbarous. The rites performed before it are shocking to think
of. You great poets should show it as it is—ugly and horrible,
not beautiful and serene. Oh, sir, had you made the campaign,
believe me, you never would have sung it so."

During this little outbreak, Mr. Addison was listening, smoking
out of his long pipe, and smiling very placidly. "What would
you have?" says he. "In our polished days, and according
to the rules of art, 'tis impossible that the Muse should depict
tortures or begrime her hands with the horrors of war. These
are indicated rather than described; as in the Greek tragedies,
that, I dare say, you have read (and sure there can be no more
elegant specimens of composition); Agamemnon is slain, or

Medea's children destroyed, away from the scene;—the chorus occupying the stage and singing of the action to pathetick musick. Something of this I attempt, my dear sir, in my humble way: 'tis a panegyrick I mean to write, and not a satire. Were I to sing as you would have me, the town would tear the poet in pieces, and burn his book by the hands of the common hangman. Do you not use tobacco? Of all the weeds grown on earth, sure the nicotian is the most soothing and salutary. We must paint our great Duke," Mr. Addison went on, "not as a man, which no doubt he is, with weaknesses like the rest of us, but as a hero. 'Tis in a triumph, not a battle, that your humble servant is riding his sleek Pegasus. We college-poets trot, you know, on very easy nags; it hath been, time out of mind, part of the poet's profession to celebrate the actions of heroes in verse, and to sing the deeds which you men of war perform. I must follow the rules of my art, and the composition of such a strain as this must be harmonious and majestick, not familiar, or too near the vulgar truth. *Si parva licet*: if Virgil could invoke the divine Augustus, a humbler poet from the banks of the Isis may celebrate a victory and a conqueror of our own nation, in whose triumphs every Briton has a share, and whose glory and genius contributes to every citizen's individual honour. When hath there been, since our Henrys' and Edwards' days, such a great feat of arms as that from which you yourself have brought away marks of distinction? If 'tis in my power to sing that song worthily, I will do so, and be thankful to my Muse. If I fail as a poet, as a Briton at least I will show my loyalty, and fling up my cap and huzzah for the conqueror:

> ——" Rheni pacator et Istri,
> Omnis in hoc uno variis discordia cessit
> Ordinibus ; lætatur eques, plauditque senator,
> Votaque patricio certant plebeia favori."

" There were as brave men on that field," says Mr. Esmond (who never could be made to love the Duke of Marlborough, nor to forget those stories which he used to hear in his youth regarding that great chief's selfishness and treachery), " there were men at Blenheim as good as the leader, whom neither knights nor senators applauded, nor voices plebeian or patrician favoured, and who lie there forgotten, under the clods. What poet is there to sing them ? "

" To sing the gallant souls of heroes sent to Hades ! " says Mr. Addison, with a smile : " would you celebrate them all? If I may venture to question anything in such an admirable work, the catalogue of the ships in Homer hath always appeared to me as somewhat wearisome; what had the poem been, supposing the writer had chronicled the names of captains, lieutenants, rank and file? One of the greatest of a great man's qualities is success; 'tis the result of all the others; 'tis a latent power in him which compels the favour of the gods, and subjugates fortune. Of all his gifts I admire that one in the great Marlborough. To be brave? every man is brave. But in being victorious, as he is, I fancy there is something divine. In presence of the occasion, the great soul of the leader shines out, and the god is confessed. Death itself respects him, and passes by him to lay others low. War and carnage flee before him to ravage other parts of the field, as Hector from before the divine Achilles. You say he hath no pity; no more have the gods, who are above it, and superhuman. The fainting battle gathers strength at his aspect; and wherever he rides, victory charges with him."

(*Henry Esmond.*)

LADY CASTLEWOOD

The instinct which led Harry Esmond to admire and love the gracious person, the fair apparition of whose beauty and kindness had so moved him when he first beheld her, became soon a devoted affection and passion of gratitude which entirely filled his young heart, that as yet, except in the case of dear Father Holt, had had very little kindness for which to be thankful. *O Dea certe*, thought he, remembering the lines out of the *Æneis* which Mr. Holt had taught him. There seemed, as the boy thought, in every look or gesture of this fair creature an angelical softness and bright pity—in motion or repose she seemed gracious alike; the tone of her voice, though she uttered words ever so trivial, gave him a pleasure that amounted almost to anguish. It cannot be called love, that a lad of twelve years of age, little more than a menial, felt for an exalted lady, his mistress : but it was worship. To catch her glance, to divine her errand and run on it before she had spoken it; to watch, follow, adore her; became the business of his life. Meanwhile, as is the way often, his idol had idols of her own, and never thought of or suspected the admiration of her little pigmy adorer.

My lady had on her side her three idols : first and foremost, Jove and supreme ruler, was her lord, Harry's patron, the good Viscount of Castlewood. All wishes of his were laws with her. If he had a headache, she was ill. If he frowned, she trembled. If he joked, she smiled and was charmed. If he went a-hunting, she was always at the window to see him ride away, her little son crowing on her arm, or on the watch till his return. She made dishes for his dinner : spiced his wine for him : made the toast for his tankard at breakfast : hushed the house when he slept in his chair, and watched for a look when he woke. If my lord was not a little proud of his beauty, my lady adored it. She clung to his arm as he paced the terrace, her two fair little hands clasped round his great one ; her eyes were never tired of looking in his face and wondering at its perfection. Her little son was his son, and had his father's looks and curly brown hair. Her daughter Beatrix was his daughter, and had his eyes—were there ever such beautiful eyes in the world ? All the house was arranged so as to bring him ease and give him pleasure. She liked the small gentry round about to come and pay him court ; never caring for admiration for herself, those who wanted to be well with the lady must admire him. Not regarding her dress, she would wear a gown to rags, because he had once liked it : and if he brought her a brooch or a ribbon would prefer it to all the most costly articles of her wardrobe.

My lord went to London every year for six weeks, and the family being too poor to appear at Court with any figure, he went alone. It was not until he was out of sight that her face showed any sorrow : and what a joy when he came back ! What preparation before his return ! The fond creature had his arm-chair at the chimney-side—delighting to put the children in it, and look at them there. Nobody took his place at the table ; but his silver tankard stood there as when my lord was present.

A pretty sight it was to see, during my lord's absence, or on those many mornings when sleep or headache kept him abed, this fair young lady of Castlewood, her little daughter at her knee, and her domesticks gathered round her, reading the Morning Prayer of the English Church. Esmond long remembered how she looked and spoke, kneeling reverently before the sacred book, the sun shining upon her golden hair until it made a halo round about her. A dozen of the servants of the house kneeled in a line opposite their mistress ; for a while Harry Esmond kept apart from these mysteries, but Doctor Tusher showing him that the prayers read were those of the Church of all ages, and the boy's own inclination prompting him to be always as near as he might to his mistress, and to think all things she did right, from listening to the prayers in the antechamber, he came presently to kneel down with the rest of the household in the parlour ; and before a couple of years my lady had made a thorough convert. Indeed, the boy loved his catechiser so much that he would have subscribed to anything she bade him, and was never tired of listening to her fond discourse and simple comments upon the book which she read to him in a voice of which it was difficult to resist the sweet persuasion, and tender appealing kindness. This friendly controversy, and the intimacy which it occasioned, bound the lad more fondly than ever to his mistress. The happiest period of all his life was this; and the young mother, with her daughter and son, and the orphan lad whom she protected, read and worked and played, and were children together. If the lady looked forward—as what fond woman does not?—towards the future, she had no plans from which Harry Esmond was left out; and a thousand and a thousand times in his passionate and impetuous way he vowed that no power should separate him from his mistress; and only asked for some chance to happen by which he might show his fidelity to her. Now, at the close of his life, as he sits and recalls in tranquillity the happy and busy scenes of it, he can think, not ungratefully, that he has been faithful to that early vow. Such a life is so simple that years may be chronicled in a few lines.

(Henry Esmond.)

CHARLES DICKENS (1812–1870)
I.—A Party at Mrs. Kenwigs's

IT was the anniversary of that happy day on which the church of England as by law established, had bestowed Mrs. Kenwigs upon Mr. Kenwigs; and in grateful commemoration of the same, Mrs. Kenwigs had invited a few select friends to cards and a supper in the first floor, and had put on a new gown to receive them in : which gown, being of a flaming colour and made upon a juvenile principle, was so successful that Mr. Kenwigs said the eight years of matrimony and the five children seemed all a dream, and Mrs. Kenwigs younger and more blooming than on the very first Sunday he had kept company with her.

Beautiful as Mrs. Kenwigs looked when she was dressed though, and so stately that you would have supposed she had a cook and housemaid at least, and nothing to do but order them about, she had a world of trouble with the preparations; more, indeed, than she, being of a delicate and genteel constitution, could have sustained, had not the pride of housewifery upheld her. At last, however, all the things that had to be got together were got together, and all the things that had to be got out of the way were got out of the way, and everything was ready, and the collector himself having promised to come, fortune smiled upon the occasion.

The party was admirably selected. There were, first of all, Mr. Kenwigs and Mrs. Kenwigs, and four olive Kenwigses who sat up to supper; firstly, because it was but right that they should have a treat on such a day; and secondly, because their going to bed, in presence of the company, would have been inconvenient, not to say improper. Then, there was a young lady who had made Mrs. Kenwigs's dress, and who—it was the most convenient thing in the world—living in the two-pair back, gave up her bed to the baby, and got a little girl to watch it. Then, to match this young lady, was a young man, who had known Mr. Kenwigs when he was a bachelor, and was much esteemed by the ladies, as bearing the reputation of a rake. To these, were added a newly married couple, who had visited Mr. and Mrs. Kenwigs in their courtship; and a sister of Mrs. Kenwigs's, who was quite a beauty; besides whom, there was another young man, supposed to entertain honourable designs upon the lady last mentioned; and Mr. Noggs, who was a genteel person to ask, because he had been a gentleman once. There were also an elderly lady from the back parlour, and one more young lady, who, next to the collector, perhaps was the great lion of the party, being the daughter of a theatrical fireman, who "went on" in the pantomine, and had the greatest turn for the stage that was ever known, being able to sing and recite in a manner that brought the tears into Mrs. Kenwigs's eyes. There was only one drawback upon the pleasure of seeing such friends, and that was, that the lady in the back parlour, who was very fat, and turned of sixty, came in a low book-muslin dress and short kid gloves, which so exasperated Mrs. Kenwigs, that that lady assured her visitors, in private, that if it hadn't happened that the supper was cooking at the back-parlour grate at that moment, she certainly would have requested its representative to withdraw.

"My dear," said Mr. Kenwigs, "wouldn't it be better to begin a round game?"

"Kenwigs, my dear," returned his wife, "I am surprised at you. Would you begin without my uncle?"

"I forgot the collector," said Kenwigs; "oh no, that would never do."

"He's so particular," said Mrs. Kenwigs, turning to the other married lady, "that if we began without him, I should be out of his will for ever."

" Dear ! " cried the married lady.

" You've no idea what he is," replied Mrs. Kenwigs; " and yet as good a creature as ever breathed."

" The kindest-hearted man as ever was," said Kenwigs.

" It goes to his heart, I believe, to be forced to cut the water off, when the people don't pay," observed the bachelor friend, intending a joke.

" George," said Mr. Kenwigs, solemnly, " none of that, if you please."

" It was only my joke," said the friend, abashed.

" George," rejoined Mr. Kenwigs, " a joke is a wery good thing—a wery good thing—but when that joke is made at the expense of Mrs. Kenwigs's feelings, I set my face against it. A man in public life expects to be sneered at—it is the fault of his elewated sitiwation, and not of himself. Mrs. Kenwigs's relation is a public man, and that he knows, George, and that he can bear; but putting Mrs. Kenwigs out of the question (if I *could* put Mrs. Kenwigs out of the question on such an occasion as this), I have the honour to be connected with the collector by marriage; and I cannot allow these remarks in my——" Mr. Kenwigs was going to say " house," but he rounded the sentence with " apartments."

At the conclusion of these observations, which drew forth evidences of acute feeling from Mrs. Kenwigs, and had the intended effect of impressing the company with a deep sense of the collector's dignity, a ring was heard at the bell.

" That's him," whispered Mr. Kenwigs, greatly excited. " Morleena, my dear, run down and let your uncle in, and kiss him directly you get the door open. Hem ! Let's be talking."

Adopting Mr. Kenwigs's suggestion, the company spoke very loudly, to look easy and unembarrassed; and almost as soon as they had begun to do so, a short old gentleman in drabs and gaiters, with a face that might have been carved out of *lignum vitæ*, for anything that appeared to the contrary, was led playfully in by Miss Morleena Kenwigs, regarding whose uncommon Christian name it may be here remarked that it had been invented and composed by Mrs. Kenwigs previous to her first lying-in, for the special distinction of her eldest child, in case it should prove a daughter.

" Oh uncle, I am *so* glad to see you," said Mrs. Kenwigs, kissing the collector affectionately on both cheeks. " So glad ! "

" Many happy returns of the day, my dear," replied the collector, returning the compliment.

Now, this was an interesting thing. Here was a collector of

water-rates, without his book, without his pen and ink, without his double knock, without his intimidation, kissing—actually kissing—an agreeable female, and leaving taxes, summonses, notices that he had called, or announcements that he would never call again, for two quarters' due, wholly out of the question. It was pleasant to see how the company looked on, quite absorbed in the sight, and to behold the nods and winks with which they expressed their gratification at finding so much humanity in a tax-gatherer.

"Where will you sit, uncle?" said Mrs. Kenwigs, in the full glow of family pride, which the appearance of her distinguished relation occasioned.

"Anywheres, my dear," said the collector, "I am not particular."

Not particular! What a meek collector. If he had been an author, who knew his place, he couldn't have been more humble.

"Mr. Lillyvick," said Kenwigs, addressing the collector, "some friends here, sir, are very anxious for the honour of —thank you—Mr. and Mrs. Cutler, Mr. Lillyvick."

"Proud to know you, sir," said Mr. Cutler, "I've heerd of you very often." These were not mere words of ceremony; for, Mr. Cutler, having kept house in Mr. Lillyvick's parish, had heard of him very often indeed. His attention in calling had been quite extraordinary.

"George, you know, I think, Mr. Lillyvick," said Kenwigs; "lady from downstairs—Mr. Lillyvick. Mr. Snewkes—Mr. Lillyvick. Miss Green—Mr. Lillyvick. Mr. Lillyvick—Miss Petowker of the Theatre Royal, Drury Lane. Very glad to make two public characters acquainted! Mrs. Kenwigs, my dear, will you sort the counters?"

Mrs. Kenwigs, with the assistance of Newman Noggs (who, as he performed sundry little acts of kindness for the children, at all times and seasons, was humoured in his request to be taken no notice of, and was merely spoken about, in a whisper, as the decayed gentleman), did as she was desired; and the greater part of the guests sat down to speculation, while Newman himself, Mrs. Kenwigs, and Miss Petowker of the Theatre Royal, Drury Lane, looked after the supper-table.

While the ladies were thus busying themselves, Mr. Lillyvick was intent upon the game in progress, and as all should be fish that comes to a water-collector's net, the dear old gentleman was by no means scrupulous in appropriating to himself the property of his neighbours, which, on the contrary, he abstracted whenever an opportunity presented itself, smiling good-humouredly all the while, and making so many condescending speeches to the owners, that they were delighted with his amiability, and thought in their hearts that he deserved to be Chancellor of the Exchequer at least.

After a great deal of trouble, and the administration of many slaps on the head to the infant Kenwigses, whereof two of the most rebellious were summarily banished, the cloth was laid with much elegance, and a pair of boiled fowls, a large piece of pork, apple-pie, potatoes and greens, were served; at sight of which, the worthy Mr. Lillyvick vented a great many witticisms, and plucked up amazingly: to the immense delight and satisfaction of the whole body of admirers.

Very well and very fast the supper went off; no more serious difficulties occurring than those which arose from the incesssant demand for clean knives and forks: which made poor Mrs. Kenwigs wish, more than once, that private society adopted the principle of schools and required that every guest should bring his own knife, fork, and spoon; which doubtless would be a great accommodation in many cases, and to no one more so than to the lady and gentleman of the house, especially if the school principle were carried out to the full extent; and the articles were expected, as a matter of delicacy, not to be taken away again.

Everybody had eaten everything, the table was cleared in a most alarming hurry, and with great noise; and the spirits, whereat the eyes of Newman Noggs glistened, being arranged in order, with water both hot and cold, the party composed themselves for conviviality; Mr. Lillyvick being stationed in a large arm-chair by the fire-side, and the four little Kenwigses disposed on a small form in front of the company with their flaxen tails towards them, and their faces to the fire; an arrangement which was no sooner perfected, than Mrs. Kenwigs was overpowered by the feelings of a mother, and fell upon the left shoulder of Mr. Kenwigs dissolved in tears.

" They are so beautiful! " said Mrs. Kenwigs, sobbing.

" Oh, dear," said all the ladies, " so they are! it's very natural you should feel proud of that; but don't give way, don't."

" I can—not help it, and it don't signify," sobbed Mrs. Kenwigs; " oh! they're too beautiful to live, much too beautiful! "

On hearing this alarming presentiment of their being doomed to an early death in the flower of their infancy, all four little girls raised a hideous cry, and burying their heads in their mother's lap simultaneously, screamed until the eight flaxen tails vibrated again; Mrs. Kenwigs meanwhile clasping them alternately to her bosom, with attitudes expressive of distraction, which Miss Petowker herself might have copied.

At length, the anxious mother permitted herself to be soothed into a more tranquil state, and the little Kenwigses, being also composed, were distributed among the company, to prevent the possibility of Mrs. Kenwigs being again overcome by the blaze of their combined beauty. This done, the ladies and gentlemen united in prophesying that they would live for many, many years, and that there was no occasion at all for Mrs. Kenwigs to distress herself : which, in good truth, there did not appear to be; the loveliness of the children by no means justifying her apprehensions.

"This day eight year," said Mr. Kenwigs after a pause. "Dear me—ah ! "

This reflection was echoed by all present, who said "Ah ! " first, and "dear me," afterwards.

"I was younger then," tittered Mrs. Kenwigs.

"No," said the collector.

"Certainly not," added everybody.

"I remember my niece," said Mr. Lillyvick, surveying his audience with a grave air; "I remember her, on that very afternoon, when she first acknowledged to her mother a partiality for Kenwigs. 'Mother,' she says, 'I love him.' "

" 'Adore him,' I said, uncle," interposed Mrs. Kenwigs.

" 'Love him,' I think, my dear," said the collector, firmly.

"Perhaps you are right, uncle," replied Mrs. Kenwigs, submissively. "I thought it was 'adore.' "

" 'Love,' my dear," retorted Mr. Lillyvick. " 'Mother,' she says, 'I love him !' ' What do I hear ? ' cried her mother; and instantly falls into strong conwulsions."

A general exclamation of astonishment burst from the company.

"Into strong conwulsions," repeated Mr. Lillyvick, regarding them with a rigid look. "Kenwigs will excuse my saying, in the presence of friends, that there was a very great objection to him, on the ground that he was beneath the family, and would disgrace it. You remember, Kenwigs ? "

"Certainly," replied that gentleman, in no way displeased at the reminiscence, inasmuch, as it proved, beyond all doubt, what a high family Mrs. Kenwigs came of.

"I shared in that feeling," said Mr. Lillyvick : "perhaps it was natural; perhaps it wasn't."

A gentle murmur seemed to say, that, in one of Mr. Lillyvick's station, the objection was not only natural, but highly praise-worthy.

" I came round to him in time," said Mr. Lillyvick. " After they were married, and there was no help for it, I was one of the first to say that Kenwigs must be taken notice of. The family *did* take notice of him, in consequence, and on my repre-sentation; and I am bound to say—and proud to say—that I have always found him a very honest, well-behaved, upright, respectable sort of man. Kenwigs, shake hands."

" I am proud to do it, sir," said Mr. Kenwigs.

" So am I, Kenwigs," rejoined Mr. Lillyvick.

" A very happy life I have led with your niece, sir," said Kenwigs.

" It would have been your own fault if you had not, sir," remarked Mr. Lillyvick.

" Morleena Kenwigs," cried her mother, at this crisis, much affected, " kiss your dear uncle ! "

The young lady did as she was requested, and the three other little girls were successively hoisted up to the collector's counten-ance, and subjected to the same process, which was afterwards repeated on them by the majority of those present.

" Oh dear, Mrs. Kenwigs," said Miss Petowker, " while Mr. Noggs is making that punch to drink happy returns in, do let Morleena go through that figure dance before Mr. Lillyvick."

" No, no, my dear," replied Mrs. Kenwigs, " it will only worry my uncle."

" It can't worry him, I am sure," said Miss Petowker. " You will be very much pleased, won't you, sir ? "

" That I am sure I shall," replied the collector, glancing at the punch-mixer.

" Well then, I'll tell you what," said Mrs. Kenwigs, " Morleena shall do the steps, if uncle can persuade Miss Petowker to recite us the Blood-Drinker's Burial, afterwards."

There was a great clapping of hands and stamping of feet, at this proposition; the subject whereof, gently inclined her head several times, in acknowledgment of the reception.

" You know," said Miss Petowker, reproachfully, " that I dislike doing anything professional in private parties."

" Oh, but not here ! " said Mrs. Kenwigs. " We are all so very friendly and pleasant, that you might as well be going through it in your own room; besides, the occasion——"

" I can't resist that," interrupted Miss Petowker; " anything in my humble power I shall be delighted to do."

Mrs. Kenwigs and Miss Petowker had arranged a small *programme* of the entertainments between them, of which this was the prescribed order, but they had settled to have a little pressing on both sides, because it looked more natural. The company being all ready, Miss Petowker hummed a tune, and Morleena danced a dance; having previously had the soles of her shoes chalked, with as much care as if she were going on the tight-rope. It was a very beautiful figure, comprising a great deal of work for the arms, and was received with unbounded applause.

" If I was blessed with a——a child—" said Miss Petowker, blushing, " of such genius as that, I would have her out at the Opera instantly."

Mrs. Kenwigs sighed, and looked at Mr. Kenwigs, who shook his head, and observed that he was doubtful about it.

" Kenwigs is afraid," said Mrs. K.

" What of ? " inquired Miss Petowker, " not of her failing ? "

" Oh, no," replied Mrs. Kenwigs, " but if she grew up what she is now,—only think of the young dukes and marquises."

" Very right," said the collector.

" Still," submitted Miss Petowker, " if she took a proper pride in herself, you know——"

" There's a good deal in that," observed Mrs. Kenwigs, looking at her husband.

" I only know—" faltered Miss Petowker,—" it may be no rule to be sure—but *I* have never found any inconvenience or unpleasantness of that sort."

Mr. Kenwigs, with becoming gallantry, said that settled the question at once, and that he would take the subject into his serious consideration. This being resolved upon, Miss Petowker was entreated to begin the Blood-Drinker's Burial; to which end, that young lady let down her back hair, and taking up her position at the other end of the room, with the bachelor friend posted in a corner, to rush out at the cue " in death expire," and catch her in his arms when she died raving mad, went through the performance with extraordinary spirit, and to the great terror of the little Kenwigses, who were all but frightened into fits.

The ecstacies consequent upon the effort had not yet subsided, and Newman (who had not been thoroughly sober at so late an hour for a long time), had not yet been able to put in a word of announcement, that the punch was ready, when a hasty knock was heard at the room-door, which elicited a shriek from Mrs. Kenwigs, who immediately divined that the baby had fallen out of bed.

" Who is that ? " demanded Mr. Kenwigs, sharply.

" Don't be alarmed, it's only me," said Crowl, looking in, in his nightcap. " The baby is very comfortable, for I peeped into the room as I came down, and it's fast asleep, and so is the girl; and I don't think the candle will set fire to the bed-curtain, unless a draught was to get into the room—it's Mr. Noggs that's wanted."

" Me ! " cried Newman, much astonished.

" Why, it *is* a queer hour, isn't it ? " replied Crowl, who was not best pleased at the prospect of losing his fire; " and they are queer-looking people, too, all covered with rain and mud. Shall I tell them to go away ? "

" No," said Newman, rising. " People? How many ? "

" Two," rejoined Crowl.

" Want me? By name? " asked Newman.

" By name," replied Crowl. " Mr. Newman Noggs, as pat as need be."

Newman reflected for a few seconds, and then hurried away, muttering that he would be back directly. He was as good as his word; for, in an exceedingly short time, he burst into the room, and seizing, without a word of apology or explanation, a lighted candle and tumbler of hot punch from the table, darted away like a madman.

" What the deuce is the matter with him? " exclaimed Crowl, throwing the door open. " Hark ! Is there any noise above ? "

The guests rose in great confusion, and, looking in each other's faces with much perplexity and some fear, stretched their necks forward, and listened attentively.

(*Nicholas Nickleby*.)

II.—EARLY IMPRESSIONS

The first objects that assume a distinct presence before me, as I look far back, into the blank of my infancy, are my mother with her pretty hair and youthful shape, and Peggotty, with no shape at all, and eyes so dark that they seemed to darken their whole neighbourhood in her face, and cheeks and arms so hard and red that I wondered the birds didn't peck her in preference to apples.

I believe I can remember these two at a little distance apart, dwarfed to my sight by stooping down or kneeling on the floor, and I going unsteadily from the one to the other. I have an impression on my mind which I cannot distinguish from actual remembrance, of the touch of Peggotty's fore-finger as she used to hold it out to me, and of its being roughened by needlework, like a pocket nutmeg-grater.

This may be fancy, though I think the memory of most of us

can go farther back into such times than many of us suppose; just as I believe the power of observation in numbers of very young children to be quite wonderful for its closeness and accuracy. Indeed, I think that most grown men who are remarkable in this respect, may with greater propriety be said not to have lost the faculty, than to have acquired it; the rather, as I generally observe such men to retain a certain freshness, and gentleness, and capacity of being pleased, which are also an inheritance they have preserved from their childhood.

I might have a misgiving that I am " meandering " in stopping to say this, but that it brings me to remark that I build these conclusions, in part upon my own experience of myself; and if it should appear from anything I may set down in this narrative that I was a child of close observation, or that as a man I have a strong memory of my childhood, I undoubtedly lay claim to both of these characteristics.

Looking back, as I was saying, into the blank of my infancy, the first objects I can remember as standing out by themselves from a confusion of things, are my mother and Peggotty. What else do I remember? Let me see.

There comes out of the cloud, our house—not new to me, but quite familiar, in its earliest remembrance. On the ground-floor is Peggotty's kitchen, opening into a back yard; with a pigeon-house on a pole, in the centre, without any pigeons in it; a great dog-kennel in a corner, without any dog; and a quantity of fowls that look terribly tall to me, walking about, in a menacing and ferocious manner. There is one cock who gets upon a post to crow, and seems to take particular notice of me as I look at him through the kitchen window, who makes me shiver, he is so fierce. Of the geese outside the side-gate who come waddling after me with their long necks stretched out when I go that way, I dream at night; as a man environed by wild beasts might dream of lions.

Here is a long passage—what an enormous perspective I make of it!—leading from Peggotty's kitchen to the front-door. A dark store-room opens out of it, and that is a place to be run past at night; for I don't know what may be among those tubs and jars and old tea-chests, when there is nobody in there with a dimly-burning light, letting a mouldy air come out at the door, in which there is the smell of soap, pickles, pepper, candles, and coffee, all at one whiff. Then there are the two parlours; the parlour in which we sit of an evening, my mother and I and Peggotty—for Peggotty is quite our companion, when her work is done and we are alone—and the best parlour where we sit on a Sunday; grandly, but not so comfortably. There is something of a doleful air about that room to me, for Peggotty has told me—I don't know when, but apparently ages ago—about my father's funeral, and the company having their black cloaks put on. One Sunday night my mother reads to Peggotty and me in there, how Lazarus was raised up from the dead. And I am so frightened that they are afterwards obliged to take me out of bed, and shew me the quiet churchyard out of the bed-room window, with the dead all lying in their graves at rest, below the solemn moon.

There is nothing half so green that I know anywhere, as the grass of that churchyard; nothing half so shady as its trees; nothing half so quiet as its tombstones. The sheep are feeding there, when I kneel up, early in the morning, in my little bed in a closet within my mother's room, to look out at it; and I see the red light shining on the sun-dial, and think within myself, "Is the sun-dial glad, I wonder, that it can tell the time again?"

Here is our pew in the church. What a high-backed pew! With a window near it, out of which our house can be seen, and *is* seen many times during the morning's service, by Peggotty, who likes to make herself as sure as she can that it's not being robbed, or is not in flames. But though Peggotty's eye wanders, she is much offended if mine does, and frowns to me, as I stand upon the seat, that I am to look at the clergyman. But I can't always look at him—I know him without that white thing on, and I am afraid of his wondering why I stare so, and perhaps stopping the service to inquire—and what am I to do? It's a dreadful thing to gape, but I must do something. I look at my mother, but *she* pretends not to see me. I look at a boy in the aisle, and *he* makes faces at me. I look at the sun-light coming in at the open door through the porch, and there I see a stray sheep—I don't mean a sinner, but mutton—half making up his mind to come into the church. I feel that if I looked at him any longer, I might be tempted to say something out loud; and what would become of me then! I look up at the monumental tablets on the wall, and try to think of Mr. Bodgers late of this parish, and what the feelings of Mrs. Bodgers must have been, when affliction sore, long time Mr. Bodgers bore, and physicians were in vain. I wonder whether they called in Mr. Chillip, and he was in vain; and if so, how he likes to be reminded of it once a week. I look from Mr. Chillip, in his Sunday neckcloth, to the pulpit; and think what a good place it would be to play in, and what a castle it would make, with another boy coming up the stairs to attack it, and having the velvet cushion with the tassels thrown down on his head. In time my eyes gradually shut up; and, from seeming to hear the clergyman singing a drowsy song in the heat, I hear nothing, until I fall off the seat with a crash, and am taken out, more dead than alive, by Peggotty.

And now I see the outside of our house, with the latticed bedroom windows standing open to let in the sweet-smelling air, and the ragged old rooks'-nests still dangling in the elm-trees at the bottom of the front garden. Now I am in the garden at the back, beyond the yard where the empty pigeon-house and dog-kennel are—a very preserve of butterflies, as I remember it, with a high fence, and a gate and padlock; where the fruit clusters on the trees, riper and richer than fruit has ever been since, in any other garden, and where my mother gathers some in a basket, while I stand by, bolting furtive gooseberries, and trying to look unmoved. A great wind rises, and the summer is gone in a moment. We are playing in the winter twilight, dancing about the parlour. When my mother is out of breath and rests herself in an elbow-chair, I watch her winding her bright curls round her fingers, and straightening her waist, and nobody knows better than I do that she likes to look so well, and is proud of being so pretty.

(David Copperfield.)

CHARLOTTE BRONTË (1816–1855)

I.—SHIRLEY AND CAROLINE

SHIRLEY showed she had been sincere in saying she should be glad of Caroline's society, by frequently seeking it : and, indeed, if she had not sought it, she would not have had it; for Miss Helstone was slow to make fresh acquaintances. She was always held back by the idea that people could not want her—that she could not amuse them; and a brilliant, happy, youthful creature, like the heiress of Fieldhead, seemed to her too completely independent of society so uninteresting as hers, ever to find it really welcome.

Shirley might be brilliant, and probably happy likewise, but no one is independent of genial society; and though in about a month she had made the acquaintance of most of the families round, and was on quite free and easy terms with all the Misses Sykes, and all the Misses Pearson, and the two superlative Misses Wynne of Walden Hall; yet, it appeared, she found none amongst them very genial : she fraternised with none of them, to use her own words. If she had had the bliss to be really

Shirley Keeldar, Esq., Lord of the Manor of Briarfield, there was not a single fair one in this and the two neighbouring parishes, whom she should have felt disposed to request to become Mrs. Keeldar, lady of the manor. This declaration she made to Mrs. Pryor, who received it very quietly, as she did most of her pupil's off-hand speeches, responding—" My dear, do not allow that habit of alluding to yourself as a gentleman to be confirmed : it is a strange one. Those who do not know you, hearing you speak thus, would think you affected masculine manners."

Shirley never laughed at her former governess : even the little formalities and harmless peculiarities of that lady were respectable in her eyes : had it been otherwise, she would have proved herself a weak character at once : for it is only the weak who make a butt of quiet worth ; therefore she took her remonstrance in silence. She stood quietly near the window, looking at the grand cedar on her lawn, watching a bird on one of its lower boughs. Presently she began to chirrup to the bird : soon her chirrup grew clearer ; erelong she was whistling ; the whistle struck into a tune, and very sweetly and deftly it was executed.

" My dear ! " expostulated Mrs. Pryor.

" Was I whistling ? " said Shirley ; " I forgot. I beg your pardon, ma'am. I had resolved to take care not to whistle before you."

" But, Miss Keeldar, where did you learn to whistle ? You must have got the habit since you came down into Yorkshire. I never knew you guilty of it before."

" Oh ! I learned to whistle a long while ago."

" Who taught you ? "

" No one : I took it up by listening, and I had laid it down again ; but lately, yesterday evening, as I was coming up our lane, I heard a gentleman whistling that very tune in the field on the other side of the hedge, and that reminded me."

" What gentleman was it ? "

" We have only one gentleman in this region, ma'am, and that is Mr. Moore ; at least he is the only gentleman who is not grey-haired : my two venerable favourites, Mr. Helstone and Mr. Yorke, it is true, are fine old beaux ; infinitely better than any of the stupid young ones."

Mrs. Pryor was silent.

" You do like Mr. Helstone, ma'am ? "

" My dear, Mr. Helstone's office secures him from criticism."

" You generally contrive to leave the room when he is announced. "

" Do you walk out this morning, my dear ? "

"Yes, I shall go to the Rectory, and seek and find Caroline Helstone, and make her take some exercise : she shall have a breezy walk over Nunnely Common."

"If you go in that direction, my dear, have the goodness to remind Miss Helstone to wrap up well, as there is a fresh wind, and she appears to me to require care."

"You shall be minutely obeyed, Mrs. Pryor : meantime, will you not accompany us yourself ? "

"No, my love ; I should be a restraint upon you : I am stout, and cannot walk so quickly as you would wish to do."

Shirley easily persuaded Caroline to go with her : and when they were fairly out on the quiet road, traversing the extensive and solitary sweep of Nunnely Common, she as easily drew her into conversation. The first feelings of diffidence overcome, Caroline soon felt glad to talk with Miss Keeldar. The very first interchange of slight observations sufficed to give each an idea of what the other was. Shirley said she liked the green sweep of the common turf, and, better still, the heath on its ridges, for the heath reminded her of moors : she had seen moors when she was travelling on the borders near Scotland. She remembered particularly a district traversed one long afternoon, on a sultry but sunless day in summer : they journeyed from noon till sunset, over what seemed a boundless waste of deep heath, and nothing had they seen but wild sheep ; nothing heard but the cries of wild birds.

"I know how the heath would look on such a day," said Caroline ; "purple-black : a deeper shade of the sky-tint, and that would be livid."

"Yes—quite livid, with brassy edges to the clouds, and here and there a white gleam, more ghastly than the lurid tinge, which, as you looked at it, you momentarily expected would kindle into blinding lightning."

"Did it thunder ? "

"It muttered distant peals, but the storm did not break till evening, after we had reached our inn : that inn being an isolated house at the foot of a range of mountains."

"Did you watch the clouds come down over the mountains ? "

"I did : I stood at the window an hour watching them. The hills seemed rolled in a sullen mist, and when the rain fell in whitening sheets, suddenly they were blotted from the prospect : they were washed from the world."

"I have seen such storms in hilly districts in Yorkshire ; and at their riotous climax, while the sky was all cataract, the earth all flood, I have remembered the Deluge."

"It is singularly reviving after such hurricanes to feel calm return, and from the opening clouds to receive a consolatory gleam, softly testifying that the sun is not quenched."

"Miss Keeldar, just stand still now, and look down at Nunnely dale and wood."

They both halted on the green brow of the Common: they looked down on the deep valley robed in May raiment; on varied meads, some pearled with daisies, and some golden with king-cups: to-day all this young verdure smiled clear in sunlight; transparent emerald and amber gleams played over it. On Nunnwood—the sole remnant of antique British forest in a region whose lowlands were once all sylvan chase, as its highlands were breast-deep heather—slept the shadow of a cloud; the distant hills were dappled, the horizon was shaded and tinted like mother-of-pearl; silvery blues, soft purples, evanescent greens and rose-shades, all melting into fleeces of white cloud, pure as azury snow, allured the eye as with a remote glimpse of heaven's foundations. The air blowing on the brow was fresh, and sweet, and bracing.

"Our England is a bonnie island," said Shirley, "and Yorkshire is one of her bonniest nooks."

"You are a Yorkshire girl too?"

"I am—Yorkshire in blood and birth. Five generations of my race sleep under the aisles of Briarfield Church: I drew my first breath in the old black hall behind us."

Hereupon Caroline presented her hand, which was accordingly taken and shaken. "We are compatriots," said she.

"Yes," agreed Shirley, with a grave nod.

"And that," asked Miss Keeldar, pointing to the forest— "that is Nunnwood?"

"It is."

"Were you ever there?"

"Many a time."

"In the heart of it?"

"Yes."

"What is it like?"

"It is like an encampment of forest sons of Anak. The trees are huge and old. When you stand at their roots, the summits seem in another region: the trunks remain still and firm as pillars, while the boughs sway to every breeze. In the deepest calm their leaves are never quite hushed, and in high wind a flood rushes—a sea thunders above you."

"Was it not one of Robin Hood's haunts?"

"Yes, and there are mementos of him still existing. To

penetrate into Nunnwood, Miss Keeldar, is to go far back into the dim days of eld. Can you see a break in the forest, about the centre ? "

" Yes, distinctly."

" That break is a dell; a deep, hollow cup, lined with turf as green and short as the sod of this Common : the very oldest of the trees, gnarled mighty oaks, crowd about the brink of this dell : in the bottom lie the ruins of a nunnery."

" We will go—you and I alone, Caroline—to that wood, early some fine summer morning, and spend a long day there. We can take pencils and sketch-books, and any interesting reading-book we like; and of course we shall take something to eat. I have two little baskets, in which Mrs. Gill, my housekeeper, might pack our provisions, and we could each carry our own. It would not tire you too much to walk so far ? "

" Oh, no; especially if we rested the whole day in the wood, and I know all the pleasant spots : I know where we could get nuts in nutting time; I know where wild strawberries abound : I know certain lonely, quite untrodden glades, carpeted with strange mosses, some yellow as if gilded, some a sober grey, some gem-green. I know groups of trees that ravish the eye with their perfect, picture-like effects : rude oak, delicate birch, glossy beech, clustered in contrast; and ash trees stately as Saul, standing isolated, and superannuated wood-giants clad in bright shrouds of ivy. Miss Keeldar, I could guide you."

" You would be dull with me alone ? "

" I should not. I think we should suit : and what third person is there whose presence would not spoil our pleasure ? "

" Indeed, I know of none about our own ages—no lady at least, and as to gentlemen——"

" An excursion becomes quite a different thing when there are gentlemen of the party," interrupted Caroline.

" I agree with you—quite a different thing to what we were proposing."

" We were going simply to see the old trees, the old ruins; to pass a day in old times, surrounded by olden silence, and above all by quietude."

" You are right; and the presence of gentlemen dispels the last charm, I think. If they are of the wrong sort, like your Malones, and your young Sykes, and Wynnes, irritation takes the place of serenity. If they are of the right sort, there is still a change—I can hardly tell what change, one easy to feel, difficult to describe."

" We forget nature, imprimis."

" And then Nature forgets us; covers her vast calm brow with a dim veil, conceals her face, and withdraws the peaceful joy with which, if we had been content to worship her only, she would have filled our hearts."

(Shirley.)

JAMES ANTHONY FROUDE (1818–1894)

MONASTIC ASCETICISM

LEAVING, however, for the present, the meaning of monastic asceticism, it seems necessary to insist that there really was such a thing; there is no doubt about it. If the particular actions told of each saint are not literally true, as belonging to him, abundance of men did for many centuries lead the sort of life which they are said to have led. We have got a notion that the friars were a snug, comfortable set, after all; and the life in a monastery pretty much like that in a modern university, where the old monks' language and affectation of unworldliness does somehow contrive to co-exist with as large a mass of bodily enjoyment as man's nature can well appropriate; and very likely this was the state into which many of the monasteries had fallen in the fifteenth century. It had begun to be, and it was a symptom of a very rapid disorder in them, promptly terminating in dissolution; but long, long ages lay behind the fifteenth century, in which wisely or foolishly these old monks and hermits did make themselves a very hard life of it; and the legend only exceeded the reality, in being a very slightly idealised portrait of it. We are not speaking of the miracles; that is a wholly different question. When men knew little of the order of nature, whatever came to pass without an obvious cause was at once set down to influences beyond nature and above it; and so long as there were witches and enchanters, strong with the help of the bad powers, of course the especial servants of God would not be left without graces to outmatch and overcome the devil. And there were many other reasons why the saints should work miracles. They had done so under the old dispensation, and there was no obvious reason why Christians should be worse off than Jews. And again, although it be true, in the modern phrase, which is beginning to savour a little of cant, that the highest natural is the highest supernatural, it is not everybody that is able to see that; natural facts permit us to be so easily familiar with them, that they have an air of commonness; and when we have a vast idea to express, there is always a disposition to the extraordinary. But the miracles are not the chief thing; nor ever were they so. Men did not become saints by working miracles, but they worked miracles because they had become saints; and the instructiveness and value of their lives lay in the means which they had used to make themselves what they were; and as we said, in this part of the business there is unquestionable basis of truth—scarcely even exaggeration. We have documentary evidence, which has been passed through the sharp ordeal of party hatred, of the way some men (and those, men of vast mind and vast influence in their day, not mere ignorant fanatics), conducted themselves, where *myth* has no room to enter. We know something of the hair-shirt of Thomas à Becket, and other uneasy penances of his; and there was another poor monk, whose asceticism imagination could not easily outrun: that was he who, when the earth's mighty ones were banded together to crush him under their armed heels, spoke but one little word; and it fell among them like the spear of Cadmus; the strong ones turned their hands against each other, and the armies melted away; and the proudest monarch of the earth lay at that monk's threshold three winter nights in the scanty clothing of penance, suing miserably for forgiveness. Or again, to take a fairer figure: there is a poem extant, the genuineness of which we believe has not been challenged, composed by Columbkill, commonly called St. Columba. He was a hermit in Aran, a rocky island in the Atlantic, outside Galway Bay; from which he was summoned, we do not know how, but in a manner which appeared to him to be a divine call, to go away and be bishop of Iona. The poem is a " Farewell to Aran," which he wrote on leaving it; and he lets us see something of a hermit's life there. " Farewell," he begins (we are obliged to quote from memory), " a long farewell to thee, Aran of my heart. Paradise is with thee, the garden of God within the sound of thy bells. The angels love Aran. Each day an angel comes there to join in its services." And then he goes on to describe his " dear cell," and the holy happy hours which he had spent there, " with the wind whistling through the loose stones, and the sea spray hanging on his hair." Aran is no better than a wild rock. It is strewed over with the ruins which may still be seen of the old hermitages; and at their best they could have been but such places as sheep would huddle under in a storm, and shiver in the cold and wet which would pierce through to them.

Or, if written evidence be too untrustworthy, there are silent witnesses which cannot lie, that tell the same touching story. Whoever loiters among the ruins of a monastery will see, commonly leading out of the cloisters, rows of cellars half under-ground, low, damp, and wretched-looking; an earthen floor, bearing no trace of pavement; a roof from which the mortar and the damp keep up (and always must have kept up) a perpetual ooze : for a window a narrow slip in the wall, through which the cold and the wind find as free an access as the light. Such as they are, a well-kept dog would object to accept a night's lodging in them; and if they had been prison cells, thousands of philanthropic tongues would have trumpeted out their horrors. The stranger perhaps supposes that they were the very dungeons of which he has heard such terrible things. He asks his guide, and his guide tells him they were the monks' dormitories. Yes; there on that wet soil, with that dripping roof above them, was the self-chosen home of those poor men. Through winter frost, through rain and storm, through summer sunshine, generation after generation of them, there they lived and prayed, and at last lay down and died.

It is all gone now—gone as if it had never been; and it was as foolish as, if the attempt had succeeded, it would have been mischievous, to revive a devotional interest in the Lives of the Saints. It would have produced but one more unreality in an age already too full of such. No one supposes we should have set to work to live as they lived; that any man, however earnest in his religion, would have gone looking for earth floors and wet dungeons, or wild islands to live in, when he could get anything better. Either we are wiser, or more humane, or more self-indulgent; at any rate we are something which divides us from mediæval Christianity by an impassable gulf which this age or this epoch will not see bridged over. Nevertheless, these modern hagiologists, however wrongly they went to work at it, had detected, and were endeavouring to fill, a very serious blank in our educational system; a very serious blank indeed, and one which, somehow, we must contrive to get filled if the education of character is ever to be more than a name with us. To try and teach people how to live without giving them examples in which our rules are illustrated, is like teaching them to draw by the rules of perspective, and of light and shade, without designs to study them in; or to write verse by the laws of rhyme and metre without song or poem in which rhyme and metre are seen in their effects. It is a principle which we have forgotten, and it is one which the old Catholics did not forget. We do not mean that they set out with saying to themselves " we must have examples, we must have ideals;" very likely they never thought about it at all; love for their holy men, and a thirst to know about them, produced the histories; and love unconsciously working gave them the best for which they could have wished. The boy at school at the monastery, the young monk disciplining himself as yet with difficulty under the austerities to which he had devoted himself, the old halting on toward the close of his pilgrimage, all of them had before their eyes, in the legend of the patron saint, a personal realisation of all they were trying after; leading them on, beckoning to them, and pointing, as they stumbled among their difficulties, to the marks which his own footsteps had left, as he had trod that hard path before them. It was as if the church was for ever saying to them:— " You have doubts and fears, and trials and temptations outward and inward; you have sinned, perhaps, and feel the burden of your sin. Here was one who, like you, *in this very spot*, under the same sky, treading the same soil, among the same hills and woods and rocks and rivers, was tried like you, tempted like you, sinned like you; but here he prayed, and persevered, and did penance, and washed out his sins; he fought the fight, he vanquished the evil one, he triumphed, and now he reigns a saint with Christ in heaven. The same ground which yields you your food, once supplied him; he breathed and lived, and felt, and died *here;* and now, from his throne in the sky, he is still looking down lovingly on his children, making intercession for you that you may have grace to follow him, that by-and-by he may himself offer you at God's throne as his own." It is impossible to measure the influence which a personal reality of this kind must have exercised on the mind, thus daily and hourly impressed upon it through a life; there is nothing vague any more, no abstract excellences to strain after; all is distinct, personal, palpable. It is no dream. The saint's bones are under the altar; nay, perhaps, his very form and features undissolved. Under some late abbot the coffin may have been opened and the body seen without mark or taint of decay. Such things have been, and the emaciation of a saint will account for it without a miracle. Daily some incident of his story is read aloud, or spoken of, or preached upon. In quaint beautiful forms it lives in light in the long chapel windows; and in the summer matins his figure, lighted up in splendour, gleams down on them as they pray, or streams in mysterious shadowy tints along the pavement, clad, as it seems, in soft celestial glory, and shining as he shines in heaven. Alas, alas, where is it all gone?

(*Essays on Literature and History*.)

JOHN RUSKIN (1819–1900)
I.—BOOKS

THE good book of the hour, then,—I do not speak of the bad ones—is simply the useful or pleasant talk of some person whom you cannot otherwise converse with, printed for you. Very useful often, telling you what you need to know; very pleasant often, as a sensible friend's present talk would be. These bright accounts of travels; good-humoured and witty discussions of question; lively or pathetic story-telling in the form of novel; firm fact-telling, by the real agents concerned in the events of passing history;—all these books of the hour, multiplying among us as education becomes more general, are a peculiar characteristic and possession of the present age : we ought to be entirely thankful for them, and entirely ashamed of ourselves if we make no good use of them. But we make the worst possible use, if we allow them to usurp the place of true books : for, strictly speaking, they are not books at all, but merely letters or newspapers in good print. Our friend's letter may be delightful, or necessary, to-day : whether worth keeping or not, is to be considered. The newspaper may be entirely proper at breakfast time, but assuredly it is not reading for all day. So, though bound up in a volume, the long letter which gives you so pleasant an account of the inns, and roads, and weather last year at such a place, or which tells you that amusing story, or gives you the real circumstances of such and such events, however valuable for occasional reference, may not be, in the real sense of the word, a " book " at all, nor, in the real sense, to be " read." A book is essentially not a talked thing, but a written thing; and written, not with the view of mere communication, but of permanence. The book of talk is printed only because its author cannot speak to thousands of people at once; if he could, he would—the volume is mere *multiplication* of his voice. You cannot talk to your friend in India; if you could, you would; you write instead : that is mere *conveyance* of voice. But a book is written, not to multiply the voice merely, not to carry it merely, but to preserve it. The author has something to say which he perceives to be true and useful, or helpfully beautiful. So far as he knows, no one has yet said it; so far as he knows, no one else can say it. He is bound to say it, clearly and melodiously if he may; clearly, at all events. In the sum of his life he finds this to be the thing, or group of things, manifest to him;—this the piece of true knowledge, or sight, which his share of sunshine and earth has permitted him to seize. He would fain set it down for ever; engrave it on rock, if he could; saying, "This is the best of me; for the rest, I ate, and drank, and slept, loved, and hated, like another; my life was as the vapour, and is not; but this I saw and knew: this, if anything of mine, is worth your memory." That is his "writing;" it is, in his small human way, and with whatever degree of true inspiration is in him, his inscription, or scripture. That is a "Book."

Perhaps you think no books were ever so written?

But, again, I ask you, do you at all believe in honesty, or at all in kindness? or do you think there is never any honesty or benevolence in wise people? None of us, I hope, are so unhappy as to think that. Well, whatever bit of a wise man's work is honestly and benevolently done, that bit is his book, or his piece of art. It is mixed always with evil fragments— ill-done, redundant, affected work. But if you read rightly, you will easily discover the true bits, and those *are* the book.

Now books of this kind have been written in all ages by their greatest men:—by great leaders, great statesmen, and great thinkers. These are all at your choice; and life is short. You have heard as much before;—yet have you measured and mapped out this short life and its possibilities? Do you know, if you read this, that you cannot read that—that what you lose to-day you cannot gain to-morrow? Will you go and gossip with your housemaid, or your stable-boy, when you may talk with queens and kings; or flatter yourselves that it is with any worthy consciousness of your own claims to respect that you jostle with the common crowd for *entree* here, and audience there, when all the while this eternal court is open to you, with its society wide as the world, multitudinous as its days, the chosen, and the mighty, of every place and time? Into that you may enter always; in that you may take fellowship and rank according to your wish; from that, once entered into it, you can never be outcast but by your own fault; by your aristocracy of companionship there, your own inherent aristocracy will be assuredly tested, and the motives with which you strive to take high place in the society of the living, measured, as to all the truth and sincerity that are in them, by the place you desire to take in this company of the Dead.

"The place you desire," and the place you *fit yourself for*, I must also say; because, observe, this court of the past differs from all living aristocracy in this:—it is open to labour and to merit, but to nothing else. No wealth will bribe, no name overawe, no artifice deceive, the guardian of those Elysian gates.

in the deep sense, no vile or vulgar person ever enters there. At the portières of that silent Faubourg St. Germain, there is but brief question, "Do you deserve to enter? Pass. Do you ask to be the companion of nobles? Make yourself noble, and you shall be. Do you long for the conversation of the wise? Learn to understand it, and you shall hear it. But on other terms?—no. If you will not rise to us, we cannot stoop to you. The living lord may assume courtesy, the living philosopher explain his thought to you with considerate pain; but here we neither feign nor interpret; you must rise to the level of our thoughts if you would be gladdened by them, and share our feelings, if you would recognise our presence."

This, then, is what you have to do, and I admit that it is much. You must, in a word, love these people, if you are to be among them. No ambition is of any use. They scorn your ambition. You must love them, and show your love in these two following ways.

First, by a true desire to be taught by them, and to enter into their thoughts. To enter into theirs, observe; not to find your own expressed by them. If the person who wrote the book is not wiser than you, you need not read it; if he be, he will think differently from you in many respects.

Very ready we are to say of a book, "How good this is—that's exactly what I think!" But the right feeling is, "How strange that is! I never thought of that before, and yet I see it is true; or if I do not now, I hope I shall, some day." But whether thus submissively or not, at least be sure that you go to the author to get at *his* meaning, not to find yours. Judge it afterwards, if you think yourself qualified to do so; but ascertain it first. And be sure also, if the author is worth anything, that you will not get at his meaning all at once;—nay, that at his whole meaning you will not for a long time arrive in any wise. Not that he does not say what he means, and in strong words too; but he cannot say it all; and what is more strange, will not, but in a hidden way and in parables, in order that he may be sure you want it. I cannot quite see the reason of this, nor analyse that cruel reticence in the breasts of wise men which makes them always hide their deeper thought. They do not give it you by way of help, but of reward, and will make themselves sure that you deserve it before they allow you to reach it. But it is the same with the physical type of wisdom, gold. There seems, to you and me, no reason why the electric forces of the earth should not carry whatever there is of gold within it at once to the mountain tops, so that kings and people might know that all the gold they could get was there; and without any trouble of digging, or anxiety, or chance, or waste of time, cut it away, and coin as much as they needed. But Nature does not manage it so. She puts it in little fissures in the earth, nobody knows where: you may dig long and find none; you must dig painfully to find any.

And it is just the same with men's best wisdom. When you come to a good book, you must ask yourself, "Am I inclined to work as an Australian miner would? Are my pickaxes and shovels in good order, and am I in good trim myself, my sleeves well up to the elbow, and my breath good, and my temper?" And, keeping the figure a little longer, even at cost of tiresomeness, for it is a thoroughly useful one, the metal you are in search of being the author's mind or meaning, his words are as the rock which you have to crush and smelt in order to get at it. And your pickaxes are your own care, wit, and learning; your smelting furnace is your own thoughtful soul. Do not hope to get at any good author's meaning without those tools and that fire; often you will need sharpest, finest chiselling, and patientest fusing, before you can gather one grain of the metal.

(Sesame and Lilies.)

II.—St. Mark's, Venice

And now I wish that the reader, before I bring him into St. Mark's Place, would imagine himself for a little time in a quiet English cathedral town, and walk with me to the west front of its cathedral. Let us go together up the more retired street, at the end of which we can see the pinnacles of one of the towers, and then through the low grey gateway, with its battlemented top and small latticed window in the centre, into the inner private-looking road or close, where nothing goes in but the carts of the tradesmen who supply the bishop and the chapter, and where there are little shaven grass-plots, fenced in by neat rails, before old-fashioned groups of somewhat diminutive and excessively trim houses, with little oriel and bay windows jutting out here and there, and deep wooden cornices and eaves painted cream colour and white, and small porches to their doors in the shape of cockle-shells, or little, crooked, thick, indescribable wooden gables warped a little on one side; and so forward till we come to larger houses, also old-fashioned, but of red brick, and with gardens behind them, and fruit walls, which show here and there, among the nectarines, the vestiges of an old cloister arch or shaft, and looking in front on the cathedral square itself, laid out in rigid divisions

of smooth grass and gravel walk, yet not uncheerful, especially
on the sunny side where the canons' children are walking with
their nursery-maids. And so, taking care not to tread on the
grass, we will go along the straight walk to the west front, and
there stand for a time, looking up at its deep-pointed porches
and the dark places between their pillars where there were
statues once, and where the fragments, here and there, of a
stately figure are still left, which has in it the likeness of a king,
perhaps indeed a king on earth, perhaps a saintly king long
ago in heaven; and so higher and higher up to the great mouldering wall of rugged sculpture and confused arcades, shattered,
and grey, and grisly with heads of dragons and mocking fiends,
worn by the rain and swirling winds into yet unseemlier shape,
and coloured on their stony scales by the deep russet-orange
lichen, melancholy gold; and so, higher still, to the bleak towers,
so far above that the eye loses itself among the bosses of their
traceries, though they are rude and strong, and only sees like a
drift of eddying black points, now closing, now scattering, and
now settling suddenly into invisible places among the bosses
and flowers, the crowd of restless birds that fill the old square
with that strange clangour of theirs, so harsh and yet so soothing,
like the cries of birds on a solitary coast between the cliffs and sea.

Think for a little while of that scene, and the meaning of all
its small formalisms, mixed with its serene sublimity. Estimate
its secluded, continuous, drowsy felicities, and its evidence of
the sense and steady performance of such kind of duties as can
be regulated by the cathedral clock; and weigh the influence
of those dark towers on all who have passed through the lonely
square at their feet for centuries, and on all who have seen them
rising far away over the wooded plain, or catching on their
square masses the last rays of the sunset, when the city at their
feet was indicated only by the mist at the bend of the river.
And then let us quickly recollect that we are in Venice, and land
at the extremity of the Calla Lunga San Moisè, which may
be considered as there answering to the secluded street that
led us to our English cathedral gateway.

We find ourselves in a paved alley, some seven feet wide
where it is widest, full of people, and resonant with cries of itinerant salesmen,—a shriek in their beginning, and dying away into
a kind of brazen ringing, all the worse for its confinement between
the high houses of the passage along which we have to make
our way. Over-head an inextricable confusion of rugged
shutters, and iron balconies and chimney flues pushed out on
brackets to save room, and arched windows with projecting

sills of Istrian stone, and gleams of green leaves here and there where a fig-tree branch escapes over a lower wall from some inner cortile, leading the eye up to the narrow stream of blue sky high over all. On each side, a row of shops, as densely set as may be, occupying, in fact, intervals between the square stone shafts, about eight feet high, which carry the first floors: intervals of which one is narrow and serves as a door; the other is, in the more respectable shops, wainscotted to the height of the counter and glazed above, but in those of the poorer tradesmen left open to the ground, and the wares laid on benches and tables in the open air, the light in all cases entering at the front only, and fading away in a few feet from the threshold into a gloom which the eye from without cannot penetrate, but which is generally broken by a ray or two from a feeble lamp at the back of the shop, suspended before a print of the Virgin. The less pious shopkeeper sometimes leaves his lamp unlighted, and is contented with a penny print; the more religious one has his print coloured and set in a little shrine with a gilded or figured fringe, with perhaps a faded flower or two on each side, and his lamp burning brilliantly. Here at the fruiterer's, where the dark-green water-melons are heaped upon the counter like cannon balls, the Madonna has a tabernacle of fresh laurel leaves; but the pewterer next door has let his lamp out, and there is nothing to be seen in his shop but the dull gleam of the studded patterns on the copper pans, hanging from his roof in the darkness. Next comes a "Vendita Frittole e Liquori," where the Virgin, enthroned in a very humble manner beside a tallow candle on a back shelf, presides over certain ambrosial morsels of a nature too ambiguous to be defined or enumerated. But a few steps farther on, at the regular wine-shop of the calle, where we are offered "Vino Nostriani a Soldi 28.32," the Madonna is in great glory, enthroned above ten or a dozen large red casks of three-year-old vintage, and flanked by goodly ranks of bottles of Maraschino, and two crimson lamps; and for the evening, when the gondoliers will come to drink out, under her auspices, the money they have gained during the day, she will have a whole chandelier.

A yard or two farther, we pass the hostelry of the Black Eagle, and, glancing as we pass through the square door of marble, deeply moulded, in the outer wall, we see the shadows of its pergola of vines resting on an ancient well, with a pointed shield carved on its side; and so presently emerge on the bridge and Campo San Moisè, whence to the entrance into St. Mark's Place, called the Bocca di Piazza (mouth of the square), the Venetian character is nearly destroyed, first by the frightful façade of San Moisè, which we will pause at another time to examine, and then by the modernising of the shops as they near the piazza, and the mingling with the lower Venetian populace of lounging groups of English and Austrians. We will push fast through them into the shadow of the pillars at the end of the " Bocca di Piazza," and then we forget them all; for between those pillars there opens a great light, and, in the midst of it, as we advance slowly, the vast tower of St. Mark seems to lift itself visibly forth from the level field of chequered stones; and, on each side, the countless arches prolong themselves into ranged symmetry, as if the rugged and irregular houses that pressed together above us in the dark alley had been struck back into sudden obedience and lovely order, and all their rude casements and broken walls had been transformed into arches charged with goodly sculpture, and fluted shafts of delicate stone.

And well may they fall back, for beyond those troops of ordered arches there rises a vision out of the earth, and all the great square seems to have opened from it in a kind of awe that we may see it far away;—a multitude of pillars and white domes, clustered into a long low pyramid of coloured light; a treasure-heap, it seems, partly of gold, and partly of opal and mother-of-pearl, hollowed beneath into five great vaulted porches, ceiled with fair mosaic, and beset with sculpture of alabaster, clear as amber and delicate as ivory,—sculpture fantastic and involved, of palm leaves and lilies, and grapes and pomegranates, and birds clinging and fluttering among the branches, all twined together into an endless network of buds and plumes; and, in the midst of it, the solemn forms of angels, sceptred, and robed to the feet, and leaning to each other across the gates, their figures indistinct among the gleam-ing of the golden ground through the leaves beside them, inter-rupted and dim, like the morning light as it faded back among the branches of Eden, when first its gates were angel-guarded long ago. And round the walls of the porches there are set pillars of variegated stones, jasper and porphyry, and deep-green serpentine spotted with flakes of snow, and marbles, that half refuse and half yield to the sunshine, Cleopatra-like, " their bluest veins to kiss "—the shadow, as it steals back from them, revealing line after line of azure undulation, as a receding tide leaves the waved sand; their capitals rich with interwoven tracery, rooted knots of herbage, and drifting leaves of acanthus and vine, and mystical signs, all beginning and ending in the Cross; and above them, in the broad archivolts, a continuous chain of language and of life—angels, and the signs of heaven, and the labours of men, each in its appointed season upon the earth; and above these, another range of glittering pinnacles, mixed with white arches edged with scarlet flowers,—a confusion of delight, amidst which the breasts of the Greek horses are seen blazing in their breadth of golden strength, and the St. Mark's Lion, lifted on a blue field covered with stars, until at last, as if in ecstasy, the crests of the arches break into a marble foam, and toss themselves far into the blue sky in flashes and wreaths of sculptured spray, as if the breakers on the Lido shore had been frost-bound before they fell, and the sea-nymphs had inlaid them with coral and amethyst.

Between that grim cathedral of England and this, what an interval! There is a type of it in the very birds that haunt them; for, instead of the restless crowd, hoarse-voiced and sable-winged, drifting on the bleak upper air, the St. Mark's porches are full of doves, that nestle among the marble foliage, and mingle the soft iridescence of their living plumes, changing at every motion, with the tints, hardly less lovely, that have stood unchanged for seven hundred years.

And what effect has this splendour on those who pass beneath it? You may walk from sunrise to sunset, to and fro, before the gateway of St. Mark's, and you will not see an eye lifted to it, nor a countenance brightened by it. Priest and layman, soldier and civilian, rich and poor, pass by it alike regardlessly. Up to the very recesses of the porches, the meanest tradesmen of the city push their counters; nay, the foundations of its pillars are themselves the seats—not " of them that sell doves " for sacrifice, but of the venders of toys and caricatures. Round the whole square in front of the church there is almost a continuous line of cafés, where the idle Venetians of the middle classes lounge, and read empty journals; in its centre the Austrian bands play during the time of vespers, their martial music jarring with the organ notes,—the march drowning the miserere, and the sullen crowds thickening round them,—a crowd, which, if it had its will, would stiletto every soldier that pipes to it. And in the recesses of the porches, all day long, knots of men of the lowest classes, unemployed and listless, lie basking in the sun like lizards; and unregarded children,—every heavy glance of their young eyes full of desperation and stony depravity and their throats hoarse with cursing,—gamble, and fight, and snarl, and sleep, hour after hour, clashing their bruised centesimi upon the marble ledges of the church porch. And the images of Christ and His angels look down upon it continually.

That we may not enter the church out of the midst of the horror of this, let us turn aside under the portico which looks towards the sea, and passing round within the two massive pillars brought from St. Jean d'Acre, we shall find the gate of the Baptistery; let us enter there. The heavy door closes behind us instantly, and the light, and the turbulence of the Piazzetta, are together shut out by it.

We are in a low vaulted room; vaulted, not with arches, but with small cupolas starred with gold, and chequered with gloomy figures : in the centre is a bronze font charged with rich bas-reliefs, a small figure of the Baptist standing above it in a single ray of light that glances across the narrow room, dying as it falls from a window high in the wall, and the first thing that it strikes, and the only thing that it strikes brightly, is a tomb. We hardly know if it be a tomb indeed; for it is like a narrow couch set beside the window, low-roofed and curtained, so that it might seem, but that it is some height above the pavement, to have been drawn towards the window, that the sleeper might be wakened early;—only there are two angels who have drawn the curtain back, and are looking down upon him. Let us look also, and thank that gentle light that rests upon his forehead for ever, and dies away upon his breast.

The face is of a man in middle life, but there are two deep furrows right across the forehead, dividing it like the foundations of a tower : the height of it above is bound by the fillet of the ducal cap. The rest of the features are singularly small and delicate, the lips sharp, perhaps the sharpness of death being added to that of the natural lines; but there is a sweet smile upon them, and a deep serenity upon the whole countenance. The roof of the canopy above has been blue, filled with stars; beneath, in the centre of the tomb on which the figure rests, is a seated figure of the Virgin, and the border of it all around is of flowers and soft leaves, growing rich and deep, as if in a field in summer.

It is the Doge Andrea Dandolo, a man early great among the great of Venice; and early lost. She chose him for her king in his 36th year; he died ten years later, leaving behind him that history to which we owe half of what we know of her former fortunes.

Look round at the room in which he lies. The floor of it is of rich mosaic, encompassed by a low seat of red marble, and its walls are of alabaster, but worn and shattered, and darkly stained with age, almost a ruin,—in places the slabs of marble have fallen away altogether, and the rugged brickwork is seen through the rents, but all beautiful; the ravaging fissures fretting their way among the islands and channelled zones of the alabaster, and the time-stains on its translucent masses darkened into fields of rich golden brown, like the colour of seaweed when the sun strikes on it through deep sea. The light fades away into the recess of the chamber towards the altar, and the eye can hardly trace the lines of the bas-relief behind it of the baptism of Christ; but on the vaulting of the roof the figures are distinct, and there are seen upon it two great circles, one surrounded by the "Principalities and powers in heavenly places," of which Milton has expressed the ancient division in the single massy line,

"Thrones, Dominations, Princedoms, Virtues, Powers,"

and around the other, the Apostles; Christ the centre of both : and upon the walls, again and again repeated, the gaunt figure of the Baptist, in every circumstance of his life and death; and the streams of the Jordan running down between their cloven rocks; the axe laid to the root of a fruitless tree that springs upon their shore. "Every tree that bringeth not forth good fruit shall be hewn down, and cast into the fire." Yes, verily : to be baptized with fire, or to be cast therein; it is the choice set before all men. The march-notes still murmur through the grated window, and mingle with the sounding in our ears of the sentence of judgment, which the old Greek has written on that Baptistery wall. Venice has made her choice.

He who lies under that stony canopy would have taught her another choice, in his day, if she would have listened to him; but he and his counsels have long been forgotten by her, and the dust lies upon his lips.

Through the heavy door whose bronze network closes the place of his rest, let us enter the church itself. It is lost in still deeper twilight, to which the eye must be accustomed for some moments before the form of the building can be traced; and then there opens before us a vast cave, hewn out into the form of a Cross, and divided into shadowy aisles by many pillars. Round the domes of its roof the light enters only through narrow apertures like large stars; and here and there a ray or two from some far away casement wanders into the darkness, and casts a narrow phosphoric stream upon the waves of marble that heave and fall in a thousand colours along the floor. What else there is of light is from torches, or silver lamps, burning ceaselessly in the recesses of the chapels; the roof sheeted with gold, and the polished walls covered with alabaster, give back at every curve and angle some feeble gleaming to the flames; and the glories round the heads of the sculptured saints flash out upon us as we pass them, and sink again into the gloom. Under foot and over head, a continual succession of crowded imagery, one picture passing into another, as in a dream; forms beautiful and terrible mixed together; dragons and serpents, and ravening beasts of prey, and graceful birds that in the midst of them drink from running fountains and feed from vases of crystal; the passions and the pleasures of human life symbolised together, and the mystery of its redemption; for the mazes of interwoven lines and changeful pictures lead always at last to the Cross, lifted and carved in every place and upon every stone; sometimes with the serpent of eternity wrapt round it, sometimes with doves beneath its arms, and sweet herbage growing forth from its feet; but conspicuous most of all on the great rood that crosses the church before the altar, raised in bright blazonry against the shadow of the apse. And although in the recesses of the aisles and chapels, when the mist of the incense hangs heavily, we may see continually a figure traced in faint lines upon their marble, a woman standing with her eyes raised to heaven, and the inscription above her, " Mother of God," she is not here the presiding deity. It is the Cross that is first seen, and always, burning in the centre of the temple; and every dome and hollow of its roof has the figure of Christ in the utmost height of it, raised in power, or returning in judgment.

(Stones of Venice.)

GEORGE ELIOT (1819–1880)

IN THE HALL FARM GARDEN

ADAM walked by the rick-yard, at present empty of ricks, to the little wooden gate leading into the garden—once the well-tended kitchen-garden of a manor-house; now, but for the handsome brick wall with stone coping that ran along one side of it, a true farmhouse garden, with hardy perennial flowers, unpruned fruit-trees, and kitchen vegetables growing together in careless, half-neglected abundance. In that leafy, flowery, bushy time, to look for any one in this garden was like playing at " hide-and-seek." There were the tall hollyhocks beginning to flower, and dazzle the eye with their pink, white, and yellow; there were the syringas and Gueldres roses, all large and disorderly for want of trimming; there were leafy walls of scarlet beans and late peas; there was a row of bushy filberts in one direction, and in another a huge apple-tree making a barren circle under its low-spreading boughs. But what signified a barren patch or two? The garden was so large. There was always a superfluity of broad beans—it took nine or ten of Adam's strides to get to the end of the uncut grass walk that ran by the side of them; and as for other vegetables, there was so much more room than was necessary for them, that in the rotation of crops a large flourishing bed of groundsel was of yearly occurrence on one spot or other. The very rose-trees, at which Adam stopped to pluck one, looked as if they grew wild; they were all huddled together in bushy masses, now flaunting with wide open petals, almost all of them of the streaked pink-and-white kind, which doubtless dated from the union of the houses of York and Lancaster. Adam was wise enough to choose a compact Provence rose that peeped out half-smothered by its flaunting scentless neighbours, and held it in his hand—he thought he should be more at ease holding something in his hand—as he walked on to the far end of the garden, where he remembered there was the largest row of currant-trees, not far off from the great yew-tree arbour.

But he had not gone many steps beyond the roses, when he heard the shaking of a bough, and a boy's voice saying—

" Now, then, Totty, hold out your pinny—there's a duck."

The voice came from the boughs of a tall cherry-tree, where Adam had no difficulty in discerning a small blue-pinafored figure perched in a commodious position where the fruit was thickest. Doubtless Totty was below, behind the screen of peas. Yes—with her bonnet hanging down her back, and her fat face, dreadfully smeared with red juice, turned up towards the cherry-tree, while she held her little round hole of a mouth and her red-stained pinafore to receive the promised downfall. I am sorry to say, more than half the cherries that fell were hard and yellow instead of juicy and red; but Totty spent no time in useless regrets, and she was already sucking the third juiciest when Adam said, " There now, Totty, you've got your cherries. Run into the house with 'em to mother—she wants you—she's in the dairy. Run in this minute—there's a good little girl."

He lifted her up in his strong arms and kissed her as he spoke, a ceremony which Totty regarded as a tiresome interruption to cherry-eating; and when he set her down she trotted off quite silently towards the house, sucking her cherries as she went along.

" Tommy, my lad, take care you're not shot for a little thieving bird," said Adam, as he walked on towards the currant-trees.

He could see there was a large basket at the end of the row : Hetty would not be far off, and Adam already felt as if she were looking at him. Yet when he turned the corner she was standing with her back towards him, and stooping to gather the low-hanging fruit. Strange that she had not heard him coming ! perhaps it was because she was making the leaves rustle. She started when she became conscious that some one was near—started so violently that she dropped the basin with the currants in it, and then, when she saw it was Adam, she turned from pale to deep red. That blush made his heart beat with a new happiness. Hetty had never blushed at seeing him before.

"I frightened you," he said, with a delicious sense that it didn't signify what he said, since Hetty seemed to feel as much as he did; "let *me* pick the currants up."

That was soon done, for they had only fallen in a tangled mass on the grass-plot, and Adam, as he rose and gave her the basin again, looked straight into her eyes with the subdued tenderness that belongs to the first moments of hopeful love.

Hetty did not turn away her eyes; her blush had subsided, and she met his glance with a quiet sadness, which contented Adam, because it was so unlike anything he had seen in her before.

"There's not many more currants to get," she said; "I shall soon ha' done now."

"I'll help you," said Adam; and he fetched the large basket which was nearly full of currants, and set it close to them.

Not a word more was spoken as they gathered the currants. Adam's heart was too full to speak, and he thought Hetty knew all that was in it. She was not indifferent to his presence after all; she had blushed when she saw him, and then there was that touch of sadness about her which must surely mean love, since it was the opposite of her usual manner, which had often impressed him as indifference. And he could glance at her continually as she bent over the fruit, while the level evening sunbeams stole through the thick apple-tree boughs, and rested on her round cheek and neck as if they too were in love with her. It was to Adam the time that a man can least forget in after-life,—the time when he believes that the first woman he has ever loved betrays by a slight something—a word, a tone, a glance, the quivering of an eye or an eyelid—that she is at least beginning to love him in return. The sign is so slight, it is scarcely perceptible to the ear or eye—he could describe it to no one—it is a mere feather-touch, yet it seems to have changed his whole being, to have merged an uneasy yearning into a delicious unconsciousness of everything but the present moment. So much of our early gladness vanishes utterly from our memory : we can never recall the joy with which we laid our heads on our mother's bosom or rode on our father's back in childhood ; doubtless that joy is wrought up into our nature, as the sunlight of long-past mornings is wrought up in the soft mellowness of the apricot; but it is gone for ever from our imagination, and we can only *believe* in the joy of childhood. But the first glad moment in our first love is a vision which returns to us to the last, and brings with it a thrill of feeling intense and special as the recurrent sensation of a sweet odour breathed in a far-off hour of happiness. It is a memory that gives a more exquisite touch to tenderness, that feels the madness of jealousy, and adds the last keenness to the agony of despair.

Hetty bending over the red bunches, the level rays piercing the screen of apple-tree boughs, the length of bushy garden beyond, his own emotion as he looked at her and believed that she was thinking of him, and that there was no need for them to talk—Adam remembered it all to the last moment of his life.

And Hetty ? You know quite well that Adam was mistaken about her. Like many other men, he thought the signs of love for another were signs of love towards himself. When Adam was approaching unseen by her, she was absorbed as usual in thinking and wondering about Arthur's possible return : the sound of any man's footstep would have affected her just in the same way—she would have *felt* it might be Arthur before she had time to see, and the blood that forsook her cheek in the agitation of that momentary feeling would have rushed back again at the sight of any one else just as much as at the sight of Adam. He was not wrong in thinking that a change had come over Hetty : the anxieties and fears of a first passion, with which she was trembling, had become stronger than vanity, had given her for the first time that sense of helpless dependence on another's feeling which awakens the clinging deprecating womanhood even in the shallowest girl that can ever experience it, and creates in her a sensibility to kindness which found her quite hard before. For the first time Hetty felt that there was something soothing to her in Adam's timid yet manly tenderness : she wanted to be treated lovingly—oh, it was very hard to bear this blank of absence, silence, apparent indifference, after those moments of glowing love ! She was not afraid that Adam would tease her with love-making and flattering speeches like her other admirers : he had always been so reserved to her : she could enjoy without any fear the sense that this strong brave man loved her, and was near her. It never entered into her mind that Adam was pitiable too—that Adam, too, must suffer one day.

Hetty, we know, was not the first woman that had behaved more gently to the man who loved her in vain, because she had herself begun to love another. It was a very old story; but Adam knew nothing about it, so he drank in the sweet delusion.

"That'll do," said Hetty, after a little while. "Aunt wants me to leave some on the trees. I'll take 'em in now."

"It's very well I came to carry the basket," said Adam, "for it 'ud ha' been too heavy for your little arms."

"No; I could ha' carried it with both hands."

"Oh, I daresay," said Adam, smiling, "and been as long getting into the house as a little ant carrying a caterpillar. Have you ever seen those tiny fellows carrying things four times as big as themselves?"

"No," said Hetty, indifferently, not caring to know the difficulties of ant-life.

"Oh, I used to watch 'em often when I was a lad. But now, you see, I can carry the basket with one arm, as if it was an empty nutshell, and give you th' other arm to lean on. Won't you? Such big arms as mine were made for little arms like yours to lean on."

Hetty smiled faintly, and put her arm within his. Adam looked down at her, but her eyes were turned dreamily towards another corner of the garden.

"Have you ever been to Eagledale?" she said, as they walked slowly along.

"Yes," said Adam, pleased to have her ask a question about himself; "ten years ago, when I was a lad, I went with father to see about some work there. It's a wonderful sight—rocks and caves such as you never saw in your life. I never had a right notion o' rocks till I went there."

"How long did it take to get there?"

"Why, it took us the best part o' two days' walking. But it's nothing of a day's journey for anybody as has got a first-rate nag. The Captain 'ud get there in nine or ten hours, I'll be bound, he's such a rider. And I shouldn't wonder if he's back again to-morrow; he's too active to rest long in that lonely place, all by himself, for there's nothing but a bit of a inn i' that part where he's gone to fish. I wish he'd got th' estate in his hands; that 'ud be the right thing for him, for it 'ud give him plenty to do, and he'd do't well too, for all he's so young; he's got better notions o' things than many a man twice his age. He spoke very handsome to me th' other day about lending me money to set up i' business; and if things came round that way, I'd rather be beholding to him than to any other man i' the world."

Poor Adam was led on to speak about Arthur because he thought Hetty would be pleased to know that the young squire was so ready to befriend him; the fact entered into his future prospects, which he would like to seem promising in her eyes. And it was true that Hetty listened with an interest which brought a new light into her eyes and a half smile upon her lips.

"How pretty the roses are now!" Adam continued, pausing to look at them. "See! I stole the prettiest, but I didna mean to keep it myself. I think these as are all pink, and have got a finer sort o' green leaves, are prettier than the striped uns, don't you?"

He set down the basket, and took the rose from his button-hole.

"It smells very sweet," he said; "those striped uns have no smell. Stick it in your frock, and then you can put it in water after. It 'ud be a pity to let it fade."

Hetty took the rose, smiling as she did so at the pleasant thought that Arthur could so soon get back if he liked. There was a flash of hope and happiness in her mind, and with a sudden impulse of gaiety she did what she had very often done before—stuck the rose in her hair a little above the left ear. Then tender admiration in Adam's face was slightly shadowed by reluctant disapproval. Hetty's love of finery was just the thing that would most provoke his mother, and he himself disliked it as much as it was possible for him to dislike anything that belonged to her.

"Ah," he said, "that's like the ladies in the pictures at the Chase; they've mostly got flowers or feathers or gold things i' their hair, but somehow I don't like to see 'em: they allays put me i' mind o' the painted women outside the shows at Treddles'on fair. What can a woman have to set her off better than her own hair, when it curls so, like yours? If a woman's young and pretty, I think you can see her good looks all the better for her being plain dressed. Why, Dinah Morris looks very nice, for all she wears such a plain cap and gown. It seems to me as a woman's face doesna want flowers; it's almost like a flower itself. I'm sure yours is."

"Oh, very well," said Hetty, with a little playful pout,

taking the rose out of her hair. "I'll put one o' Dinah's caps on when we go in, and you'll see if I look better in it. She left one behind, so I can take the pattern."

"Nay, nay, I don't want you to wear a Methodist cap like Dinah's. I daresay it's a very ugly cap, and I used to think when I saw her here, as it was nonsense for her to dress different t' other people; but I never rightly noticed her till she came to see mother last week, and then I thought the cap seemed to fit her face somehow as th' acorn cup fits th' acorn, and I shouldn't like to see her so well without it. But you've got another sort o' face; I'd have you just as you are now, without anything t' interfere with your own looks. It's like when a man's singing a good tune, you don't want t' hear bells tinkling and interfering wi' the sound."

He took her arm and put it within his again, looking down on her fondly. He was afraid she should think he had lectured her; imagining, as we are apt to do, that she had perceived all the thoughts he had only half expressed. And the thing he dreaded most was lest any cloud should come over this evening's happiness. For the world he would not have spoken of his love to Hetty yet, till this commencing kindness towards him should have grown into unmistakable love. In his imagination he saw long years of his future life stretching before him, blest with the right to call Hetty his own: he could be content with very little at present. So he took up the basket of currants once more, and they went on towards the house.

(Adam Bede.)

CHARLES KINGSLEY (1819-1875)

THE BARBADOS

"The sun's rim dips; the stars rush out;
At one stride comes the dark."—COLERIDGE.

LAND! land! land! Yes, there it was, far away to the south and west, beside the setting sun, a long blue bar between the crimson sea and golden sky. Land at last, with fresh streams and cooling fruits, and free room for cramped and scurvy-weakened limbs. And there, too, might be gold, and gems, and all the wealth of Ind. Who knew? Why not? The old world of fact and prose lay thousands of miles behind them, and before them and around them was the realm of wonder and fable, of boundless hope and possibility. Sick men crawled up out of their stifling hammocks; strong men fell on their knees and gave God thanks; and all eyes and hands were stretched eagerly toward the far blue cloud, fading as the sun sank down, yet rising higher and broader as the ship rushed on before the rich trade-wind, which whispered lovingly round brow and sail, " I am the faithful friend of those who dare ! " " Blow freshly, freshlier yet, thou good trade-wind, of whom it is written that He makes the winds His angels, ministering breaths to the heirs of His salvation. Blow freshlier yet, and save, if not me from death, yet her from worse than death. Blow on, and land me at her feet, to call the lost lamb home, and die ! "

So murmured Frank to himself, as with straining eyes he gazed upon that first outlier of the New World which held his all. His cheeks were thin and wasted, and the hectic spot on each glowed crimson in the crimson light of the setting sun. A few minutes more, and the rainbows of the West were gone ; emerald and topaz, amethyst and ruby, had faded into silver-grey ; and overhead, through the dark sapphire depths, the Moon and Venus reigned above the sea.

" That should be Barbados, your worship," said Drew, the master ; " unless my reckoning is far out, which, Heaven knows, it has no right to be, after such a passage, and God be praised."

" Barbados ? I never heard of it."

" Very like, sir ; but Yeo and I were here with Captain Drake, and I was here after, too, with poor Captain Barlow ; and there is good harbourage to the south and west of it, I remember."

" And neither Spaniard, cannibal, or other evil beast," said Yeo. " A very garden of the Lord, sir, hid away in the seas, for an inheritance to those who love Him. I heard Captain Drake talk of planting it, if ever he had a chance."

" I recollect now," said Amyas, " some talk between him and poor Sir Humphrey about an island here. Would God he had gone thither instead of to Newfoundland ! "

" Nay, then," said Yeo, " he is in bliss now with the Lord ; and you would not have kept him from that, sir ? "

" He would have waited as willingly as he went, if he could have served his Queen thereby. But what say you, my masters ? How can we do better than to spend a few days here, to get our sick round, before we make the Main, and set to our work ? "

All approved the counsel except Frank, who was silent.

" Come, fellow-adventurer," said Cary, " we must have your voice too."

" To my impatience, Will," said he, aside in a low voice, " there is but one place on earth, and I am all day longing for wings to fly thither : but the counsel is right. I approve it."

So the verdict was announced, and received with a hearty cheer by the crew; and long before morning they had run along the southern shore of the island, and were feeling their way into the bay where Bridgetown now stands. All eyes were eagerly fixed on the low wooded hills which slept in the moonlight, spangled by fire-flies with a million dancing stars; all nostrils drank greedily the fragrant air, which swept from the land, laden with the scent of a thousand flowers; all ears welcomed, as a grateful change from the monotonous whisper and lap of the water, the hum of insects, the snore of the tree-toads, the plaintive notes of the shore-fowl, which fill a tropic night with noisy life.

At last she stopped; at last the cable rattled through the hawsehole; and then, careless of the chance of lurking Spaniard or Carib, an instinctive cheer burst from every throat. Poor fellows! Amyas had much ado to prevent them going on shore at once, dark as it was, by reminding them that it wanted but two hours of day.

"Never were two such long hours," said one young lad, fidgeting up and down.

"You never were in the Inquisition," said Yeo, "or you'd know better how slow time can run. Stand you still, and give God thanks you're where you are."

"I say, Gunner, be there goold to that island?"

"Never heard of none; and so much the better for it," said Yeo, drily.

"But, I say, Gunner," said a poor scurvy-stricken cripple, licking his lips, "be there oranges and limmons there?"

"Not of my seeing; but plenty of good fruit down to the beach, thank the Lord. There comes the dawn at last."

Up flushed the rose, up rushed the sun, and the level rays glittered on the smooth stems of the palm-trees, and threw rainbows across the foam upon the coral-reefs, and gilded lonely uplands far away, where now stands many a stately country-seat and busy engine-house. Long lines of pelicans went clanging out to sea; the hum of the insects hushed, and a thousand birds burst into jubilant song; a thin blue mist crept upward toward the inner downs, and vanished, leaving them to quiver in the burning glare; the land-breeze, which had blown fresh out to sea all night, died away into glassy calm, and the tropic day was begun.

The sick were lifted over the side, and landed boat-load after boat-load on the beach, to stretch themselves in the shade of the palms; and in half-an-hour the whole crew were scattered on the shore, except some dozen worthy men, who had volunteered to keep watch and ward on board till noon.

And now the first instinctive cry of nature was for fruit! fruit! fruit! The poor lame wretches crawled from place to place plucking greedily the violet grapes of the creeping shore vine, and staining their mouths and blistering their lips with the prickly pears, in spite of Yeo's entreaties and warnings against the thorns. Some of the healthy began hewing down cocoa-nut trees to get at the nuts, doing little thereby but blunt their hatchets; till Yeo and Drew, having mustered half-a-dozen reasonable men, went off inland, and returned in an hour laden with the dainties of that primeval orchard—with acid junipa-apples, luscious guavas, and crowned ananas, queen of all the fruits, which they had found by hundreds on the broiling ledges of the low tufa-cliffs; and then all, sitting on the sandy turf, defiant of galliwasps and jackspaniards, and all the weapons of the insect host, partook of the equal banquet, while old blue land-crabs sat in their house-doors and brandished their fists in defiance at the invaders, and solemn cranes stood in the water on the shoals with their heads on one side, and meditated how long it was since they had seen bipeds without feathers breaking the solitude of their isle.

And Frank wandered up and down, silent, but rather in wonder than in sadness, while great Amyas walked after him, his mouth full of junipa-apples, and enacted the part of showman, with a sort of patronising air, as one who had seen the wonders already, and was above being astonished at them.

"New, new; everything new!" said Frank, meditatively. "Oh, awful feeling! All things changed around us, even to the tiniest fly and flower; yet we the same; the same for ever!"

Amyas, to whom such utterances were altogether sibylline and unintelligible, answered by—

"Look, Frank, that's a colibri. You've heard of colibris?"

Frank looked at the living gem, which hung, loud humming, over some fantastic bloom, and then dashed away, seemingly to call its mate, and whirred and danced with it round and round the flower-starred bushes, flashing fresh rainbows at every shifting of the lights.

Frank watched solemnly awhile, and then—

"*Qualis Natura formatrix, si talis formata?* Oh, my God, how fair must be Thy real world, if even Thy phantoms are so fair!"

"Phantoms?" asked Amyas, uneasily. "That's no ghost,

Frank, but a jolly little honey-sucker, with a wee wife, and children no bigger than peas, but yet solid greedy little fellows enough, I'll warrant."

" Not phantoms in thy sense, good fellow, but in the sense of those who know the worthlessness of all below."

" I'll tell you what, brother Frank, you are a great deal wiser than me, I know ; but I can't abide to see you turn up your nose as it were at God's good earth. See now, God made all these things ; and never a man, perhaps, set eyes on them till fifty years agone ; and yet they were as pretty as they are now, ever since the making of the world. And why do you think God could have put them here, then, but to please Himself "— and Amyas took off his hat—" with the sight of them ? Now, I say, brother Frank, what's good enough to please God, is good enough to please you and me."

" Your rebuke is just, dear old simple-hearted fellow ; and God forgive me, if with all my learning, which has brought me no profit, and my longings, which have brought me no peace, I presume at moments, sinner that I am, to be more dainty than the Lord Himself. He walked in Paradise among the trees of the garden, Amyas ; and so will we, and be content with what He sends. Why should we long for the next world, before we are fit even for this one ? "

" And in the meanwhile," said Amyas, " this earth's quite good enough, at least here in Barbados."

" Do you believe," asked Frank, trying to turn his own thoughts, " in those tales of the Spaniards, that the Sirens and Tritons are heard singing in these seas ? "

" I can't tell. There's more fish in the water than ever came out of it, and more wonders in the world, I'll warrant, than we ever dreamt of ; but I was never in these parts before ; and in the South Sea, I must say, I never came across any, though Yeo says he has heard fair music at night up in the Gulf, far away from land."

" The Spaniards report, that at certain seasons choirs of these nymphs assemble in the sea, and with ravishing music sing their watery loves. It may be so. For Nature, which has peopled the land with rational souls, may not have left the sea altogether barren of them ; above all, when we remember that the ocean is as it were the very fount of all fertility, and its slime (as the most learned hold with Thales of Miletus) that *prima materia* out of which all things were one by one concocted. Therefore, the ancients feigned wisely that Venus, the mother of all living things, whereby they designed the plastic force of nature, was born of the sea-foam, and rising from the deep, floated ashore upon the isles of Greece."

"I don't know what plastic force is; but I wish I had had the luck to be by when the pretty poppet came up : however, the nearest thing I ever saw to that was maidens swimming alongside us when we were in the South Seas, and would have come aboard, too; but Drake sent them all off again for a lot of naughty packs, and I verily believe they were no better. Look at the butterflies, now ! Don't you wish you were a boy again, and not too proud to go catching them in your cap ? "

And so the two wandered on together through the glorious tropic woods, and then returned to the beach to find the sick already grown cheerful, and many who that morning could not stir from their hammocks, pacing up and down, and gaining strength with every step.

"Well done, lads ! " cried Amyas, " keep a cheerful mind. We will have the music ashore after dinner, for want of mermaids to sing to us, and those that can dance may."

And so those four days were spent; and the men, like school-boys on a holiday, gave themselves up to simple merriment, not forgetting, however, to wash the clothes, take in fresh water, and store up a good supply of such fruit as seemed likely to keep; until, tired with fruitless rambles after gold, which they expected to find in every bush, in spite of Yeo's warnings that none had been heard of on the island, they were fain to lounge about, full-grown babies, picking up shells and sea-fans to take home to their sweethearts, smoking agoutis out of the hollow trees, with shout and laughter, and tormenting every living thing they could come near, till not a land-crab dare look out of his hole, or an armadillo unroll himself, till they were safe out of the bay, and off again to the westward, unconscious pioneers of all the wealth, and commerce, and beauty, and science, which has in later centuries made that lovely isle the richest gem of all the tropic seas.

(Westward Ho !)

MATTHEW ARNOLD (1822–1888)
THE SPIRIT OF THE ENGLISH NATION

WHAT are the essential characteristics of the spirit of our nation ? Not, certainly, an open and clear mind, not a quick and flexible intelligence. Our greatest admirers would not claim for us that we have these in a pre-eminent degree; they might say that we had more of them than our detractors gave us credit for; but they would not assert them to be our essential characteristics. They would rather allege, as our chief spiritual characteristics, energy and honesty; and, if we are judged favourably and positively, not invidiously and negatively, our chief characteristics are no doubt these : energy and honesty, not an open and clear mind, not a quick and flexible intelligence. Openness of mind and flexibility of intelligence were very signal characteristics of the Athenian people in ancient times; everybody will feel that. Openness of mind, and flexibility of intelligence are remarkable characteristics of the French people in modern times; at any rate they strikingly characterise them as compared with us; I think everybody, or almost everybody, will feel that. I will not now ask what more the Athenian or the French spirit has than this, nor what short-comings either of them may have as a set-off against this; all I want now to point out is that they have this, and that we have it in a much lesser degree. Let me remark, however, that not only in the moral sphere, but also in the intellectual and spiritual sphere, energy and honesty are most important and fruitful qualities; that, for instance, of what we call genius, energy is the most essential part. So, by assigning to a nation energy and honesty as its chief spiritual characteristics—by refusing to it, as at all eminent characteristics, openness of mind and flexibility of intelligence—we do not by any means, as some people might at first suppose, relegate its importance and its power of manifesting itself with effect from the intellectual to the moral sphere. We only indicate its probable special line of successful activity in the intellectual sphere, and, it is true, certain imperfections and failings to which, in this sphere, it will always be subject. Genius is mainly an affair of energy, and poetry is mainly an affair of genius; therefore a nation whose spirit is characterised by energy may well be eminent in poetry;—and we have Shakespeare. Again, the highest reach of science is, one may say, an inventive power, a faculty of divination, akin to the highest power exercised in poetry; therefore a nation whose spirit is characterised by energy may well be eminent in science;—and we have Newton. Shakespeare and Newton : in the intellectual sphere there can be no higher names. And what that energy, which is the life of genius, above everything demands and insists upon, is freedom; entire independence of all authority, prescription, and routine—the fullest room to expand as it will. Therefore, a nation whose chief spiritual characteristic is energy, will not be very apt to set up in intellectual matters, a fixed standard, an authority, like an academy. By this it certainly escapes certain real inconveniences and dangers, and it can, at the same time, as we have seen, reach undeniably splendid heights in poetry and science. On the other hand, some of the requisites of intellectual work are specially the affair of quickness of mind and flexibility of intelligence. The form, the method of evolution, the precision, the proportions, the relations of the parts to the whole, in an intellectual work, depend mainly upon them. And these are the elements of an intellectual work which are really most communicable from it, which can most be learned and adopted from it, which have, therefore, the greatest effect upon the intellectual performance of others. Even in poetry these requisites are very important; and the poetry of a nation, not eminent for the gifts on which they depend, will, more or less, suffer by this short coming. In poetry, however, they are, after all, secondary, and energy is the first thing; but in prose they are of first-rate importance. In its prose literature, therefore, and in the routine of intellectual work generally, a nation with no particular gifts for these will not be so successful. These are what, as I have said, can to a certain degree be learned and appropriated, while the free activity of genius cannot. Academies consecrate and maintain them, and, therefore, a nation with an eminent turn for them naturally establishes academies. So far as routine and authority tend to embarrass energy and inventive genius, academies may be said to be obstructive to energy and inventive genius, and, to this extent, to the human spirit's general advance. But then this evil is so much compensated by the propagation, on a large scale, of the mental aptitudes and demands which an open mind and a flexible intelligence naturally engender, genius itself, in the long run, so greatly finds its account in this propagation, and bodies like the French Academy have such power for promoting it, that the general advance of the human spirit is, perhaps, on the whole, rather furthered than impeded by their existence.

How much greater is our nation in poetry than in prose! How much better, in general, do the productions of its spirit show in the qualities of genius than in the qualities of intelligence! One may constantly remark this in the work of individuals; how much more striking, in general, does any Englishman—of some vigour of mind, but by no means a poet—seem in his verse than in his prose! His verse partly suffers from his not being really a poet, partly, no doubt, from the very same defects which impair his prose, and he cannot express himself with thorough success in it. But how much more powerful a personage does he appear in it, by dint of feeling, and of originality and movement of ideas, than when he is writing prose ! With a Frenchman of like stamp it is just the reverse : set him to write poetry, he is limited, artificial, and impotent; set him to write prose, he is free, natural and effective. The power of French literature is in its prose-writers, the power of English literature is in its poets.

(The Literary Influence of Academies.)

GEORGE MEREDITH (1828–1909)

DAWN IN THE MOUNTAINS

BEYOND the fir-wood light was visibly the dawn's. Halfway down the ravines it resembled the light cast off a torrent water. It lay on the grass like a sheet of unreflecting steel, and was a face without a smile above. Their childhood ran along the tracks to the forest by the light, which was neither dim nor cold, but grave; presenting tree and shrub and dwarf growth and grass austerely, not deepening or confusing them. They wound their way by borders of crag, seeing in a dell below the mouth of the idle mine begirt with weedy and shrub-hung rock, a dripping semi-circle. Farther up they came on the flat juniper and crossed a wet ground-thicket of whortleberry : their feet were in the moist moss among sprigs of heath; and a great fir-tree stretched his length, a pealed multitude of his dead fellows leaned and stood upright in the midst of scattered fire-stained members, and through their skeleton limbs the sheer precipice of slate-rock of the bulk across the chasm, nursery of hawk and eagle, wore a thin blue tinge, the sign of warmer light abroad.

" This way, my brother ! " cried Carinthia, shuddering at a path he was about to follow.

Dawn in the mountain-land is a meeting of many friends. The pinnacle, the forest-head, the latschen-tufted mound, rockbastion and defiant cliff and giant of the triple peak, were in view, clearly lined for a common recognition, but all were figures of solid gloom, unfeatured and bloomless. Another minute and they had flung off their mail and changed to various, indented, intricate, succinct in ridge, scar and channel; and they had all a look of watchfulness that made them one company. The smell of rock-waters and roots of herb and moss grew keen; air became a wine that raised the breast high to breathe it; an uplifting coolness pervaded the heights. What wonder that the mountain-bred girl should let fly her voice. The natural carol woke an echo. She did not repeat it.

"And we will not forget our home, Chillon," she said, touching him gently to comfort some saddened feeling.

The plumes of cloud now slowly entered into the lofty arch of dawn and melted from brown to purple-black. The upper sky swam with violet; and in a moment each stray cloud-feather was edged with rose, and then suffused. It seemed that the heights fronted East to eye the interflooding of colours, and it was imaginable that all turned to the giant whose forehead first kindled to the sun : a greeting of god and king.

On the morning of a farewell we fluctuate sharply between the very distant and the close and homely : and even in memory the fluctuation occurs, the grander scene casting us back on the modestly nestling, and that, when it has refreshed us, conjuring imagination to embrace the splendour and wonder. But the wrench of an immediate division from what we love makes the things within reach the dearest, we put out our hands for them, as violently-parted lovers do, though the soul in days to come would know a craving, and imagination flap a leaden wing, if we had not looked beyond them.

"Shall we go down?" said Carinthia, for she knew a little cascade near the house, showering on rock and fern, and longed to have it round her.

They descended, Chillon saying that they would soon have the mists rising, and must not delay to start on their journey.

The armies of the young sunrise in mountain-lands neigh-bouring the plains, vast shadows, were marching over woods and meads, black against the edge of golden; and great heights were cut with them, and bounding waters took the leap in a silvery radiance to gloom; the bright and dark-banded valleys were like night and morning taking hands down the sweep of their rivers. Immense was the range of vision scudding the peaks and over the illimitable eastward plains flat to the very East and sources of the sun.

(The Amazing Marriage.)

"LEWIS CARROLL," CHARLES L. DODGSON (1832–1898)

A MAD TEA-PARTY

THERE was a table set out under a tree in front of the house, and the March Hare and the Hatter were having tea at it: a Dormouse was sitting between them, fast asleep, and the other two were using it as a cushion resting their elbows on it, and talking over its head. "Very uncomfortable for the Dormouse," thought Alice; "only, as it's asleep, I suppose it doesn't mind."

The table was a large one, but the three were all crowded together at one corner of it. "No room! No room!" they cried out when they saw Alice coming. "There's *plenty* of room!" said Alice indignantly, and she sat down in a large armchair at one end of the table.

"Have some wine," the March Hare said in an encouraging tone.

Alice looked all round the table, but there was nothing on it but tea. "I don't see any wine," she remarked.

"There isn't any," said the March Hare.

"Then it wasn't very civil of you to offer it," said Alice angrily.

"It wasn't very civil of you to sit down without being invited," said the March Hare.

"I didn't know it was *your* table," said Alice; "it's laid for a great many more than three."

"Your hair wants cutting," said the Hatter. He had been looking at Alice for some time with great curiosity, and this was his first speech.

"You should learn not to make personal remarks," Alice said with some severity; "it's very rude."

The Hatter opened his eyes very wide on hearing this; but all he *said* was "Why is a raven like a writing-desk?"

"Come, we shall have some fun now!" thought Alice. "I'm glad they've begun asking riddles,—I believe I can guess that," she added aloud.

"Do you mean that you think you can find out the answer to it?" said the March Hare.

"Exactly so," said Alice.

"Then you should say what you mean," the March Hare went on.

"I do," Alice hastily replied; "at least—at least I mean what I say—that's the same thing, you know."

"Not the same thing a bit!" said the Hatter. "Why, you might just as well say that 'I see what I eat' is the same thing as 'I eat what I see'!"

"You might just as well say," added the March Hare, "that 'I like what I get' is the same thing as 'I get what I like'!"

"You might just as well say," added the Dormouse, which seemed to be talking in his sleep, "that 'I breathe when I sleep is the same thing as 'I sleep when I breathe'!"

"It *is* the same thing with you," said the Hatter; and here the conversation dropped, and the party sat silent for a minute, while Alice thought over all she could remember about ravens and writing-desks, which wasn't much.

The Hatter was the first to break the silence. "What day of the month is it?" he said, turning to Alice: he had taken his watch out of his pocket, and was looking at it uneasily, shaking it every now and then, and holding it to his ear.

Alice considered a little, and then said "The fourth."

"Two days wrong!" sighed the Hatter. "I told you butter wouldn't suit the works!" he added, looking angrily at the March Hare.

"It was the *best* butter," the March Hare meekly replied.

"Yes, but some crumbs must have got in as well," the Hatter grumbled: "you shouldn't have put it in with the bread-knife."

The March Hare took the watch and looked at it gloomily: then he dipped it into his cup of tea, and looked at it again: but he could think of nothing better to say than his first remark, "It was the *best* butter, you know."

Alice had been looking over his shoulder with some curiosity. "What a funny watch!" she remarked. "It tells the day of the month, and doesn't tell what o'clock it is!"

"Why should it?" muttered the Hatter. "Does *your* watch tell you what year it is?"

"Of course not," Alice replied very readily: "but that's because it stays the same year for such a long time together."

"Which is just the case with *mine*," said the Hatter.

Alice felt dreadfully puzzled. The Hatter's remark seemed to have no meaning in it, and yet it was certainly English. "I don't quite understand," she said as politely as she could.

"The Dormouse is asleep again," said the Hatter, and he poured a little hot tea upon its nose.

The Dormouse shook its head impatiently, and said, without opening its eyes, "Of course, of course; just what I was going to remark myself."

"Have you guessed the riddle yet?" the Hatter said, turning to Alice again.

"No, I give it up," Alice replied: "what's the answer?"

"I haven't the slightest idea," said the Hatter.

"Nor I," said the Hare.

Alice sighed wearily. "I think you might do something better with the time," she said, "than waste it asking riddles with no answers."

"If you knew Time as well as I do," said the Hatter, "you wouldn't talk about wasting *it*. It's *him*."

"I don't know what you mean," said Alice.

"Of course you don't!" the Hatter said tossing his head contemptuously. "I dare say you never even spoke to Time!"

"Perhaps not," Alice cautiously replied: "but I know I have to beat time when I learn music."

"Ah! that accounts for it," said the Hatter. "He won't stand beating. Now, if you only kept on good terms with him, he'd do almost anything you liked with the clock. For instance, suppose it were nine o'clock in the morning, just time to begin lessons: you'd only have to whisper a hint to Time, and round goes the clock in a twinkling! Half-past one, time for dinner!"

("I only wish it was," the March Hare said to itself in a whisper.)

"That would be grand, certainly," said Alice thoughtfully: "but then—I shouldn't be hungry for it, you know."

"Not at first, perhaps," said the Hatter: "but you could keep it to half-past one as long as you liked."

"Is that the way *you* manage?" Alice asked.

The Hatter shook his head mournfully. "Not I!" he replied. "We quarrelled last March—just before *he* went mad you know——" (pointing with his tea-spoon at the March Hare), "——it was at the great concert given by the Queen of Hearts, and I had to sing

'Twinkle, twinkle, little bat!
How I wonder what you're at!'

You know the song, perhaps?"

"I've heard something like it," said Alice.

"It goes on, you know," the Hatter continued, "in this way:—

'Up above the world you fly,
Like a tea-tray in the sky.
Twinkle, twinkle——'"

Here the Dormouse shook itself, and began singing in its sleep "*Twinkle, twinkle, twinkle, twinkle*——" and went on so long that they had to pinch it to make it stop.

"Well, I'd hardly finished the first verse," said the Hatter, "when the Queen jumped up and bawled out 'He's murdering the time! Off with his head!'"

"How dreadfully savage!" exclaimed Alice.

"And ever since that," the Hatter went on in a mournful tone, "he won't do a thing I ask! It's always six o'clock now."

A bright idea came into Alice's head. "Is that the reason so many tea-things are put out here?" she asked.

"Yes, that's it," said the Hatter with a sigh: "it's always tea-time, and we've no time to wash the things between whiles."

"Then you keep moving round, I suppose?" said Alice.

"Exactly so," said the Hatter: "as the things get used up."

"But what happens when you come to the beginning again?" Alice ventured to ask.

"Suppose we change the subject," the March Hare interrupted, yawning. "I'm getting tired of this. I vote the young lady tells us a story."

"I'm afraid I don't know one," said Alice, rather alarmed at the proposal.

"Then the Dormouse shall!" they both cried. "Wake up, Dormouse!" And they pinched it on both sides at once.

The Dormouse slowly opened his eyes. "I wasn't asleep," he said in a hoarse, feeble voice: "I heard every word you fellows were saying."

"Tell us a story!" said the March Hare.

"Yes, please do!" pleaded Alice.

"And be quick about it," added the Hatter, "or you'll be asleep again before it's done."

"Once upon a time there were three little sisters," the Dormouse began in a great hurry; "and their names were Elsie, Lacie, and Tillie; and they lived at the bottom of a well——"

"What did they live on?" said Alice, who always took a great interest in questions of eating and drinking.

"They lived on treacle," said the Dormouse, after thinking a minute or two.

"They couldn't have done that, you know," Alice gently remarked; "they'd have been ill."

"So they were," said the Dormouse; "*very* ill."

Alice tried a little to fancy to herself what such an extraordinary way of living would be like, but it puzzled her too much, so she went on: "But why did they live at the bottom of a well?"

"Take some more tea," the March Hare said to Alice, very earnestly.

"I've had nothing yet," Alice replied in an offended tone, "so I can't take more."

"You mean you can't take *less*," said the Hatter: "it's very easy to take *more* than nothing."

"Nobody asked *your* opinion," said Alice.

"Who's making personal remarks now?" the Hatter asked triumphantly.

Alice did not quite know what to say to this: so she helped herself to some tea and bread-and-butter, and then turned to the Dormouse, and repeated her question. "Why did they live at the bottom of a well?"

The Dormouse again took a minute or two to think about it, and then said, " It was a treacle-well."

" There's no such thing ! " Alice was beginning very angrily, but the Hatter and the March Hare went " Sh ! sh ! " and the Dormouse sulkily remarked " If you can't be civil, you'd better finish the story for yourself."

" No, please go on ! " Alice said very humbly. " I won't interrupt you again. I dare say there may be *one*."

" One, indeed ! " said the Dormouse indignantly. However, he consented to go on. " And so these three little sisters—they were learning to draw, you know——"

" What did they draw ? " said Alice, quite forgetting her promise.

" Treacle," said the Dormouse, without considering at all this time.

" I want a clean cup," interrupted the Hatter : " let's all move one place on."

He moved on as he spoke, and the Dormouse followed him : the March Hare moved into the Dormouse's place, and Alice rather unwillingly took the place of the March Hare. The Hatter was the only one who got any advantage from the change : and Alice was a good deal worse off than before, as the March Hare had just upset the milk-jug into his plate.

Alice did not wish to offend the Dormouse again, so she began very cautiously : " But I don't understand. Where did they draw the treacle from ? "

" You can draw water out of a water-well," said the Hatter ; " so I should think you could draw treacle out of a treacle-well —eh, stupid ? "

" But they were *in* the well," Alice said to the Dormouse, not choosing to notice this last remark.

" Of course they were," said the Dormouse ; " ——well in."

This answer so confused poor Alice, that she let the Dormouse go on for some time without interrupting it.

" They were learning to draw," the Dormouse went on, yawning and rubbing its eyes, for it was getting very sleepy ; " and they drew all manner of things—everything that begins with an M——"

" Why with an M ? " said Alice.

" Why not ? " said the March Hare.

Alice was silent.

The Dormouse had closed its eyes by this time, and was going off into a doze ; but, on being pinched by the Hatter, it woke up again with a little shriek, and went on : " ——that begins with an M, such as mouse-traps, and the moon, and memory, and muchness—you know you say things are ' much of a muchness '—did you ever see such a thing as a drawing of a muchness ? "

" Really, now you ask me," said Alice, very much confused, " I don't think——"

" Then you shouldn't talk," said the Hatter.

This piece of rudeness was more than Alice could bear : she got up in great disgust, and walked off ; the Dormouse fell asleep instantly, and neither of the others took the least notice of her going, though she looked back once or twice, half hoping that they would call after her : the last time she saw them, they were trying to put the Dormouse into the teapot.

" At any rate I'll never go *there* again ! " said Alice as she picked her way through the wood. " It's the stupidest tea-party I ever was at in all my life ! "

(*Alice's Adventures in Wonderland.*)

WILLIAM MORRIS (1834–1896)
THE HOLLOW LAND

WHEN I woke I was on the bank of that river ; the flooded waters went hurrying past me ; no boat on them now ; from the river the ground went up in gentle slopes till it grew a great hill, and there, on that hill-top,—Yes, I might forget many things, almost everything, but not that, not the old castle of my fathers up among the hills, its towers blackened now and shattered, yet still no enemy's banner waved from it.

So I said I would go and die there ; and at this thought I drew my sword, which yet hung about my neck, and shook it in the air till the true steel quivered ; then began to pace towards the castle. I was quite naked, no rag about me ; I took no heed of that, only thanking God that my sword was left, and so toiled up the hill. I entered the castle soon by the outer court ; I knew the way so well, that I did not lift my eyes from the ground, but walked on over the lowered drawbridge through the unguarded gates, and stood in the great hall at last—my father's hall—as bare of everything but my sword as when I came into the world fifty years before : I had as little clothes, as little wealth, less memory and thought, I verily believe, than then.

So I lifted up my eyes and gazed ; no glass in the windows, no hangings on the walls ; the vaulting yet held good throughout, but seemed to be going; the mortar had fallen out from between the stones, and grass and fern grew in the joints; the marble pavement was in some places gone, and water stood about in puddles, though one scarce knew how it had got there.

No hangings on the walls—no; yet, strange to say, instead of them, the walls blazed from end to end with scarlet paintings, only striped across with green damp-marks in many places, some falling bodily from the wall, the plaster hanging down with the fading colour on it.

In all of them, except for the shadows and the faces of the figures, there was scarce any colour but scarlet and yellow; here and there it seemed the painter, whoever it was, had tried to make his trees or his grass green, but it would not do; some ghastly thoughts must have filled his head, for all the green went presently into yellow, out-sweeping through the picture dismally. But the faces were painted to the very life, or it seemed so;—there were only five of them, however, that were very marked or came much in the foreground; and four of these I knew well, though I did not then remember the names of those that had borne them. They were Red Harald, Swanhilda, Arnald, and myself. The fifth I did not know; it was a woman's, and very beautiful.

Then I saw that in some parts a small penthouse roof had been built over the paintings, to keep them from the weather. Near one of these stood a man painting, clothed in red, with stripes of yellow and black: then I knew that it was the same man who had saved me from drowning by spearing me through the shoulder; so I went up to him, and saw furthermore that he was girt with a heavy sword.

He turned round when he saw me coming, and asked me fiercely what I did there.

I asked why he was painting in my castle.

Thereupon, with that same grim smile widening his mouth as heretofore, he said, "I paint God's judgments."

And as he spoke, he rattled the sword in his scabbard; but I said:

"Well, then, you paint them very badly. Listen; I know God's judgments much better than you do. See now; I will teach you God's judgments, and you shall teach me painting."

While I spoke he still rattled his sword, and when I had done, shut his right eye tight, screwing his nose on one side; then said:

"You have got no clothes on, and may go to the devil! What do *you* know about God's judgments?"

"Well, they are not all yellow and red, at all events; you ought to know better."

He screamed out, "O you fool! yellow and red! Gold and blood, what do they make?"

"Well," I said; "what?"

"HELL!" And, coming close up to me, he struck me with his open hand in the face, so that the colour with which his hand was smeared was dabbed about my face. The blow almost threw me down; and, while I staggered, he rushed at me furiously with his sword. Perhaps it was good for me that I had got no clothes on; for, being utterly unencumbered, I leapt this way and that, and avoided his fierce, eager strokes till I could collect myself somewhat; while he had a heavy scarlet cloak on that trailed on the ground, and which he often trod on, so that he stumbled.

He very nearly slew me during the first few minutes, for it was not strange that, together with other matters, I should have forgotten the art of fence: but yet, as I went on, and sometimes bounded about the hall under the whizzing of his sword, as he rested sometimes, leaning on it, as the point sometimes touched my bare flesh, nay, once as the whole sword fell flatlings on my head and made my eyes start out, I remembered the old joy that I used to have, and the *swy, swy,* of the sharp edge, as one gazed between one's horse's ears; moreover, at last, one fierce swift stroke, just touching me below the throat, tore up the skin all down my body, and fell heavy on my thigh, so that I drew my breath in and turned white; then first, as I swung my sword round my head, our blades met, oh! to hear that *tchink* again! and I felt the notch my sword made in his, and swung out at him; but he guarded it and returned on me; I guarded right and left, and grew warm, and opened my mouth to shout, but knew not what to say; and our sword points fell on the floor together: then, when we had panted awhile, I wiped from my face the blood that had been dashed over it, shook my sword and cut at him, then we spun round and round in a mad waltz to the measured music of our meeting swords, and sometimes either wounded the other somewhat, but not much, till I beat down his sword on to his head, that he fell grovelling, but not cut through. Verily, thereupon my lips opened mightily with "Mary rings."

Then, when he had gotten to his feet, I went at him again, he staggering back, guarding wildly; I cut at his head; he put his sword up confusedly, so I fitted both hands to my hilt, and smote him mightily under the arm: then his shriek mingled with my shout, made a strange sound together; he rolled over and over, dead, as I thought.

I walked about the hall in great exultation at first, striking my sword point on the floor every now and then, till I grew faint with loss of blood; then I went to my enemy and stripped off some of his clothes to bind up my wounds withal; afterwards I found in a corner bread and wine, and I eat and drank thereof.

Then I went back to him, and looked, and a thought struck me, and I took some of his paints and brushes, and kneeling down, painted his face thus, with stripes of yellow and red, crossing each other at right angles; and in each of the squares so made I put a spot of black, after the manner of the painted letters in the prayer-books and romances when they are ornamented.

So I stood back as painters use, folded my arms, and admired my own handiwork. Yet there struck me as being something so utterly doleful in the man's white face, and the blood running all about him, and washing off the stains of paint from his face and hands, and splashed clothes, that my heart misgave me, and I hoped that he was not dead; I took some water from a vessel he had been using for his painting, and, kneeling, washed his face.

Was it some resemblance to my father's dead face, which I had seen when I was young, that made me pity him? I laid my hand upon his heart, and felt it beating feebly; so I lifted him up gently, and carried him towards a heap of straw that he seemed used to lie upon; there I stripped him and looked to his wounds, and used leech-craft, the memory of which God gave me for this purpose, I suppose, and within seven days I found that he would not die.

Afterwards, as I wandered about the castle, I came to a room in one of the upper stories, that had still the roof on, and windows in it with painted glass, and there I found green raiment and swords and armour, and I clothed myself.

So when he got well I asked him what his name was, and he me, and we both of us said, "truly I know not." Then said I, "but we must call each other some name, even as men call days."

"Call me Swerker," he said, "some priest I knew once had that name."

"And me Wulf," said I, "though wherefore I know not."

Then he said:

"Wull, I will teach you painting now, come and learn."

Then I tried to learn painting till I thought I should die, but at last learned it through very much pain and grief.

And, as the years went on and we grew old and grey, we painted purple pictures and green ones instead of the scarlet and yellow, so that the walls looked altered, and always we painted God's judgments.

And we would sit in the sunset and watch them with the golden light changing them, as we yet hoped God would change both us and our works.

Often too we would sit outside the walls and look at the trees and sky, and the ways of the few men and women we saw; therefrom sometimes befell adventures.

Once there went past a great funeral of some king going to his own country, not as he had hoped to go, but stiff and colourless, spices filling up the place of his heart.

And first went by very many knights, with long bright hauberks on, that fell down before their knees as they rode, and they all had tilting-helms on with the same crest, so that their faces were quite hidden: and this crest was two hands clasped together tightly as though they were the hands of one praying forgiveness from the one he loves best; and the crest was wrought in gold.

Moreover, they had on over their hauberks surcoats which were half scarlet and half purple, strewn about with golden stars.

Also long lances, that had forked knights'-pennons, half purple and half scarlet, strewn with golden stars.

And these went by with no sound but the fall of their horse-hoofs.

And they went slowly, so slowly that we counted them all, five thousand five hundred and fifty-five.

Then went by many fair maidens whose hair was loose and yellow, and who were all clad in green raiment ungirded, and shod with golden shoes.

These also we counted, being five hundred; moreover some of the outermost of them, viz., one maiden to every twenty, had long silver trumpets, which they swung out to right and left, blowing them, and their sound was very sad.

Then many priests, and bishops, and abbots, who wore white albs and golden copes over them; and they all sang together mournfully, " *Propter amnen Babylonis ;* " and these were three hundred.

After that came a great knot of the Lords, who wore tilting helmets and surcoats emblazoned with each one his own device; only each had in his hand a small staff two feet long whereon was a pennon of scarlet and purple. These also were three hundred.

And in the midst of these was a great car hung down to the ground with purple, drawn by grey horses whose trappings were half scarlet, half purple.

And on this car lay the King, whose head and hands were bare; and he had on him a surcoat, half purple and half scarlet, strewn with golden stars.

And his head rested on a tilting helmet, whose crest was the hands of one praying passionately for forgiveness.

But his own hands lay by his side as if he had just fallen asleep.

And all about the car were little banners, half purple and half scarlet, strewn with golden stars.

Then the King, who counted but as one, went by also.

And after him came again many maidens clad in ungirt white raiment strewn with scarlet flowers, and their hair was loose and yellow and their feet bare : and, except for the falling of their feet and the rustle of the wind through their raiment, they went past quite silently. These also were five hundred.

Then lastly came many young knights with long bright hauberks falling over their knees as they rode, and surcoats, half scarlet and half purple, strewn with golden stars; they bore long lances with forked pennons which were half purple, half scarlet, strewn with golden stars; their heads and their hands were bare, but they bore shields, each one of them, which were of bright steel wrought cunningly in the midst with that bearing of the two hands of one who prays for forgiveness; which was done in gold. These were but five hundred.

Then they all went by winding up and up the hill roads, and, when the last of them had departed out of our sight, we put down our heads and wept, and I said, " Sing us one of the songs of the Hollow Land."

Then he whom I had called Swerker put his hand into his bosom, and slowly drew out a long, long tress of black hair, and laid it on his knee and smoothed it, weeping on it : So then I left him there and went and armed myself, and brought armour for him.

And then came back to him and threw the armour down so that it clanged, and said :

" Oh ! Harald, let us go ! "

He did not seem surprised that I called him by the right

name, but rose and armed himself, and then he looked a good knight; so we set forth.

And in a turn of the long road we came suddenly upon a most fair woman, clothed in scarlet, who sat and sobbed, holding her face between her hands, and her hair was very black.

And when Harald saw her, he stood and gazed at her for long through the bars of his helmet, then suddenly turned, and said :

"Florian, I must stop here; do you go on to the Hollow Land. Farewell."

"Farewell." And then I went on, never turning back, and him I never saw more.

And so I went on, quite lonely, but happy, till I had reached the Hollow Land.

Into which I let myself down most carefully, by the jutting rocks and bushes and strange trailing flowers, and there lay down and fell asleep.

*   *   *   *   *

And I was waked by some one singing; I felt very happy; I felt young again; I had fair delicate raiment on, my sword was gone, and my armour; I tried to think where I was, and could not for my happiness; I tried to listen to the words of the song. Nothing, only an old echo in my ears, only all manner of strange scenes from my wretched past life before my eyes in a dim, far-off manner : then at last, slowly, without effort, I heard what she sang.

                "Christ keep the Hollow Land
                        All the summer-tide ;
                    Still we cannot understand
                        Where the waters glide ;

                    Only dimly seeing them
                        Coldly slipping through
                Many green-lipp'd cavern mouths,
                    Where the hills are blue."

"Then," she said, "come now and look for it, love, a hollow city in the Hollow Land."

I kissed Margaret, and we went.

Through the golden streets under the purple shadows of the houses we went, and the slow fanning backward and forward of the many-coloured banners cooled us : we two alone; there was no one with us, no soul will ever be able to tell what we said, how we looked.

At last we came to a fair palace, cloistered off in the old time, before the city grew golden from the din and hubbub of traffic; those who dwelt there in the old ungolden times had had their own joys, their own sorrows, apart from the joys and sorrows of the multitude : so, in like manner, was it now cloistered off from the eager leaning and brotherhood of the golden dwellings : so now it had its own gaiety, its own solemnity, apart from theirs ; unchanged, unchangeable, were its marble walls, whatever else changed about it.

We stopped before the gates and trembled, and clasped each other closer ; for there among the marble leafage and tendrils that were round and under and over the archway that held the golden valves, were wrought two figures of a man and woman, winged and garlanded, whose raiment flashed with stars ; and their faces were like faces we had seen or half seen in some dream long and long and long ago, so that we trembled with awe and delight ; and I turned, and seeing Margaret, saw that her face was that face seen or half seen long and long and long ago : and in the shining of her eyes I saw that other face, seen in that way and no other long and long and long ago—my face.

And then we walked together toward the golden gates, and opened them, and no man gainsaid us.

And before us lay a great space of flowers.

(The Hollow Land.)

LADY RITCHIE (ANNA ISABELLA THACKERAY)
(1837–1919)

REINE

CATHERINE found herself transported as if by magic, from the long dreary brick-enclosed hours to a charming world, where vine garlands were wreathing under cloudless skies. There was at once more light, more sound, more sentiment and drowsy peace in it than she had ever known in all her life before. She awakened to a dazzle streaming through the vine round her window, and flickering upon the red brick floor of her little room ; to a glitter, to a cheerful vibration of noises. Some one would bring her a little roll and a cup of steaming coffee, and then, when she was dressed, the children would come tapping and fumbling at her door. Little Henri de Tracey sometimes attempted a réveillé upon his horn, which would be instantly suppressed by a voice outside. Nanine, who was nine years old, and had elegant little manners like a lady, would wish Catherine good-morning; and Madelaine, who was four and "très raisonnable" Suzanne her nurse said, consented to be kissed through the iron-work balusters of the staircase.

The children would lead the way through the great dining-room, where Baptiste was hopping about on one leg, polishing the shining floor, across the terrace, through green avenues and gardens, looking a little neglected, but fresh with dew, and luxuriant with flowers and fruit-trees. Pumpkins, carnations, and roses were growing between vine-clad walls. There were bees, and there was an old stone well full of deep water, like Jocelyn's well—

> Dont la châine rouillée a poli la marqelle,
> Et qu'une vigne étreint de sa verte dentelle.

From the terrace there was a distant view of the sea—of the blue line of the horizon flashing beyond the golden cornfields.

One morning Nanine said, " We are to go to the Ferme, Miss George, to-day, with a commission from grandmamma. We will go out at the door in the Potager, if you'd not mind and come back the other way." It was all the same to Catherine, who followed her little conductors through the kitchen-garden door out into the open country, and along the path skirting the cornfields which spread to the sea. Henri went first, blowing his horn, Nanine loitered to pick the poppies and bleu-bleus as she called the corn-flowers, Madelaine trotted by Catherine, holding her hand. It was like the nursery rhyme. Miss George thought of the little boy blue, only the sheep were wanting.

From outside the farm at Tracy still looks more like a ruined fortress than a farm where milk is sold in cans and little pats of butter prepared, and eggs counted out in dozens, and pigs fattened for the market. All over Normandy you come upon these fortified abbayes, built for praying and fighting once, and ruined now, and turned to different uses. It is like Samson's riddle to see the carcase of the lions with honey flowing from them. " Out of the eater came forth meat; out of the strong came forth sweetness." There is a great archway at the farm at Tracy, with heavy wooden doors studded with nails. There is rust in plenty, and part of a moat still remaining. The hay is stacked in what was a chapel once ; the yellow trusses are hanging through the crumbling flamboyant east window. There is a tall watch-tower to which a pigeon-cote has been affixed, and low cloisters that are turned into out-houses and kitchens. The white walls tell a story of penance and fierce battlings which are over now, as far as they are concerned. The great harvest waggons pass through the archway without unloading ; so do the cows at milking time. Cocks and hens are pecketing the fallen grains, the pigeons circle overhead suddenly white against the sky.

As the children and Miss George pushed open the heavy doors and came into the wide sunny court, a figure descended the stone steps leading from the strong tower where the apples are kept. It was Reine in her white coiffe, who advanced with deliberate footsteps, carrying an earthenware pan under her arm, and who stood waiting in the middle of the great deserted-looking place until they should come up to her.

Catherine wondered whether all Normandy peasant girls were like this one. It was a princess keeping the cows. There she stood, straight, slender, vigorous; dressed in the Sunday dress of the women of those parts, with this difference, that instead of two plastered loops of hair like a doll's, a tawny ripple flowed under the lace of her cap and low over her arched brows. As for her eyes, they were quick dancing grey eyes, that looked black when she was angry—clouds and lightning somebody once told her they were, but the lightning became warm sunlight when she smiled upon those she liked. She smiled now, for Reine was a child-lover, and even little De Tracys were welcome as they came towards her with their bunches of flowers out of the fields, and the pretty strange lady following.

(*The Village on the Cliff.*)

WALTER HORATIO PATER (1839–1894)
The Way to Rome

The opening stage of his journey, through the firm, golden weather, for which he had lingered three days beyond the appointed time of starting—days brown with the first rains of autumn—brought him by the byways among the lower slopes of the Apennines of Luna, to the town of Luca, a station on the Cassian Way; travelling so far mainly on foot, while the baggage followed under the care of his attendants. He wore a broad felt hat, in fashion not unlike a more modern pilgrim's, the neat head projecting from the collar of his gray *pænula*, or travelling mantle, sewed closely together over the breast, but with its two sides folded up upon the shoulders, to leave the arms free in walking, and was altogether so trim and fresh, that, as he climbed the hill from Pisa, by the long steep lane through the olive-yards, and turned to gaze where he could just discern the cypresses of the old school garden, like two black lines down the yellow walls, a little child took possession of his hand, and looking up at him with entire confidence, paced on bravely at his side, for the mere pleasure of his company, to the spot where the road declined again into the valley beyond. From this point, leaving the servants behind, he surrendered himself, a willing subject, as he walked, to the impressions of the road, and was almost surprised, both at the suddenness with which evening came on, and the distance from his old home at which it found him.

And at the little town of Luca, he felt that indescribable sense of a welcoming in the mere outward appearance of things, which seems to mark out certain places for the special purpose of evening rest, and gives them always a peculiar amiability in retrospect. Under the deepening twilight, the rough-tiled roofs seem to huddle together side by side, like one continuous shelter over the whole township, spread low and broad above the snug sleeping-rooms within; and the place one sees for the first time, and must tarry in but for a night, breathes the very spirit of home. The cottagers lingered at their doors for a few minutes as the shadows grew larger, and went to rest early; though there was still a glow along the road through the shorn cornfields, and the birds were still awake about the crumbling gray heights of an old temple. So quiet and air-swept was the place, you could hardly tell where the country left off in it, and the field-paths became its streets. Next morning he must needs change the manner of his journey. The light baggage-waggon returned, and he proceeded now more quickly, travelling a stage or two by post, along the Cassian Way, where the figures and incidents of the great high-road seemed already to tell of the capital, the one centre to which all were hastening, or had lately bidden adieu. That *Way* lay through the heart of the old, mysterious and visionary country of Etruria; and what he knew of its strange religion of the dead, reinforced by the actual sight of the funeral houses scattered so plentifully among the dwelling-places of the living, revived in him for a while in all its strength, his old in-stinctive yearning towards those inhabitants of the shadowy land he had known in life. It seemed to him that he could half divine how time passed in those painted houses on the hillsides, among the gold and silver ornaments, the wrought armour and vestments, the drowsy and dead attendants; and the close consciousness of that vast population gave him no fear, but rather a sense of companionship, as he climbed the hills on foot behind the horses, through the genial afternoon.

The road, next day, passed below a town not less primitive it might seem, than its rocky perch—white rocks, that had long been glistening before him in the distance. Down the dewy paths the people were descending from it, to keep a holiday, high and low alike in rough, white-linen smocks. A homely old play was just begun in an open-air theatre, with seats hollowed out of the turf-grown slope. Marius caught the terrified expression of a child in its mother's arms, as it turned from the yawning mouth of a great mask, for refuge in her bosom. The way mounted, and descended again, down the steep street of another place, all resounding with the noise of metal under the hammer; for every house had its brazier's workshops, the bright objects of brass and copper gleaming, like lights in a cave, out of their dark roofs and corners. Around the anvils the children were watching the work, or ran to fetch water to the hissing, red-hot metal; and Marius too watched, as he took his hasty mid-day refreshment, a mess of chestnut-meal and cheese, while the swelling surface of a great copper water-vessel grew flowered all over with tiny petals under the skilful strokes. Towards dusk, a frantic woman at the roadside stood and cried out the words of some philter or malison, in verse, with weird motion of her hands, as the travellers passed, like a wild picture drawn from Virgil. . . .

But on the seventh evening there came a reaction in the cheerful flow of our traveller's thoughts, a reaction with which mere bodily fatigue, asserting itself at last over his curiosity, had much to do; and he fell into a mood known to all passably sentimental wayfarers, as night deepens again and again over their path, in which all journeying, from the known to the unknown, comes suddenly to figure as a mere foolish truancy—like a child's running away from home—with the feeling that one had best return at once even through the darkness. He had chosen to climb on foot, at his leisure, the long windings by which the road ascended to the place where that day's stage was to end, and found himself alone in the twilight, far behind the rest of his travelling companions. Would the last zigzag round and round those dark masses, half natural rock, half artificial sub-structure, ever bring him within the circuit of the walls above? It was now that a startling incident turned those misgivings almost into actual fear. From the steep slope a heavy mass of stone was detached, after some whisperings among the trees above his head, and rushing down through the stillness fell to pieces in a cloud of dust across the road just behind him, so that he felt the touch upon his heel. That was sufficient just then, to rouse out of its hiding-place his old vague fear of evil—of one's " enemies "—a distress, so much a matter of constitution with him, that at times it would seem that the best pleasures of life could but be snatched, as it were hastily, in one moment's forgetfulness of its dark besetting influence.

A sudden suspicion of hatred against him, of the nearness of "enemies," seemed all at once to alter the visible form of things, as with the child's hero, when he found the footprint on the sand of his peaceful dreamy island. His elaborate philosophy had not put beneath his feet the terror of mere bodily evil; much less of "inexorable fate, and the noise of greedy Acheron."

The resting-place to which he presently came, in the keen wholesome air of the market-place of the little hill town, was a pleasant contrast to that last effort of his journey. The room in which he sat down to supper, unlike the ordinary Roman inns at that day, was trim and sweet. The firelight danced cheerfully upon the polished, three-wicked *lucernæ* burning clearly with the best oil, upon the white-washed walls, and the bunches of scarlet carnations set in glass goblets. The white wine of the place put before him, of the true colour and flavour of the grape, and with a ring of delicate foam as it mounted in the cup, had a reviving edge or freshness he had found in no other wine. These things had relieved a little the melancholy of the hour before; and it was just then that he heard the voice of one, newly arrived at the inn, making his way to the upper floor—a youthful voice, with a reassuring clearness of note, which completed his cure.

He seemed to hear that voice again in dreams, uttering his name : then, awake in the full morning light and gazing from the window, saw the guest of the night before, a very honourable-looking youth, in the rich habit of a military knight, standing beside his horse, and already making preparations to depart. It happened that Marius, too, was to take that day's journey on horseback. Riding presently from the inn, he overtook Cornelius —of the Twelfth Legion—advancing carefully down the steep street; and before they had issued from the gates of *Urbs-vetus*, the two young men had broken into talk together. They were passing along the street of the goldsmiths; and Cornelius must needs enter one of the workshops for the repair of some button or link of his knightly trappings. Standing in the doorway, Marius watched the work, as he had watched the brazier's business a few days before, wondering most at the simplicity of its processes, a simplicity, however, on which only genius in that craft could have lighted. By what unguessed-at stroke of hand, for instance, had the grains of precious metal associated themselves with so daintily regular a roughness, over the surface of the little casket yonder? And the conversation which followed, hence arising, left the two travellers with sufficient interest in each other to insure an easy companionship for the remainder of their journey. In time to come, Marius was to depend very much on the preferences, the personal judgments, of the comrade who now laid his hand so brotherly on his shoulder, as they left the workshop.

(Marius the Epicurean.)

AUSTIN DOBSON (1840-1921)
GRAY'S LIBRARY

AMONG Gray's papers was one inscribed *Dialogue of Books*. The handwriting was that of his biographer Mason, but it was believed to be either by Gray or by West. There is a strong presumption that the author was Gray; and it is accordingly attributed to him in the Rev. D. C. Tovey's *Gray and his Friends*, where for the first time it was printed. It shows us the little great man (if it is accurately dated 1742, it must have been in the year of his fullest poetical activity) sitting tranquilly in his study chair, when he is " suddenly alarmed with a great hubbub of Tongues." He listens; and finds that his books are talking to one another. Madame de Sévigné is being what Mrs. Gamp would call " scrouded " by Aristotle, who replies to her compressed expostulations with all the brutality of a philosopher and a realist. Thereupon she appeals to her relative, the author of the *Histoire amoureuse des Gaules*. But the gallant M. Bussy-Rabutin, himself pining for an interchange of compliments with a neighbouring Catullus, is hopelessly penned in by a hulking edition of Strabo, and cannot possibly arrive to the assistance of his *belle Cousine*. Elsewhere La Bruyère comments upon the strange companions with whom Fate has acquainted him; and Locke observes, with a touch of temper, that *he* is associated with Ovid—and Ray the Naturalist![1] Virgil placidly quotes a line of his own poems; More, the Platonist, delivers himself of a neat little copy-book sentiment in praise of theological speculation; and great fat Dr. Cheyne huskily mutters his own adage, " Every man after forty is either a fool or a Physician." In another corner an ill-judged and irrelevant remark by Euclid, touching the dimensions of a point, brings down upon him the scorn both of Swift and Boileau, who clamour for the unconditional suppression of mathematics. (If there be nothing else, this in itself is almost sufficient to fix the authorship of the paper with Gray, whose hatred of mathematics was only equalled by that of Goldsmith.) Then a pert exclamation from a self-sufficient *Vade Mecum* provokes the owner of the library to so hearty an outburst of merriment that the startled tomes at once

[1] Ray's *Select Remains* with life by Derham, 1740, and many marginal notes by Gray, was recently in a London bookseller's catalogue

shrink back into "uncommunicating muteness." Laughter, it would seem, is as fatal to books as it was of old to the Coquecigrues.

Whether Gray's library ever again broke silence, his biographers have not related. But if his books were pressed for space while in his possession, they have since enjoyed ample opportunities for change of air and scene. When he died he left them, with his manuscripts, to Mason, who in turn bequeathed them to the poet's friend Stonehewer, from whom they passed, in part, to a relative, Mr. Bright of Skeffington Hall. At Mr. Bright's death, being family property, they were sold by auction. In August, 1851, they were again offered for sale; and three years later a number of them, which had apparently been reserved or bought in, once more came under the hammer at Sotheby and Wilkinson's. We have before us the catalogue of the second sale, which is naturally much fuller than that of 1854. What strikes one first is the care with which the majority of the volumes had been preserved by their later possessors. Many of the Note-Books were cushioned on velvet in special cases, while the more precious manuscripts had been skilfully inlaid, and bound in olive morocco with leather joints and linings of crimson silk. Like Prior, Gray must have preserved almost everything, " e'en from his boyish days." Among the books is *Plutarch's Lives*, with Dacier's notes, and the inscription, " E libris Thomæ Gray, Scholæ Eton : Alumn. Januar. 22, 1733 " —a year before he left for Cambridge; there is also his copy of Pope's *Iliad*, with autograph date a year earlier; there is a still more youthful (though perhaps more suspicious) possession— namely, three volumes of Dryden's *Virgil*, which were said to have actually belonged to Pope. *Ex libris A. Pope*, 1710, was written at the back of the portrait, and the same inscription recurred in each volume, though in the others some Vandal, probably a classmate, by adding a tail to the " P " and an " r " at the end, had turned the " Pope " into " Roper." Another of Gray's Eton books was a Waller, acquired in 1729, in which favourite poems and passages were underlined.

Of the classics he must have been a most unwearied and sedulous student. Euripides he read in the great folio of Joshua Barnes (Cantab. 1694), which is marked throughout by a special system of stars, inverted commas, and lines in red crayon; and his note-books bristle with extracts, neatly " arranged and digested," from all the best Greek authors—Sophocles, Thucydides, Xenophon, and even that Isocrates whom Goldsmith, from the critical altitudes of the *Monthly Review*, recommended him to study. At other "classics" he worked with equal diligence. His *Decameron*—the London *quarto* of 1725—was filled with *marginalia* identifying Boccaccio's sources of inspiration and principal imitators, while his Milton—the two-volume *duodecimo* of 1730–8—was interleaved, and annotated profusely with parallel passages drawn from the Bible, Dante, Shakespeare, and "the ancients." He had crowded Dugdale's *Baronage* with corrections and additions; he had largely "commented" the four folio volumes of Clarendon's *Rebellion*: and he had followed everywhere, with remorseless rectifications, the vagrant utterances of gossiping Gilbert Burnet. His patience, accuracy, research, were not less extraordinary than his odd, out-of-the-way knowledge. In the *Voyages de Bergeron (quarto)* that author says: "Mango Cham fut noié." No, comments Gray, decisively, "Muncacâ or Mangu-Khanw was not drowned, but in reality slain in China at the siege of Hochew in 1258." Which of us could oblige an inquisitive examiner with the biography of this Eastern potentate ! Which of us would not be reduced to "combining our information" (like the ingenious writer on Chinese Metaphysics) as to "mangoes" and "great Chams !"

But the two most interesting items of the Catalogue are yet unmentioned. One is the laborious collection of Manuscript Music that Gray compiled in Italy while frivolous Horace Walpole was eating iced fruits in a domino to the sound of a guitar. Zamperelli, Pergolesi, Arrigoni, Galuppi—he has ransacked them all, noting the school of the composer and the source of the piece selected—copying out religiously even the *Regole per l'Accompagnamento*. The other, which we who write have seen, is the famous Linnæus exhibited at Cambridge in 1885 by Mr. Ruskin. It is an interleaved copy of the *Systema Naturæ*, two volumes in three, covered as to their margins and added pages with wonderful minute notes in Latin, and illustrated by Gray himself with delicately finished pen-and-ink drawings of birds and insects. During the later part of his life these volumes, we are told, were continually on his table, and his absorbing love for natural history is everywhere manifested in his journals and pocket-books. When he is in the country, he classes the plants; when in town, he notes the skins of birds in shops; and when he eats whitebait at Greenwich, he straightway describes that dainty in the language of Tacitus. *Nullus odor nisi Piscis ; farina respersus, frixusque editur.*

Among the manuscripts proper of this collection, the place of honour belongs to one which Mason had labelled "Original Copy of the Elegy in a Country Church Yard." In addition to other variations from the printed text, erased words in this MS. showed that Cato stood originally for Hampden, and Tully and Cæsar for Milton and Cromwell—

> "Some mute inglorious Tully here may rest,
> Some Cæsar guiltless of his country's blood."

Here, too, were found those well-known but rejected "additional stanzas"—

> "The thoughtless World to Majesty may bow,
>   Exalt the brave, and idolize Success ;
> But more to Innocence their safety owe
>   Than Pow'r and Genius e'er conspir'd to bless.
>
> "And thou, who mindful of th' unhonour'd Dead,
>   Dost in these Notes their artless Tale relate,
> By Night and lonely Contemplation led
>   To linger in the gloomy Walks of Fate:
>
> "Hark ! how the sacred Calm that broods around,
>   Bids ev'ry fierce tumultuous Passion cease ;
> In still small Accents whisp'ring from the Ground.
>   A grateful Earnest of eternal Peace.
>
> "No more, with Reason and thyself at Strife,
>   Give anxious Cares and endless Wishes room ;
> But thro' the cool sequester'd Vale of Life
>   Pursue the silent Tenour of thy Doom." [1]

Another group of autographs in this volume had a special interest. The first was the notelet, or "spell," which Lady Schaub and Miss Speed left for Gray upon that first call when the nervous poet was "not at home" to his unexpected visitors. Next to this came the poem which the note elicited—that charming *Long Story*, with its echo of Matthew Prior, which has set their tune to so many later verse-spinners—

> "His bushy beard, and shoe-strings green.
>   His high-crown'd hat, and sattin-doublet,
> Mov'd the stout heart of England's Queen,
>   Tho' Pope and Spaniard could not trouble it."

Or again—

> "Who prowl'd the country far and near,
>   Bewitch'd the children of the peasants,
> Dried up the cows, and lam'd the deer,
>   And suck'd the eggs, and kill'd the pheasants."

---

[1] Another additional stanza, perhaps better known than the above, does not occur in the "Original Copy" of the Elegy, but in a later MS. at Pembroke College :—

> There scatter'd oft, the earliest of the Year,
>   By Hands unseen, are Show'rs of Violets found :
> The Red-breast loves to build, & warble there,
>   And little Footsteps lightly print the Ground."

Does not one seem to catch in this the coming cadences of another haunter of the " Poets' Walk " at Eton—of Winthrop Mackworth Praed; nay, an it be not *lèse majesté*, even of the lighter strains of Lord Tennyson himself ! To the *Long Story* followed Miss Speed's polite little acknowledgment with its invitation to dinner, and a few pages further on the verses beginning—

" Midst Beauty and Pleasure's gay Triumphs to languish,"

which Gray probably wrote for her—verses in which there is more of poetic ardour than genuine passion. Gray was not a marrying man. Yet one feels half sorry that he was never united to " Your oblig'd & obedient Henrietta Jane Speed," with her £30,000, her house in town, and her " china and old japan infinite." Still more to be resented is the freak of Fate which transformed the delightful Melissa of the *Long Story* into the berouged French Baronne who, sixteen years later, in company with her lap-dogs, piping bullfinch, and cockatoo, arrived from the Hague as Madame de la Perrière, and " Ministress at London."

The large *quarto* volume containing the above poems also included the first sketch in red crayon of Gray's unfinished Latin Poem, *De Principiis Cogitandi*, and a copy of the translation of the Ugolino episode from the *Inferno*, first printed by Mr. Gosse in 1884. Of the volumes of miscellaneous MSS. (where was to be found the *Dialogue of Books*) it is impossible to speak here. But among the rest comes a copy of the " Strawberry Hill " edition of the *Odes by Mr. Gray*—those Odes which at first he had so obstinately refused to annotate. " If a thing cannot be understood without notes," he told Walpole, " it had better not be understood at all." He must, however, have subsequently recanted, since this copy is filled with carefully written explanations of the allusions, and with indications of the sources of information. This book and the Note-books of Travel and Reading, with their methodical arrangement, their scrupulous accuracy, their unwearied pains, all help us to understand that leisurely fastidiousness, that hesitating dilettanteism, that endless preluding to unachieved performance, which make of the most literary, exact, and polished of poets, at the same time the least copious of writers. In his bust in the hall of Pembroke College, Mr. Hamo Thornycroft has happily succeeded in accentuating these qualities of refinement and intellectual precision. For the rest, is not Gray wholly contained in the vignette of Rogers to Mitford ? Gray, he says, saw little society in London. He had " a nice dinner from the Tavern brought to his lodgings, a glass or two of sweet wine, and (here is a delightful touch !) as he sipped it talked about great People." It needs but to fill the room with those scarlet martagon-lilies and double stocks for which he trudged daily to Covent Garden, to spread a meteorological register upon the writing-table, to open Gavin Douglas his *Palice of Honour* in the window-seat—and the picture is finished.

(From Eighteenth Century Vignettes)

THOMAS HARDY (1840–1928)

THE SHEEP-SHEARERS

IT was the first day of June, and the sheep-shearing season culminated, the landscape, even to the leanest pasture, being all health and colour. Every green was young, every pore was open, and every stalk was swollen with racing currents of juice. God was palpably present in the country, and the devil had gone with the world to town. Flossy catkins of the later kind, fern-sprouts like bishops' crooks, the square-headed moschatel, the odd cuckoo-pint,—like an apoplectic saint in a niche of malachite,—clear white ladies'-smocks, the tooth-wort, approximating to human flesh, the enchanter's nightshade, and the black-petalled doleful-bells, were among the quainter objects of the vegetable world in and about Weatherbury at this teeming time; and of the animal, the metamorphosed figures of Mr. Jan Coggan, the master-shearer; the second and third shearers, who travelled in the exercise of their calling, and do not require definition by name; Henery Fray the fourth shearer, Susan Tall's husband the fifth, Joseph Poorgrass the sixth, young Cain Ball as assistant-shearer, and Gabriel Oak as general supervisor. None of these were clothed to any extent worth mentioning, each appearing to have hit in the matter of raiment the decent mean between a high and low caste Hindoo. An angularity of lineament, and a fixity of facial machinery in general, proclaimed that serious work was the order of the day.

They sheared in the great barn, called for the nonce the Shearing-barn, which on ground-plan resembled a church with transepts. It not only emulated the form of the neighbouring church of the parish, but vied with it in antiquity. Whether the barn had ever formed one of a group of conventual buildings, nobody seemed to be aware ; no trace of such surroundings remained. The vast porches at the sides, lofty enough to admit a waggon laden to its highest with corn in the sheaf, were spanned by heavy-pointed arches of stone, broadly and boldly cut, whose very simplicity was the origin of a grandeur not apparent in erections where more ornament has been attempted. The dusky, filmed, chestnut roof, braced and tied in by huge collars, curves, and diagonals, was far nobler in design, because more wealthy in material, than nine-tenths of those in our modern churches. Along each side wall was a range of striding buttresses, throwing deep shadows on the spaces between them, which were perforated by lancet openings, combining in their proportions the precise requirements both of beauty and ventilation.

One could say about this barn, what could hardly be said of either the church or the castle, akin to it in age and style, that the purpose which had dictated its original erection was the same with that to which it was still applied. Unlike and superior to either of those two typical remnants of mediævalism, the old barn embodied practices which had suffered no mutilation at the hands of time. Here at least the spirit of the ancient builders was at one with the spirit of the modern beholder. Standing before this abraded pile, the eye regarded its present usage, the mind dwelt upon its past history, with a satisfied sense of functional continuity throughout—a feeling almost of gratitude, and quite of pride, at the permanence of the idea which had heaped it up. The fact that four centuries had neither proved it to be founded on a mistake, inspired any hatred of its purpose, nor given rise to any reaction that had battered it down, invested this simple grey effort of old minds with a repose, if not a grandeur, which a too curious reflection was apt to disturb in its ecclesiastical and military compeers. For once mediævalism and modernism had a common standpoint. The lanceolate windows, the time-eaten arch-stones and chamfers, the orientation of the axis, the misty chestnut work of the rafters, referred to no exploded fortifying art or worn-out religious creed. The defence and salvation of the body by daily bread is still a study, a religion, a desire.

To-day the large side doors were thrown open towards the sun to admit a bountiful light to the immediate spot of the shearers' operations, which was the wood threshing-floor in the centre, formed of thick oak, black with age and polished by the beating of flails for many generations, till it had grown as slippery and as rich in hue as the state-room floors of an Elizabethan mansion. Here the shearers knelt, the sun slanting in upon their bleached shirts, tanned arms, and the polished shears they flourished, causing them to bristle with a thousand rays strong enough to blind a weak-eyed man. Beneath them a captive sheep lay panting, quickening its pants as misgiving merged in terror, till it quivered like the hot landscape outside.

This picture of to-day with its frame of four hundred years ago did not produce that marked contrast between ancient and modern which is implied by the contrast of date. In comparison with cities Weatherbury was immutable. The citizen's *Then* is the rustic's *Now*. In London, twenty or thirty years ago are old times; in Paris ten years, or five; in Weatherbury three or four score years were included in the present, and nothing less than a century set a mark on its face or tone. Five decades hardly modified the cut of a gaiter, the embroidery of a smock-frock, by the breadth of a hair. Ten generations failed to alter the turn of a single phrase. In these Wessex nooks the busy out-sider's ancient times are only old; his old times are still new; his present is futurity.

So the barn was natural to the shearers, and the shearers were in harmony with the barn.

The spacious ends of the building, answering ecclesiastically to nave and chancel extremities, were fenced off with hurdles, the sheep being all collected in a crowd within these two en-closures; and in one angle a catching-pen was formed, in which three or four sheep were continuously kept ready for the shearers to seize without loss of time. In the background, mellowed by tawny shade, were the three women, Maryann Money, and Temperance and Soberness Miller, gathering up the fleeces and twisting ropes of wool with a wimble for tying them round. They were indifferently well assisted by the old maltster, who, when the malting season from October to April had passed, made himself useful upon any of the bordering farmsteads.

Behind all was Bathsheba, carefully watching the men to see that there was no cutting or wounding through carelessness, and that the animals were shorn close. Gabriel, who flitted and hovered under her bright eyes like a moth, did not shear continuously, half his time being spent in attending to the others and selecting the sheep for them. At the present moment he was engaged in handing round a mug of mild liquor, supplied from a barrel in the corner, and cut pieces of bread and cheese.

Bathsheba, after throwing a glance here, a caution there, and lecturing one of the younger operators who had allowed his last finished sheep to go off among the flock without re-stamping it with her initials, came again to Gabriel, as he put down the luncheon to drag a frightened ewe to his shear-station, flinging it over upon its back with a dexterous twist of the arm. He lopped off the tresses about its head, and opened up the neck and collar, his mistress quietly looking on.

" She blushes at the insult," murmured Bathsheba, watching the pink flush which arose and overspread the neck and shoulders of the ewe where they were left bare by the clicking shears—a flush which was enviable, for its delicacy, by many queens of coteries, and would have been creditable for its promptness, to any woman in the world.

Poor Gabriel's soul was fed with a luxury of content by having her over him, her eyes critically regarding his skilful shears, which apparently were going to gather up a piece of flesh at every close, and yet never did so. Like Guildenstern, Oak was happy in that he was not over happy. He had no wish to converse with her : that his bright lady and himself formed one group, exclusively their own, and containing no others in the world, was enough.

So the chatter was all on her side. There is a loquacity that tells nothing, which was Bathsheba's; and there is a silence which says much : that was Gabriel's. Full of this dim and temperate bliss, he went on to fling the ewe over upon her other side, covering her head with his knee, gradually running the shears line after line round the dewlap, thence about her flank and back, and finishing over the tail.

" Well done, and done quickly ! " said Bathsheba, looking at her watch as the last snip resounded.

" How long, miss ? " said Gabriel, wiping his brow.

" Three and twenty minutes and a half since you took the first lock from her forehead. It is the first time that I have ever seen one done in less than half-an-hour."

The clean, sleek creature arose from its fleece—how perfectly like Aphrodite rising from the foam should have been seen to be realized—looking startled and shy at the loss of its garment, which lay on the floor in one soft cloud, united throughout, the portion visible being the inner surface only, which, never before exposed, was white as snow, and without flaw or blemish of the minutest kind.

" Cain Ball ! "

" Yes, Mister Oak; here I be ! "

Cainy now runs forward with the tar-pot. " B. E." is newly stamped upon the shorn skin, and away the simple dam leaps, panting, over the board into the shirtless flock outside. Then up comes Maryann; throws the loose locks into the middle of the fleece, rolls it up, and carries it into the background as three-and-a-half pounds of unadulterated warmth for the winter enjoyment of persons unknown and far away, who will, however, never experience the superlative comfort derivable from the wool as it here exists, new and pure—before the unctuousness of its nature whilst in a living state has dried, stiffened, and been washed out—rendering it just now as superior to anything *woollen* as cream is superior to milk-and-water.

*   *   *   *   *   *

For the shearing-supper a long table was placed on the grass-plot beside the house, the end of the table being thrust over the sill of the wide parlour window and a foot or two into the room. Miss Everdene sat inside the window, facing down the table. She was thus at the head without mingling with the men.

This evening Bathsheba was unusually excited, her red cheeks and lips contrasting lustrously with the mazy skeins of her shadowy hair. She seemed to expect assistance, and the seat at the bottom of the table was at her request left vacant until after they had begun the meal. She then asked Gabriel to take the place and the duties appertaining to that end, which he did with great readiness.

At this moment Mr. Boldwood came in at the gate, and crossed the green to Bathsheba at the window. He apologized for his lateness : his arrival was evidently by arrangement.

"Gabriel," said she, "will you move again, please, and let Mr. Boldwood come there?"

Oak moved in silence back to his original seat.

The gentleman-farmer was dressed in cheerful style, in a new coat and white waistcoat, quite contrasting with his usual sober suits of grey. Inwardly, too, he was blithe, and consequently chatty to an exceptional degree. So also was Bathsheba now that he had come, though the uninvited presence of Pennyways, the bailiff who had been dismissed for theft, disturbed her equanimity for a while.

Supper being ended, Coggan began on his own private account, without reference to listeners :—

> "I've lost my love, and I care not,
> I've lost my love, and I care not ;
> I shall soon have another
> That's better than t'other ;
> I've lost my love, and I care not."

This lyric, when concluded, was received with a silently appreciative gaze at the table, implying that the performance, like a work by those established authors who are independent of notices in the papers, was a well-known delight which required no applause.

"Now, Master Poorgrass, your song!" said Coggan.

"I be all but in liquor, and the gift is wanting in me," said Joseph, diminishing himself.

"Nonsense; wou'st never be so ungrateful, Joseph—never!" said Coggan, expressing hurt feelings by an inflection of voice. "And mistress is looking hard at ye, as much as to say, 'Sing at once, Joseph Poorgrass.'"

"Faith, so she is; well, I must suffer it! . . . Just eye my features, and see if the tell-tale blood overheats me much, neighbours?"

"No, yer blushes be quite reasonable," said Coggan.

"I always tries to keep my colours from rising when a beauty's eyes get fixed on me," said Joseph, diffidently; "but if so be 'tis willed they do, they must."

"Now, Joseph, your song, please," said Bathsheba, from the window.

"Well, really, ma'am," he replied, in a yielding tone, "I don't know what to say. It would be a poor plain ballet of my own composure."

"Hear, hear!" said the supper-party.

Poorgrass, thus assured, trilled forth a flickering yet commendable piece of sentiment, the tune of which consisted of the key-note and another, the latter being the sound chiefly dwelt upon. This was so successful that he rashly plunged into a second in the same breath, after a few false starts :—

> "I sow'-ed th'-e . . . .
> I sow'-ed . . . .
> I sow'-ed the'-e seeds' of' love',
> I-it was' all' i'-in the'-e spring',
> I-in A'-pril', Ma'-ay, a'-nd sun'-ny' June',
> When sma'-all bi'-irds they' do' sing."

"Well put out of hand," said Coggan, at the end of the verse. "'They do sing,'" was a very taking paragraph."

"Ay; and there was a pretty place at 'seeds of love,' and 'twas well heaved out. Though 'love' is a nasty high corner when a man's voice is getting crazed. Next verse, Master Poorgrass."

But during this rendering young Bob Coggan exhibited one of those anomalies which will afflict little people when other persons are particularly serious : in trying to check his laughter, he pushed down his throat as much of the tablecloth as he could get hold of, when, after continuing hermetically sealed for a short time, his mirth burst out through his nose. Joseph perceived it, and with hectic cheeks of indignation instantly ceased singing. Coggan boxed Bob's ears immediately.

" Go on, Joseph—go on, and never mind the young scamp," said Coggan. " 'Tis a very catching ballet. Now then again —the next bar; I'll help ye to flourish up the shrill notes where yer wind is rather wheezy :—

> " Oh the wi'-il-lo'-ow tree' will' twist',
> And the wil'-low tre'-ee wi'-ill twine'."

But the singer could not be set going again. Bob Coggan was sent home for his ill manners, and tranquillity was restored by Jacob Smallbury, who volunteered a ballad as inclusive and interminable as that with which the worthy old toper Silenus amused on a similar occasion the swains Chromis and Mnasylus, and other jolly dogs of his day.

It was still the beaming time of evening, though night was stealthily making itself visible low down upon the ground, the western lines of light raking the earth without alighting upon it to any extent, or illuminating the dead levels at all. The sun had crept round the tree as a last effort before death, and then began to sink, the shearers' lower parts becoming steeped in embrowning twilight, whilst their heads and shoulders were still enjoying day, touched with a yellow of self-sustained brilliancy that seemed rather inherent than acquired.

The sun went down in an ochreous mist, but they sat, and talked on, and grew as merry as the gods in Homer's heaven. Bathsheba still remained enthroned inside the window, and occupied herself in knitting, from which she sometimes looked up to view the fading scene outside. The slow twilight expanded and enveloped them completely before the signs of moving were shown.

(Far from the Madding Crowd.)

ANDREW LANG (1844–1912)

To Master Geoffrey Chaucer

SIR,—I read of late the book of a learned clerk who said of you, that you were the most English of all poets, and the least read by Englishmen. Now Englishmen and even Englishwomen, read two Knights cleped Sir Edwin and Sir Lewis. The second is a Knight of the Welsh Marches, but the first dwelt hard by Fleet Street, wherein men say that you broke the head of a Gray Friar, how truly I know not. They take much delight also in a good Squire, Master Kipling, who has been in Inde and other far lands, and prays oft to St. George that he will help England, and put a stout heart into her men-at-arms. That Englishmen read not much in your books is no marvel, for, *imprimis*, the fashion of our speech is altered, and they neither know what your words mean, nor can they readily understand the letters of your spelling to-day. For consider, fair sir, in your timeless Paradise, and eternity of joy, that five hundred mortal years of time have passed since you wrote,

> " And for ther is so gret diversite
> In Englissh, and in writing of our tonge
> So prey to God that none miswrite thee
> Nor thee mismetre for defaulte of tonge !
> And, red whereso thou be, or elles songe,
> That thou be understonde God Biseche ! "

But you be not understonde—though your speech is plain English—because of the diversity of writing. Our manner of spelling is changed. To-day, I read the letter of a Queen, Dame Margaret of Scotland, to her brother Henry, the Eighth of that name ; she subscribed herself his loving " cystyr." We are now in use to write " sister," and as your Englishman is not quick-brained, he cannot guess what " cystyr " should signify. Consider then, Sir, how we shall read these verses of yours concerning Cressida and her love, which I write just as I find them in a book of your poems, that I bought for three marks,

> " And whan that she was comen into halle,
> ' Now em,' quod she, ' we wol go dine anon ! '
> And gan some of her wommen for to calle, (1172),
> And streight into her chaumbre gan she gon ;
> But of her bisinesse this was oon (1174)
> Amonges othre thinges, out of drede,
> Full prively this lettre for to reade.
>
> Avised word by word in every line,
> And fond no lak, she thoughte he coulde good,
> And up it putte, and wente her into dine ;
> But Pandarus, that in a study stood,
> Or he was war, she took him by the hood (1811)
> And seide ' Ye were caught or that ye wiste ! '
> ' I vouche sauf ! ' quod he, ' Do what you liste ! ' "

Hereto the learned add the following elucidations—

(1172) *for to*, so J. G. : a2 Cx. omit ; H4 H5 *in to* ; R *gan she* ; y8 *to her*.

(1174) *lisinesse*. Cp. *bisinesses*.

(1181) *him* by 3 omit ; R *tho*

Here you paint for us the prettiest picture of the prettiest maid, catching her uncle by the hood while he muses, and thrusting the prettiest face into it. But think you that your Englishman understands a word of it, or of these commentaries, " D, y3 omit," and the like, more akin to the cunning of the Paynim in that magic art called *Al Gebra*, than any Christian speech? No, sir, this is matter too hard for him, and indeed I know not nor care, what the crabbed commentaries may signify.

For this is the second thing which hinders men from reading you, first, the hardness of the old words (though simple enough to him that carefully considers them), and, next, the craft of the learned, who sprinkle dots and accents about, like a cook with her pepper-caster. For, Sir, you are an author that feeds many a learned man, almost as the ancient Greeks and Romans do, for we read neither the ancients nor you, but we pay the learned to write about you and them. Yet, marry, what they write we read not, for it is as dry as sawdust, also much of it is made in Almayne, and is brought hither without paying dues and customs. Yet, if one be not too hurried up and down, as many now are, to sit in a nook with your Tale of Troilus, his love and broken heart, is as pleasant as to lie beneath the hawthorn bough, where the clear brook flows by our feet, and the thrushes carol in May. What I do love is to meet your memories of old poets, as here,

> " The swalwe Proigne, with a sorwful lay (64)
> Whan morwe com gan make her waymentinge
> Why she forshapen was ; and evere lay
> Pandare a-bedde, half in a slomberinge,
> Til she so nigh him made her cheteringe
> How Tereus gan forth his suster take, (69)
> That with the noise of her he gan awake."

The learned clerk adds to make all clear—

(64) *Proigne*. See L. G. W., vii.
(69) *Tereus*, so H4 R Cx. ; a2 *Thereus* ; J. *Tereux* ; y *Tireux*.

For this verse of yours minds me how Rufinus bade the swallow cease her singing in the dawn, and let him sleep and forget the cruel Rhodocleia.

For this reason, methinks, you old poets are dear, because you tell of life and men's hearts, ever the same, whether Penelope complained upon the nightingale in days when Israel was yet in Egypt, or Rufinus heard the swallows cry, or *you* speak of the throstles, or Tennyson of the " pipe of half-awakened birds " as if all the ages were but one, and ever the birds chanting, and man setting the thought of his heart to their unchanging music. Time alters our speech and manners and habit, but never alters our hearts, or the birds' song. This, also, is a delight in you, that you marked not the change in these little things of the outside and appearance, as of arms and dress, but Troilus rides back from battle into Troy, like a knight who has kept the barriers below the walls of Orléans or Compiégne, and does not drive in a chariot, as was his manner while he lived.

> " So lik a man of armes and a knight,
> He was to sen, fulfil'd of heigh prowesse !
> For bothe he hadde a body and a might
> To don that thing, as well as hardinesse ;
> And ek to sen him in his gere him dresse,
> So fressh, so yong, so weldy seemed he
> It was an hevene upon him for to see !
>
> His helm to-hewen was in twenty places,
> That by a tissu heng his bak bihinde ;
> His sheld to-dasshed was with swerdes and maces,
> In which men mighte many an arwe finde
> That Thirled hadde horn and nerf and rinde ;
> And ay the peple cri'de, ' Her com'th our joye !
> And next his brother, holder up of Troye ! ' "

No maker, methinks, has sung so well as you the joyful surprise of two lovers brought together beyond hope :

> " O blissful night, of hem so longe y-sought,
> How blithe unto hem bothe two thou were !
> Why n'had I swich oon with my soule y-bought !
> Ye, or the leeste joye that was there ?
> Awey, thou foule daunger and thou fere,
> And lat hem in this hevene blisse dwelle,
> That is so heigh that no man can it telle ! "

You could not endure to punish fair Cresseid for her perfidy, but the tale is told out, and the punishment meted by a Scottish clerk, Robert Henryson, who shows us how Cresseid became a leper among the leper folk, and how Troilus, riding back once more from battle into Troy, saw her, and knew her not in her altered guise—

> " And with ane blenk it come into his thocht
> That he sumtyme hir face befoir had sene.
>
> " Ane spark of lufe than till his hert culd spring,
> And kendlit all his bodie in ane fyre
> With hait fevir ane sweit and trimbilling
> Him tuik, quhill he was reddie to expyre ;
> To beir his scheild, his breit began to tyre ;
> Within ane quhyle he changit mony hew
> And nevertheless not ane ane uther knew.
>
> " For knichtlie pietie and memoriall
> Of fair Cresseid, ane gyrdill can he tak,
> Ane purs of gold and mony gay jowall,

And in the skirt of Cresseid doun can swak ;
Than raid away, and not ane word he spak.
Pensive in hart, quhill he come to the toun,
And for greit cair oft syis almaist fell doun."

Surely if yours be the sweetest first meeting of young lovers,
Master Henryson's is the saddest last meeting of old lovers
parted, and shamed and smitten over hard by change of fortune
and stroke of time. Nothing of yours is so bitter and true, and
nothing of his so beautiful : thus poet helps poet, though you
are remembered, and the solitary of the Dunfermline cloister
is forgotten. For you, Sir, are the father of your country's
makers, from Edmund Spencer onwards, and you are the father
of the poets of my own land, Henryson and Dunbar, and the
best of them, the crowned singer, the only King of all the
poets in Paradise, King James.

From you they all came, but you are far greater than all of
them, in music and in mirth, in tenderness and laughter, and
knowledge of the hearts and ways of women and men. Humour
and beauty are both in your gift, as in the gift of no other but
the lord of all worlds, all knowledge, all heights and depths,
Master Shakespeare. Neither the deep places nor the high
places were trodden by you, but the middle path of life, whereby
men ride on pilgrimage or about their business, with telling of
amorous or sad tales, and pleasure in wine and in meat, flowers,
and the sun and the birds' song. So they rode to Canterbury,
Knight and Monk, and Reeve and Nun. Knights we have still,
(as witness Sir Lewis aforesaid), but " at mortal battles they
have " *not* " been fifteen." A few Nuns we may see, but
never a pretty Prioress, and a Mammoth is not more extinct
than the wanton merry Frere and the Pardoner. Time may
bring wisdom, but, for all that I can see men were wiser in
merry England, with pretty Prioresses and the Pardoners and
Freres, than in moody England, where we and our wisdom
speed by steam under black smoke, beside poisoned rivers.
Master, I see not that we have bettered the world, since the
Miller told his tale, though we have scattered the bones of
St. Thomas, and the Frere's occupation is gone with the plough-
men's tabors. In your world were room enough, and pure
light, clear air, colour, variety, and the crown of all (when
Wat Tyler was not up) content. How, prithee, have we bettered
the world by abjuring the Saints and robbing the monks, and
teaching the ploughman to read the ribald newspapers ? Indeed,
Sir, we have nothing left of your age, but the Clerks of Oxenford,
that own " but litel gold in cofre," and of " study take moost

cure and moost hede." It is an old Clerk of Oxenford and one
" that is not right fat I undertake,"

" But lookes holwe and thereto soberly"

who bids Geoffrey Chaucer hail and goodbye.

(New and Old Letters to Dead Authors.)

RICHARD JEFFERIES (1848–1887)

OUT OF DOORS IN FEBRUARY

THE cawing of the rooks in February shows that the time is
coming when their nests will be re-occupied. They resort to
the trees, and perch above the old nests to indicate their rights;
for in the rookery possession is the law, and not nine-tenths
of it only. In the slow dull cold of winter even these noisy birds
are quiet, and as the vast flocks pass over, night and morning,
to and from the woods in which they roost, there is scarcely
a sound. Through the mist their black wings advance in silence,
the jackdaws with them are chilled into unwonted quiet, and
unless you chance to look up the crowd may go over unnoticed.
But as soon as the waters begin to make a sound in February,
running in the ditches and splashing over stones, the rooks
commence the speeches and conversations which will continue
till late into the following autumn.

The general idea is that they pair in February, but there are
some reasons for thinking that the rooks, in fact, choose their
mates at the end of the preceding summer. They are then in
large flocks, and if only casually glanced at appear mixed together
without any order or arrangement. They move on the ground
and fly in the air so close, one beside the other, that at the first
glance or so you cannot distinguish them apart. Yet if you
should be lingering along the by-ways of the fields as the acorns
fall, and the leaves come rustling down in the warm sunny
autumn afternoons, and keep an observant eye upon the rooks
in the trees, or on the fresh-turned furrows, they will be seen
to act in couples. On the ground couples alight near each other,
on the trees they perch near each other, and in the air fly side
by side. Like soldiers each has his comrade. Wedged in the
ranks every man looks like his fellow, and there seems no tie
between them but a common discipline. Intimate acquaintance
with barrack or camp life would show that every one had his
friend. There is also the mess, or companionship of half-a-
dozen, a dozen, or more, and something like this exists part of
the year in the armies of the rooks. After the nest time is over
they flock together, and each family of three or four flies in

concert. Later on they apparently choose their own particular friends, that is the young birds do so. All through the winter after, say October, these pairs keep together, though lost in the general mass to the passing spectator. If you alarm them while feeding on the ground in winter, supposing you have not got a gun, they merely rise up to the nearest tree, and it may then be observed that they do this in pairs. One perches on a branch and a second comes to him. When February arrives, and they resort to the nests to look after or seize on the property there, they are in fact already paired, though the almanacs put down St. Valentine's day as the date of courtship.

There is very often a warm interval in February, sometimes a few days earlier and sometimes later, but as a rule it happens that a week or so of mild sunny weather occurs about this time. Released from the grip of the frost, the streams trickle forth from the fields and pour into the ditches, so that while walking along the footpath there is a murmur all around coming from the rush of water. The murmur of the poets is indeed louder in February than in the more pleasant days of summer, for then the growth of aquatic grasses checks the flow and stills it, whilst in February, every stone, or flint, or lump of chalk divides the current and causes a vibration. With this murmur of water, and mild time, the rooks caw incessantly, and the birds at large essay to utter their welcome of the sun. The wet furrows reflect the rays so that the dark earth gleams, and in the slight mist that stays farther away the light pauses and fills the vapour with radiance. Through this luminous mist the larks race after each other twittering, and as they turn aside, swerving in their swift flight, their white breasts appear for a moment. As while standing by a pool the fishes come into sight, emerging as they swim round from the shadow of the deeper water, so the larks dart over the low hedge, and through the mist, and pass before you, and are gone again. All at once one checks his pursuit, forgets the immediate object, and rises, singing as he soars. The notes fall from the air over the dark wet earth, over the dank grass, and broken withered fern of the hedges, and listening to them it seems for a moment spring. There is sunshine in the song : the lark and the light are one. He gives us a few minutes of summer in February days. In May he rises before as yet the dawn is come, and the sunrise flows down to us under through his notes. On his breast, high above the earth, the first rays fall as the rim of the sun edges up at the eastward hill. The lark and the light are as one, and wherever he glides over the wet furrows the glint of the sun goes with him. Anon alighting he runs between the lines of the green corn. In hot summer, when the open hillside is burned with bright light, the larks are then singing and soaring. Stepping up the hill laboriously, suddenly a lark starts into the light and pours forth a rain of unwearied notes overhead. With bright light, and sunshine, and sunrise, and blue skies the bird is so associated in the mind, that even to see him in the frosty days of winter, at least assures us that summer will certainly return.

Ought not winter, in allegorical designs, the rather to be represented with such things that might suggest hope than such as convey a cold and grim despair? The withered leaf, the snowflake, the hedging bill that cuts and destroys, why these? Why not rather the dear larks for one? They fly in flocks, and amid the white expanse of snow (in the south) their pleasant twitter or call is heard as they sweep along seeking some grassy spot cleared by the wind. The lark, the bird of the light, is there in the bitter short days. Put the lark then for winter, a sign of hope, a certainty of summer. Put, too, the sheathed bud, for if you search the hedge you will find the buds there, on tree and bush, carefully wrapped around with the case which protects them as a cloak. Put, too, the sharp needles of the green corn; let the wind clear it of snow a little way, and show that under cold clod and colder snow the green thing pushes up, knowing that summer must come. Nothing despairs but man. Set the sharp curve of the white new moon in the sky: she is white in true frost, and yellow a little if it is devising change. Set the new moon as something that symbols an increase. Set the shepherd's crook in a corner as a token that the flocks are already enlarged in number. The shepherd is the symbolic man of the hardest winter time. His work is never more important than then. Those that only roam the fields when they are pleasant in May, see the lambs at play in the meadow, and naturally think of lambs and May flowers. But the lamb was born in the adversity of snow. Or you might set the morning star, for it burns and burns and glitters in the winter dawn, and throws forth beams like those of metal consumed in oxygen. There is nought that I know by comparison with which I might indicate the glory of the morning star, while yet the dark night hides in the hollows. The lamb is born in the fold. The morning star glitters in the sky. The bud is alive in its sheath; the green corn under the snow; the lark twitters as he passes. Now these to me are the allegory of winter.

These mild hours in February check the hold which winter has been gaining, and as it were, tear his claws out of the earth, their prey. If it has not been so bitter previously, when this Gulf stream or current of warmer air enters the expanse it may bring forth a butterfly and tenderly woo the first violet into flower. But this depends on its having been only moderately cold before, and also upon the stratum, whether it is backward clay, or forward gravel and sand. Spring dates are quite different according to the locality, and when violets may be found in one district, in another there is hardly a woodbine-leaf out. The border line may be traced, and is occasionally so narrow, one may cross over it almost at a step. It would sometimes seem as if even the nut-tree bushes bore larger and finer nuts on the warmer soil, and that they ripened quicker. Any curious in the first of things, whether it be a leaf, or flower, or a bird, should bear this in mind, and not be discouraged because he hears some one else has already discovered or heard something.

A little note taken now at this bare time of the kind of earth may lead to an understanding of the district. It is plain where the plough has turned it, where the rabbits have burrowed and thrown it out, where a tree has been felled by the gales, by the brook where the bank is worn away, or by the sediment at the shallow places. Before the grass and weeds, and corn and flowers have hidden it, the character of the soil is evident at these natural sections without the aid of a spade. Going slowly along the footpath—indeed you cannot go fast in moist February—it is a good time to select the places and map them out where herbs and flowers will most likely come first. All the autumn lies prone on the ground. Dead dark leaves, some washed to their woody frames, short gray stalks, some few decayed hulls of hedge fruit, and among these the mars or stocks of the plants that do not die away, but lie as it were on the surface waiting. Here the strong teazle will presently stand high; here the ground-ivy will dot the mound with bluish-purple. But it will be necessary to walk slowly to find the ground-ivy flowers under the cover of the briers. These bushes will be a likely place for a blackbird's nest; this thick close hawthorn for a bullfinch; these bramble thickets with remnants of old nettle stalks will be frequented by the whitethroat after a while. The hedge is now but a lattice-work which will before long be hung with green. Now it can be seen through, and now is the time to arrange for future discovery. In May everything will be hidden, and unless the most promising places are selected beforehand, it will not be easy to search them out. The broad ditch will be arched over, the plants rising on the mound will meet the green boughs drooping, and all the vacancy will be filled. But having observed the spot in winter you can almost make certain of success in spring.

It is this previous knowledge which invests those who are always on the spot, those who work much in the fields or have the care of woods, with their apparent prescience. They lead the new-comer to a hedge, or the corner of a copse, or a bend of the brook, announcing beforehand that they feel assured something will be found there; and so it is. This, too, is one reason why a fixed observer usually sees more than one who rambles a great deal and covers ten times the space. The fixed observer who hardly goes a mile from home is like the man who sits still by the edge of a crowd, and by-and-by his lost companion returns to him. To walk about in search of persons in a crowd is well known to be the worst way of recovering them. Sit still and they will often come by. In a far more certain manner this is the case with birds and animals. They all come back. During a twelvemonth probably every creature would pass over a given locality: every creature that is not confined to certain places. The whole army of the woods and hedges marches across a single farm in twelve months. A single tree—especially an old tree—is visited by four-fifths of the birds that ever perch in the course of that period. Every year, too, brings something fresh, and adds new visitors to the list. Even the wild sea birds are found inland, and some that scarce seem able to fly at all are cast far ashore by the gales. It is difficult to believe that one would not see more by extending the journey, but, in fact, experience proves that the longer a single locality is studied the more is found in it. But you should know the places in winter as well as in tempting summer, when song and shade and colour attract every one to the field. You should face the mire and slippery path. Nature yields nothing to the sybarite. The meadow glows with butter-cups in spring, the hedges are green, the woods lovely; but these are not to be enjoyed in their full significance unless you have traversed the same places when bare, and have watched the slow fulfilment of the flowers.

The moist leaves that remain upon the mounds do not rustle, and the thrush moves among them unheard. The sunshine may bring out a rabbit, feeding along the slope of the mound, following the paths or runs. He picks his way, he does not like wet. Though out at night in the dewy grass of summer, in the rain-soaked grass of winter, and living all his life in the earth, often damp nearly to his burrows, no time, and no succession of generations can make him like wet. He endures it, but he picks his way round the dead fern and the decayed leaves. He sits in the bunches of long grass, but he does not like the drops of rain or dew on it to touch him. Water lays his fur close, and mats it, instead of running off and leaving him sleek. As he hops a little way at a time on the mound he chooses his route almost as we pick ours in the mud and pools of February. By the shore of the ditch there still stand a few dry, dead dock stems, with some dry reddish-brown seed adhering. Some dry brown nettle stalks remain; some grey and broken thistles; some teazles leaning on the bushes. The power of winter has reached its utmost now, and can go no farther. These bines which still hang in the bushes are those of the greater bindweed, and will be used in a month or so by many birds as conveniently curved to fit about their nests. The stem of wild clematis, grey and bowed, could scarcely look more dead. Fibres are peeling from it, they come off at the touch of the fingers. The few brown feathers that perhaps still adhere where the flowers once were are stained and discoloured by the beating of the rain. It is not dead: it will flourish again ere long. It is the sturdiest of creepers, facing the ferocious winds of the hills, the tremendous rains that blow up from the sea, and bitter frost, if only it can get its roots into soil that suits it. It some places it takes the place of the hedge proper and becomes itself the hedge. Many of the trunks of the elms are swathed in minute green vegetation which has flourished in the winter, as the clematis will in the summer. Of all, the brambles bear the wild works of winter best. Given only a little shelter, in the corner of the hedges or under trees and copses they retain green leaves till the buds burst again. The frosts tint them in autumn with crimson, but not all turn colour or fall. The brambles are the bowers of the birds; in these still leafy bowers they do the courting of the spring, and under the brambles the earliest arum, and cleaver, or avens push up. Round about them the first white nettle flowers, not long now; latest too, in the autumn. The white nettle sometimes blooms so soon (always according to locality), and again so late, that there seems but a brief interval between, as if it flowered nearly all the year round. So the berries on the holly if let alone often stay till summer is in, and new berries begin to appear shortly afterwards. The ivy, too, bears its berries far into the summer. Perhaps if the country be taken at large there is never a time when there is not a flower of some kind out, in this or that warm southern nook. The sun never sets, nor do the flowers ever die. There is life always, even in the dry fir-cone that looks so brown and sapless.

The path crosses the uplands where the lapwings stand on the parallel ridges of the ploughed field like a drilled company; if they rise they wheel as one, and in the twilight move across the fields in bands, invisible as they sweep near the ground, but seen against the sky in rising over the trees and the hedges. There is a plantation of fir and ash on the slope, and a narrow waggon-way enters it, and seems to lose itself in the wood. Always approach this spot quietly, for whatever is in the wood is sure at some time or other to come to the open space of the track. Wood-pigeons, pheasants, squirrels, magpies, hares, everything feathered or furred, down to the mole, is sure to seek the open way. Butterflies flutter through the copse by it in summer, just as you or I might use the passage between the trees. Towards the evening the partridges may run through to join their friends before roost-time on the ground. Or you may see a covey there now and then, creeping slowly with humped backs, and at a distance not unlike hedgehogs in their motions. The spot therefore should be approached with care; if it is only a thrush out it is a pleasure to see him at his ease and, as he deems, unobserved. If a bird or animal thinks itself noticed it seldom does much, some will cease singing immediately they are looked at. The day is perceptibly longer already. As the sun goes down, the western sky often takes a lovely green tint in this month, and one stays to look at it, forgetting the dark and miry way homewards. I think the moments when we forget the more of the world are the most precious. After a while the green corn rises higher out of the rude earth.

Pure colour almost always gives the idea of fire, or rather it is perhaps as if a light shone through as well as colour itself. The fresh green blade of corn is like this, so pellucid, so clear and pure in its green as to seem to shine with colour. It is not brilliant—not a surface gleam or an enamel,—it is stained through. Beside the moist clods the slender flags arise filled with the sweetness of the earth. Out of the darkness under— that darkness which knows no day save when the ploughshare opens its chinks—they have come to the light. To the light they have brought a colour which will attract the sunbeams from now till harvest. They fall more pleasantly on the corn, toned, as if they mingled with it. Seldom do we realise that the world is practically no thicker to us than the print of our foot-steps on the path. Upon that surface we walk and act our comedy of life, and what is beneath is nothing to us. But it is out from that under-world, from the dead and the unknown, from the cold moist ground, that these green blades have sprung. Yonder a steam-plough pants up the hill, groaning with its own strength, yet all that strength and might of wheels, and piston, and chains, cannot drag from the earth one single blade like these. Force cannot make it; it must grow—an easy word to speak or write, in fact full of potency. It is this mystery of growth and life, of beauty, and sweetness, and colour, starting forth from the clods that gives the corn its power over me. Somehow I identify myself with it; I live again as I see it. Year by year it is the same, and when I see it I feel that I have once more entered on a new life. And I think the spring, with its green corn, its violets, and hawthorn-leaves, and increasing song, grows yearly dearer and more dear to this our ancient earth. So many centuries have flown! Now it is the manner with all natural things to gather as it were by smallest particles. The merest grain of sand drifts unseen into a crevice, and by-and-by another; after a while there is a heap; a century and it is a mound, and then every one observes and comments on it. Time itself has gone on like this; the years have accumulated, first in drifts, then in heaps, and now a vast mound, to which the mountains are knolls, rises up and over-shadows us. Time lies heavy on the world. The old, old earth is glad to turn from the cark and care of drifted centuries to the first sweet blades of green.

There is sunshine to-day after rain, and every lark is singing. Across the vale a broad cloud-shadow descends the hillside, is lost in the hollow, and presently, without warning, slips over the edge, coming swiftly along the green tips. The sunshine follows—the warmer for its momentary absence. Far, far down in a grassy coomb stands a solitary cornrick, conical roofed, casting a lonely shadow—marked because so solitary, and beyond it on the rising slope is a brown copse. The leafless branches take a brown tint in the sunlight; on the summit above there is furze; then more hill lines drawn against the sky. In the tops of the dark pines at the corner of the copse, could the glance sustain itself to see them, there are finches warming themselves in the sunbeams. The thick needles shelter them from the current of air, and the sky is bluer above the pines. Their hearts are full already of the happy days to come, when the moss yonder by the beech, and the lichen on the fir-trunk, and the loose fibres caught in the fork of an unbending bough, shall furnish forth a sufficient mansion for their young. Another broad cloud-shadow, and another warm embrace of sunlight. All the serried ranks of the green corn bow at the word of command as the wind rushes over them.

There is largeness and freedom here. Broad as the down and free as the wind, the thought can roam high over the narrow roofs in the vale. Nature has affixed no bounds to thought. All the palings, and walls, and crooked fences deep down yonder are artificial. The fetters and traditions, the routine, the dull roundabout which deadens the spirit like the cold moist earth, are the merest nothings. Here it is easy with the physical eye to look over the highest roof. The moment the eye of the mind is filled with the beauty of things natural an equal freedom and width of view come to it. Step aside from the trodden footpath of personal experience, throwing away the petty cynicism born of petty hopes disappointed. Step out upon the broad down beside the green corn, and let its freshness become part of life.

The wind passes, and it bends—let the wind, too, pass over the spirit. From the cloud-shadow it emerges to the sunshine— let the heart come out from the shadow of roofs to the open glow of the sky. High above, the songs of the larks fall as rain —receive it with open hands. Pure is the colour of the green flags, the slender-pointed blades—let the thought be pure as the light that shines through that colour. Broad are the downs and open the aspect—gather the breadth and largeness of view. Never can that view be wide enough and large enough, there will always be room to aim higher. As the air of the hills enriches the blood, so let the presence of these beautiful things enrich the inner sense. One memory of the green corn, fresh beneath the sun and wind, will lift up the heart from the clods.

(The Open Air.)

"FIONA MACLEOD," WILLIAM SHARP (1856–1905)

I.—THE FISHER OF MEN

OLD Sheen put her head back wearily on the chair, and let her hands lie, long and white, palm-downward upon her knees. The peat-glow warmed the dull grey that lurked under her closed eyes and about her mouth, and in the furrowed cheeks. Alasdair moved nearer and took her right hand in his, where it lay like a tired sheep between two scarped rocks. Gently he smoothed her hand, and wondered why so frail and slight a creature as this small, old wizened woman could have mothered a great swarthy man like himself—he a man now, with his twoscore and ten years, and yet but a boy there at the dear side of her.

"It was this way, Alasdair-mochree," she went on, in her low thin voice—like a wind-worn leaf, the man that was her son thought. "It was this way. I went down to the burn to wash the *claar*, and when I was there I saw a wounded fawn in the bracken. The big, sad eyes of it were like those of Maisie, poor lass, when she had the birthing that was her going-call. I went through the bracken, and down by the Gorromalt, and into the glen of The Willows.

"And when I was there, and standing by the running water, I saw a man by the stream-side. He was tall, but spare and weary: and the clothes upon him were poor and worn. He had sorrow. When he lifted his head at me, I saw the tears. Dark, wonderful, sweet eyes they were. His face was pale. It was not the face of a man of the hills. There was no red in it, and the eyes looked in upon themselves. He was a fair man, with the white hands that a woman has, a woman like the Bantighearna of Glenchaisteal over yonder. His voice, too, was a voice like that: in the softness, and the sweet, quiet sorrow, I am meaning.

"The word that I gave him was in the English: for I thought he was like a man out of *Sasunn*, or of the southlands somewhere. But he answered me in the Gaelic: sweet, good Gaelic like that of the Bioball over there, to Himself be the praise.

"'And is it the way down the Strath you are seeking,' I asked: 'and will you not be coming up to the house yonder, poor cot though it is, and have a sup of milk, and a rest if it's weary you are?'

"'You are having my thanks for that,' he said, 'and it is as though I had both the good rest and the cool sweet drink. But I am following the flowing water here.'

"'Is it for the fishing?' I asked.

"'I am a Fisher,' he said, and the voice of him was low and sad.

"He had no hat on his head, and the light that streamed through a rowan-tree was in his long hair. He had the pity of the poor in his sorrowful grey eyes.

"'And will you not sleep with us?' I asked again: 'that is, if you have no place to go to, and are a stranger in this country, as I am thinking you are; for I have never had sight of you in the home-straths before.'

"'I am a stranger,' he said, 'and I have no home, and my father's house is a great way off.'

"'Do not tell me, poor man,' I said gently, for fear of the

pain, ' do not tell me if you would fain not; but it is glad I will be if you will give me the name you have.'

" ' My name is Mac-an-t'-Saoir,' he answered with the quiet deep gaze that was his. And with that he bowed his head, and went on his way, brooding deep.

" Well, it was with a heavy heart I turned, and went back through the bracken. A heavy heart, for sure, and yet, oh peace too, cool dews of peace. And the fawn was there : healed, Alasdair, healed, and whinny-bleating for its doe, that stood on a rock wi' lifted hoof an' stared down the glen to where the Fisher was.

" When I was at the burn side, a woman came down the brae. She was fair to see, but the tears were upon her.

" ' Oh,' she cried, ' have you seen a man going this way? '

" ' Ay, for sure,' I answered, ' but what man would he be? '

" ' He is called Mac-an-t'-Saoir.'

" ' Well, there are many men that are called Son of the Carpenter. What will his own name be? '

" ' Iosa,' she said.

" And when I looked at her she was weaving the wavy branches of a thorn near by, and sobbing low, and it was like a wreath or crown that she made.

" ' And who will you be, poor woman? ' I asked.

" ' O my Son, my Son,' she said, and put her apron over her head and went down into the glen of the Willows, she weeping sore, too, at that, poor woman.

" So now, Alasdair, my son, tell me what thought you have about this thing that I have told you. For I know well, whom I met on the brae there, and who the Fisher was. And when I was at the peats here once more I sat down, and my mind sank into myself. And it is knowing the knowledge I am."

" Well, well, dear, it is sore tired you are. Have rest now. But sure there are many men called Macintyre? "

" Ay, an' what Gael that you know will be for giving you his surname like that."

Alasdair had no word for that. He rose to put some more peats on the fire. When he had done this, he gave a cry.

The whiteness that was on the mother's hair was now in the face. There was no blood there, or in the drawn lips. The light in the old, dim eyes was like water after frost.

He took her hand in his. Clay-cold it was. He let it go, and it fell straight by the chair, stiff as the cromak he carried when he was with the sheep.

" Oh my God and my God," he whispered, white with the awe, and the bitter cruel pain.

Then it was that he heard a knocking at the door.

" Who is there? " he cried hoarsely.

" Open, and let me in." It was a low, sweet voice, but was that grey hour the time for a welcome?

" Go, but go in peace, whoever you are. There is death here."

" Open, and let me in."

At that, Alasdair, shaking like a reed in the wind, unclasped the latch. A tall, fair man, ill-clad and weary, pale, too, and with dreaming eyes, came in.

" *Beannachd Dhe an Tigh*," he said, " God's blessing on this house, and on all here."

" The same upon yourself," Alasdair said, with the weary pain in his voice. " And who will you be? and forgive the asking."

" I am called Mac-an-t'-Saoir, and Iosa is the name I bear—Jesus, the Son of the Carpenter."

" It is a good name. And is it good you are seeking this night? "

" I am a Fisher."

" Well, that's here an' that's there. But will you go to the Strath over the hill, and tell the good man that is there, the minister, Lachlan MacLachlan, that old Sheen nic Lèoïd, wife of Alasdair Ruadh, is dead."

" I know that, Alasdair 'Og."

" And how will you be knowing that, and my name too, you that are called Macintyre? "

" I met the white soul of Sheen as it went down by the Glen of the Willows a brief while ago. She was singing a glad song, she was. She had green youth in her eyes. And a man was holding her by the hand. It was Alasdair Ruadh."

At that Alasdair fell on his knees. When he looked up there was no one there. Through the darkness outside the door, he saw a star shining white, and leaping like a pulse.

It was three days after that day of shadow that Sheen Macleod was put under the green turf.

On each night, Alasdair 'Og walked in the Glen of the Willows, and there he saw a man fishing, though ever afar off. Stooping he was, always, and like a shadow at times. But he was the man that was called Iosa Mac-an-t'-Saoir—Jesus, the Son of the Carpenter.

And on the night of the earthing he saw the Fisher close by.

"Lord God," he said, with the hush on his voice, and deep awe in his wondering eyes : "Lord God ! "

And the man looked at him.

"Night and day, Alasdair MacAlasdair," he said, "night and day I fish in the waters of the world. And these waters are the waters of grief, and the waters of sorrow, and the waters of despair. And it is the souls of the living I fish for. And lo, I say this thing unto you : *Go in peace.* Go in peace, good soul of a poor man, for thou hast seen the Fisher of Men."

(*Collected Works, Vol. II. The Sin Eater.*)

ROBERT LOUIS STEVENSON (1850–1894)

ADDRESS TO THE CHIEFS ON THE OPENING OF THE ROAD OF GRATITUDE, OCTOBER 1894

I WILL tell you, chiefs, that when I saw you working on that road, my heart grew warm ; not with gratitude only, but with hope. It seemed to me that I read the promise of something good for Samoa ; it seemed to me, as I looked at you, that you were a company of warriors in a battle, fighting for the defence of our common country against all aggression. For there is a time to fight, and a time to dig. You Samoans may fight, you may conquer twenty times and thirty times, and all will be in vain. There is but one way to defend Samoa. Hear it before it is too late. It is to make roads, and gardens, and care for your trees, and sell their produce wisely, and, in one word, to occupy and use your country. If you do not others will. . . . What are you doing with your talent, Samoa ? Your three talents, Savaii, Upolu, and Tutuila ? Have you buried it in a napkin ? Not Upolu at least. You have rather given it out to be trodden under feet of swine : and the swine cut down food trees and burn houses, according to the nature of swine, or of that much worse animal, foolish man, acting according to his folly. "Thou knewest that I reap where I sowed not, and gather where I have not strawed." But God has both sown and strawed for you here in Samoa ; He has given you a rich soil, a splendid sun, copious rain ; all is ready to your hand, half done. And I repeat to you that thing which is sure : if you do not occupy and use your country, others will. It will not continue to be yours or your children's, if you occupy it for nothing. You and your children will in that case be cast out into outer darkness, where shall be weeping and gnashing of teeth ; for that is the law of God which passeth not away. I who speak to you have seen these things. I have seen them with my eyes—these judgments

of God. I have seen them in Ireland, and I have seen them in
the mountains of my own country—Scotland—and my heart was
sad. These were a fine people in the past—brave, gay, faithful,
and very much like Samoans, except in one particular, that they
were much wiser and better at that business of fighting of which
you think so much. But the time came to them as it now comes
to you, and it did not find them ready. The messenger came into
their villages and they did not know him; they were told, as
you are told, to use and occupy their country, and they would
not hear. And now you may go through great tracts of the land
and scarce meet a man or a smoking house, and see nothing but
sheep feeding. The other people that I tell you of have come
upon them like a foe in the night, and these are the other people's
sheep who browse upon the foundation of their houses. To
come nearer; and I have seen this judgment in Oahu also.
I have ridden there the whole day along the coast of an island.
Hour after hour went by and I saw the face of no living man
except that of the guide who rode with me. All along that
desolate coast, in one bay after another, we saw, still standing,
the churches that have been built by the Hawaiians of old.
There must have been many hundreds, many thousands, dwelling there in old times, and worshipping God in these now empty
churches. For to-day they were empty; the doors were closed,
the villages had disappeared, the people were dead and gone;
only the church stood on like a tombstone over a grave, in the
midst of the white men's sugar fields. The other people had
come and used that country, and the Hawaiians who occupied
it for nothing had been swept away, "where is weeping and
gnashing of teeth."

I do not speak of this lightly, because I love Samoa and her
people. I love the land, I have chosen it to be my home while
I live, and my grave after I am dead; and I love the people,
and have chosen them to be my people to live and die with. And
I see that the day is come now of the great battle; of the great
and the last opportunity by which it shall be decided, whether
you are to pass away like these other races of which I have been
speaking, or to stand fast and have your children living on and
honouring your memory in the land you received of your fathers.

The Land Commission and the Chief Justice will soon have
ended their labours. Much of your land will be restored to you
to do what you can with. Now is the time the messenger is
come into your villages to summon you; the man is come with
the measuring rod; the fire is lighted in which you shall be
tried; whether you are gold or dross. Now is the time for the

true champions of Samoa to stand forth. And who is the true champion of Samoa? It is not the man who blackens his face, and cuts down trees, and kills pigs and wounded men. It is the man who makes roads, who plants food trees, who gathers harvests, and is a profitable servant before the Lord, using and improving that great talent that has been given him in trust. That is the brave soldier; that is the true champion; because all things in a country hang together like the links of the anchor cable, one by another: but the anchor itself is industry.

There is a friend of most of us, who is far away; not to be forgotten where I am, where Tupuola is, where Poè Lelei, Mataafa, Solevao, Poè Teleso, Tupuola Lotofaga, Tupuola Amaile, Muliaiga, Ifopa, Fatialoga, Lemusu are. He knew what I am telling you; no man better. He saw the day was come when Samoa had to walk a new path, and to be defended, not only with guns and blackened faces, and the noise of men shouting, but by digging and planting, reaping and sowing. When he was still here amongst us, he busied himself planting cacao; he was anxious and eager about agriculture and commerce and spoke and wrote continuously; so that when we turn our minds to the same matters, we may tell ourselves that we are still obeying Mataafa. Ua tautala mai pea o ia ua mamao.

I know that I do not speak to idle or foolish hearers. I speak to those who are not too proud to work for gratitude. Chiefs! You have worked for Tusitala, and he thanks you from his heart. In this, I wish you could be an example to all Samoa— I wish every chief in these islands would turn to, and work, and build roads, and sow fields, and plant food trees, and educate his children and improve his talents—not for love of Tusitala, but for the love of his brothers, and his children, and the whole body of generations yet unborn.

Chiefs! On this road that you have made many feet shall follow. The Romans were the bravest and greatest of people! Mighty men of their hands, glorious fighters and conquerors. To this day in Europe you may go through parts of the country where all is marsh and bush, and perhaps after struggling through a thicket, you shall come forth upon an ancient road, solid and useful as the day it was made. You shall see men and women bearing their burdens along that even way, and you may tell yourself that it was built for them perhaps fifteen hundred years before—perhaps before the coming of Christ—by the Romans. And the people still remember and bless them for that convenience, and say to one another, that as the Romans were the bravest men to fight, so they were the best at building roads.

Chiefs ! Our road is not built to last a thousand years, yet in a sense it is. When a road is once built, it is a strange thing how it collects traffic, how every year as it goes on, more and more people are found to walk thereon, and others are raised up to repair and perpetuate it, and keep it alive ; so that perhaps even this road of ours may, from reparation to reparation, continue to exist and be useful hundreds and hundreds of years after we are mingled in the dust. And it is my hope that our far-away descendants may remember and bless those who laboured for them to-day.

(Vailima Letters.)

ALPHABETICAL LIST OF AUTHORS

1. ADDISON, Joseph (1672—1719)
2. Alfred, King (849—901)
3. Anglo-Saxon Chronicle, The
4. Arnold, Matthew (1822—1888)
5. Ascham, Roger (1515—1568)
6. Austen, Jane (1775—1817)
7. Bacon, Francis, Viscount St. Albans (1561—1626)
8. Bede (673—735)
9. Berners, John Bourchier, Lord (1467—1533)
10. Bible, The English, 1611
11. Boswell, James (1740—1795)
12. Bright, John (1811—1889)
13. Brontë, Charlotte (1816—1855)
14. Brown, Dr. John (1810—1882)
15. Browne, Sir Thomas (1605—1682)
16. Bunyan, John (1628—1688)
17. Burke, Edmund (1729—1797)
18. Carlyle, Thomas (1795—1881)
19. Carroll, Lewis (Charles L. Dodgson) (1832—1898)
20. Caxton, William (1422?—1491)
21. Clarendon, Edward Hyde, Earl of (1609—1674)
22. Coleridge, Samuel Taylor (1772—1834)
23. Cowley, Abraham (1618—1667)
24. Defoe, Daniel (1661—1731)
25. Dekker, Thomas (1570?—1641)
26. Dickens, Charles (1812—1870)
27. Dobson, Austin (1840—1921)
28. Dryden, John (1631—1700)
29. Earle, John (1601?—1665)
30. Eliot, George (Mary Ann Evans) (1819—1880)
31. Elyot, Sir Thomas (1499?—1546)
32. Evelyn, John (1620—1706)
33. Fielding, Henry (1707—1754)
34. Froude, James Anthony (1818—1894)
35. Fuller, Thomas (1608—1661)
36. Gaskell, Elizabeth Cleghorn (1810—1865)
37. Geoffrey of Monmouth (c. 1120)
38. Gibbon, Edward (1737—1796)
39. Gladstone, William Ewart (1809—1898)
40. Goldsmith, Oliver (1728—1774)
41. Gray, Thomas (1716—1771)
42. Greene, Robert (1560—1592)
43. Hakluyt, Richard (1552?—1616)
44. Hardy, Thomas (1840—1928)
45. Hazlitt, William (1778—1830)
46. Hobbes, Thomas (1588—1679)
47. Holinshed, Raphael (1515?—1580?)
48. Hooker, Richard (1554?—1600)
49. Hunt, James Henry Leigh (1784—1859)
50. Jefferies, Richard (1848—1887)
51. Johnson, Samuel (1709—1784)